Alex Gray was born and educated in Glasgow and is the author of the bestselling William Lorimer series. After studying English and Philosophy at the University of Strathclyde, she worked as a visiting officer for the DHSS, a time she looks upon as postgraduate education since it proved a rich source of character studies. She then trained as a secondary school teacher of English. Alex began writing professionally in 1993 and had immediate success with short stories, articles and commissions for BBC radio programmes. A regular on Scottish bestseller lists, she has been awarded the Scottish Association of Writers' Constable and Pitlochry trophies for her crime writing. She is also the co-founder of the international Scottish crime writing festival, Bloody Scotland, which had its inaugural year in 2012.

ALSO BY ALEX GRAY

Never Somewhere Else
A Small Weeping
Shadows of Sounds
The Riverman
Pitch Black
Glasgow Kiss
Five Ways to Kill a Man
Sleep Like the Dead
A Pound of Flesh
The Swedish Girl
The Bird That Did Not Sing
Keep the Midnight Out
The Darkest Goodbye
Still Dark
Only the Dead Can Tell
The Stalker

Alex Gray

WHEN SHADOWS FALL

sphere

SPHERE

First published in Great Britain in 2020 by Sphere
This paperback edition published by Sphere in 2020

1 3 5 7 9 10 8 6 4 2

Copyright © Alex Gray 2020

The moral right of the author has been asserted.

Quotation from *The Fellowship of the Ring* by J. R. R. Tolkien reprinted
by permission of Harper Collins Publishers Ltd. © The Tolkien
Estate Limited 1954, 1961

*All characters and events in this publication, other than those
clearly in the public domain, are fictitious and any resemblance
to real persons, living or dead, is purely coincidental.*

All rights reserved.
No part of this publication may be reproduced, stored in a
retrieval system, or transmitted, in any form or by any means, without
the prior permission in writing of the publisher, nor be otherwise circulated
in any form of binding or cover other than that in which it is published
and without a similar condition including this condition being
imposed on the subsequent purchaser.

A CIP catalogue record for this book
is available from the British Library.

ISBN 978-0-7515-7642-9

Typeset in Caslon by M Rules
Printed and bound in Great Britain by
Clays Ltd, Elcograf S.p.A.

Papers used by Sphere are from well-managed forests
and other responsible sources.

Sphere
An imprint of
Little, Brown Book Group
Carmelite House
50 Victoria Embankment
London EC4Y 0DZ

An Hachette UK Company
www.hachette.co.uk

www.littlebrown.co.uk

For John, who loves the freedom of the hills

'Deserves it! I daresay he does. Many that live deserve death. And some that die deserve life. Can you give it to them? Then do not be too eager to deal out death in judgement. For even the very wise cannot see all ends.'

J. R. R. TOLKIEN, *The Fellowship of the Ring*

Come now, let us reason together,
    says the Lord:
though your sins are like scarlet, they
    shall be as white as snow;
though they are red like crimson, they
    shall become like wool.

ISAIAH 1:18

CHAPTER ONE

Joseph Alexander Flynn whistled as he turned into the driveway of the big house. He could see the storm doors beyond the front porch were shut and there was no sign of any vehicle parked outside. That suited him just fine. No interruptions from the owner of the house, who occasionally worked from home, meant that Flynn would have a clear run at the job today. It was a cold morning but thankfully there was no sign of frost. Digging at this time of year was always problematic, October mornings might bring icy windscreens and ground hard as iron but today looked ideal for a bit of landscaping.

Flynn stopped the truck around the side of the house, as previously instructed by his client, and looked at the place with a critical eye. Hedges on one side with white cobwebs sewn together, dewdrops twinkling as the sun rose weakly in a misty sky; a steeply sloping lawn that would need a mower before the year's end and, hidden from the sight of anyone looking out from the big house, a derelict patch that had once been a kitchen garden but was now little more than a mass of brambles and weeds. Clearing this area and turning it into raised beds for growing vegetables was the task that Flynn had agreed to take on for a reasonable fee.

His breath clouded in front of him as he trudged downhill, a spade and fork in each gloved hand. It should take him the best part of a week to clear the ground, he'd told the owner of the garden, several days more to build the raised beds and create new places for planting. Now, two days into his task, Flynn could see what the client had in mind. Almost half of the neglected patch had been tackled, a heap of tangled foliage piled high in one corner, to be carted away when the whole lot was uprooted. Once the entire space had been cleared Flynn would dig it over again, rake it to a finer tilth then set the wooden frames around the rectangle of soil. His expert eye already saw the end result and he was keen to add the client to his list of regulars, knowing what work a garden this size demanded.

'Right,' he muttered aloud, placing one booted foot against the fork, and eyeing the next bramble bush with a determined glint in his eye. 'Here we go again.'

It was not going to be an easy job to get at the roots of this one, he soon discovered, plunging the fork repeatedly into the soil. Taking a pair of secateurs from his jacket pocket, Flynn began to cut back the whip-like stems and fling them towards the path. Once more he dug around the stump of the bramble bush, heaving at the embedded plant to reach its deepest root. At last he felt a shift beneath the tines of the fork and with an extra push the roots began to emerge from the ground, scattering clumps of soil.

He wiped a hand across his eyes, blinking to rid himself of the tiny bits of dirt that had hit his face. Next he'd have to dig up the rest of these thread-like roots in order to clear another bit of ground.

Flynn blinked once more, a frown creasing his brow.

It was not just more of the bush's root system that caught his attention and he bent down to examine it more closely, pushing the soil to one side.

At first Flynn thought it must be something a dog had buried, the bone a pale shape against the dark earth. But when his gloved hand scooped out more loose soil, Flynn sat back on his haunches, blinking in disbelief.

Somewhere a robin was piping its frosty note, a harbinger of winter to come, but all that Flynn could hear was a ringing in his ears as he stared at the skull grinning up at him from the place where it had been buried.

CHAPTER TWO

'Say that again.' Detective Superintendent William Lorimer sat back in his chair, a frown creasing the space between his blue eyes. 'You've found what?'

'A body,' Flynn said. 'A body buried in this garden I'm workin' in the now. C'mon, Lorimer, you huv tae dae something, man. I cannae stay here on my own.'

'You're kidding me, right?' Lorimer began, but he'd caught the edge of fear in his friend's voice and knew that this was no joking matter. Joseph Alexander Flynn had a strange sense of humour but even he would hesitate to call the head of the MIT at work with a daft story.

'Where are you?' Lorimer asked, listening and jotting down the address in the West Renfrewshire countryside that Flynn gave him.

'Okay, stay there, touch nothing else and make sure nobody else sees it till the officers arrive. Got that? I'll send someone to you right away.'

'C'n you no' come here yerself?'

Lorimer heard the pleading in the younger man's voice and instantly recalled the days when Flynn had recuperated at his own home, an ex-druggie knocked down in the street as he was chased by one of his officers. From the beginning there had been something vulnerable about him that had tugged at Lorimer's conscience, prompting him to offer sanctuary to the skinny lad.

'I'll see,' was all he could promise.

It was less than half an hour's drive to the village of Houston from Glasgow city centre, the client's house on the outskirts, up a farm road and along a deserted tree-lined avenue.

A squad car was already parked in the driveway, a uniformed officer standing by the doorway of the house when the detective superintendent arrived.

'Sir.' The man came forward as soon as Lorimer stepped out of the Lexus.

'You've secured the scene.' Lorimer nodded approvingly as he caught sight of the blue and white tape stretched either side of the house to prevent any unauthorised access. 'That was quick.' He gave the officer a smile.

'Mr Flynn's in his truck, sir,' the officer told him, pointing to the left-hand side of the building.

Lorimer raised his hand in thanks before ducking under the tape and heading to the familiar green truck several yards away. Flynn had been employed by Glasgow District Council for some years before setting up on his own, the maintenance of the Lorimers' garden becoming one of his regular jobs.

'All right?' Lorimer opened the driver's door and regarded

his friend. The younger man's normally ruddy complexion was pale and his eyes flicked nervously from Lorimer back towards the place where he had found the skeleton.

Flynn nodded silently, exhaling a long breath. 'Aye,' he answered shortly. 'Cannae believe it, mind. Wan minute I'm diggin' up that big bramble, the next thing I sees this skeleton grinnin' up at me. Fair gied me the willies.' He shook his head.

'Where's the owner of the property?' Lorimer asked.

'Dunno. I gied they other polis Mr Mathieson's number, though. He and the wife both work in Glasgow. The kids are all at school the now. Thon private place over in Kilmacolm, he telt me.'

'What do you know about him, your client?'

'No' an awfie lot,' Flynn replied, scratching his head. 'His name's Lawrence Mathieson. Works in a bank. Telt me they'd bought the place last year, moved in before the summer when they came up frae England. Wanted the garden done before the winter.'

'How did he get in touch with you?'

Flynn shrugged. 'Word o' mouth. Ah dae the gardens for the estate agent he bought this place from,' he said, jerking a thumb at the blond-sandstone villa.

Lorimer gave the house a quick glance. It was probably Victorian, a solid three-storey building, and now he noticed a large conservatory at the far side as he looked back. From this vantage point close to the back of the property he could see a large curve of paving slabs that provided a pleasant terrace for a weatherworn table and chairs placed opposite French windows. He looked up at the sky: the original architect had chosen a south-facing aspect and whoever lived here would enjoy sunshine from early morning to sunset. Beyond the extensive terrace a large area of the lawn was flat then it sloped away steeply to the neglected area below where Flynn had been working. The grass near the house had been tended and there were large pots of chrysanthemums close to the French doors but the lower part of the garden had grown wild. Over how many years? Lorimer wondered.

'Have they taken a statement from you?' he asked.

'Naw, jist telt me tae stay put the now.'

'You okay with that?' Lorimer patted his shoulder.

'Aye, s'pose so,' Flynn sighed. 'This wis meant tae keep me busy all week,' he grumbled. 'Nothin' else in the diary onyway.'

Lorimer stood up and looked down the garden path where a couple of uniformed officers stood watching him.

'I'll try not to keep you too long,' he promised. 'Just wait here meantime, all right?'

Flynn nodded but the expression on his face was glum as Lorimer began to make his way along the beaten earth pathway, its edges green with moss.

Autumn leaves whirled about his feet as he descended the slope and took his first sight of the place where Flynn had been digging. A garden fork was still lodged in the soil at one side, a perfect perch for the beady-eyed robin that was regarding him intently as he approached.

Forensics would be here within the hour but by the look of the site, there was no danger of contamination to the surrounding paths. Flynn had thrown down a plank of wood close to the area he'd been digging, possibly to prevent his boots sinking into the damp earth, so Lorimer picked his way gingerly along and looked down into the hole.

A pale skull looked up at him, its grinning teeth like some macabre mask better suited to Hallowe'en. Once upon a time someone had wrapped the body in layers of black plastic, shreds of which were still visible where Flynn had been digging. And not only the gardener – foxes, probably, scenting fresh meat at some time, tearing the covering with hungry teeth and claws. This skeleton was probably not going to be found intact, he guessed. It was not the first cadaver Lorimer had seen buried deep in a makeshift grave but he still felt a shiver down his spine as he gazed at the bones. Whoever this was, it had to be identified. He shifted his position, hunkering down on the plank, and tried to examine the skull more carefully without touching anything.

Was that a bit of dirt . . . ? He bent more closely and took a quick breath. No, that was not dirt, but a neat hole in the side of the skull.

The sun had risen higher in the sky by the time the scene of crime officers arrived and now there were several white-suited figures at the foot of this garden, a forensic tent erected over the remains lest a sudden shower of rain flood the grave.

Lorimer looked up to see another figure approaching, his familiar long, loping stride a welcome sight.

Iain Mackintosh, the Procurator Fiscal, did not always grace a scene of crime with his presence but today he was evidently curious enough to see this for himself after

Lorimer had called him. There was no doubt in Lorimer's mind that this was a suspicious death and as such, a matter for the Fiscal. Under Scots law, a body belonged to the Crown at this stage of an investigation and so Mackintosh's arrival was not so unusual.

'Iain.' Lorimer grasped the outstretched hand, already clad in double layers of latex, like his own.

'What have we got here?' Mackintosh asked, his eyebrows raised in expectation.

Lorimer shrugged. 'Who knows? Pathologist reckons it to be male, but until they get him along to the mortuary for further examination, we won't know much more.'

'Any identification?'

Lorimer shook his head. 'Nothing yet. He might have been naked when he was buried there, the officers have found no trace of any clothing, wallet, shoes ... looks to me like he was killed a long time ago, but that's something we can't even guess at right now.'

Mackintosh turned to look up at the house. 'What about the owner of this place?'

'Chap called Mathieson. Lawrence Mathieson. He's coming from Glasgow as we speak. Just bought the house a year ago, or less. Flynn there was doing a landscape job for him,' he added, pointing up the pathway to the gardener's truck.

'*Your* Flynn?' Mackintosh's eyes widened. 'Lad that stayed with you during the Royal Concert Hall case?'

'The very same. Has his own business now, garden maintenance and landscaping. He's made a good fist of it too,' Lorimer told the Fiscal, a tinge of pride in his voice.

9

'Bet that gave him a queer fright,' Mackintosh said, turning back towards the forensic tent where the skeleton lay.

'Aye, but I think his fright's worn off now and he's cursing the loss of a decent commission,' Lorimer chuckled. 'Time's money when you work for yourself.'

'Any idea about previous owners?'

'Still to find out but hopefully we'll know soon enough. I'm guessing that's Mr Mathieson heading our way now,' he replied, looking up to where two uniformed officers were engaged in conversation with a man in a dark coat.

'Shall we?' Mackintosh gestured for Lorimer to accompany him up the steep path to where the owner of the house, and this garden, stood watching them, hands thrust into his pockets.

Lawrence Mathieson was a man in his late forties, Lorimer reckoned, sandy-haired and smartly dressed in a grey chalk stripe suit beneath a navy blue coat. As he shook the man's hand, Lorimer glimpsed the Rolex watch on Mathieson's wrist, noting the man's quizzical expression as he made the necessary introductions.

'What's going on?' Mathieson's well-bred voice showed a degree of irritation, though he was clearly too polite to vent his annoyance on a senior police officer and a Crown official. 'Nobody gave me a reason why I suddenly needed to be here. Official police business, they said.'

'Sorry to drag you out from the city, sir.' Lorimer paused for a moment, searching for words to tell the man that a skeleton had been found in his garden. 'Mr Flynn, your gardener, was digging the patch at the bottom of the garden when he made a discovery,' he began. 'Sorry to have to tell you this, sir, but human remains have been found.'

'Human remains, you say? Who on earth is it? And what are they doing in *my* garden?'

'It looks as if this person was buried in your garden a long time ago, sir,' Iain Mackintosh told him. 'The remains are skeletal so that would indicate a historic burial.'

'Historic? You mean it might be centuries old? Something of significance?'

'That cannot be determined just yet, sir, but of course anything that we can tell you at a future date, we will,' Mackintosh assured him.

'Perhaps we might go inside, Mr Mathieson,' Lorimer suggested. 'What we'd like to know is something about the previous owners and a bit about the house itself. How old it is, land registration, that sort of thing.' He phrased his words to keep them deliberately vague. It was highly unlikely that the banker had any connection with the buried body, but Lorimer wanted to find out a bit more about Lawrence Mathieson and his choice of home out here, miles from the city. A family man, with kids in school, yet he'd chosen this remote house. It was a small thing, but caused Lorimer to ask himself: why?

The two men watched as the banker produced a set of keys and proceeded to unlock the storm doors and open them wide. There was a glass door beyond that required two different sets of keys to unlock.

Lorimer exchanged raised eyebrows with the Fiscal as they stood behind Mathieson: evidently there was some need for all this extra security. And each man's mind was buzzing with the possibilities. A safe full of important work-related documents? Personal effects worth a lot of money? That Rolex certainly suggested that the Mathiesons weren't short of a bob or two. Perhaps, reasoned Lorimer, it was simply the remoteness of this place that justified extra care when leaving it unattended.

As the banker stepped inside an alarm began to sound but he quickly opened a small cabinet fixed to the wall and disarmed it with a few clicks before closing it once more. The security code would be something known only to the owner and his wife and from the way he shielded the digital keypad it was evident that Mathieson had no intention of letting a stranger see what it was, police officer or not.

'Do come in, gentlemen,' Mathieson said at last, standing aside and beckoning them forward.

Inside, the reception hall yawned to reveal a corridor that led left and right with a set of closed double doors directly ahead.

Sunlight streamed into the large room as Mathieson pushed them open, leading the two men forwards, the French windows opposite letting his visitors see the grounds outside as far as the edge of the lawn, the steep slope masking the current activity where Flynn had made his discovery.

Mathieson shed his coat, tossing it on the back of an antique chair that sat in one corner of the room next to a long glass-fronted cabinet gleaming with silverware.

'Please take a seat, gentlemen.' He gestured towards a pair of pale apricot-coloured sofas that were angled to give the best view of the terrace and garden.

Lorimer was used to seeing the change that often came

over the owner of a house when he or she was visited by the police; the proprietorial look on the householder's face, the advantage over strangers that came from being in their own home. Yet this chap had not lived here very long, he reminded himself as Mathieson leaned back and crossed his legs. Perhaps the man was used to asserting himself in his everyday life and a visit from the police held no terrors for him.

'Lovely property, how did you come to choose it?' he began, glancing around the room with an appreciative smile on his face. It had been recently decorated, he guessed, the wall coverings fresh and modern, yet in a leaf pattern that was timeless and well suited to the antique furniture.

'Usual way,' Mathieson said, his tone a shade sarcastic as though the question was elementary. 'Estate agent sent us particulars of several places. I'd given them a brief that included a decent-sized house with enough garden grounds but not anywhere that was overlooked by other properties. We value our privacy,' he added with a smirk.

'Certainly fits the bill,' Mackintosh remarked. 'I take it you viewed the place before buying it?'

Mathieson uncrossed his legs and shifted a little in his seat. 'Just once,' he told them. 'My wife liked it immediately. She's a keen gardener and wanted to have plots where she could grow vegetables. That's why we hired this Flynn character to clear the overgrown area and make raised beds. He's a bit rough around the edges but came with good references,' he explained.

Lorimer made no comment, hoarding the remark to tell Maggie, his wife, later on. Joseph Alexander Flynn had been a particular favourite of Maggie's late mother and the Lorimers still regarded him as a close friend.

'The previous owner—'

'In a care home,' Mathieson interrupted. 'The place was too much for her, seemingly, and had to be sold. Probably to help fund the woman's expenses, I imagine. The house lay empty for about a year, I believe.'

'And nobody lived here at all during that time?' Lorimer asked.

Mathieson shook his head. 'It was in the hands of the agents till we bought it. Must say we did get it at a good price, but then anything up here is dirt cheap compared to London prices.'

Was that another smirk? Lorimer felt a prickle of annoyance, as if this man was deliberately trying to needle them, remind the two Scots that they were in some way inferior to the English banker. Yet, he mused, why had Mathieson chosen to come north if he felt this way? Was it just the availability of bigger and cheaper housing? The banking crisis had made many of his fellow workers redundant but somehow this man had survived and was reaping the rewards only a few could enjoy. *The privileged few* – the phrase came into his mind. That was what Mathieson reeked of, he told himself. Privilege. *We're all Jock Tamson's bairns*, Maggie's mother used to tell them and Lorimer had loved her for it. In his profession all the members of the public he met were treated the same, irrespective of creed or class, and Lorimer had sat beside weeping relatives from every sector of society.

He set aside these feelings and concentrated on

Mathieson, the owner of a property where a murder might have been committed.

'What else do you know about the previous owner? Where exactly is she now?' he asked.

Mathieson frowned for a moment as though he were trying to recall enough to answer the detective superintendent's question.

'Ah, yes,' he said, sitting up a little straighter, his brow clearing. 'Not too far from here, in fact. Erskine Hospital, I think it's called, the place for ex-servicemen. And women,' he added hastily. 'I think she may have been in the forces during World War Two. That's about all I know. You really ought to contact the estate agency. Their people would be able to tell you more.' Mathieson wagged an instructive finger at them as though Lorimer and the Fiscal needed his advice.

'Indeed,' Iain Mackintosh murmured. 'I think the police already have that in hand, sir.'

Lorimer risked a glance at the Fiscal, seeing a red tide wash across his neck and jaw. Mackintosh was clearly struggling to keep his cool.

'What happens now?' Mathieson asked, sitting on the edge of his seat to indicate that it was time to wrap up their interview. Lorimer looked at the body language: the head held high, hands on each side as though he wanted to stand up and bid them goodbye.

'I can see you want to get back to work,' Lorimer told him, standing up and making the first move, an amused smile on his face.

Mathieson jumped to his feet and looked up at the tall

detective towering over him. 'Right, I'll show you both out,' he declared and strode across the room, coming to stop at the large double doors, a fixed smile on his face that did not reach his eyes.

'Thank you, sir,' Lorimer said, stopping deliberately in the doorway. 'We will be in touch later today but meantime if you would ensure that nobody from the house goes near the bottom of the garden.' It was not a request and there was no doubt in his mind that Mathieson realised that as he nodded.

'Of course, of course.'

'There will be officers here for the rest of the day and possibly for several days to come,' Lorimer added gravely.

Mackintosh turned towards the banker as he closed the doors of the huge sitting room behind him, waiting patiently till he had Mathieson's attention.

'The cadaver is the possession of the Crown at the moment. That is something you may not understand. Scots law is rather different from what goes on down south,' he said, a tinge of pride in his voice. 'You would do well to remember that.'

Lorimer heard the front door thud shut behind them as he walked away from the house, Mackintosh at his side.

There was no need to express his feelings, Lorimer thought, seeing the Fiscal shake his head and raise his eyes heavenwards. Iain Mackintosh had clearly taken a scunner to the owner of the property. Though, Lorimer told himself, Lawrence Mathieson would probably not know the meaning of the word.

CHAPTER THREE

Geoorge Phillips groaned as he tried to stand up. The arthritis was worse today, his knees complaining from kneeling by the flower beds for the past three-quarters of an hour. George straightened up, fingers searching around his lower back to rub at the aches under his belt. His painful joints were like a sullen headache, always present and hard to ignore. Years of being out of doors at scenes of crime in all the vagaries of Scottish weather had taken their toll yet Phillips still missed the challenges he'd faced during those years. Now, in his retirement, he was enjoying his garden and the tasks that each changing season demanded.

It had been a good morning so far, however, and the ex-policeman surveyed the rich brown soil with satisfaction, a rubber container full of weeds ready to tip into his brown bin. Every couple of weeks the council came to remove it, though that was not often enough for a keen gardener like George Phillips. The beds were still full of royal blue lobelia and scarlet geraniums, though he'd have to lift the latter before the frosts came. Across the lawn was a small drift of leaves, his Japanese maple tree a crowning glory at this time of year. The azaleas, too, had donned their autumn hues of russet and gold, their long leaves poised to shed as soon as the October gales began.

Time for a cuppa, George told himself, turning away with a sigh of satisfaction from those neat borders and the bushes burnished by a sun that was low in the sky. He picked up the heavy container of weeds, carrying it in both hands.

It was the last thing that George Phillips ever saw.

The bullet came swiftly, striking the side of his head. The old man fell with a thud, his body hitting the garden path, weeds scattering all around as they flew out of George's hands.

There was no sudden silence. Cars passed by on the road nearby, wheels skimming over the tarmac, drivers oblivious to the moment of death they had failed to witness. On the rooftop a magpie screeched, dipping its body as though to see what had happened below.

Only one man stood watching and waiting as though to be certain the bullet had done its job. He bent down to pick up the spent cartridge, secreting it into his pocket.

Then, like a shadow, he was gone.

CHAPTER FOUR

'George Phillips? My God, what happened?'

Lorimer was on his feet, hands clutching the edges of his desk as he stared in disbelief at the woman who had walked into his room moments ago to deliver the worst sort of news.

DCC Caroline Flint motioned for him to sit down again.

'He was your old boss, I gather?' she said solemnly, her eyes searching Lorimer's face as he slumped into his chair.

The detective superintendent nodded mutely, the woman's words still ringing in his ears.

I am sorry to have to tell you but George Phillips was shot dead in his garden this morning.

'Shot? What happened? A gun went off? Tell me this was some sort of accident ... surely ... ?'

'We don't think so.' Caroline Flint shook her head. 'Looks like a deliberate assassination. Ballistics confirmed the gunman's position. They think he was standing in the lane next to the victim's house.'

Victim! *George Phillips, a victim!* It didn't make sense, Lorimer thought, his mind in a turmoil, still trying to get to grips with the reality of his friend's death.

'What . . . ? Why . . . ?' he whispered. He swallowed hard as a surge of emotion threatened to overwhelm him.

'Did anybody see what happened?' he asked at last, his voice husky.

Flint shook her head. 'Not as far as we know. A friend passing by on a cycle noticed him lying on the ground and sent for an ambulance. Too late, of course, but at least the local cops got to the scene pretty quickly. I'll send on their initial report as soon as we receive it.'

Lorimer nodded, too full of emotion to reply.

George Phillips. Gunned down in his own garden. It was beyond all reason. Lorimer knew a moment of regret for all the invitations George had issued over the years, he and Maggie too busy to make time to visit their old friend in his cottage near Inverkip. They'd been once, after George's wife had died, but life had always a way of intruding on good intentions. Lorimer sighed ruefully. Now it was too late and he would never grasp that gnarled hand again or hear his friend's throaty chuckle.

'A good age. Nearly eighty,' Flint remarked. 'And you can console yourself that he would not have known a thing. Death was instantaneous, the pathologist reckons. One second he was here in the world, the next in the hereafter.'

And he would not even have heard the gunshot, had there been any to hear, Lorimer knew. If that bullet had struck him as Flint described, George Phillips had a swift though brutal passing.

'Who would want to . . . ?'

'We're asking ourselves the selfsame question. And, hopefully, there will be answers before much longer. Scene of crime team are still down there and the PM will take place as soon as possible.'

'You want me to be there?'

She looked directly at him, neither nodding nor shaking her head.

'Do you want to?' she asked softly. And Lorimer understood that it was her way of offering him a chance to say a last farewell to the man who had been both his superior officer and old friend.

'What time?' he asked.

'Dr Fergusson said she would give you a ring.'

Lorimer nodded in reply. Rosie Fergusson had been a colleague of George's too during the latter part of his career and she knew how much this would mean. He cast his mind back to a case just before George Phillips's retirement when Rosie had first made the acquaintance of Solomon Brightman, a psychologist and sometime criminal profiler. Now that unlikely pair were married with two young children, the Lorimers godparents to Abby and Ben. That case had put a violent psychopath behind bars, one less threat to the safety of ordinary people.

Yes, he decided, it would be the right thing to do. He would attend the post-mortem with Rosie Fergusson officiating and make his own silent farewell to George.

It was odd how death made people change, Lorimer thought, looking down from his position behind the glazed viewing

21

window. Once a big man, the former detective superinten-dent appeared shrunken, his limbs twisted a little from the arthritis that had stricken him. Lorimer's gaze fell on the hands that had once cuffed so many Glasgow neds. Now they seemed brittle like dried twigs, their knotted veins standing out. Despite his condition, George had been work-ing out of doors right till the end, the report had told him: his clothes showed signs of the old man having been busy in the garden that morning, the spillage of weeds from his fallen tub testament to a few hours of toil.

It was perhaps the way he'd have wanted to go, Lorimer mused. Not death by a gunman's bullet, of course, but out-side in his beloved garden close to the river Clyde, his last breath one of fresh sea air.

He watched as Rosie bent to search the source of the wound, her gloved hands holding a pair of plastic-tipped forceps. It was essential to take the utmost care in removing a bullet so that any rifling mark could be used by ballistics in an attempt to match with any weapon on their database.

There was a silence until he heard the satisfied murmur as Rosie drew out the bullet from the side of the victim's skull. She turned towards Lorimer, holding it up before placing it into a stainless steel dish, the metal object making a tinny sound as it rolled to one side.

It was such a tiny thing yet capable of piercing flesh and bone, destroying the brain within in a split second of fury. Soon enough the bullet would be put under a microscope and then a story might begin. A story that included a sniper, perhaps; certainly an assassin who had intended to kill and more than likely been paid for firing that single shot.

Yet it was not his story to tell, Lorimer reminded himself, glancing to the woman at his side. DI Heather McDougall was senior investigating officer in this case and it would be her team of officers from the Greenock Division that made the enquiries and searched for the perpetrator. He was simply here to observe and pay his respects to the body lying on its side beneath their gaze.

DI McDougall glanced at the tall man by her side.

'Never met him. Believe he was a decent guy from all I've heard, though,' she offered.

'Aye, he was,' Lorimer replied gruffly. 'One of the best.'

'Don't worry, sir, we'll catch whoever did this. Not going to spare a moment for one of our own,' the woman said firmly.

Lorimer believed her. The officers in Greenock would work tirelessly to locate the gunman, already trawling the streets of every village along the coast in their search for answers.

CHAPTER FIVE

'First one down, then,' he muttered into the mobile phone tucked against his ear.

'Aye. Phillips. Easy as pie. On his own, not a soul around to see him falling,' the voice on the other end chuckled.

'Well, that's a start. But I want the whole lot of them running about like headless chickens by the time we're finished.'

There was a short pause then the sound of a throat clearing. 'I've got my instructions,' the man at the other end said. 'To hand it all over after the next one. But who gets the ones after that? And why can't it be me?'

'We've gone over this before,' he growled. 'I've my own reasons for doing it this way. Besides, it keeps them guessing, never lets them have a clue who's going to be next.'

There was another pause filled with the sound of traffic in the distance and he imagined the man standing somewhere out in the cold air, shuffling his feet to keep warm.

'Aye, okay.' The man sounded reluctant to accept his

instructions. 'But if you need someone to do a job again after tomorrow, you just have to ask.'

He clicked the phone, cutting off the sound of the man's voice, its tone a shade too whiny for his liking. It was all very well having a hitman that was capable of doing a job to his satisfaction but he would never allow any of them to become trigger-happy.

Besides, there were several people who had signed up to see this particular business through.

He smiled as he thought about another list of names, mentally taking a pencil and scoring off the name George Phillips. Wondering about the next one.

CHAPTER SIX

Maggie Lorimer closed the laptop with a sigh. It had been a long day at Muirpark Secondary School, some of her pupils less willing than others to pay attention to their English teacher, their recent holiday from school making them more restless than usual. At least the October break had given Maggie time to finish her second children's story but there were elements that wanted tidying up and she knew that careful editing would pay off in the long term.

Her thoughts turned to the telephone call that had come not long after arriving home late afternoon, the news about George Phillips making all the little irritations of her day pale into insignificance. Now she must think of what to say when Bill walked through that door, though words were pretty inadequate to sum up a horror like this.

A memory flickered in her brain, George standing at his retirement dinner, putting on a hey-you-Jimmy hat and making everybody laugh. The former detective superintendent had been full of life that night, telling stories from his past making each and every person in that room feel that here was a man who had seen the best and worst of human nature and survived it. Maggie remembered George's hearty laugh, his deep baritone voice and a smile that encompassed all who had come to wish him well that night.

And afterwards? There had been a couple of cruises with his wife before she had succumbed to the disease that had taken her from George, treasured memories no doubt comforting him on the lonely nights in the cottage by the sea.

Bill had met up with him occasionally in town, the pair meeting at an Italian restaurant close by Glasgow Central Station, sometimes simply for the company, other times to pick the older man's brains.

Maggie saw the headlights swinging round to the drive and watched as the Lexus came to a halt. Taking a deep breath she stepped away from the desk in the bay window and pulled the curtain cord, shutting out the night.

The sound of his key in the lock then the front door closing were usually enough to lift her heart in a moment of joy but tonight their embrace would be for mutual comfort.

'Hi,' was all he said as she took him in her arms, her head nestling against his chest.

'I'm so sorry,' Maggie whispered. 'It's hard to believe . . .'

She felt his hands stroke her hair, heard the deep sigh that said more than any words.

'Come on, I think a wee whisky would do us both some good,' Maggie said at last, breaking away from the warmth of her husband's arms.

*

Lorimer stretched out his long legs and let the glass sink onto the carpet by his side. They'd eaten later than usual, Maggie's casserole and a slice of home-made apple pie welcome consolations after the horrors of the day.

'He was found by a local man who knew him,' he began. 'Chap who'd been a friend of sorts after they'd bought the cottage. Must have given the poor fellow a hell of a fright.'

Maggie nodded, listening. It was her husband's habit to relate things from his day, though many events would always remain untold, the newspapers giving the details of grislier cases that Lorimer chose to keep from his wife.

'Rosie did the PM late this afternoon. Won't know anything more till ballistics get a look at the bullet. One shot,' he added, glancing across at Maggie. 'She said it was enough to kill him instantly. Wouldn't have known a thing about it.'

He saw his wife press her lips together, a look of doubt in her sea-grey eyes.

'Really,' he insisted. 'I'm not making this up to spare you any anxiety. Whoever took a shot at George knew exactly what they were doing.' He looked away again. 'My money would be on a weapon with a silencer. He'd have had the exact spot he wanted to aim for in the gun sights.'

He felt rather than saw Maggie shudder.

'Sorry,' he said, holding out his hand in apology. 'Shouldn't have told you, but what I'm trying to say is he didn't suffer. That's small consolation, I know. But let's hold on to that, eh?'

He could hear Maggie breathing quietly at his side, shoulders tucked beneath the duvet, warm body close to his.

Sound asleep, thank goodness, Lorimer thought. Tomorrow would bring another busy day, he knew, and she must try to put aside all thoughts of their dead friend and concentrate on teaching her classes.

All evening they had reminisced about the man who had been Lorimer's boss back in Stewart Street. He blinked suddenly, realising with a jolt that he had forgotten to tell Maggie anything about his morning out in Houston. *Flynn and the skeleton*, he'd wanted to joke as if it might be a title for one of his wife's stories. But any pithy comments Lorimer might have prepared had been swept aside by the DCC's visit to break the news about George's murder. Even as he had been examining that patch of ground out in West Renfrewshire mid-morning, George Phillips had been gunned down, the pathologist's estimation of time of death putting it around eleven a.m. Coffee time, Lorimer guessed, George carting a load of weeds from his flower beds, a hitman waiting for the right moment to pull that trigger.

Sleep eluded the detective now, the image of George on that steel table, his remains pored over by the pathologist in an effort to tell some sort of story about how his life had been snuffed out. And his spirit? Lorimer had seen many cadavers in the mortuary and none held any terror for him. They were the leftovers of a life, not the essential part of the person who had lived it. That would endure in the minds of those whose own lives the former detective had touched, though there were some, like the woman sleeping by his side, who believed a soul continued elsewhere for eternity.

As he closed his eyes at last, felt the heaviness in his limbs,

Lorimer wondered for a fleeting second who else might have been affected by the life of George Phillips.

Enough to want to kill him.

Professor Solomon Brightman walked up and down, the little child in his arms. Ben's earlier whimpers were now replaced by a great sigh as the little boy finally slept. Solly had forgotten the nights of broken sleep when their daughter, Abby, had been teething and now these times came back, making the psychologist grin. How like human nature to blot out the bad bits of rearing an infant! He turned at the end of the corridor, enjoying the weight of his baby son in his arms, not yet ready to lay him back in the cot.

Rosie had been late home, reaching for the bottle of wine in their fridge before dinner, a needful antidote to the post-mortem examination of the man who was only a vague memory to Solly. George Phillips had been someone that William Lorimer had respected and that was enough in Solly's book to make the former detective one of the good guys.

What if . . . ? The psychologist turned the usual motives for murder in his mind. What if the gunman had sought out the old man to seek revenge for a past arrest? Had there been any cases in Phillips's past that had carried a shade of doubt? A prisoner wrongly incarcerated and now seeking some sort of payback? Solly rocked his son gently as he considered this. The police would no doubt have already taken this idea on board and would be looking at any prisoner recently discharged that fitted the bill. What other reason would there be? George was surely too old to have had an affair that sparked a conflagration of passion in another man's breast. And money? He had appeared to be comfortably off, though who knew what habits a lonely fellow might acquire that brought him into the clutches of unscrupulous money-lenders. Motives for his murder would be investigated by the CID squad down in Greenock. But for a moment, Solly Brightman wished that he might be included in their team, the mystery of why the old man had been killed piquing his curiosity.

CHAPTER SEVEN

The October sun was low in the sky as he drove home from Aviemore, trees on either side ablaze with yellow birch and golden beech, the occasional red acer a flame-bright torch. Already the roadsides were fringed with tawny larch fall, obscuring the edges till winter snows blanketed the landscape. Behind him lay the mighty Cairngorm Mountains, their tops already white against the afternoon skies. Ahead, the road wound between the trees, dark Scots pines planted firmly like stalwart Highlanders of old.

Stephen McAlpine hummed along to the music from his car radio, a familiar tune he couldn't have put a name to, though he recalled a cartoon where Mickey Mouse was dressed in wizard's clothing. He tapped the steering wheel, a smile on his weather-beaten face, thinking of the days ahead and the grandchildren he had delivered home safely to their mum after nursery. It was a routine that Stephen loved and he was looking forward to helping them dress up for Hallowe'en at the end of this month.

It was grand, this retirement, with time to spend playing with the wee ones.

Stephen gave a little sigh. Their own kids had missed out on quite a lot, Daddy often away from home if there was a major case to investigate. But that had been back in the days when they'd lived in Dundee; now Ailsa was married with two lovely bairns and another on the way, Connor following his father's footsteps down in Glasgow where there was enough crime to keep every young police constable busy.

Just a couple of miles more and then he'd be home, ready to cook the evening meal for Ellen and himself, a task that Stephen had taken to with relish after his thirty years as a cop.

The music quickened and Stephen began to hum along, grinning as he suddenly remembered the title of the music: *The Sorcerer's Apprentice*. Had the wee ones ever seen *Fantasia*? Probably not. He and Ellen must put it on next time they came for a sleepover with Nana and Papa.

He glanced in the rear-view mirror, seeing a large white van close to his rear, evidently ready to overtake on the straight stretch ahead. Stephen slowed down, sensible to the needs of those to whom deadlines still mattered. A delivery man, maybe, heading towards Grantown or even Elgin with a tight schedule to keep. Poor soul, he told himself, a smug sense of satisfaction that he himself was no longer in thrall to the clock. It had taken a while to adjust after the years spent chasing criminals but nowadays former DI McAlpine was just fine about how he spent his days.

Stephen's foot was on the brake as he saw the van overtake him then accelerate. It moved swiftly ahead then roared off and disappeared around the next corner, Stephen shaking his head at its speed. A few more bends then he'd turn off the road and drive through the forest, the narrower road taking him higher into the hills until he reached their cottage.

The ex-cop gave a sigh of satisfaction, anticipating the first sight of the old house that had taken him the best part of a year to renovate. Now it was like a new home, the old slates changed to red roof tiles, thick white walls dazzling white in the afternoon sunlight. He'd lit the wood burner before setting out to collect the bairns and soon he'd be rewarded by a thin skein of grey smoke issuing from the old chimney stack. All these years of hard graft had paid off and now Stephen McAlpine was free to enjoy the fruits of his thirty years' labour.

He slowed down as the turning approached, noticing a large Transit van with coloured day-glo chevrons along its side. Two workmen in hi-vis jackets were apparently digging in the ditch alongside the path, a protective barrier shielding them from the traffic. Stephen paid them little attention. There was always something going on these days; laying new pipes, dredging the ditches or even putting in something to speed up the broadband. He gave a grin as he drove around the bend and headed uphill, hoping it might be that, a downside to living in a remote area being that the Wi-Fi was lamentably slow.

Trees crowded in on either side, sombre fir and spruce, the dark green blotting out the sky in places, no bright autumnal colours here to relieve the gloom. The music had changed too, that rhythmic beat banished in an instant by sad dreamy notes.

His hand was on the gear stick, ready to drop down for the steep incline and the hairpin bend, then the road would twist up and down before opening out of the trees and into the daylight once again. He had just mounted the crest of the hill when he saw it.

Slewed across the road at a crazy angle was the white van that had overtaken him just a few minutes before.

Slamming on the brake, Stephen swore loudly.

What the ...?

Had the guy hit a deer? Was there oil spilled on the road? He squinted at the tarmac, his mind seeking a logical explanation.

Above the sound of his own engine he heard the slam of a door and saw a figure dressed in black leap down from the cab.

Stephen let out a sigh of relief. Thank God! The driver was all right.

The glare from a stray sunbeam piercing the treetops made him blink. Was the man limping? And, was that a walking stick he held in his gloved hand?

Stephen rolled down the window, leaning out to offer help. 'Everything okay, mate?'

The man raised his stick and in that moment Stephen McAlpine saw it for what it really was.

He heard no sound, the first shot finding its mark in one split second.

In moments the gunman was back in the van and driving away from the scene, crows cawing their protest as they rose in one black wave from the treetops. There was no need to check on the body slumped against the steering wheel. No contact, no trace. Besides, he knew that he'd fulfilled his mission and that this former cop was well and truly dead.

Down at the road end, the two workmen pulled the Road Closed sign back to allow a white van room to speed away. They would follow soon, once their props were safely stowed away. As it passed, one of them nodded to the driver, his thumb raised to confirm a job well done.

The carrion crows settled once again after wheeling through the skies. Below, there was a smell of blood and one by one they would flutter down to investigate.

The final notes of music from the car radio played out. Stephen McAlpine would never hear that final flourish as it ended, never see his grandchildren dressed up for future Hallowe'ens nor see the woodsmoke from his own home drifting upwards into the endless skies.

CHAPTER EIGHT

The police road block was a blasted nuisance for anyone trying to access this particular road but a necessary one to keep away prying eyes until they could tow away the car and take the body to Raigmore Hospital. Terry Finnegan sighed. She'd been in the job less than twenty-four hours and now here was her first homicide as senior investigating officer. An anonymous phone call from a payphone had alerted them to this remote spot; that in itself raising suspicions.

The former Glasgow cop stood by the red Audi, her attention focused on the man whose body lay across the wheel. Flies were already buzzing through the open window and she'd chased away a couple of hopeful crows, attracted by the smell of blood. Terry swayed a little, sudden dizziness reminding her that she'd had nothing to eat since breakfast. And that had been hours ago.

'You all right, ma'am?' A burly constable whose name

Terry had already forgotten was by her side, a concerned look on his florid face.

'It's not the first time I've seen a dead body,' Terry snapped. 'How about you, Constable?'

'Aye, well, there was yon laddie a few years back took his own life ... hanged hisself in the woods ower yonder,' he remarked, waving a large hand in the direction of the tree-lined road.

Terry nodded. It was part and parcel of this job to have to deal with the horrible stuff that folk did to themselves or to others. There was no sign of a weapon here, however, so Terry knew without any doubt that this fellow's hand had not been instrumental in bringing about his own demise. Besides, the caller had told them that a 'man had been killed', words that had dispatched the DI and a small team including local officers from Aviemore to the wooded road above the A95.

She looked up as a second uniformed officer walked hurriedly towards them, phone to his ear. From the startled look he directed her way, Terry knew that there was something he was going to tell her; something she guessed that she would not like to hear.

Ma'am.' The newcomer cleared his throat and jerked his head in the direction of the red car. 'We've just been told who that is.'

Terry waited, watching the man's face, seeing the bit lip, the reluctance to impart whatever it was.

'Stephen McAlpine, ma'am. Former DI from Dundee. Leastwise, that's his car.'

Terry felt a sudden chill as she approached the vehicle

again. She'd ordered the officers not to touch a thing, but now she felt her fingers itching to pick up that jacket lying on the back seat of the Audi, just to see if there was any ID. Couldn't do any harm to look?

Hands that were already gloved pulled at the rear door handle, but it was stuck fast. Walking purposefully round the car, she yanked at the door handle on the passenger side and immediately the buzzing became louder, swarms of flies evidently rejoicing in this unexpected feast. Terry batted a few away, wishing she could raise the driver's window, but knowing that she must do nothing that might compromise this scene of crime.

Leaning in towards the dashboard, she released the child lock, her head turning ever so slightly to stare at the dead man.

He'd been shot twice, from what Terry could see. Once in the head, once in the chest. Heart head, she recited mentally, recognising it for what it was: a typical assassination by a hitman. Wasn't the first time DI Finnegan had seen this pattern of wounds on a body, Glasgow gangsters favouring the sniper approach beloved of the military. That anonymous call would be subjected to some scrutiny if their tech department was up to it. Terry sighed, experiencing a longing for Glasgow and its nearby Scottish Crime Campus in Gartcosh.

The SIO straightened up and opened the back door, careful not to let her arm touch anything. *Every contact leaves a trace* had been dinned into her years ago and there was no way she was going to leave her own DNA all over this crime scene. Picking up the discarded jacket between gloved finger and thumb, Terry rifled through the inside pocket, feeling the shape of a wallet. She drew it out and snapped it open, hardly daring to breathe.

Pushing up the plastic credit card with her gloved thumb, Terry saw what she was after.

S J MCALPINE

It was enough.

Terry drew herself up to her full five feet eight inches and nodded at the two uniformed officers staring at her.

'Aye, that's who it is. One of our own,' she said quietly, a mulish expression on her downturned mouth.

Staff Nurse Ellen McAlpine saw the two officers at the open door of her patient's room and straightened up from where she had been replacing Mr Jones's catheter.

For a moment she felt a rush of blood as though she'd stood up too quickly. One of the cops, a woman, stepped into the room, hand outstretched.

'Mrs McAlpine?'

Ellen froze, unable to move. *Connor? Ailsa?* Her mind whirled with deadly possibilities.

Then a hand was on her elbow, steering the nurse into the corridor, a cop on either side as Ellen McAlpine was walked briskly into the empty office.

'I'm very sorry to have to tell you . . .'

Ellen listened to the words, her mind refusing to take in the truth of what she was hearing.

'No,' she whispered. 'No, it can't be . . .' Then, as she

looked from one face to the other and saw their dismay, she uttered a howl of anguish, doubling up as though in pain, her legs suddenly buckling under her.

Terry flopped down on the suede-covered armchair with a sigh. What a bloody day! They'd taken the body to Raigmore and been informed that it would be at least tomorrow afternoon before a PM could be done. She'd visited the widow last of all, making sure the family liaison officer was with her to smooth things along. It was the part of the job that everyone hated and Terry was humbly grateful for the FLO's expertise.

'I never thought anything like this could ever happen,' the bereaved woman had whispered at last. 'All these years in the job, and now this?' She'd looked pleadingly into Terry's eyes. 'Was it a mistake, do you think? Case of mistaken identity?'

Terry had made all the right sort of non-committal noises whilst knowing all the time that the chances of Stephen McAlpine's death being an accident were round about nil.

She pulled herself out of the chair, heading towards the kitchen. God, how she needed a drink!

Moments later she was back on the same seat, the red wine her new colleagues had given her that morning unscrewed, necking it straight from the bottle, too weary to be bothered finding a glass.

Stephen McAlpine. The name was new to her, the former cop hailing from the Dundee area. But DI Terry Finnegan had been no stranger to another dead man who was uppermost in her thoughts at that moment.

41

'George Phillips,' she said aloud, raising the bottle as if in a toast to her late boss, remembering how proud he'd been to hear about her promotion.

'Come on up for a holiday,' she'd suggested as they'd parted at George's garden gate. But George Phillips would never make that journey, a gunman making sure of that.

Two former cops. Two gunmen? Bit of a coincidence, Terry told herself with a cynical twist to her mouth. There was someone she knew who was fond of saying how he never really believed in coincidences, Terry reminded herself. Someone who had also been fond of old George.

'Hello? Who? Oh, yes, he is, just wait a moment, please. Who shall I say is calling?' Maggie Lorimer covered the telephone with one hand.

'It's for you,' she told her husband. 'A DI Finnegan.' She frowned. 'Do you know her?'

Lorimer nodded silently, taking the phone from Maggie's outstretched hand.

He was aware of the television being turned to mute then Maggie giving his shoulder a pat before she left the room, leaving him to whatever police business had encroached on their evening.

'Lorimer.'

'It's Theresa Finnegan, sir, don't know if you remember me from Stewart Street? I was a DC there before George Phillips retired,' the woman's voice said.

'You'll have heard the news, then?'

'Aye, horrible,' Terry sighed. 'I kept in touch with George, just saw him a couple of weeks back, in fact, down in Inverkip.'

Lorimer frowned, puzzled.

'You must be wondering why I'm calling, sir,' she went on. 'I'm up in Inverness now, brand-new posting as it happens.' He could hear a tinge of irony in her voice. 'First day on the job, and we have a murder.' She sighed. 'Chap name of Stephen McAlpine.'

Lorimer's frown deepened. 'Should I have heard of him?'

'No, but you will.' There was a pause before the woman added, 'Former Detective Inspector Stephen McAlpine, sir. One of our own. Two shots. One to the head, other to the heart.' There was another pause as Lorimer let out a long breath of astonishment.

'Thought you might want to think about that. I've already been in touch with Heather McDougall in Greenock, but . . .'

Lorimer waited, wondering if the woman was trying to justify her late-night call.

'Well, I thought you ought to know. Seeing as how we were both George's friends.'

It was more than that, of course, Lorimer realised. As head of the Major Investigation Team based at Helen Street in Govan he could pull some strings to have these two cases brought under his own scrutiny. Was that the purpose behind this call?

Theresa Finnegan was speaking again, a low chuckle in her voice.

'Always mind you telling us how you didn't believe in coincidences,' she said.

Lorimer chewed his lip thoughtfully, glad that the woman could not see the expression on his face. It was true, but that didn't mean that he was going to step all over two other detectives' cases with his size elevens. Was the woman trying to pass her case off to the MIT? He frowned. Surely not.

'You quite happy to lead this one, DI Finnegan?' he asked.

'Yes, sir,' came back the sharp retort.

'Good. You can keep me in the loop if you like, but I'm sure both you and DI McDougall are more than capable of carrying out your own investigations,' he told her, still wondering why Theresa Finnegan had chosen to call him here tonight. Her first day on the job and she'd wanted to speak to him. They'd not been especially chummy at Stewart Street, after all. Why call him at home? Why not wait till the morning or email him at his office? The lines between his eyes deepened. It had been a long day and he'd wanted to relax in front of the television, Maggie by his side.

Was that an indrawn breath he heard? Perhaps he'd been a little abrupt?

'Really, thanks for calling,' he said, an attempt to redress any irritation he'd let slip. 'This is dreadful news coming so soon after George's death and I appreciate your concern. But I'm sure there will be plenty of resources at your disposal. After all, as you said, it's one of our own.'

'Yes.' He heard the woman's voice again, recognising disappointment.

'Well, good night, then. And good luck. You can always email me at Govan if you think there's anything I can do to help.'

'Thanks. Goodnight, sir,' she said, then the call was ended.

Lorimer sat still for a few moments. He'd handled that badly. Should have made more sympathetic noises, maybe?

Yet the woman was SIO in a murder case, should be more than capable of carrying out the necessary actions. For a moment his hand reached out to pick up the phone, call her again and apologise, but he drew back. Leave her be, an inner voice argued; let her get on with it her way. If the powers on high gave a command to the MIT that would be a different story, but meantime the investigations should be carried out by the local detective inspectors.

Lorimer sank back into his chair with a sigh, one hand grasping the remote control, but not yet pressing the button to release the sound from the television. He stared into space, wondering about the dead man up in the Highlands. From experience he could imagine the torrent of grief flooding out to family and friends, the agony they would all be going through right now. Plus the usual unwelcome intrusion from the press.

He must resist empathising too closely with strangers he had never even met, that inner voice reminded him. With a sigh, Lorimer clenched his right fist, making himself remember the mindfulness techniques he had been taught up in Castlebrae, the Police Treatment Centre. If he tried to put himself into the shoes of each and every single victim there would be no energy left to do the job he loved.

Closing his eyes, he began to breathe deeply, relaxing his muscles and concentrating on a soft voice he now knew by heart. But, try as he might, it was Terry Finnegan's insistent voice that kept reminding him that he was a man who didn't believe in coincidences. Despite the two-hundred-mile distance between them Lorimer had to acknowledge that it might not be mere chance that in less than forty-eight hours two retired police officers had been gunned down near their own homes.

Terry Finnegan pulled off her thin crew-neck sweater and tossed it on the bedside chair then sat down on the bed, exhausted. Somewhere she had clean pyjamas but tonight she'd just sleep in the same old T-shirt. Terry pulled back the duvet, glad that she'd simply made up the bed as a priority after the removal van had offloaded her furniture.

Lorimer had sounded a bit cross and she couldn't blame him. Goodness alone knows what sort of workload he had down in Govan. The wife had sounded nice answering the phone, Terry thought. Lovely voice. Wasn't she a school-teacher and a children's author?

She closed her eyes, thinking back to her early days at Stewart Street and the big man who'd been the boss there. Hard to think of George not being in the world any more. Someone gunning him down. Perhaps there were a good few folk up in this neck of the woods thinking just those thoughts about Stephen McAlpine. Terry sighed. This was her patch now and she must try to put herself into the shoes of her fellow officers, feel the pain they were feeling. As sleep began to overtake her, Terry heard again the murmuring sound of flies as they sought out that body slumped across the steering wheel.

CHAPTER NINE

Rosie Fergusson had seen worse things in her life than the decomposed remains that had been placed on the table in front of her, each and every corpse that came her way commanding her undivided attention. Today, curiosity was tempered by a need to find answers to the questions demanded of her, answers that might help to put a name to this bundle of bones and create a history for him. The skeleton had already been established as male, both long bones from one leg and the man's pelvis remaining intact, but the age was more difficult to determine, certainly an adult, but with no sign of any arthritis or osteoporosis in these bones she could only say with some hesitation that he might be between thirty and sixty. It had taken some time to excavate the remains from its makeshift grave, officers at great pains to preserve as much of the fibrous material as possible. Scraps of dark plastic were being preserved along with soil samples, just in case any further scrutiny was required.

Rosie gave a wintry smile, thinking of Flynn. He'd been

badly shaken by the discovery, Lorimer had told her, but at least he'd had the sense to call his old friend and set a procedure in motion, something that now involved Dr Rosie Fergusson, head of the Department of Forensic Medicine and Science at the University of Glasgow.

She had seen the bullet hole in the parietal bone of the skull, of course, knew they were dealing with a probable murder, but who this was and when he'd been killed remained one of the questions. Finding these things out might take quite a bit of time. The victim had been shot through the head from a certain distance, but that was now impossible to calculate, with no telltale marks of powder residue tattooing on the skin.

Still, one thing that had been found, nestling within the skull, was a bullet that was currently up at Gartcosh, the Scottish Crime Campus, with their ballistics division. Rosie had seen a bullet displaced once before, the missile entering the victim's chest then hitting solid bone before tumbling around and ending up inside the man's woollen jumper. A freak of luck for the investigating team, like this one, though there had been no trace of clothing in the Houston grave after all this time, any material having degraded over the years.

There was nothing else to see inside this empty skull now, of course, but Rosie imagined that bullet would have forced all the brain tissue away from the central impact point and lodged there as the victim fell. How long the body had lain in that weed-covered garden was for others to determine, but she hazarded a guess that as many as two decades might have passed since this fellow had lived and breathed. As for identifying him, well, that was going to be a tricky one for the investigators since nothing had been found by the body apart from the bullet.

Rosie bent a little further forward, examining the dental structure. A forensic odontologist might make some observations about the man, she thought, noticing the squint front tooth that overlapped its neighbour. There were gaps, too, she noticed. Fellow hadn't taken much care of his teeth so there was probably no point in alerting any local dentists. Besides, who was to say the man had even come from that part of West Renfrewshire? Could have been buried after being transported from anywhere. And if he'd lain there for a long time, maybe there would be no dentist left alive to identify these particular teeth.

Their best bet was matching the man's DNA, *if* he'd been on any database back then, but perhaps he'd been killed before such lists had been compiled.

The pathologist made a face under her mask. Her task was to report on cause of death, not to speculate on who he'd been or why he'd been shot dead and buried in that garden out near Houston. Yet it was a fascinating puzzle, one that Rosie would gladly have pursued.

The Erskine Home for ex-servicemen was a modern low-lying building set amongst neatly landscaped grounds a short drive from the Erskine Bridge and the modern township that bore its name. Lorimer closed the car door and looked around. The nearby Kilpatrick Hills were bronze now, clad in dried bracken that would be like a winter coat until spring came around once more. He could see traffic crossing the bridge but heard nothing from this distance; peace and quiet for residents in their latter years, he thought, no inner city noises disturbing their rest.

Ladybank House had been sold by Mrs Riddoch partly to fund her retirement here, the estate agent had explained, and she was as intrigued by the officers who were to pay her a visit as they surely were, the agent had told him.

DI Brodie was waiting for him in the foyer of the home and stood up as Lorimer entered. The case had been handed over to CID in Paisley, a DI from Mill Street in overall charge.

'Superintendent.' A man about Lorimer's age strode forward, hand outstretched. His grip was strong, Lorimer noted, seeing past the bulky figure straining in its suit to the ruddy cheeks, close-cropped hair and a pair of dark, intelligent eyes that were looking at him with interest.

'DI Brodie, I think we've met before?' Lorimer smiled, his brow furrowing.

'I was at your lecture earlier this year,' Brodie replied. 'Scottish Medico Legal Society. I try to make it each month if I can,' he added.

'Ah, yes.' Lorimer's face cleared. 'We spoke in the pub afterwards, didn't we? Talked about historic cases. Looks like you've got another one here.'

'Cold cases are a particular speciality of mine,' Brodie admitted. 'I was seconded to the unit a couple of years ago and never found any reason to leave.' He grinned. 'It can be frustrating at times but helluva rewarding when you manage to hand a body over to any relatives after a long time.'

'Let's hope you manage with this one,' Lorimer agreed

as they walked along a corridor that led to the lifts and the upper floor where Mary Riddoch had her room.

As they walked, Lorimer noticed several pictures: officers in uniform, a display of remembrance poppies that commemorated a hundred years since the Great War, and black and white images of the former hospital building not far away that was now a luxury hotel.

'The estate agent tells me that the house lay empty for more than a year,' Brodie said. 'Nothing had been done to the lower gardens for decades. Hopefully this lady will be able to put a date to the time when a gardener was at work in that part of the property.'

Lorimer nodded. He'd wanted to come here with the DI from the Cold Case Unit, partly out of loyalty to Flynn and partly since he had been the first senior officer at the scene. Lorimer had also requested that he be present when the old lady was interviewed today, his curiosity piqued by Flynn's discovery out in Houston.

The home was divided into several houses, each of them containing single rooms plus a communal dining area and spacious lounge where residents could meet. Downstairs they passed a large recreation room and Lorimer paused to read the list of activities for that week, his eyebrows lifting in surprise at a visit from members of Scottish Opera. Not just games of cribbage and being planked in front of a large-screen TV, then, he realised, his admiration for those who ran this place going up several notches.

A lift took them up to the second floor to where Pearson House was located and the two men walked towards the apartment where Mrs Mary Riddoch was now living out her twilight years.

There was a nurses' station halfway along the corridor, past several break-out areas with comfy settees and occasional tables, made homely by vases of flowers and pictures on the walls; places where residents might talk to their visitors in a more intimate setting.

'Good afternoon, may I help you?' A red-haired woman in purple uniform rose to her feet as the two men approached.

'Detective Superintendent Lorimer, Detective Inspector Brodie,' he said, letting the nurse have a good look at his warrant card. 'You're expecting us. We're here to see Mrs Riddoch.'

The woman beamed at them. 'Oh, she's fair excited about this,' she told them. 'These old folk have been talking about nothing else since it came on last night's news. Bit of a stir, eh? The orderlies were teasing her this morning about having bumped off an old boyfriend,' she laughed.

Lorimer smiled thinly but said nothing. Many a true story was told in jest, though he doubted whether anyone would be careless or foolish enough to bury a body in their own backyard.

'Mary's along there in room seven,' she said. 'Just knock the door and go in. She's expecting you.'

'Hello?' Lorimer pushed the door and entered the room to see an old woman in a wheelchair looking up expectantly. Her white hair looked freshly permed and it was hard to tell if those rosy cheeks were the result of a healthy constitution or a clever application of rouge.

'I'm Detective Superintendent Lorimer and this is my colleague, Detective Inspector Brodie,' Lorimer said, bending low to shake the woman's papery hand.

A pair of bright eyes looked back at him, reminding Lorimer for all the world of a curious robin.

'Well now, this is a turn-up for the book, isn't it? Two senior police officers paying an old biddy like me a visit!' She twinkled at them, a smile tugging the corners of her mouth as though Mary Riddoch was finding the whole thing an amusing diversion.

'You are the only person that can tell us the recent history of Ladybank House,' Lorimer remarked.

'Sit down, the pair of you,' Mary Riddoch commanded, waving a hand towards her bed. 'There's not a lot of room for big fellows like you but that will have to do for now.'

'We could take you along the corridor?' Brodie suggested.

'No. Too many nosy parkers,' she replied with a short laugh. 'They're all dying to see you. Find out what's been happening. Now,' she nodded as the two detectives sat side by side on the pink counterpane, the bed sinking under their weight, 'tell me all about this body you found down in my old garden.'

Lorimer smiled despite himself. Mary Riddoch was clearly used to being in command of a situation and he did not envy any nurse or orderly who tried to coerce her into doing something she didn't appreciate.

'We'd like to ask you some questions, ma'am,' he began.

'None of that nonsense!' she exclaimed. 'I'm Mary to all the staff in here so that is what you can call me.' The old lady smiled again, a pair of dimples showing beside her apple-red cheeks, glancing coquettishly from one of the men to the other. Lorimer bit his lip, stopping the ripple of laughter that threatened to explode. She must be ninety if she was a day, he thought, yet here she was flirting with two men half her age!

'Well, Mary, you seem to know the basic facts already,' Lorimer said. 'Yes, human remains have been found in your old garden. But what DI Brodie and I would like to know is how they came to be there and how long it was since they were buried. Can you enlighten us?' he asked, grinning back at her.

'Well, I didn't bury anybody there,' Mary laughed. 'Silly thing to do if I'd done away with anyone! I'd have dissolved their body in a bath of acid or . . . well, one of the methods Agatha Christie used in her stories. I love a good detective story, you know. None of these modern ones, mind. Too much blood and gore. No, give me *Murder on the Orient Express* any time,' she said, wagging a finger at them.

'How long did you live there?' Brodie asked.

'Oh, let me see. I've been in here over a year now.' The old lady stopped and gazed to one side, her lips moving as she calculated. 'We lived in Paisley after we got married. Hm. Must have been fifty-two years,' she said at last. 'Roderick and I had celebrated our golden wedding the year before he died and that was the spring of 2009.' Her face fell as though recalling the sadness of that particular memory. 'We had a good life together and several years of travelling after he retired.'

Lorimer nodded to himself. Roderick Riddoch; he knew that name, the haulier's lorries travelling the length and breadth of the country. The business had been bought by a multinational, he remembered. At the time there had been a bit of a stooshie about it contravening the monopolies guide-lines but somehow the new owners had got away with it. Between the sale of that business and her large Renfrewshire home, Lorimer suspected that he was sitting right opposite one of Scotland's wealthiest women. Whatever Lawrence Mathieson or his estate agent had thought, there had surely been no need to sell Ladybank House to fund the old lady's retirement here.

'You travelled a lot?' Brodie asked.

'Oh, yes.' Mary nodded. 'Our two children moved to Australia after they graduated, one lives in Perth, the other in Brisbane. We spent several months with them every winter.'

'A long way to fly,' Brodie remarked.

'Oh, we never flew, Inspector,' Mary shook her head. 'Roddy hated flying. So we always took a cruise. Left home around the middle of November and would rarely be back before the end of March.' She sighed. 'Such lovely ships in those days. The *QE2* was our favourite, of course. An elegant ship. So sad that it has become nothing but a floating hotel now.'

Lorimer saw Brodie glance at him, realised what he was probably thinking.

'The house was left empty each winter, then?'

'Yes,' Mary said firmly. 'Locked up each year. Wattie, the gardener, took away all our house plants to look after then brought them back after we had returned home. Nice chap, he was. Died a few years ago,' she murmured.

'And, did he tend to the bottom of the garden?' Brodie asked, breathlessly.

'Ah, I see where you're going,' Mary laughed. 'No, Inspector, that was left fallow for years and years. Too much shade under the lime trees to grow anything well. So we just let it go wild. Foxes used to have a den there,' she mused. 'And the nettles attracted all sorts of butterflies. I suppose we were a bit ahead of the trend to have a wildlife patch.'

'The current owner wants to grow vegetables there,' Lorimer told her.

'Good luck to him!' Mary retorted. 'He'll never get anything to survive down there. Too dark and the soil always had too much clay for Roddy's liking.'

'You never noticed any disturbance in the soil when you returned from your holidays?' Brodie asked hopefully.

Mary pursed her lips thoughtfully. 'We did have foxes,' she began. 'Sometimes they'd make deep holes in the ground looking for another entrance to their den. But ...' She tailed off, shaking her head. 'I couldn't possibly say when that might have been, or whether it was a two-legged fox.' She smiled at them both in turn.

Lorimer imagined a red-coated animal digging in the bramble patch, attracted by the smell of a decomposing body. It had been buried deeply, though, and those tangled bushes had grown over the grave, hiding it for years. Had Joseph Alexander Flynn not dug right under those roots, the body might have lain there for decades more.

'Nobody looked after the house while you were abroad?' Brodie persisted.

'We always phoned the police,' Mary said at last. 'That was what you did in those days. So, I suppose someone from the local police station might have called in a few times when we weren't there. Probably just drove past to check. But there was no key holder or that sort of thing. Just locked everything up, doors, windows ... ' She shrugged. 'It's a mystery.' She leant forward and fixed Lorimer with those beady eyes. 'But I'd like to know how it ends.'

DI Brodie had taken down notes of the years when the Riddochs had been in Australia, asked about the gardener, Malcolm Watt, who had passed away before Mary Riddoch sold up, and took down the details of the families still living overseas. A son and a daughter, she'd told them with a glint of pride in her voice, the girl a successful architect, their son a doctor. Mary Riddoch's head had turned to a series of colour photographs on her wall and the two officers had followed her gaze, seeing images of a man and woman in graduation gowns, then wedding pictures and family photos complete with adoring grandparents. She would never return there again, Mary had told them wistfully. But perhaps one of the grandchildren might visit next summer. Though it was a long way to go, she'd added, looking away from them as if to hide the longing they could both hear in her voice.

CHAPTER TEN

Back in his schooldays it might have been a cause for derision if Douglas Petrie had told anyone that he had wanted to become a minister of the Kirk. He'd mumbled things about university and a possible degree in engineering during those periods set aside to speak to their careers advisors. Being a son of the manse was bad enough for a self-conscious lad who excelled at football and was popular amongst the lassies without revealing the secret ambition hidden in the schoolboy's heart.

Things changed for ever the year that Douglas left high school and headed south to attend the University of Glasgow. The joy of studying subjects that were part of a Divinity degree combined with the camaraderie of like-minded souls gave the young man a sure direction of where he was going and why. Now, fifteen years down the line and the Revd Petrie had still not fulfilled his early ambition. Sure, he had a ministry of sorts, but it was not the traditional parish that he had known as a boy.

Douglas looked up at the front of Barlinnie Prison as he parked his car in the area reserved for staff. Being chaplain here was not an easy option but he knew that, for now at least, it was where God wanted him to be.

As he made his way through the usual high security check, Petrie thought about the man he was going to see this morning. John Ramsay had recently been discharged from the hospital and was first on his list for counselling today. Petrie had read through the man's notes, dismayed as ever to see the catalogue of crimes the man had committed over his lifetime. Petty theft as a youngster had escalated to some brutal assaults, then armed robbery, until the last sentence had been passed. The security guard at the factory where the raid had taken place had died of his injuries a few days later, Ramsay named as one of the five that had attacked the defenceless father of three.

The chaplain closed the door to his office and sat down with a sigh. What kind of man was he going to be faced with now? It was not his place to judge the men in this prison, as he'd often reminded them, but he would never condone the actions that had brought them here.

Petrie closed his eyes, as was his habit, and concentrated on praying to his heavenly father. There were so many things in this place that he could not change, so many lives wasted by wrong choices. There were times he wanted to make a difference but it was not through his own powers or gifts that anything could be altered. Only God could make these changes. And the Reverend Petrie trusted his Lord day by day to do the things that were simply beyond him.

*

The chapel was quiet, the prison officer in attendance standing a discreet distance from where the man sat, head bowed, near the front of the room. There was a fresh smell within, like pine, reminding Ramsay of the trees around the loch though it was more than likely from some cleaning product. Nothing really fresh came into this place except at Christmas when baskets of pine cones appeared by the raised platform or underneath the artificial Christmas tree.

He bit the hard, calloused skin at the side of his finger, nails bitten to the quick. There was no clock in here and he turned his head several times, looking for the man he was supposed to be meeting. Maybe he'd been held up? Maybe he was too busy to bother with an old con like John Ramsay, he told himself bitterly. Wouldn't blame the man for that. After all, what could a nice clean-living person like the chaplain do for someone like him?

The tickle in his throat became a full-blown cough and Ramsay bent over, knowing the pain that would follow. He gasped, trying to find some air, stop the next spasm, but it was no use. Waves of pain crowded in his chest, until the hard dry coughs ceased. A low moan issued from the old man as he straightened up again, one hand rubbing his chest.

'You all right?'

Ramsay jumped as the chaplain sat beside him.

'Aye. Well, no' really.' Ramsay attempted a faint grin. Being a hard man was second nature to them all and any show of weakness in this place was dangerous. You kept yourself to yourself as far as possible, never letting the slightest vulnerability be seen. No tears during those long lonely nights, no sighing as you read bad news in the letters that came every so often, and certainly no complaining about your lot. The whiners soon learned to put up and shut up, their mantra of *I really shouldn't be in here, you know*, earning them the odd slap in the face.

He coughed again, a harsh rasping noise, tears filming his eyes.

'That sounded sore.'

Ramsay nodded but said nothing.

'You wanted to see me,' the chaplain continued.

'Aye.' Ramsay glanced sideways at the man by his side, assessing what sort of person he really was. Sunday services showed one side of him, the dutiful sermons aimed at making life bearable for the men, the Gospel message of good news usually going straight over their heads. But that had been till last week when something the Padre had said had niggled away at John Ramsay until he made the request to see Reverend Petrie for a quiet half-hour.

He was looking at him intently, the Padre's soft brown eyes searching his face as though asking lots of questions. No hardness in those features, though, not like the screws who stared, emotionless, or looked over your head.

Ramsay blinked and bent his head again. 'That sermon you gave ... ' He bit his lip, wondering how to put his feelings into words. 'It made me wonder ... '

'About yourself?'

Ramsay nodded. 'The thing about blood ... and wool ... where does that all come from, eh?' He looked at the quiet young man by his side, those gentle eyes regarding him thoughtfully. 'What was that thing you read out, again?'

Petrie gave him a faint grin. 'You were nearly right,' he

61

told the older man. 'But it's not blood that's mentioned.' He drew a little closer to Ramsay and lifted a well-worn Bible from the shelf in front of them. Ramsay watched attentively as the chaplain flicked easily through the book as if he knew it so intimately that each verse came readily to hand.

'Here we are,' Petrie murmured. Then, in a clear voice he read, ' "Come now, let us reason together, says the Lord; though your sins are like scarlet, they shall be as white as snow; though they are red like crimson, they shall become like wool.'

He placed the book on his lap and folded his hands on top of it. 'That was the verse I read out last Sunday,' he said.

Ramsay nodded, his lips tightening. He'd remembered blood, not words like scarlet or crimson. Just a mistake. Or an association of ideas? The old man felt a shudder down his spine. He'd shed plenty of other men's scarlet blood over the years, hadn't he? Sins that could not possibly be wiped clean.

'You wanted to talk to me about that?' Petrie asked quietly.

Ramsay nodded. 'Aye. Didn't really get it the first time,' he lied.

'In the Old Testament Isaiah was probably the most respected of the prophets,' Petrie told him. 'And in the time of Christ everyone in the Jewish community would know his words from the sermons in their synagogues. But, no matter what age we live in, everyone wants to know they have a chance of forgiveness, right?'

Ramsay glanced at him again, There was no feverish light in the chaplain's eyes, no desire to push him into a corner and confess his sins; just a sort of friendly expression as though he understood.

For the next few minutes he listened as the chaplain explained about the prophet's words and how they related to the Israelites way back then.

'Can I give you this to read for yourself?' Petrie asked at last, handing Ramsay the leather-bound book.

Ramsay hesitated. If he refused it would be really rude after asking the man to talk to him. But he'd need to keep it hidden from his co-pilot, the youngster who'd been in his cell when he'd returned from the hospital. No way was he going to appear like a soppy old man needing a Bible for comfort. And yet . . .

'Aye, aw right,' he said at last, stretching out his hand and taking the book. 'Thanks, Padre.'

'Can we say a wee prayer before you go?' Petrie asked. And Ramsay nodded again, closing his eyes and screwing them tight. Thank God none of the other inmates were here to listen to all of this stuff. Yet, as the chaplain spoke a few words, it really did seem as if he were talking to someone else and that the unseen recipient of his prayer was actually listening.

Petrie looked at the old man and saw the bowed head, those gnarled hands that had been involved in some dreadful crimes. Had the thief on the cross beside Jesus looked like that? Beaten and in despair?

There was no response from the man by his side, no sigh of recognition or remorse. So, did John Ramsay believe those words of scripture? Or was he so far past any belief in redemption that he was prepared to end his sorry life in misery?

*

Ramsay pushed the old book under his mattress. It was unlikely that he'd ever bother looking at it and he felt a bit ashamed of having taken up the young chaplain's time. Ach, he'd just need to reconcile himself to spending his last few weeks in here until his release date came up at last. He'd have no need of chaplains or ancient books then, he told himself. Just somewhere warm to lay down his old bones and sleep.

Yet, as he sank back on his bed, the chaplain's words kept returning, words that had not been about blood after all, just bright colours changing completely to white. He'd been the shedder of blood and perhaps it was his punishment to be eternally haunted by the things he had done.

Besides, how could he even have begun to think that forgiveness was within his grasp when he was already mired in plans that meant he would have to kill again?

CHAPTER ELEVEN

Flynn worried at the raggle on his fingernail. It had been a bad habit in his teens, exacerbated by the drugs he'd been using back then, and he'd gradually weaned himself off both. But the anxiety he felt did not stop when he thrust his hand back into his old jacket pocket. Having nothing to do today but cool his heels in this police station had given the young man a few bad memories from his past. The times he'd stood outside the concert hall shaking a polystyrene cup in the hope that enough punters would see past his dirty appearance and drop in some coins, their own consciences assuaged by a small act of what could be construed as kindness. His big eyes had been his best asset, looking puppy-like into their faces, a beaten creature ready to express so much gratitude, if that was what they wanted to hear.

As it was, Joseph Alexander Flynn was now losing money by sitting on this bench, waiting for the man who'd ordered him here to Paisley's Mill Street police HQ. Every hour that he lost was another few quid leaking from his business. For, now that he had kicked the old ways of his misspent youth, Flynn was working for himself with a modicum of success. A few years with Glasgow City Council had taught him enough to set the gardener on his own path of self-employment, his taxes filed carefully and his bank account in a reasonably healthy state. And while he doubted that his enterprise would ever make him a wealthy man, the work itself was reward enough. Being out of doors in all seasons was what Flynn needed, the cold winds and the blustery days rarely holding him back. And for those times when landscaping was impossible, he caught up with paperwork or busied himself with the computer that had been given to him by Maggie Lorimer, his skill at creating garden landscapes on paper a new-found joy.

The police office was like every one Flynn remembered, blue-covered benches attached to the floor (so that neds couldn't chuck them at any of the police officers on duty), a noticeboard with posters urging the community to be vigilant about this or that or to report any suspicions to their local cops. And this waiting: that was something Flynn had all but forgotten over the years since he had attended a police office. They always made you wait. Was that to drive you into a state of sheer nervousness? Or because behind the scenes they really were that busy?

He pushed his hair out of his eyes, making a mental note to drop into a local barber's up the High Street after he'd finished here.

'Mr Flynn?' The swing doors were open and a pleasant-faced woman about his own age stood looking down at him.

Flynn sprang to his feet.

'I'm DC Finlay,' she told him. 'Would you come this way please? DS Evans is waiting for you upstairs.'

Flynn followed her along a corridor then up two flights of stairs, passing a man in a dark grey suit who nodded briefly at the detective constable but completely ignored Flynn. As he climbed the stairs after her, Flynn admired her slim ankles and curvaceous figure then inwardly cursed himself. It wasn't right to look at a female police officer this way, was it? Anyway, a nice-looking lassie like this was way out of his league. Yet, as they came to the top of the stairs, Flynn found himself looking for a ring on DC Finlay's left hand. In spite of himself, he felt a surge of pleasure to see that her fingers were bare.

'Did you ever meet a pal of mine, Detective Superintendent Lorimer?' he blurted out.

DC Finlay's eyebrows rose. 'He's a friend of yours?' she asked, surprise etched on her features.

'Oh, aye,' Flynn assured her. 'We go way back, so we do. To tell you the truth, I probably wouldn't be here the day if it wasnae for Lorimer. And I don't mean this place.' He grinned, sticking a thumb up at the walls beside them.

'Really?' The detective constable smiled again, obviously intrigued.

'Buy you a coffee later and tell you all about it, if you want?' Flynn offered with a chuckle.

The woman smiled again, this time showing twin dimples in her cheeks. 'You're a chancer, aren't you?' she laughed.

'That's what the Lorimers' old cat's called,' Flynn told her, grinning back. 'Chancer. I look after it sometimes when they're away.'

DC Finlay tilted her head, looking at Flynn as though for the first time and liking what she saw.

'I'm not off shift till five o'clock,' she whispered.

'Well, how about a drink, then? Somewhere nice and handy?'

DC Finlay raised her eyebrows. 'My, you don't waste much time, do you, Mr Flynn?'

'Off today because of this.' Flynn shrugged, still looking at her with what he hoped was his old disarming smile.

'Aye, why not,' she replied, her lips twitching with suppressed laughter. 'How about the Watermill. Just after five?'

'I'll be there,' he replied swiftly, trying to hide his surprise.

DC Finlay pushed open a double set of doors and led Flynn through a large room where several officers sat at desks and computers, a few glancing their way as if curious to know who the stranger was. She stopped at the far end and knocked on a glass-fronted door.

'The DS says sorry he kept you waiting, by the way,' she whispered. 'It's been hell in here this morning.'

'Mr Flynn, please come in.' A dark-suited man about Flynn's height opened the door and ushered him to a seat. Flynn's first impression was that this guy was just back from a holiday in the sun or he spent a lot of time in a tanning salon, his teeth dazzling white below a scrubby moustache.

'Thanks, Erin.' He nodded to the woman who stood beside Flynn, dismissing her at once.

Flynn glanced behind as the door closed. Well, if he was lucky enough, that wouldn't be the last he'd see of the detective constable. And now he knew that her name was Erin.

'Right, Mr Flynn, or is it Joseph?'

'Everyone just calls me Flynn,' he replied. 'No need for first names.'

'Just so.' Evans nodded brusquely. 'Well, it looks as if you've uncovered a fair old can of worms, if you'll excuse the pun.' Evans attempted a smile that did not reach his eyes. 'We, that is the Cold Case Unit, are looking into the death of this chap as homicide. The initial examination shows that and hopefully in time we'll have sufficient forensic evidence to put a name to him.'

Evans lifted a pencil and began to twirl it absently between his fingers. 'I don't suppose you had ever been in that place before?'

'Couple of days previously, doing the same big patch,' Flynn told him. 'But I'd never been out that way at all. Houston was new to me, though the place is a wee bit out of the actual village.'

'You sure about that? Sure you've never been there in the past?' The DS's eyes bored into his own, making Flynn feel hot under the collar. He was stricken with a sudden desire to look away from that steely gaze but held the other man's stare, knowing that a sideways look could be misinterpreted as an impulse to lie.

'Quite sure,' he said firmly.

'Not even in your bad old days?' Evans asked, a condescending smile on his tanned face.

'No,' Flynn replied, resisting the urge to rise to the man's bait. 'Not even then.'

Evans looked down at a notepad on his desk. 'Right,' he repeated. 'So, what can you tell me about the job you took on for Mr Mathieson?'

The next half hour was spent with Flynn going over the same ground as before, wondering all the time just why he had been brought into the police HQ and if his past had anything at all to do with the skeleton he had uncovered. Knowing the head of the Major Incident Team did not cut any ice with this guy, apparently, nor had his statement shown anything other than his willingness to assist the police in this inquiry. At last, the interview was over, a firm handshake given and DS Evans had called a different female officer to escort Flynn from the police office.

His eyes roamed across the room, seeking out DC Erin Finlay, but she was nowhere to be seen. With a heavy heart, Flynn climbed down the steps back into the cold afternoon, wondering if she was likely to turn up at the Watermill and if he would ever see her again. She must know about his past, after all, if that DS had been poking about. Why would she even think about meeting him after work? Flynn shivered, thrusting hands into his jacket pocket, telling himself that it really didn't matter, but there was still a wee voice inside that told him DC Erin Finlay was a woman he would love to get to know.

Learning the truth about an unidentified body takes a great deal of skill and patience, especially one that has been dead and buried for a considerable length of time. Rosie Fergusson sat back at her desk with a sigh. Forensic anthropology was not her speciality but she had seen enough corpses over her career to learn the basic techniques of that particular science. The skeletal remains that the gardener had discovered were surprisingly intact, depredations by animals, particularly foxes, not unexpected in a case like this. Rosie had examined the numerous photographic images over and over again since her first careful scrutiny of the bones that lay in her department. The skull was of greatest interest to the police, of course, the hole showing exactly where that fatal bullet had entered, probably killing the victim instantly. No exit wound on the opposite side of the skull and the pathologist guessed that the bullet had pierced the bone as the man had fallen, but had stayed there, lodged tightly until skin and brain matter had dissolved in the dark earth where he had been buried.

What did she know about him? A young man, she believed from the formation of his limbs, and certainly an adult, the wisdom teeth well formed, though neglected as if his diet had suffered. Or, she mused, leaning forward once more and enlarging the picture, was that missing incisor a sign of something else? No tissue remained to show if the tooth had been wrenched from the man's mouth or knocked out by a blow. Rosie sighed and rubbed the base of her spine. She'd been sitting there for hours, looking at these images, willing them to reveal anything at all of the life that had gone from the bones. Forensic odontology might be the way to go, she told herself, if only they could find a timescale to begin with. Often a victim of violent crime had been part of a gang himself, possibly with a police record. A prison dentist might keep records of the patients he or she saw in the course of their work, but which prison and when?

These were questions best answered by the woman who was now making her way north to the University of Glasgow's Forensic Medicine department. The forensic anthropologist had seen countless skeletons over her own career, both here and in Kosovo where the dead from mass graves had been identified after a time, their flesh disintegrating into pulpy masses. A clean skeleton held no terrors for Alice Morton CBE, the diminutive lady who had taught Rosie so much in her own undergraduate years. Now nearing retirement, Professor Morton was the foremost woman in her particular field and the person Rosie hoped might shed some light on this case. She closed down the file with a yawn. Time to go home now to baby Ben and Abby. Solly would be there already, waiting for her, knowing that her work so often made Rosie the last of the family to arrive back at their West End flat. Tomorrow she would meet with Alice Morton and then, perhaps, she might be able to add something to the existing forensic report.

So many people were waiting for answers: the pathologist, the police, not to mention the man who had first glimpsed these bones deep in the soil of that country garden. Rosie flexed her tired shoulders as she thought about Joseph Alexander Flynn, imagining the moment when his eyes and brain told him just what he had dug up, the realisation making him recoil in horror.

Flynn jumped out of his seat as soon as he felt the tap on his shoulder.

The woman smiled down at him, evidently amused by the surprise in his eyes.

'Didn't think I'd come, eh?' Erin Finlay slid onto the vacant seat beside Flynn.

'Glad you did, though.' Flynn's eyebrows rose as he regarded the policewoman thoughtfully. 'What would you like to drink?'

'Oh, just a diet Coke for me.' She wrinkled her nose (a very pretty, pert little nose, Flynn noticed). 'Driving, can't afford to be caught in my line of work,' she added with a grin.

Flynn laid a hand on her shoulder as he rose to head for the bar. It was a small gesture, not meant as anything more than an assurance that he was glad that she had come to meet him. But when her fingers closed over his own, he felt as though this young woman could see inside his head, understand the tumble of emotions that filled him with a strange joy.

She was watching for him when he brought the drinks back from the bar, a Coke for her, a ginger beer and lime for himself.

'You driving too?' she asked, eyebrows raised at the two glasses.

'Yep, brought the van down. Actually, it's all I've got. Don't have a second car. Too many overheads in my business to afford anything else,' he explained. 'It's a decent van, though I'd need to clean it out before I gave a lady a lift anywhere.' He grinned ruefully. 'Always has loads of gear and with my mucky boots and everything, it never has a chance to be that smart.'

'And would you?' Erin Finlay asked, tilting her head to one side.

'Would I what?'

'Give me a lift anywhere?' she asked, lips twitching with suppressed laughter.

Flynn grinned back at her. 'Course I would. Where do you fancy?'

Erin laughed out loud then, a real hoot, not a girlish giggle, and Flynn found himself warming to her even more.

'Cheers,' he said, raising his glass to hers. 'Tae our first outing in my van!'

The policewoman's smile faded just a little as they clinked glasses. But she kept her eyes fixed on his, giving a little nod as if to agree on that. Or was he reading too much into that salutation? Was his sudden hope for a proper relationship with this nice-looking woman clouding the reality of the situation?

Flynn looked down at his drink, doubt taking the edge off his pleasure.

'Why did you really come down to meet me?' he asked quietly. 'A nice girl like you?'

Erin didn't answer for a moment, simply regarding him thoughtfully.

'I get that a lot. Not the nice girl bit,' she began. 'The fact that I'm a polis. It kind of gets in the way sometimes. Especially if I meet someone at work.' She shrugged.

'No ulterior motive, then?' Flynn asked, half-joking, but giving her the opportunity to come clean if she really had wanted to talk to him about the case.

'Well,' she nodded again, 'maybe just a wee bit of one. I was curious about your pal, Lorimer. How did you come to know him?'

'Ah, it's the big guy that brought you here, then, no' a burnin' desire tae see this poor hard-done-by gardener?'

Erin dunted him with her elbow. 'Fishing for compliments already?' she laughed. 'I admit I was interested in your relationship with the head of the MIT but I wouldn't be here if you hadn't asked me so nicely.'

For a moment Flynn held her gaze and knew that he wanted to believe her. So many people in his past had lied to him but those days were gone. Now he was leading a decent life, mixing with clients who could afford his services, and making a living from his own hard work. Why shouldn't a girl like Erin want to get to know him better?

'Is there anywhere you have to be or can I buy you dinner?' he asked.

'That's nice of you,' Erin told him. 'I live on my own so there's nobody expecting me home. But I think if we have dinner together we should go Dutch. Not as if it's a first date or anything.' She bit her lip, cheeks reddening a little.

'Sure,' Flynn chuckled. 'And we can always discuss the possibility of a date over our meal, hm?'

She nodded at him, meeting his eyes and then looking down again as though taken with sudden shyness.

As he waved her off from the hotel car park, Flynn watched the red tail-lights until they disappeared into the traffic. Erin lived in one of the new flats near Braehead, she'd told him, but that was all he knew about her home. They'd exchanged mobile numbers and he'd promised to call her, knowing that it would take every ounce of strength not to text her as soon as he reached his own place. He'd moved from the flat in

Govanhill that Maggie Lorimer's mum had helped him to furnish. Now Flynn rented a one-bedroom apartment on the south side of the River Clyde, the private parking ideal for his van. The rent was pretty steep, though, and Flynn had been saving over the last few years, knowing that a mortgage for a home of his own was the better option.

As he set off from the Watermill, he reflected on the evening spent with a woman who'd been a complete stranger just a few hours earlier. Erin was easy to talk to and Flynn had found himself opening up about his past, making a joke about his bad-boy days. He'd skipped a few details, right enough, but had told her the truth about how Lorimer had rescued him from a life of drugs on the street, giving him a place in his own home to recuperate from the accident that had nearly killed him.

After that Erin had told him a bit about herself: she'd wanted to join the police after a talk at school from a couple of officers from Mill Street and had been happy when she'd been sent there after her stint at Tullyallan, the Scottish Police college. She'd had her fair share of seeing the bad side of humanity; that was to be expected after all, but doing a job that was worthwhile gave Erin Finlay more satisfaction than anything she could imagine. Now that she worked in the Cold Case Unit in Mill Street, she had lots of fun searching into the past, trying to put names to victims of homicide, like the one Flynn had uncovered.

Her eyes had lit up as she told him a couple of stories about relatives she'd managed to speak to at the conclusion of a successful case, no names given, of course, and Flynn had found himself liking this young woman more and more.

By the time he reached the Clydeside flats and parked the van, Flynn's hands were itching to pull out his mobile and text her. After a few hesitant starts and several deletions, he finally pressed send, hoping that his simple message about how much he'd enjoyed the evening and 'how about a coffee soon?', would be rewarded with a positive answer.

The lift took him to the top floor and Flynn stepped out into the small landing. In three strides he was unlocking his door and, as he closed it behind him, the ring tone from his mobile made him whip it out eagerly.

Tomorrow? Same time same place? it read.

His fingers fairly flew over the tiny keyboard as he tapped out his reply.

See you there.

He hesitated for a moment then added an X, pressing send before he could change his mind.

CHAPTER TWELVE

He was a bad man; that was one thing he knew for certain, no matter what the chaplain said. There were certain things that were impossible to do in this life and one was to erase the past. Oh, aye, he spoke about forgiveness, redemption and all that stuff, but what was done was done and you couldn't ever bring back to life the folk you'd sent to an early grave, could you?

Being inside was what he'd deserved and pleading guilty had been the right way to go, taking the sentence handed down and making the best of it during these years of incarceration.

John Ramsay turned in the narrow bed. It was still dark outside and lights in here wouldn't come on for a while yet. It had become a habit to wake in the night, those dreary hours between three and four when his spirit was at its lowest ebb. The man in the adjacent bed was snoring quietly. They'd come and gone during Ramsay's time here, younger men still displaying the sort of bravado that would get them arrested time after time until they learned how to keep out of trouble, or at least under the radar. Thank God this one wasn't a druggie, he thought, remembering his last co-pilot who'd fretted and moaned night after night, fidgeting and talking non-stop during the day, driving the old man to the point where he wanted to give the bloke a belting. Ramsay had complained instead and asked for him to be moved. They'd just laughed at him, of course, but the druggie had been out in a matter of months, Ramsay glad to see the back of him.

His window in Barlinnie faced east and sometimes Ramsay was rewarded with a faint pink glow as the sun rose above these bleak grey walls. All he could see from his cell was another block that blotted out much of the sky. That was what John Ramsay missed most; waking up and being able to look out of a window, feel fresh air on his face. It wouldn't be long now, though. His release date was just about to be agreed and he would be a free man this side of Christmas.

The thought should have given him a warm feeling of pleasure but as Ramsay closed his eyes once more, all he could see was the figure of the man who was to be his next target. It had been decided for him, of course. There was no way he'd have had any say about the mark. That was up to others more powerful than himself. The killing had begun and two of the names on the list were already scored off as if they were just numbers. That was how it had been put to him at the start, Ramsay recalled. It was just a job to these polismen and -women, the Big Man had explained: they didn't lose any sleep over putting the likes of John Ramsay away for a very long time, did they? So, in his turn, it was just to be regarded as another job to the old hitman.

Except this time it wasn't like that.

Had the years inside made him lose his touch? Had old age and infirmity made him feeble and sentimental? The Big Man didn't think so, or he wouldn't have demanded that John Ramsay seek out the armourer on his release from prison. A suitable weapon would be waiting for him, he'd been told. He'd be given all the info he'd need to study the mark, taking his time to decide on a place of execution.

In the past Ramsay had done the jobs thoroughly and with a professionalism that had earned him the respect of those at the head of various criminal organisations. He should have been pleased to be chosen for this job, of course he should. And part of his reward was seeing an old adversary scored off the list.

It was just when he'd been given the name that the gnawing doubts had crept into John Ramsay's mind. He'd come across the man several times in the past and bore him no ill will.

The famous line from *The Godfather* had resonated in his brain: *It's not personal . . . it's strictly business.*

But was he capable of taking yet another life? And, in particular, this man's life? Shedding more blood and adding to the weight of his all-consuming guilt? The Padre's words came back to him now and Ramsay closed his eyes, craving the sleep that would bring oblivion to his mind, knowing full well that the hours would tick by slowly till he would hear the sound of a key turning in the lock and another day begin at last.

CHAPTER THIRTEEN

'No significant bone loss, apart from the ones the foxes got,' Alice Morton's eyes twinkled as she smiled at the pathologist to share in her joke, 'so he's not that advanced in age.' She had already scanned the X-rays Rosie had shown her, nodding as the pathologist remarked on the extent of ossification, the bones thickening as a human aged.

'Look here,' she said, indicating a faint squiggly line running across the top of the skull. 'That's what we call the sagittal suture,' she explained. 'See how it is completely fused?' She eyed Rosie, who nodded attentively. 'Then we know he was older than thirty-five. Now, see here.' She moved a little to one side and pointed at a second line to the front of the skull, bending close and peering at it through her thick spectacles. 'Hm, that's handy,' she murmured. 'Not fully closed, see? So he didn't reach forty, poor man.' The forensic anthropologist straightened up and looked into the distance. ' "Forever wilt thou love, and she be fair . . . Forever panting, and forever young.",' she quoted.

Then, smiling at Rosie's puzzled frown, Alice Morton nodded. 'Keats. "Ode on a Grecian Urn",' she explained. 'Always think of these lines whenever I see a young person's remains. Not that he was so very young, and by the looks of him he led an interesting life.'

'Keats? I think I remember that one from school,' Rosie admitted slowly.

'The figures carved onto that Grecian Urn were immortalised by him,' Alice told her. 'Frozen in time and marble.' She nodded once more. 'Unlike this chap who was left in the Scottish soil to deteriorate, decompose ... but fret not, Rosie, my dear, we can tell a good bit more about him already.'

Rosie grinned back at Alice, who had stepped nimbly around the table where the skeleton lay.

'Looking at the pubic symphysis here,' said Alice, indicating a joint at the man's pelvis, 'we can see very little sign of pits or cragginess, confirming that he wasn't an old man when he was shot.'

Rosie remained silent, afraid to stop the older woman's flow as she was getting into her stride. 'His teeth help a lot too, don't they?' Alice Morton exclaimed. 'Worn down like that at his age? Sign of a poor diet, I reckon. What do you think? Lad from a deprived part of town? Got into bad company? Falls out with his mates then, bang!' She aimed at the skeleton with her fingers shaped like a gun. 'He's gone!' Alice grinned at her former student. 'And he's been gone for quite a long time, haven't you, lad?' she added, turning to address the skeleton. 'Need to get along with carbon dating, eh? Determine just when you were laid to rest in that country garden.'

The older woman fixed Rosie with a stare. 'You should call on Lorna Dawson, of course. She could tell you much more about this fellow's grave than I ever could. Best soil scientist in the UK.'

'Not my shout,' Rosie told her. 'Depends on Police Scotland's budget. In any case there doesn't seem to be any great rush to find out this man's identity. It's not as if he is linked to an ongoing case or part of an older one that could present any danger to the public.' She shrugged.

'Ah, well. At least you got me here. Fortunate about those guest lectures at the university,' Alice twinkled.

Rosie suppressed a laugh. The lectures had been swiftly arranged as soon as Alice Morton had agreed to come north, making the celebrated forensic anthropologist's visit to Glasgow worthwhile.

'By the way, is there any chance you might lend me this chap's skull? Just for a while. It might be nice to try a facial reconstruction.'

'I'll ask the officers in charge, shall I? I bet they'd jump at a chance to have you do this. Imagine having a three-dimensional picture of him!'

Alice Morton laughed. 'It takes time, of course, so don't expect miracles, my dear.'

As the two women turned to go, leaving an assistant to cover up the skeleton and wheel it back to its temporary lodging, Rosie gave a sigh of pleasure. Tonight she would be free to entertain this fascinating woman to dinner, Solly joining them once Morag, their nanny, arrived. It was a rare night out, though she could guess that the talk around the restaurant table would be about the case. Her husband would be interested to know not so much how the victim died, but why.

Solly gazed out at the city lights spread below his window. Glasgow was now his home city, a strange admission perhaps for a born-and-bred Londoner, but Solomon Brightman preferred the smaller city, whose citizens shared a pawky sort of humour and a friendliness. Glaswegians did not take themselves or others too seriously, yet had the capacity for genuine warmth and compassion. He felt part of the place after all these years, at one with the student life around this part of the city. Ben and Abby would grow up here, he told himself contentedly, free to choose their own route once schooldays were over, but that was a long way off yet, years ahead.

A sigh escaped the psychologist as his thoughts flicked to the unidentified victim his wife had been examining earlier in the day. A man whose life had been cut short; a man, Rosie had told him, who had probably not even seen his fortieth birthday. Solly blinked behind his horn-rimmed spectacles. His own fortieth birthday had passed in a haze of night feeds and nappies, neither he nor Rosie desiring more than a decent night's sleep in lieu of a party.

'Ready?'

He turned and smiled at Rosie standing there, looking fresh and gorgeous in a deep crimson coat, a patterned pashmina in hues of pink and violet slung across one shoulder. Just two hours before, she had hurried home, dark circles under her eyes, yet now, with that magic some women seemed to possess, she had transformed herself into this radiant creature, sparkling with the anticipation of a night out.

'You look wonderful,' he said simply, bending towards her and planting a kiss on her cheek. 'Let's go, shall we?'

'Have a nice time, you two,' Morag called out from the lounge where Abby was doing her best to prolong the time till she was packed off to bed, pretending to read a story to baby Ben who was bouncing on Morag's knee.

The night was calm and still, though there was a distinct chill in the air as they crossed the park. They were to meet Alice Morton in Stravaigin, one of their favourite restaurants in nearby Gibson Street, a short walk from their top-storey flat in Park Circus. He and Rosie walked to and from work most days, except when she had appointments further afield like the city's mortuary; Rosie was the driver in the family, Solly preferring to take a taxi or public transport whenever necessary. He had never had the notion to obtain a driver's licence and had sufficient self-knowledge to understand that he might be a liability on the roads, given his tendency to become too easily engrossed in his thoughts.

Soon they were entering the brightly lit restaurant, the maître d' coming forward to greet them like the old friend that she now was.

'Your guest is here already.' The woman smiled at them in turn. 'Let me take your coats.'

Alice half rose from her seat as they approached a table in the corner, Rosie hurrying to give her a hug.

'This is Solly, my husband,' she said, turning and beaming at the bearded man standing quietly to one side.

Alice Morton stood up now and smiled. 'Ah, the celebrated

Professor Brightman,' she exclaimed, allowing Solly to kiss her on each cheek. 'I've read your work on female killers,' she added, taking her seat again and following Solly with her eyes. 'Most informative, I must say.'

'Solly's working on a new book,' Rosie told her, an unmistakable note of pride in her tone. 'It's about the psychology behind recidivism.'

'Hm, you follow the recent trends in prisons regarding rehabilitation, then, Professor?'

'Please, call me Solly,' he replied, dipping his head modestly. 'It's a fascinating area, of course, and we are lamentably behind many of our European counterparts when it comes to rehabilitating offenders.'

Just then a waiter approached bearing three menus and for the next few minutes each of them pored over the choices for dinner. Solly breathed a grateful sigh. He wasn't one for talking about a work in progress, preferring to sit and think on his own with no distractions, something that happened less and less at home since Ben's arrival.

At last, their selections made, Alice Morton swept a glance at the couple seated opposite her.

'Thank you for this,' she began. 'It's not often I have a dinner date with two such interesting people.' A smile twitched at the corners of her mouth. 'But then don't you find that death makes for the best sort of conversation?'

Solly could hear the flippant tone and gave a polite smile, just what was required at the moment, but his thoughts had immediately gone from the skeletal remains that both women were examining to the disturbing deaths of two police officers.

'Oh, have I said something wrong?' Alice Morton's eyes clouded for a moment as she looked at Solly. 'I have, haven't I? What is it, my dear?' She laid a kindly hand across the table and gripped Solly's fingers.

Then he found himself telling the forensic anthropologist about the shootings in Inverkip and near Inverness. As he spoke, Solly was aware of the older woman's attention and Rosie by his side, nodding occasionally as he related the details in hushed tones, careful not to be overheard in a public place.

'And he was a friend?' Alice asked at last.

'More a friend of a friend,' Solly explained. 'But we both worked on the same case with George's colleague, William Lorimer.' He gave a shy smile and looked affectionately at Rosie. 'That's how we met,' he added.

'Goodness knows what he saw in me under that white forensic suit,' Rosie protested, picking up her glass of wine with a giggle.

'Same goes for me,' Solly laughed. 'A chap that can't stand the sight of blood . . . you won't see me in any mortuary, I can assure you. My hat goes off to professionals like you both.' He gave a slight bow in Alice's direction.

'What do you make of the two shootings?' Alice asked as she picked at her prawn starter. 'Are they related, do you think?'

Rosie and Solly shared a questioning look.

'Far too early to tell,' Rosie pointed out. 'Ballistic reports still to come in. Haven't heard if either officer had known the other or worked a case together. George's time on the force was before Police Scotland was formed so it's less likely that they had ever met through work.'

Solly remained silent, unwilling to speculate on the possibility that the same gunman had dispatched each former police officer to the hereafter. Earlier today he had spoken to Lorimer and heard the latest details about Stephen McAlpine. The detective superintendent was obviously still reeling from the death of his old boss and the news of this second shooting up north had come as a real shock. Questions were being asked, tests carried out, but as yet there was nothing to link these two men apart from the method of their deaths.

The main courses had given way to desserts, Solly choosing a selection of Scottish cheeses to which he was especially partial. He sipped his mineral water from time to time, listening as the two women chatted about their workload and the perennial problems of university politics. Rosie and Alice were enjoying what the latter had proclaimed a very decent bottle of Merlot, though such praise was lost on Solly who simply did not care for alcohol or its effects.

His mind roamed back to the discussion about the killings. How easy it was to take a gun and shoot someone dead, he thought. Yet perhaps not. Some planning had to have gone into the time these men were killed, the opportunity to have them in the gunman's sights taken into careful consideration. For, he believed, neither of these had been a random act of violence. Rather, it seemed to Solomon Brightman, these shootings showed an intelligent mind that had worked out just where and when they would take place.

There had to be a link, he told himself, staring past the women opposite and gazing into the middle distance. It was just a matter of time before the investigating teams found just what that was.

There was a solemn silence as the figures walked along the corridor, DC Connor McAlpine supporting his mother, his sister clutching the woman's arm on the other side. From a distance it might look as if they were almost dragging Ellen McAlpine along to the viewing room, but the truth was that their mother was heavily sedated, her eyes half closed, still red from weeping.

The attendant stood aside and a deep pink curtain was drawn back to reveal a small plain room where a man lay on a narrow bed, the white sheet drawn up and folded under his chin. They had positioned him so that the wound was not visible from this side but the dead man's face was waxy pale now, his lips closed. It was as though he had no more to say about the world, his life cut off suddenly, all thoughts and imagination ceasing in the seconds after that shot had been fired.

'Oh, Dad,' the young man blurted out, a catch in his voice.

'It's okay, Connor, son.' Ellen McAlpine patted his hand. 'It's okay,' she repeated, looking dreamily through the pane of glass.

But of course nothing would be okay ever again for this family, each autumn season a reminder of their loss.

CHAPTER FOURTEEN

'You're kidding me.' Terry Finnegan sat down heavily, the phone pressed to her ear.

'It's true,' the woman on the other end of the line insisted.

There was a short silence as Terry digested the news that her DI counterpart, Heather McDougall, had uttered.

It had been two days since Stephen McAlpine had been shot dead on that lonely woodland track, three since George Phillips had been found lying in his garden. A short time to have this sort of information, but things moved fast when it concerned one of their own, Terry reminded herself.

'I'm looking at the ballistics report right now. Expect it will be on your own news feed,' she added.

Terry groped towards her laptop, phone tucked under her chin.

'Gimme a minute,' she gasped, then, laying down the phone, she grabbed the laptop and in seconds was scrolling down to the page that DI McDougall had indicated.

'Not sure I want to believe this,' she muttered to herself, then, picking up the mobile, she swallowed hard.

'Okay, I suppose we ought to have been prepared for it,' she said, her voice thick with emotion. 'Difficult enough to take in that George was murdered, but *this*?'

'I know,' McDougall agreed. 'And all in the space of a day or so. Doesn't take that long to drive up your way ...' She tailed off, letting Terry fill in the details.

'It was well planned out,' Terry told her. 'Road blocks in place, other persons involved. They must have done a recce on our man's movements to know exactly when he would return from dropping off his grandkids. It wasn't just some random gunman running amok.'

'No,' McDougall agreed. 'There's one hell of a lot more to this than two separate shootings, don't you think?'

Terry bit her lip. Should she mention Lorimer? Tell the DI down in Greenock about the detective super's insistence that coincidences like this deserved more scrutiny? But, faced with this ballistics report, it was no longer a matter of conjecture whether the two killings were completely coincidental.

'Same gun. Same gunman?' she murmured.

Heather McDougall put down the phone and gave a deep sigh. If there was another link between these two former officers it was up to the two teams to find it. Otherwise the cases would be taken over by a bigger group altogether. She found herself thinking back to Lorimer at the city mortuary gazing sadly at the body of his old boss. It might come down to that, right enough, she thought, closing her lips in a grim line. The head of the MIT could easily have stepped in and demanded to take over both cases by now but had not so much as hinted that could happen. Till things changed she and DI Finnegan were still SIOs and her own team was moving heaven and earth, seeking out as much background info as they could about the late George Phillips and what had made him a target for that hitman.

It had to be something about one of his old cases, surely? George had been a good cop, had maintained a reputation for honest dealing with his fellow officers and there had never been the slightest rumour of taking backhanders from crooks. But was that really the situation? Had he kept some secrets hidden? And was his death to be the catalyst for uncovering things about the man, things that none of his friends wanted to believe?

Lorimer's eyes clouded over as he read the email a second time. The SIO in Greenock had done the decent thing, forwarding the ballistics report to him, and the short note attached was simply courteous, no sign of DI McDougall asking for any favours from him.

Just wanted you to know that the two cases have now been linked. Still no other area of common ground between the deceased officers but working to establish that.

And she would be, he thought. If he had been SIO in either of these cases he would have his team working their butts off to see if Stephen McAlpine or George Phillips had ever come into contact through the job or in any other capacity.

There had to be a link, Lorimer told himself. It was too

much of a coincidence that a gunman had selected these officers without some deeper reason. The police might work on the assumption that the same gunman was involved since the ballistics report now confirmed that each victim had been shot dead by the same weapon. Small as it was, a bullet could provide a huge amount of information; from the simple fact of its calibre to the specific rifling marks that identified its provenance.

And it would not just be the police themselves making some assumptions, he knew. Once this came out, the media would have a field day. Already the newspapers and online reports were headlining the two deaths and it was just a matter of time before some idiot leaked the information about the bullets. He trusted the officers up in Gartcosh, though, men and women who devoted their days to studying ballistics. But would tongues begin to wag in Inverness or Inverclyde? Theresa Finnegan was the new girl up there and that might mean a bit of resentment from any officer that had been overlooked for promotion. Lorimer knew from bitter experience how these things worked and feared that it would not take long for the *Inverness Courier* to get hold of this juicy snippet of information.

A dry chuckle came from the man reading the latest report about the killings of the two cops. It was more than satisfying to imagine the consternation within Police Scotland and the head scratching that these deaths had caused. Oh, aye, they might boast about the wonderful new technologies they had and that new place out in Gartcosh. But he was cleverer than those sorts. And besides, wasn't he already several steps ahead of them?

The list was folded neatly and hidden behind the fly leaf of the book next to his bed. But he had no need of reading it. Each name on that list was burned onto his memory and he had the satisfaction of knowing that it would be his hand that wielded the pencil to score out their names.

Taking a deep breath, he savoured the sense of satisfaction that came from being in control of it all. No matter where he was or what he was doing on a day-to-day basis, he had this God-like power, omnipotent in the decision of where and when the next hit would take place.

His closed his eyes and sat back, hands folded behind his head, dreaming about the chaos that was only just beginning.

CHAPTER FIFTEEN

HUNT FOR COP KILLER: POLICE STEP UP ENQUIRIES

Following the shooting of former Detective Inspector Stephen McAlpine, Police Scotland have said that their investigation is now being linked to that of the death of George Phillips, a former senior officer who was based largely in the Glasgow area. Mr McAlpine had served in Dundee for thirty years, retiring four years ago when he and his wife, Ellen, relocated to the Grantown area to be closer to their family in Aviemore. Detective Inspector Theresa Finnegan, senior investigating officer, has said that, despite their enquiries being at an early stage, she is confident that extra resources from Police Scotland will be put into the case and that the killer will be found. Stephen McAlpine was a well-respected officer and a loving family man who had enjoyed caring for his two grandchildren since his retirement from the force.

He leaves a wife, Ellen, a nurse at Raigmore Hospital, a daughter and son. Forensic officers have been at the scene of the shooting in recent days and it is speculated that the two former police officers were deliberately targeted by the same gunman. Police here and in Inverclyde are asking anyone who may have seen anything suspicious prior to the shootings to come forward.

'There's nothing to be worried about, is there?' Terry Finnegan held the phone to her ear, waiting impatiently for the other woman to respond.

'Doesn't look like it,' McDougall agreed. 'They're fishing here as well, only to be expected. But so far all the press knows is the timings of the incidents and a bit about the two officers' background. Squeaky clean, the pair of them, by all accounts.'

'Aye, nothing seemed to have stuck to McAlpine as far as I can see. Decent cop, decent man. Rumours are flying around, of course. That is always going to happen, isn't it? What they don't know they make up,' she said bitterly. 'Still, the local journos up here have toed the line. But it's just a matter of time till they put two and two together.'

'There's no chance of it coming out at this end,' Heather McDougall insisted. 'It's been impressed on everyone associated with the case that they keep their mouths shut about the ballistics. Once that gets out then the press will be screaming about a gunman on the loose and police getting nowhere fast.'

'As usual,' agreed Terry with a weary sigh. 'What do you think, though? Same guy? A loner picking off two cops for some reason?'

'Hm, same weapon, so more than likely same hitman. But was it out of some malicious intent or was he paid to take them both out? And, million-dollar question, why?'

Terry Finnegan stifled a yawn. She had not slept more than five hours a night since her arrival in Inverness and the case was becoming all-consuming. In an odd way it was comforting to be able to talk to McDougall, know that she was not alone in trying to find a reason behind this shooting.

'You still there?' DI McDougall asked.

Terry sniffed. 'Aye, but better get back to work. There's a pile of paperwork to get through. Thirty years' worth. There must be some kind of link. Did they put away the same perp, for instance?'

'We're looking at that too,' McDougall agreed. 'Something will turn up. Just stick in there. Speak later, okay? And thanks for the call. Bit of a relief to know that the press are still unaware of what they found at Gartcosh.'

Nothing troubling about Lawrence Mathieson had been found and it seemed that the Englishman was entirely innocent of anything to do with the skeleton discovered in his own backyard. Once it had become clear that its provenance predated Mathieson's arrival at the house, the banker had assumed what Lorimer guessed was an air of natural belligerence, the peculiar authority adopted by some men whose work involved dealing in big money. He'd seen it in gangsters as well as in those professionals who were well on the side of the law, an attitude of superiority that made some men bullies. Most people had secrets, Lorimer mused as he closed down his computer and readied himself for the journey home. He would put out a few more feelers if the time and trouble could be justified but he felt that Mathieson and his wife really had no prior knowledge of what had been buried in their garden. Lorimer dismissed the new owners, turning to other matters. He was interested to see if Rosie and her forensic anthropologist friend could come up with anything that might identify Flynn's skeleton.

The case had helped keep Lorimer's mind off George Phillips's death, but then, as he picked up his coat and headed downstairs, the detective superintendent's face became grim. Nobody should have served the public the way George had and come to such an end. The injustice of it rankled almost as much as the need to find out who had killed him and why. But that was a job for DI McDougall, he reminded himself. Treading on another officer's case was not on, especially when that officer was a young ambitious woman. It was high time that there were more women in senior positions like DCC Caroline Flint and he knew that any sign of interference by the MIT would only be counterproductive. His mind roamed back several years to the discovery of a body on the shores of Fishnish Bay and the subsequent investigation, a case he had eventually shared with a female detective but not until she had ceased to see him as a threat.

As he stepped into the Lexus, Lorimer glanced upwards. Clouds were scudding across the darkening sky and the wind was rising. Soon the trees would be swept by autumn storms, their spent leaves cast adrift for another season. Flynn might come by at the weekend and sweep them up from the Lorimers' garden, the Houston property still out of bounds. He'd send the young man a text to see if he wanted to fit them in, he decided, swinging away from the red-brick building and heading for home. And, if there was anything more that he could tell Flynn about the skeleton he had found in that overgrown patch of ground, then he would.

The scene of crime tape fluttered in the darkness, a reminder not to venture towards the place where the excavation had taken place, but Lawrence Mathieson had no intention of further disturbing the dead. He shuddered as he looked across the lawn, feeling the rising wind chill his face. Indoors his wife was preparing for their trip to the ballet, a corporate event that demanded their presence and was something that she enjoyed. But Mathieson dreaded the inevitable questions and raised eyebrows over glasses of champagne and canapés. He would require every ounce of charm to deflect the probing words that threatened to destroy the fragile barriers he had built since his arrival in the Scottish banking scene.

A body, an old body, a skeleton, found in his garden! What pleasure that might give to his fellow bankers and their guests! It would be best to make light of it, of course, but Mathieson knew he was defective in bringing a natural humour to any situation. Perhaps this move north had been a mistake, after all, the lure of a more senior position and cheaper housing taking them from a place where he felt more at home. London, with all its melting pot of humanity and problems, suddenly seemed a far more desirable city than this bleak and windswept part of Scotland.

CHAPTER SIXTEEN

'I don't agree,' Caroline Flint said, eyes staring at the man on the opposite side of the table. 'Both these officers are eminently capable of dealing with the situation. I know for a fact that they have been in regular contact.'

'But have they made any progress?' the Chief Constable asked, his bushy eyebrows raised a fraction.

Alan Marshall's deputy tried not to appear ruffled though inwardly she was seething. The shootings were linked by that bullet, of course, but so far that was all they had to make some sort of connection with the two dead officers. It was not right to hand this over to the MIT, no matter that it concerned such a high-profile case. 'No danger to the public' were words that hovered between them. But was that true? A lone gunman on the loose was a danger, of course it was. But meantime what needed to be done was to reassure the public to whom they owed a duty of protection.

'What's needed is to reassure the public,' Caroline avowed stoutly, giving voice to her thoughts.

Marshall nodded but avoided her eyes. She could see the worry lines etched deeply there, the grey hair turning white above his ears. His was not the job that every officer coveted, but Caroline Flint was close enough in the police hierarchy to understand his internal struggles.

'Wait and see what happens,' she advised. 'There may be some new forensic evidence from the scene up north. And we have to let those two SIOs do their job, Alan.'

She saw him look to the side, noticed the rise and fall of his chest as he sighed, knowing she was right.

Flint appreciated his need to speed things along, however. A previous felon, jailed by Phillips and McAlpine at different times, had been an initial thought but that had petered out pretty quickly, no such criminal seeming to exist. Their paths had not crossed during their service either, according to the records that had been meticulously gone over by both investigation teams. So, what was it? Two random killings? A message to Police Scotland of some sort? She looked across at the Chief Constable again and nodded.

'They'll let us know the moment anything turns up,' she assured him.

Marshall grunted then waved his hand, sensing that his deputy was ready to depart.

Caroline Flint stood up and turned to go, hesitating for a moment as she saw Marshall shake his head wearily.

'Shit's going to hit the fan as soon as the press get hold of the ballistics report. And that's just a matter of time, I expect.'

Flint pursed her lips, resisting the temptation to stick up for the detective inspectors. Anything could happen, despite their best intentions. She gave him a nod and headed for the door but not before hearing his parting words.

'Anything serious comes to light, I want Lorimer on it right away.'

Lorimer. It had to be him, of course, but that was the last name he'd hoped to be given. There were plenty of others whose demise he'd not lose sleep over, men and women who had left courtrooms with a smirk after the judge had pronounced his sentence. But William Lorimer wasn't one of them.

It was only a few weeks until Christmas and by then he would be out of here and enjoying what time he had as a free man. But, if he were to mess up, get caught or, worse still, fail to carry out his orders, that time would be very limited indeed. John Ramsay shifted uneasily in his seat. There had been several takers for library books but now he was left for a spell alone behind the desk, the librarian off to the toilet, leaving him in charge. His eyes flicked over the pile of returned volumes but there was nothing there that he fancied reading.

Books had been his solace in here, a 'get-out-of-jail-free card', one visiting author had suggested with a sympathetic smile. And for Ramsay, at least, it had worked. Reading had taken him away from the day-to-day drudgery, the bleak colour of washed out clothes on poorly washed bodies.

The book he'd been handed earlier was another crime novel, but one that had held an important message. The Big Man would never risk a face-to-face meeting, only ordering his lesser henchmen to visit when it was absolutely necessary. Instead he preferred to send his instructions this way, pencil marks ready to be deciphered by men like him who had plenty of time on their hands. And he'd read the marks easily enough the first time, these seven letters spelling out the target's name. This time he'd be getting further information, an address perhaps, or a date and time to collect whatever weapon had been selected for the job, letters in this novel faintly underscored over random pages.

Ramsay's thoughts returned to the well-thumbed book that he had hidden beneath his mattress. The chaplain had encouraged him to think about things, not making a fuss, not urging him to seek a God he wasn't even sure existed. At least not for the likes of John Ramsay.

He was walking back along the narrow corridor when it happened. The man in regulation prison garb wasn't anyone he knew yet his eyes caught Ramsay's in a feverish glare as he drew nearer.

The metal glinted briefly as the chib was raised above the man's head and Ramsay ducked instinctively, his fists pumping straight into the man's stomach.

'Agh!' The single cry was muffled as Ramsay delivered a well-aimed boot to his face and dodged sideways, leaving the bigger man twisting in pain on the cold floor.

His heart thudded as he increased his pace. No running here or that would be a dead giveaway. Screws would find the guy and see the chib, draw their own sorry conclusions. No one would bother looking for the old man who helped out in the library. He had to get away, and fast. Any trouble at this stage might mean his release date being delayed and right now that was more important than a confrontation with a stranger.

But who the hell was he? Some nutter put into the wrong wing? Or was it some sort of message?

A grin of satisfaction crossed his face as John Ramsay rubbed his knuckles and headed back into the recreation area, sliding quietly behind a group of men that were watching a game of snooker.

That had felt good, the sheer physical buzz from giving the guy a doing. It reminded him of the old days when he'd been younger and stronger. Hell, he wasn't finished yet and hadn't he just proved to himself that he still had it in him to cut an opponent down to size? A sudden yearning seized him and for a moment Ramsay was almost grateful for the chance of violent confrontation that awaited him on release from this place.

Later, the light dying, Ramsay had found himself alone in his cell. Taking out the Bible, he gave a smile. He'd see what this could do for him, though he doubted anything would appeal in these thin, papery pages.

He'd play a game, he chuckled, letting the old book fall open at a random place, put that God of the chaplain's to the test.

It opened first at an Old Testament book, Ezekiel, a character he had only vaguely heard of but didn't know who he had been or why he was in the Bible at all.

The words at the start of chapter 37 sprang out at him.

*The hand of the Lord was upon me, and he brought
me out in the Spirit of the Lord and set me down in
the middle of the valley; it was full of bones.*

Ramsay shivered at that. Wasn't he in a place like this where men were set down till their flesh and bones became old and weary? Or was he just reading something into this that wasn't there at all? He hesitated, ready to chuck the book to one side, but reluctant in a superstitious way to do anything quite so violent, quite so profane. Still, he gave it a quick shake as if there was a dice somewhere inside, taking a gamble on the next page that fell open.

Maybe it had been well read, the way it opened so easily. The Gospel According to John. He'd grinned at that, his namesake opening up to him, then he'd read the first few verses, intrigued but not understanding what they meant. Was it to do with creation? How could the Word be made flesh? That didn't make any sense at all. But one verse did bother John Ramsay:

> *The light shines in the darkness, and the darkness has*
> *not overcome it.*

Too right, he'd thought cynically. He was a man who had worked in the dark often enough, fearful of any light that might shine on him to uncover his misdeeds. He remembered that night when they'd been caught, the torchlight shining into his face before he'd been grabbed roughly, cuffed then bundled into the police van. Fifteen-year stretch. But now that was coming to its end and John Ramsay had a chance to begin afresh. His lip curled at the idea. As if.

Third time lucky, he told himself.

It was a longer passage than he'd anticipated. A story about a man in court, a man, it seemed, who had done nothing to deserve imprisonment. Plenty in here who bleated that sort of thing, right enough, but this was different. There was a guy who'd accused him of creating a disturbance but it was a load of pish, Ramsay decided, reading the story of Paul from the start of Acts chapter 24. Wanting to find out what happened to him, he'd read on. Seemed this Paul had been on the other side originally, out to get these new Christians and stick them in jail. Or worse. He'd been *enraged*, the story said, persecuting them ... a right wee Hitler he sounded.

And then it had happened, one of the most famous stories that even John Ramsay had heard of. Except he had never actually read it for himself.

A bright light, a voice, then a complete change of direction ...

This man is doing nothing to deserve death or imprisonment, the court decided. No, Ramsay, thought, but he'd put plenty of folk to death before this conversion, hadn't he? Like *he* had. Like he still would ... and what would he deserve for that?

He closed the book with a thump, heart pumping. What the hell had just happened? Was that mere chance, three different passages opened from this book yet telling him something? It was as if whoever had written it was speaking to him, challenging the stupid game he'd been playing and coming up with something real.

John Ramsay closed his eyes. It was all a load of tosh, wasn't it? How old was the Bible anyway? And how could it affect a man living in the twenty-first century with all its technology, men in space and new cures for different diseases ... ?

But there was no cure for him, was there? Nothing that could change his life, no bright light shining into this cell.

As if on cue the lights in the prison went out as they did every night.

But this evening found John Ramsay clutching the covers of his bunk and shivering.

Elsewhere in the night another man smiled as remembered the telephone call. Ramsay had done all right, the voice had assured him. Knocked this crazy guy flying, left him with one front tooth dislodged. John Ramsay might be older now but with that unexpected incident he had shown that he was still capable of causing damage.

And that was what mattered.

CHAPTER SEVENTEEN

It felt good waking up every morning with nobody telling her what to do, where to go. She smiled and stretched lazily, contemplating the day ahead. A game of golf had been arranged for just after lunch but until then Eileen was free to do anything she wanted. There was no longer any routine to her life, something they had all told her she'd miss. But they'd been wrong. Living alone had been a bonus, of course, in a small bungalow (mortgage paid off last year) that she kept tidy mainly because she was the sort of person who eschewed too many possessions. Some mornings she'd get up, head off to the local pool for a swim then grab a newly baked croissant from the local coffee shop to take home for breakfast. But, really, there was no pattern to her days any more.

She drew open the curtains and gazed out at the far-off hill that soared high above the rooftops of the houses that backed onto her garden, looking at the sheep grazing there. Suburbia had not quite blotted out the rural landscape of her childhood and it was good to see traces of farmland. The flats on the other side of the street were thankfully far enough along not to block out her view of trees and sky, something she'd worried about when planning permission had been sought. Still, they were only three storeys high and occupied mainly by pensioners who had downsized. Eileen knew a few of them by sight: the old man who wore a NY Giants baseball cap all year round and who tipped its peak with a finger whenever he saw her; a grey-haired woman who gleefully careered around in a mobility scooter as though hoping to knock over any unwary pedestrians; and Mrs Brogan, the only one who had ever stopped in the street to talk to Eileen. It had begun when the old lady had waved a frantic hand as she saw Eileen emerging from the garage. She'd lost her cat, had Eileen seen it?

It had been obvious from that initial encounter that Mrs Brogan was finding it hard to settle in and Eileen had made a point of stopping to chat whenever she saw her out on the strip of communal garden bordering the flats. Usually just a short hello, how are you, then off she'd drive, occasionally a longer conversation about their past lives. Perhaps she might go and visit the old dear one day, she thought. After all, her time was her own to do as she pleased and she warmed to the idea of listening to the old lady talking about her life.

The cat had returned home (Eileen had seen it sitting on the window sill inside the flat) and her main communication with its owner since then had been a desultory wave as they'd passed one another by.

She sauntered through to her kitchen, thoughts of a lingering coffee and a half-finished paperback tempting Eileen to sit back and indulge herself with after breakfast.

*

He waited outside, tapping his fingers on the steering wheel, looking from time to time at the windows, the front door and the garage. Every day had been different so far, no discernible routine to her day. It was annoying but patience was one of the only virtues he had left. He'd taken the trouble to arrive in vans that bore the logos of some well-known firms, never the same one twice. She'd been a top detective, after all, and might notice something strange in the same vehicle parked at an angle across the road, near to the block of flats.

The garage door had been a grave disappointment, an electronic job that simply lifted up and closed behind her white Ford Focus. But she had to come out sometime on foot. Alone. Nobody around to see what was happening.

A movement to his right made him stiffen, the gun ready, car window lowering silently. But it was just the blinds of her bedroom being lowered. He waited, watching the front door, willing her to come out and stand where he could see her.

Eileen pressed the key fob and watched as the door began to rise then pressed her foot on the accelerator. The sound of the engine drowned out any noise of the metal door swaying behind her in a deep and sonorous clang. As she drove out of the cul-de-sac, the woman stared straight ahead, completely oblivious to the man in the blue van across the road whose face was a mask of impotent fury.

There was no sense of being watched, nothing in all her years of training as a police officer that gave her a frisson of danger. Even as the man lying in wait lowered his gun, Eileen Ormiston, former detective chief inspector, felt only glad to be alive on this late October morning, quite unaware of the irony in her delight.

CHAPTER EIGHTEEN

'Nothing more, not a single lead,' Lorimer told the bearded man sitting with his back to the large bay window that overlooked University Avenue.

Solomon Brightman nodded gravely, his expression sombre. The professor had asked to be kept up to date with the ongoing investigation, not out of any desire to be part of it (though his work as a criminal profiler had often taken him into Lorimer's team) but rather because he had felt a desire to give some support to his friend.

'Caroline Flint says it might be a matter of time till they bring us in, but I can't honestly see why they would,' Lorimer added.

'Politics,' Solly said briefly, stroking his beard. 'The public will expect some sort of escalation in the investigations. And if the media keep on churning out their suppositions about what is behind the killings, well, maybe the MIT being brought in could satisfy everybody.'

'Everybody except two bright SIOs in two separate

divisions,' Lorimer growled. 'Those women would have every right to feel aggrieved if their cases were turned over to me.'

Solly sighed quietly, saying nothing. He had a bad feeling about the deaths of those two men.

One day after the other.

A gunman? Gunmen? Someone with the same gun, at any rate, had shot the retired officers.

Why? That was what Solly wanted to know. Lorimer was right, though. Not a thing had turned up to help the case since the ballistics report. Yet with each passing day the professor had a horrid expectation that this was not the end and that news would come in of some further tragedy.

If, or when, that happened, there was no doubt in anyone's mind that Lorimer would be forced to take over the entire investigation.

'Interesting to see what is happening with Flynn's discovery,' he said.

Lorimer's brow cleared as the conversation turned away from the deaths of the two police officers, a simple but deliberate ploy of Solly's to spare his friend further grief. George Phillips's death had hit him hard and he could see that Lorimer was caught in a dilemma, chafing to do something about finding George's killer yet knowing the case was in other competent hands.

'Rosie had her forensic anthropologist friend give a guest lecture to the students,' he went on. 'She's a talented woman, Alice, not just an expert in her particular field, but a very good communicator. Had the youngsters eating out of her hand, Rosie said.'

'And she did manage to give us a better idea of the victim's age,' agreed Lorimer. 'Not quite forty, perhaps around thirty-seven. There aren't enough resources to do much more, however. If the team in Mill Street can't find any identification from the odontology database they might decide to shelve the case.'

'His teeth were in quite a poor state. Rosie thought he might have been in prison at some time?'

'Aye, that's the lead the Mill Street unit is currently following up. And there's the ballistics aspect too, though that'll take time to be examined. Too many current cases . . . ' He tailed off, biting his lip as if unwilling to bring up the subject of his old boss's shooting once more.

Behind his horn-rimmed spectacles, Solly's brown eyes looked across at his friend, knowing just how much passion he would put into finding the gunman. Each murder case was different yet William Lorimer always seemed to make it his personal mission to bring the perpetrator to justice. Catching the killer behind the police officers' deaths would drive him to the limits, should he be forced to take on the case. The psychologist felt a wave of sympathy for Lorimer as he watched the detective run restless fingers through his unruly dark hair. It was not all that long ago that the detective superintendent had thought about giving up his career altogether, a horrific incident involving children's deaths tipping him over the edge. There was only so much any human could endure but Lorimer appeared to have come back from that time stronger for the experience. Still, Solly cared about his friend, the man who was godfather to his two children. In a very few years he would be eligible for retirement, his thirty years of service complete. Would he take that? Solly wondered. Or would he continue to be driven by that innate sense of justice that kept him working these complex cases, investigations that often displayed the worst excesses of humanity?

Flynn brushed down his jeans and shrugged on his parka. It was a chilly evening and the nights were drawing in, autumn closing around like the swirl of a magician's cloak. Once outside the flat he raised his face to the cold and took a deep breath, inhaling the fragrant smell of something woody. Smouldering logs, maybe, or it could be a garden bonfire, though he could see no telltale column of smoke.

He gave a quiet smile of satisfaction as he approached the van parked out in the forecourt of the flats. Who would have thought that digging up an old skeleton would have brought him into contact with a woman like Erin? It was a mystery to Flynn why the young policewoman had taken a shine to him.

His past life was still something that nagged at the gardener, his self-esteem clouded by the years when he'd been low-life; a druggie begging in the streets of Glasgow. All that had changed the day William Lorimer had offered Flynn a place to recuperate after he had dashed out in front of a Transit van, the boy fleeing pursuit of one of Lorimer's colleagues. The accident could have been fatal, the doctors had warned him afterwards, that alone making the teenager reflect on the sort of chaotic existence he had been leading. Time spent with the senior detective had gradually made a difference in the life of Joseph Alexander Flynn, and he had been shown a kindness that he'd never be fully able to repay.

'Just get on and do something useful,' Maggie Lorimer's mum had scolded him. And he had, buoyed up by the older woman's practical manner and the signs that she had really cared for him. She was gone now, sadly, but Flynn cherished her memory and was proud that he had fulfilled the promise he'd made to her to make something of himself.

Erin had the evening off and they were going to see a film together along at the Quayside cinema close to the River Clyde. He could have walked along to the place but wanted to have the van handy in case Erin needed a lift home afterwards.

Just as Flynn swung himself up into the driver's seat he heard the familiar ring of his mobile. Whipping it from his jacket pocket, he read the text, the smile fading from his face.

Sorry, have to work late. Something came up. Text you later.

He sank back into his seat, cursing the life of a police officer. Okay, it wasn't her fault and might even be laid at his own door if this overtime was anything to do with the skeleton he had found. But his earlier carefree mood had evaporated and now Flynn was left with a long empty evening ahead.

Erin Finlay sat amongst her team, eyes glowing.

'It's been double checked but there is absolutely no doubt that the bullet we found was fired from the same gun,' DI Brodie told them. The police officer scratched his head. 'Hard to believe, I know. They must have done

115

some great work on that bullet, badly corroded though it was, and of course weapons can be kept in a decent condition for decades. Problem for us now is who was this man? Not a serving police officer, from what the forensic people have told us, more likely to have been detained at Her Majesty's pleasure, though the odontology work has still some way to go.'

He looked around the room, a gleam in his eye that told them there was more to come.

'That's not all,' DI Brodie said. 'We've agreed to allow a forensic anthropologist, name of Professor Morton, to do a facial reconstruction job on our skull.'

There was a buzz in the room tonight. Not only was this a massive breakthrough in the investigation into the skeleton Flynn had found in the garden, it was now linked to the high-profile shootings of two retired police officers.

Erin had completed a course at the University of Glasgow on Forensic Medical Science along with a couple of her younger colleagues and had been fascinated by the detailed information that both dental records and ballistics could throw up to help a case. For a while she had toyed with the idea of applying to join the ballistics division but had grown to love the work here instead, where several different strands of knowledge could be applied in identifying the remains of missing persons. She bit her lip, feeling only a tiny bit guilty for feeling so enthusiastic about this latest development, knowing that Flynn would be disappointed to miss their date. Wait till she told him about Professor Morton, though!

The smile returned to her lips. Her chosen profession had brought her more than mere job satisfaction; it had led to her having a boyfriend who was lighting up her life outside her working hours.

Lorimer sat back, listening to DCC Flint's words.

'There's no mistake?'

'None. They checked the bullets several times. Same striation marks. No doubt about it, Lorimer. Whoever fired the bullet that killed your chap out in Houston used the very same weapon that killed George Phillips and Stephen McAlpine.'

'What now?' he asked, his voice dry.

'Nothing changes yet,' she told him. 'Each of the investigation teams carries on with what they have to do. And, until we have a name for the man shot dead a couple of decades ago we might not make a lot of progress in linking them all up any further than we have now. However,' she paused to clear her throat, 'we will be asking Professor Dawson to have a look at the soil samples retrieved from the burial site. You never know, that might not have been the locus of his death.'

'Right,' he replied. 'Good.' And it was good that more resources were being tapped to solve this case. Though it was surely a long call to expect Professor Dawson to come up with anything after all the time that body had spent mouldering in the earth.

'That's all, Lorimer. I'll keep you informed of any other developments, naturally. Goodnight.'

'Goodnight, ma'am,' he replied then clicked off his phone, sinking back into the comfort of his favourite armchair.

'What was all that about?' Maggie asked. 'Something happening?'

He shook his head and sighed. 'It's almost impossible to believe,' he began, 'but ballistics have made a rather odd discovery.'

'Oh?'

'Seems that our skeleton man that Flynn dug up was shot with the same gun that killed George.'

'No!'

'Can't fault the ballistics folk out at Gartcosh, Maggie. These men and women are probably the best in Europe right now. Okay, it is a weird coincidence given the time difference, but guns have a habit of being passed around in the underworld. Could be that one was kept for a lengthy period of time till it was sold on. Makes sense ...'

'What does?'

'The time scale ...' he murmured, sitting up a little straighter. 'If that gun had been used in a hit all those years back perhaps it was returned to the armourer.'

'Who?'

'Hitmen don't normally own their guns,' he explained. 'Whoever decides the assassination also gives instructions to the killer about picking up the weapon. It's then returned to the guy who dishes out the guns, someone who makes a tidy profit from that.'

'You mean he rents them out?' Maggie's eyebrows rose in astonishment.

'That's sometimes the way of it,' Lorimer agreed. 'And we rarely find the people behind that particular activity. They aren't killers themselves, just experts in their chosen field.'

'So, this gun wasn't used for, what? About twenty years?

Then all of a sudden it's used twice to kill two police officers?'

Lorimer nodded. 'And that, believe it or not, might be the very thing that helps us trace whoever pulled the trigger.'

They would never find him, not in a million years. He lay back, hands behind his grizzled head, closed his eyes and smiled. It had taken him years to plan but it would be a mere matter of weeks to execute.

He gave a sigh of pleasure, pleased with the choice of word that had come to mind. Executions. That's exactly what they were. And he had a familiar sense of satisfaction that nobody could ever lay the blame at his door.

CHAPTER NINETEEN

In the end it was so simple he could have cried tears of mirth.

Thursday night was when the wheelie bins were rolled out onto the pavement for emptying by the council next day, something he could have found out easily enough had it crossed his mind.

Seeing the grey bins in another part of the city had triggered the idea and the internet had provided the rest.

The ex-cop would have to come out of her house now, even for a few minutes, and he would be ready, waiting for her. The light was fading from the skies but he could see perfectly well from his vantage point. The window was rolled down and chill air had filled the cab but he felt no cold, only a thrill of anticipation as his eyes drilled the space in front of the house.

The cat yowled in fright at the sudden noise, making Mrs Brogan pick her up and breathe soothing words into the long fur.

But the animal refused to be placated and squirmed out of her grasp.

'Blooming kids, blooming fireworks,' the old lady muttered, moving towards the window, expecting to see boys running past her window.

Instead she caught sight of a van moving off down the street. Perhaps that was it, the sound she'd heard?

Then Rita Brogan froze.

Lying below the street lamp was a figure in a familiar grey tracksuit, arms flung out at a strange angle.

She knew without having to be told that Eileen was dead. And that the sound she had heard was nothing to do with fireworks.

Fingers trembling, the old lady picked up her telephone and began to dial.

'Lorimer.'

'Caroline Flint here.'

There was an ominous pause. Then, almost as though he knew what she was going to say, Lorimer swallowed hard.

'There's been another one. You'd better be prepared to take a team to the scene.'

'Anyone I know?' Lorimer held his breath, his chest tightening.

'Eileen Ormiston.'

He felt the blood pounding in his head. Former DCI Ormiston had been deputy divisional commander in Kilmarnock until her retirement last year. But Lorimer had known the woman well enough, their paths crossing at conferences and training sessions over the years.

'Lorimer?'

'Yes,' he replied thickly. 'I knew her. Good cop. Unblemished record. Who the hell . . . ?'

'That's for you to find out,' Flint replied crisply. 'I'm going to be there myself. Meet you there.' She read out an address and Lorimer scribbled it down.

'Less than ten minutes from my place,' he murmured. 'Just off the Ayr Road. I'm on my way.'

Maggie caught his sleeve and he pressed a kiss on top of her head.

'Don't wait up, love,' he murmured softly. 'This may take some time.'

As Lorimer parked the Lexus in Eileen Ormiston's street he could see several white-suited figures moving around in the dark, among them one diminutive female that he recognised as Rosie Fergusson. The scene of crime tent was erected already as he gazed around at the block of nearby flats, many of their windows lit up, faces peering out to see why there were so many Police Scotland vehicles casting arcs of blue light heavenward. It was human nature, after all, this urge to know what was happening in their street. It was only a matter of time before a reporter caught a whiff of something newsworthy to satisfy this overburdening curiosity. He rubbed his hands together briefly, the shiver coming more from disgust than from the chill night air.

'Lorimer.'

He turned at the sound of the English accent and nodded to the Deputy Chief Constable who was walking briskly towards him.

'Ma'am.' Lorimer saw the white-suited figure moving towards him, flat-soled shoes encased in scene of crime bootees that made no sound over the pavement. Yet even under the forensic hood he could see Caroline Flint's grim expression. This was a bad business and she was ready to tackle it.

'One bullet straight into the forehead,' she told him.

'Killed outright?'

Flint nodded. 'She wouldn't have known a thing. Wouldn't even have heard the shot before everything went black.'

'If there was even a sound to be heard.'

'Oh, there was. A neighbour called it in. Elderly lady name of Rita Brogan. Heard the gunshot and saw the victim lying on the ground.'

Lorimer looked across the street where several police vehicles were parked, blue lights flashing through the gloom next to an ambulance. It was standard procedure in emergency calls to alert both services, though he guessed it might be the neighbour receiving treatment for shock inside the ambulance, certainly not the victim, who would not be moved for some time yet.

'When did it happen?'

'About an hour ago. Pretty good response,' the DCC commented approvingly, glancing round at the activity. 'And Dr Fergusson was on call. If you want to suit up we can see for ourselves.'

Eileen Ormiston lay where she had fallen, the harsh artificial light inside the scene of crime tent making her dead face more ghastly than it really was. A single bullet hole through her forehead was the first thing Lorimer noticed, then that stare, her expression one of mute surprise. She would be for ever caught in that final moment, he thought: stupefied by the bullet now lodged somewhere in her brain.

He backed out of the tent, blinking hard to adjust his eyes to the darkness. A grey wheelie bin was part-way across the driveway. Bin night, one of the uniforms had told him, and Lorimer saw for himself the familiar shapes on the pavement outside each adjacent property. One simple act, a habitual chore, yet it had been her last. Putting out the bin. Had the gunman watched and waited for her to emerge from her home? And had he known the exact time that his mark would step onto that pavement?

A uniformed officer stood at the door of the victim's house. That door was shut fast, Lorimer could see. So, had Eileen come out of the back door to wheel her bin along the path that ran to the far side of the integral garage straight into the firing range of a gunman?

Lorimer had known DCI Ormiston, but not well enough to say whether she had been so set in her ways that it made her an easy target for the killer. Had she been a woman predictable in her habits? That was perhaps something that would be asked of those who'd known her best.

She'd been married once, that Lorimer did know, but divorced long before she'd risen to her rank of detective chief inspector, her ex-husband a uniformed cop who'd never even made his sergeant's stripes. An unequal partnership, someone once told him, and Lorimer had felt sad for each of them, if that really was at the root of the split. Tommy Ormiston would have to be informed. And asked to keep away from the media.

Lorimer heaved a sigh, unable for once to summon up the energy to begin a major investigation. This was all wrong; these police officers being targeted was something so horrific that he felt sickened in a way he had never experienced before. Yet he had to carry out his duties and the routine of setting up his team had already begun. He'd contacted several officers in Govan since the DCC's call, alerting them to the fact that the MIT were now taking over two major homicides from other SIOs as well as covering the initial investigation into this latest shooting. One of his DCIs would be sent to Inverness-shire and another down to Greenock. His face grew grim at the thought of what each of the SIOs would say at their cases being taken over. But, with Eileen Ormiston's death, everything had changed and the sooner the MIT with its superior resources began to spread their net across the country, the better it would be for all concerned.

Already things were in motion, CCTV cameras from the nearest locations being swooped upon by police officers and all the footage over the past few hours relayed to his team. He pulled off his protective suit and glanced across at the ambulance. First things first, he told himself, and headed towards the vehicle to meet the woman who had alerted the police to her neighbour's death.

Rita Brogan was a surprise. Somehow he had expected a frail wee lady, but the woman sitting in the ambulance, blanket draped neatly across her shoulders, was tall and well built. She sat with a mug of tea clutched in both hands and Lorimer noticed the fingers knotted with arthritis, but the faded blue eyes that looked his way were bright and curious.

'Mrs Brogan? I'm Detective Superintendent Lorimer,' he told her. 'Thanks for staying here to meet me.'

'Oh, they said you would want to ask me things.' Mrs Brogan nodded then looked past him into the darkness.

'How are you feeling?'

He saw the rounded shoulders heave up and sink down again. 'I'd be lying if I didn't say it was a shock,' she began. 'But I knew as soon as I saw her . . . it was the way she was lying there, so still . . . and, I suppose after I'd heard the gun going off . . . well, it took me a moment to put two and two together then . . . ' She tailed off, her eyes looking down at the mug in her hands.

'You rang the police.'

'Oh, yes.' She shrugged slightly. 'I knew there was nothing I could do for poor Eileen. No point in going over to touch her body . . . I could see she was dead. I've seen dead bodies before, you know,' she added, meeting his eyes for a moment with a tired smile.

Lorimer raised questioning eyebrows.

'I was a theatre sister. Long time ago now, of course. But not every patient survived major surgeries,' she sighed. 'All part of the job, it was.' She shook her head. 'I sometimes managed a wee chat with Eileen after she retired. Told her a few stories about my own working life.'

'And did she tell you any of hers?' Lorimer asked, smiling gently.

The elderly lady looked away for a moment, her expression sad. 'Not a lot. She hadn't been away from the job all that long, really. I think she missed it, though. Didn't seem as if she had any notion of finding another job. You usually

126

do, don't you? Far too young just to do nothing at that age, aren't you?'

Lorimer nodded. 'Usually if an officer is fit they find some other sort of work to keep them busy. Now, can you tell me, Mrs Brogan, exactly what you saw and heard?' he asked, steering her back to the moment when the shot had rung out, hoping every detail might still be fresh in her mind.

'I thought it might be kids setting off a firework, one of these horrible noisy ones, or a car backfiring. It was very loud,' she insisted. 'My cat was terrified. She hates fireworks. Or any loud bangs.'

'What did you do?'

'Well, I looked out of the window, of course.' The woman frowned at Lorimer. 'Saw a dark-coloured van driving down the street. At first I thought that was it. The noise, I mean. And then I saw Eileen. Just lying there. So still.'

Lorimer watched Rita Brogan swallow back tears, her hands shaking as she held out her mug. He took it from her outstretched hands then she pulled a cotton handkerchief from the sleeve of her cardigan and wiped her nose.

'It ... it was getting dark, so, you know ... hard to make out very much.' She nodded, biting her lip. 'But I knew it was Eileen. She wears that grey tracksuit nearly all the time now. Goes to a gym, I think, or the swimming pool. '

'Can you tell me any more about the van? What make was it? What size?'

'Oh, I don't know much about makes of vans, Superintendent, but it wasn't a big van, more like the one the gardener uses, you know? About the size of a normal car, but van-shaped. Oh, I'm not describing it right at all!' she exclaimed.

'That's all right, you're doing fine,' he assured her. 'Do you remember what colour it was?'

Rita Brogan screwed up her eyes in determined concentration. 'Dark,' she said at last. 'But not black. Maybe blue or brown?'

'Any writing on the side?'

She shook her head. 'Not that I recall. I think it was a plain van. The kind that has doors in the back, no windows.'

'Thank you,' Lorimer said gravely. 'That may well be of great help to us. Is there anyone we can call for you? Anyone you want to keep you company tonight?'

The audible sigh was answer enough and Lorimer guessed what the answer would be even as Rita Brogan shook her grey head.

'I'll be all right, son,' she assured him. 'I'll lock my door, I promise.'

'Do you feel fit enough to go back to your flat now?'

'Och, yes. But if you wanted to take my arm, that would be nice,' she added with a tremulous smile.

Rita Bogan would have to be collected from her flat again in the morning and escorted to Helen Street to give a witness statement, but meantime Lorimer was curious about Eileen Ormiston. He had shed the forensic suit but pulled on a pair of rubber gloves before crossing the road once more. The garage was attached to the house, a narrow path running alongside, wide enough for a wheelie bin to be dragged out onto the pavement at the front. A high hedge cast deep shadows on to the ground as Lorimer left the activity and walked silently along the path. He gave a small smile of approval as he turned the corner, his movement triggering a beam of light: Eileen Ormiston had practised what she preached, he thought, conscious of the need for security, a woman living on her own. Or, he thought, the smile instantly fading, had she needed that extra security for a different reason? Was there something of which DCI Ormiston had been afraid?

There was, as he'd expected, another officer standing guard at the back door of the property, a clipboard under his arm.

'Sir.' The constable nodded, recognising the man from the MIT and holding out the clipboard for Lorimer to sign his name and write down the time he was entering the premises.

The back door remained ajar, just the way it had when Eileen had left it, no doubt expecting to return within a minute. But that short walk along her pathway was fated to be her last. Lorimer pushed the door wider, his hand searching for a light switch and finding one. He blinked as the kitchen was lit up and stood for a moment, looking around. It was a habitual skill that Lorimer had honed over the years; reading a house to make some sense of its owner, often the home of a victim who could not tell their story any more. The first thing he noticed was the smell of recently cooked food and he saw a couple of pots on the hob, though no gas was lit under them now. His gloved hand lifted the lids to see the remains of some home-made vegetable soup in one and a few strands of dried up spaghetti in the other. Had she eaten her evening meal then cleared almost everything away, waiting for the leftover food to cool?

Lorimer glanced around the kitchen. It was not a homely room, like his own cluttered kitchen in nearby Giffnock, no sign of books left on the counter or plants by the window sill, but rather stark as though Eileen had preferred a minimalist look. Pulling out a couple of drawers intensified this notion: everything was clean and in its place. Almost clinically neat, Lorimer thought, wondering what life had been like for Tommy Ormiston.

The rest of the house came as no surprise. The lounge to the front, its blinds already pulled shut, contained a pale beige leather suite and a large flat-screen television, a stack of nesting tables pushed against one wall. The original fire had been replaced with a modern glass-fronted one, its flames flickering in the gloom. So, she'd been in here just before going out to wheel the bin into the street, he told himself, noticing the TV handset lying to one side of the settee. He could imagine Eileen watching the evening news programme as she ate her dinner then switching it off right on the dot of seven o'clock. That certainly fitted in with the time scale as they knew it. He glanced up at a brass-coloured carriage clock on a nearby shelf. It was almost ten o'clock now and he wondered if this had made the late news headlines already.

Along the corridor he found two bedrooms, one with a single bed and a desk where the former officer might have worked at night, the MacBook closed flat for now.

The second bedroom had obviously been Eileen's own, the double bed arranged with several cushions and a folded throw, a bedside chair angled close by, all in contemporary shades of grey that were reflected in her choice of darker velvet cushions and gunmetal throw. It was a room that might have come straight from a catalogue, he thought;

impersonal and— A small pile of books caught his eye, halting his judgemental thoughts.

Sweeping them up in gloved hands he gave a smile. So, Eileen Ormiston had preferred to visit her local library and patronised the crime fiction section. He recognised the author, a bestselling writer whose name he'd seen in the *Sunday Times* charts. Eileen might have left the life of catching criminals but her interest in the subject had evidently continued. There was a bookmark in the volume at the top of the stack and Lorimer gave a small sigh, sad that Eileen would never now read to the end of that particular story.

What would the papers make of her existence? Would her life as a hard-working police officer be for ever tainted by the manner of her death? Probably, he thought, replacing the books where he had found them and looking out of the window at the scene below where other officers were still trying to make sense of what had happened.

CHAPTER TWENTY

He was nice, she thought absently, tall with a gentle voice. Lewis accent, wasn't it?

'Thanks for coming so quickly.' DI Terry Finnegan shook the hand of DCI Cameron, the man from the MIT who had spoken to her just a few hours previously. Terry had been woken by the call and had not even tried to get back to sleep, instead coming straight to the station.

'It's escalated to a stage where we have to assume that this gunman is a serious danger to the public,' DCI Cameron told her.

Terry nodded. As soon as she had been given the news she realised that the McAlpine case would be taken away from her, yet somehow her personal involvement did not matter. This was far more serious than anything she had encountered in her entire career and it was a relief to have this man standing in her office.

'Please,' she said, waving her hand. 'Sit down. Can I get you a coffee?'

'A cup of tea would be nice,' DCI Cameron replied. 'Didn't stop all the way here. Lucky to leave early enough to miss the worst of the traffic on the A9.'

Terry looked across at him, noting the smart grey suit and pale blue silk tie. And the gold band on his wedding ring finger. Some lucky lady back in Glasgow looked after this fellow well, she thought.

She strode to the door of her room and lifted a hand to alert the nearest of her team out in the larger open-plan area.

'Jamie, two cups of tea, please,' she asked, relieved to see the young man rise rapidly from his desk and head off with a 'Yes, ma'am.' Jamie, like the rest of the team, knew fine that the MIT was here to take over the McAlpine case and he would be curious to see this DCI Cameron for himself.

'Lorimer sends his regards,' Cameron told her. 'I think he felt sorry that this was being snatched away from you so soon after your arrival here.'

Terry shrugged. 'Can't be helped. More important to see the bigger picture now,' she told him.

'All the same, it would be good if you'd continue to liaise with us on this one. Your officers know the territory up here. We need to see how much they've covered already, see if any further forensic searches are required.'

'We did a fairly extensive search,' Terry told him. 'And I had officers looking back at DI McAlpine's record of service to see if there was anything that linked him to George Phillips.'

'You knew George,' Cameron said.

'Aye, he was a decent man, a good boss,' Terry sighed. 'I just hope to God that we get whoever is doing this.'

*

133

Maggie Lorimer looked out of her classroom window. The sounds of children laughing and squabbling in the playground was so familiar. Normal life continued for these kids down there, didn't it? It was Friday, excitement mounting for the weekend, especially for Hallowe'en, and Maggie could imagine the sorts of discussions taking place this morning interval, particularly amongst the juniors who still went out guising after dark.

She gave an involuntary shudder, remembering the words from her husband describing his latest case. *Eileen Ormiston*, he'd told her, though the name meant nothing to Maggie. She'd never met the policewoman, couldn't recall Bill ever mentioning her name before. But how terrible to have to see a former colleague dead in the street like that! If anything like that ever happened to her husband ... Maggie closed her eyes for a moment, a silent prayer to keep him safe. Not to be attacked for doing his job like those officers who had been gunned down.

She moved away from the window, fingers clenched into fists. It didn't bear thinking about and in a few minutes she would have to turn her thoughts to the class coming in for their lesson. Her Advanced Higher class was next, a few students whose enthusiasm for her subject made Maggie warm to them. Exams were still several weeks away and they were at that enviable stage where they had delved deeply enough into a text to be able to discuss its finer points with confidence. *The Great Gatsby* was a novel they all appeared to have enjoyed yet there was still a division of opinion about some of the characters. The girls were harder on Daisy, whose careless attitude had taken away the life of another.

Maggie sighed as she heard the bell ring out, the shouts from the playground increasing in volume. Real life and death were issues her husband dealt with, whereas she was simply looking at them through the prism of another man's writing.

The press conference was inevitable, of course, the need to disseminate information on a national scale something that simply could not be avoided. Yet, what to say? How to appear in front of television cameras as if this was just another major murder case? Every death was tragic, he knew that well enough, and no matter a victim's background they each had the right to be given justice. There was always a grieving mother, wife or child in the end and that never changed. But this. This was surely one of the biggest pieces of news to hit in years. Three police officers gunned down in cold blood and very little progress in finding their killer. That was all they needed to say right now; other information about the link to a twenty-year-old skeleton would be held back from the public meantime.

Lorimer straightened the knot on his tie and strode out of the room.

The Police Scotland logo on the opposite wall of this room was a reminder, if that was needed, of just what he had signed up for: *Semper Vigilo*, or, as it was shown in other versions, *Keeping People Safe*, which was a fairly watered down translation of Ever Vigilant but came to the same thing in the end, give or take the sorts of bureaucracy with which officers had to contend.

The buzz of chatter quietened as soon as Detective

Superintendent Lorimer and the woman in uniform stepped on to the platform and sat down behind the table with its bank of microphones. Caroline Flint was there to observe, not to pass any comment or to answer questions, she had insisted, though Lorimer would have been grateful for her input right now.

'You know why we are here,' Lorimer began, determined not to go into any preamble. 'Three of our former officers have been shot dead in the past few days and I want to bring you all up to date with such information regarding the investigations as I am permitted.'

He paused and stared out at the throng of press men and women. They were all perfectly aware of the need for police to keep some aspects of an ongoing case away from the public but they would always try to lift the lid on Pandora's box.

'I can say with a degree of certainty that there is ballistic evidence to tie all three of these cases together.'

The murmur that had died down began again until the swell of noise made Lorimer lift a hand again to ask for silence.

'This suggests that it may be the same killer who carried out these atrocious deeds,' he continued, 'and so, given that they have occurred in different parts of the country, we are stepping up the investigation.'

'You're taking over?' one reporter at the front called out and Lorimer nodded.

'I have been asked by the Chief Constable to make this a major incident and yes, the Major Incident Team from Govan are already in charge of the investigations as I speak.'

'Why retired officers?' another asked, their eyes looking meaningfully at Lorimer.

He swallowed hard, a sudden memory of George Phillips laughing at his retirement dinner, head thrown back, a glass of whisky in his hand.

'One aspect of that is to think from the viewpoint of those who want to target police officers at all,' Lorimer replied. 'Retired officers, like any ordinary citizens, have more of a pattern to their daily lives, making them more vulnerable to anyone seeking an opportunity to make them a target, whereas serving officers often do not know where they might be or what they might be required to do on a daily basis. In other words, these dead officers would have been easier targets.'

A woman that Lorimer knew and disliked stood up and tossed her mane of red curls, a supercilious grin on her face. 'Anything dodgy in their past?' she asked. Her question was met instantly with a growl of disapproval from those seated around her.

'Not as far as we know,' Lorimer replied stiffly. 'And extensive background checks have been made to verify that.'

'But it might be something in their past that made someone want to shoot them dead,' she insisted, not put off in the slightest by the glares from a few of her neighbours.

'That is an obvious line of inquiry,' Lorimer agreed, 'but as yet we have nothing to link these officers in their lives, only the manner of their death. However,' and he held up a commanding hand once more, 'I would ask that members of the public be vigilant at this time. Any person that you see carrying what looks like a shotgun should be reported to the police. Do not, I repeat, do not approach anyone carrying a weapon that looks in the least bit suspicious. We are dealing with a gunman who is a crack shot and whom we now consider to be a danger to the public.'

He was conscious of Caroline Flint's eyes on him. They had discussed just what ought to be said on camera and how much to emphasise the danger without creating a sense of panic.

'That is all I have to say at present. But please, if you have any information that might help do get in touch with a member of the Major Incident Team at this number.'

He stood up then and accompanied his superior officer off the stage, knowing that the cameras would have panned in on the screen behind them, the telephone number and email address clear for all to see.

He bent forward and made a gun with his fingers, aiming it at the television screen.

'Bang!' he said, pointing at the figure on the screen. Then, sitting back on the chair he smiled quietly, wanting to laugh out loud but canny enough not to give in to that impulse. So, Lorimer was taking over, was he? That would create a nice bit of fun for them all, watching him run around and chase their mystery killer.

Then it'll be your turn, he thought, his face creasing into a wide grin as he watched the tall detective leave the platform, imagining how Detective Superintendent Lorimer might crash to the ground, a fatal bullet lodged in his forehead.

Maggie Lorimer gave a sigh as she switched channels. He'd done a good job, she thought, that grave expression on his face as he was telling the public to be careful yet asking for their help too. She stood up and strode to the window, pulling the curtains closed. The sky was dark now at this time and she dreaded the coming weeks when every journey to and from work would require headlights. He'd be home soon, Maggie consoled herself, then they would eat their evening meal together, a chicken and mushroom curry that was Bill's favourite, some naan bread just to slip under the grill when she heard his key in the door.

Life as the wife of a senior detective was not easy but Maggie had spent years adjusting to the uncertainty of mealtimes together, her own days spent in the classroom and in front of her laptop. The stories about her little ghost boy had been a surprising success and Maggie enjoyed her new career as a children's author. Now, sometimes, *she* was the one to come home late from a meeting with her agent in Edinburgh or a library visit some miles away. She had chuckled the first time one of her publicity ladies had introduced Bill as 'Mr Lorimer, Maggie's husband'. Now she had a public profile of her own and a life outside these four walls. Yet nothing made Maggie Lorimer happier than the sound of her husband's voice as he called to her from the doorway each evening.

Being home together felt so good, so secure in those strong arms and she would do anything to keep their life just that way. And yet, his job as a police officer was fraught with dangers every single day, something that preyed on Maggie Lorimer's mind in the wake of these dreadful shootings.

Maggie sat back in her comfortable armchair, watching a favourite quiz programme, knowing that she would press the pause button the minute she heard the sound of his car on the driveway. Her husband dealt with some terrible things, matters of life and death his daily task, but he always came home to a place where they could be together, the darkness shut out, cocooned in their own private world.

CHAPTER TWENTY-ONE

I n some ways he was lucky, his dad had chuckled, with a captive audience for his Sunday sermons. Douglas had smiled back, sharing the gentle quip, but it wasn't quite like that, the men incarcerated inside Barlinnie prison being given the choice as to whether they wished to attend Sunday service or not. Plus, there were regular visits from Father Peter Kearney, an older priest with whom Douglas sometimes shared services, especially at Christmas. This very morning he was to meet the white-haired cleric to discuss the sorts of things they might bring to that season.

Douglas submitted to the rigorous security check, something that was now a daily habit, and pushed his way through the metal arms of the barrier to where a prison officer stood waiting.

'Good morning, Jock.' Douglas nodded at the middle-aged man as they fell into step, the officer's hand on the chain full of keys that were required to unlock several doors on their way to the chapel. 'How are things today?'

'No' bad,' the man replied. 'Quiet night, thank Goad. Nae real trouble since thon mad bloke took a run at the wall.'

'Still in the hospital, is he?' Douglas asked.

'Naw, they transferred him tae Shotts. Nae chance o' him taking anither maddie, either. Ah wis telt they'd pit him oan some medication tae calm him doon, like.'

Douglas nod silently. The young man, a repeat offender and known drug addict, had been found lying on the floor of a corridor and it was assumed that he had run straight into the stone wall during recreation time, knocking himself out cold and damaging his skull. He'd been clutching a home-made chib in his fist too, something that made his warders guess it had been fashioned to self-harm. It had been a deliberate act, he'd been told, but Douglas sometimes wondered just what had been behind that. Had there been a build-up of frustration that had overflowed into that crazy dash against the solid wall? Had he intended to end his life, perhaps? Sometimes it happened, no matter how careful the prison officers were to keep a close eye on their more vulnerable charges.

He cleared his throat, wondering how to ask his next question without causing any ripples for the prisoner. 'And John Ramsay? How is he doing?'

'Old Ramsay?' the officer scoffed. 'Aye, his days are numbered, I reckon. The hospital did whit they could, right enough, but ah dinnae think he'll be alive this time next year. Lungs shot tae buggery, if ye'll pardon the expression, Reverend.' He grinned. 'But at least he'll have a wee bit o' time tae breathe in the Scottish winter. Wi' a bit o' luck that might finish him aff fur good. Nae mair than he deserves, bad wee toerag.'

Douglas winced at the officer's tone. It was true enough that John Ramsay had committed some dreadful deeds in his past, but Douglas Petrie had begun to wonder if it was not too late to point the old man to the route of remorse. He wouldn't be here at Christmas, of course, but maybe if he came again to Douglas, asking for more help with passages of scripture . . . ? It was hard for the minister to pick out individuals, the repercussions from other inmates often being worse than the spiritual pain a man was suffering. *Going to the Padre* or *getting religion* was looked on as a sort of weakness to be stamped out by those bullies inside who commanded far too much authority in Barlinnie, as far as Douglas was concerned.

'Right, here you are, Padre.' The officer stood by the final door that led to the chapel where Father Kearney was already seated at the front of the chapel. 'Ah'll leave youse two tae it. Jist shout when you want tae get back intae yer office.'

The door to the chapel remained open, the officer stationing himself outside, his duty to protect the two men of the cloth continuing.

Days could pass quickly or slowly depending on how busy the library was, but today there were few takers for books and that suited John Ramsay just fine. He'd been reading a new book about Johnny Ramensky, a safe blower whose fame had spread during the Second World War. Part of Ramsay's interest had been piqued because, despite being born Yonas Ramanauckas to Lithuanian parents who had moved to Lanarkshire, Ramensky adopted many names, one of them being John Ramsay.

143

Safe blowing might have been a better option, he thought. Like Ramensky, he'd begun as a youngster with burglary, but his criminal career had escalated into violence whereas the safe blower had been known for his aversion to anything like that, hence the nickname Gentleman Johnny. Ramsay sighed. He'd never be known with a name like that, would he? His reputation as a hard man capable of violent crimes had followed him into every prison he'd been in. And now, as a known killer, sometimes acting as a hitman who could be relied upon to carry out an order, he'd been selected for his final job.

And it would be the last one, the Big Man must have known, despite the sum of money guaranteed to ease Ramsay into several years of comfort, years he knew that he simply did not have left. A hit, just one hit, and the mark was a senior cop, one of several on a list that the Big Man had compiled. Ramsay hadn't asked any questions, simply listened as the order had been issued one day during visiting time.

Ramsay piled up the books in front of him, hands trembling. What would happen if he couldn't go through with it? He'd be out soon, could disappear anywhere in the world. But they would still find him, wouldn't they? If he failed to carry out the hit then they'd come after him and John Ramsay knew the penalty for disobeying an order from the Big Man. He'd watched it before, the drawn-out torturing of a man either too weak or mired in double-dealing to stay true to his command. He had heard the endless screams in nightmares since, remembered the blood and the dismembered body parts, knowing full well that such a fate lay ahead of him should he refuse to carry out one particular assassination. You simply did not say no to the man who wielded all the power from a place where nobody could reach him.

But the question he'd wanted to ask, had almost blurted out, was *Why?*

And in particular, *Why Lorimer?*

Lorimer had been not far off the mark when he'd spoken to Maggie about the gun that had been used to dispatch three police officers to eternity as well as the man found in that West Renfrewshire garden. He nodded silently as he listened to the woman from the ballistics team in Gartcosh, the telephone close to his ear.

'There are a few possibilities,' she told him, 'but we are tending towards a .303 rifle, an old one from around the Second World War.'

'That old?' Lorimer's eyebrows rose in surprise.

'Yes,' she replied. 'There were plenty of British Enfield Number 4s hanging about after the war ended, lots of them converted to sporting rifles.'

'Go on,' Lorimer said.

'A sawn-off rifle is the more likely weapon we are associating with the bullets.' She paused then added, 'You know you can saw off both part of the barrel and the wooden stock? Hm? Anyway, that's what we have concluded in our report so far.' She hesitated. 'Eileen Ormiston's death was also down to that sort of weapon,' she murmured. 'Not hard for a gunman to conceal such a thing under his jacket. Bit of string or rope and they hang it over their shoulder, all set to carry out an attack.'

Lorimer tried to imagine the gunman lying in wait for George Phillips, an innocuous figure strolling along near the cottage, rifle hidden beneath his clothing until the time was right to aim and fire without being seen.

'The old bullet found inside the skull gave us far more trouble,' the ballistics expert grumbled. 'Terribly corroded, of course and was difficult at first to assess but we are pretty certain it was fired from the same gun.'

'Thanks,' Lorimer said, though such a simple word was not nearly enough to express what he felt for the expertise shown out there in the Scottish Crime Campus.

'It's a pleasure. And if it helps catch whoever killed those officers . . . ' she said with a sigh that Lorimer could hear over the airwaves.

The detective superintendent put down the phone and looked out of the window, not seeing the storm clouds scudding across a violet blue sky but imagining the rifle that had been used for so many tasks. A British Enfield No. 4 might well have been used to shoot the enemy back in the 1940s and then, what? Taken and converted into a gun to be used by gentlemen in some sporting estate up in the Highlands? Or, he wondered, perhaps not that far away. Had this gun been used by someone closer to home? Houston, maybe? That was a question he had not asked Mary Riddoch, but perhaps now he might have to ask her that very thing: had her husband ever owned a gun?

The sound of music flowed along the corridor as Lorimer strode towards the recreation room where, he'd been advised, Mary Riddoch was enjoying an afternoon watching black and white movies of the Rat Pack, their songs part of the old folks' own young days. Standing at the entrance to the long room he looked at the residents, their backs to him as they stared at the large screen, and wondered just how many of them had been on active service way back when the British Enfield rifle had been a weapon of war. Had any of those men sitting nodding in time to the rhythm of the big band music ever carried such a thing? Had any of them shot or wounded a soldier from the enemy's ranks?

He waited until the song was finished and the clapping broke out from the audience then made his way to where she was sitting, a uniformed carer by the side of her wheelchair.

'Oh, a visitor for you, Mary,' the carer exclaimed, standing up and beaming at Lorimer.

'Hello, again.' Mary looked up at him. 'Do you want to wheel me back upstairs?' she asked, her head to one side, those intelligent eyes assessing his face as though trying to read the reason he had come back to see her. 'Not just a courtesy visit, I suppose?'

'No,' he affirmed, stepping around and undoing the brakes before wheeling her out of the room.

'Anything to do with those awful murders?' Mary asked, shaking her soft white curls. 'Terrible thing to kill a police officer, just terrible.'

Lorimer did not reply until they were in the lift that took them from the ground floor to the next level where Pearson House was located.

'It might be,' was all he said. 'But you must understand that I can give you no information about an ongoing case, Mary.'

He saw her shoulders heave in a sigh.

147

'Something bad's come up,' she said at last. 'I saw it in your face.'

Lorimer's jaw tightened but he said nothing as the doors slid open again and he rolled the wheelchair along to room 7.

Once inside he made sure that Mary was comfortable with the position he'd parked her, close enough to see her television and still able to look up at her visitor who now sat on the edge of her bed.

'I need to ask you something, Mary, but first I have to be sure you won't say a word to any of the other residents or medical staff, okay? This is a confidential chat we're having, something that might help me solve a very difficult case.'

Mary Riddoch nodded, her expression grave as she watched him.

'I understand,' she said. 'I might have lost the use of my legs but this,' she tapped the side of her head, 'is in perfect working order.'

'Okay.' Lorimer smiled gently at her. 'What I need to know is this. Did your husband or anyone in your household ever have a licence for a gun?'

Mary frowned for a moment. 'A gun? What sort of a gun? D'you mean the old thing we kept for shooting foxes?'

Lorimer's pulse quickened. 'Maybe,' he replied, leaning forward a little. 'What was it? Can you remember?'

'Oh, it was so long ago,' Mary replied, looking down at her hands. 'There was a rifle, not a big affair, really. I think it had been made a wee bit smaller after the war.' She looked up at him suddenly. 'Lots of men brought them back, you know. Times were hard and they fetched a few bob in those days.

We kept it wrapped up in old oilcloth in a cupboard when we lived in Paisley, as I remember.'

'And took it with you to Houston?'

'Yes, we did,' she agreed. 'The gardener used it for shooting foxes. Dashed nuisance they were when we were all trying to raise chickens, you know. One of the drawbacks of living in the countryside. Same with the deer before we got proper fences put up around the place.'

'Can you remember what type of gun it was, Mary?'

She gave a small laugh. 'Sorry, I never took much interest in those sorts of things. Not my part of the ship, I used to tell him.'

'And what happened to the gun? Can you remember that?'

Mary frowned again, her little face creased with the effort of remembering.

'I really don't know,' she said at last. 'I don't think I remember seeing it for years, certainly not when the children were growing up. Was it even in the house?' She shook her head. 'Maybe the gardener kept it,' she murmured. 'I do remember telling Roddy not to have it anywhere near the bairns. I never liked guns,' she said suddenly, looking at Lorimer with a serious expression. 'Saw what they could do one time when I was taken to a military hospital to help wounded men just back from the front.'

'Did your gardener keep it at his house?'

Mary paused for a moment then nodded, her face clearing. 'Yes,' she said, tapping one hand with the other. 'That is what happened right enough. I remember now. Roddy gave it to Malcolm Watt and ... well, come to think of it, Superintendent, I never saw that gun again.'

*

If DI Brodie was surprised to see the detective superintendent at his office door he concealed it well.

'I've just come from Erskine,' Lorimer explained. 'Mary Riddoch told me something you ought to know.' He went on to tell the detective inspector what he and Mary had discussed.

'So, an old gun,' Brodie mused. 'What do you think? British Enfield, maybe?'

'Lots of them were adapted for use in sporting estates and farms. Mrs Riddoch reckons theirs was mainly used to keep down foxes.'

'And she has no idea when it went missing?' Brodie asked.

'Remember she told us that their gardener had died a few years ago,' Lorimer reminded him.

'That's where we should start, then,' Brodie agreed. 'I'll have someone look into whoever inherited the gardener's own home, that sort of thing. You never know,' he added, looking at Lorimer with a twinkle in his eye, 'we might even find who fell heir to that gun.'

He stroked the wooden barrel fondly with the piece of soft cloth that he kept specially for that purpose, the gun resting on a support that was actually an old kitchen stool turned upside down. He loved this particular process, the scent of linseed oil filling the small room. Close your eyes, he sometimes told himself, and you might be in an artist's studio. And, in some respects, he was an artist or perhaps a craftsman, an armourer who cared deeply for these particular weapons.

It was almost clean once again and he would ensure that

no trace of any fingerprints remained on the old rifle. It had been one of his favourites all those years back, of course, sometimes lent out, more often hired for a fee, the amount rising over the years as inflation made everything more expensive, including his particular sorts of services. Grease had been applied on the fore part of the weapon where metal met wood, his fingers clad in double layers of latex gloves, and now all that remained to do was buff the stock up to a smooth polish. He breathed in the smell, his hands now rubbing the stock. It was a little sad that this old gun was not as it had been way back when it had been manufactured but those who needed it from time to time were happier with the present sawn-off version.

Walter McBride knew perfectly well what use had been made of the weapon he held in his hands, but there was nothing written down that could ever associate the armourer with this current spate of assassinations. Walter had learned the hard way about keeping written records of his transactions, a lengthy spell in Peterhead prison the reward for past deeds that had been presented as evidence in court. These days everything was done by mobile phone: the date when a hitman would turn up on the doorstep of his workshop for a gun then a time and place to have it returned to him. Few ever came to his home and only at Walter's request.

Aberdeen had been fine in the old days, a thriving place full of folk making a pile from the offshore oil that was flowing into Scotland. But on his release from Peterhead the armourer had decided to head down south, making his home in the bigger city of Glasgow, where he had no difficulty finding new clients for his specialist services. Walter was now the possessor of a senior rail card and a bus pass that allowed him free transport all over the country, something of which he was taking advantage on a regular basis these days.

Walter gave a sigh as he placed the rifle in its cover and laid it carefully to one side of the cabinet. It would remain there until the telephone rang once more, an unfamiliar voice telling him what was needed and when.

Outside it was bitterly cold after the warmth of the workshop and Walter pulled his coat collar up before double-locking the front door and pocketing the keys.

A scream made him step back in alarm then three young children careered past him, their faces painted in lurid shades of green, black clothing fluttering from their arms as they ran.

Hallowe'en, Walter thought. October 31, the night when ghosts and witches roamed the city streets, though nowadays it was all trick or treat, not the old-fashioned guising of his own schooldays. He watched as the figures raced around the corner of the street and out of sight. There were no wee ones left in his family to help dress up for a night like this. After Jess had died nobody had kept in touch with Uncle Walter, both her relatives and his keen to distance themselves from the old ex-con. That suited Walter fine, though. He had nobody busybodying into his affairs and if when he passed away there was a gasp at the vast amount he had accumulated over the years, then he'd have a chuckle to himself from the other side of the grave.

The old man walked towards the bus stop and slipped into the shelter, his eyes fixed on the road, waiting for the number 103 to take him back into the city where he would hop into a taxi and be driven to the comfort of his bungalow. Out here in Nitshill there were too many wee fly men watching and waiting for an opportunity to rip off some poor soul and Walter was careful to make his own visits to the workshop in daylight, shuffling off like any other sensible senior citizen to the bus stop before the rush hour began, only the pick-ups being done under cover of darkness. The single-decker McGill's bus arrived on time, as it usually did, and Walter stepped on, flicking his bus pass on the screen by the driver's cab, then settled down on a seat next to the window. To anyone who cared to observe, this was just another elderly fellow dressed in an old tweed coat, a tartan scarf pulled around his neck, nobody worth a second look.

CHAPTER TWENTY-TWO

She had to go. There was no other way if he wanted to be happy again. He sat on the edge of his bed, nursing the glass of whisky, contemplating the where and when that this would take place. The how was easy enough. He'd handled guns often enough in his time and knew that one shot would be sufficient.

Tonight might be the best time to catch her unawares, no kids running round. He'd already checked the times of the Hallowe'en disco, knowing she would be alone in that house. He drained the glass and looked at it before setting it down on the worn carpet. Dutch courage? Perhaps. He stood up, jaw tightening in determination. It was now or never, he told himself, heading towards the bedroom door and picking up the long bag that lay propped against the wall.

Sharon pressed the mute button as she heard the doorbell ring. It had to be kids, though there had never been anyone calling on Hallowe'en night in all the years they'd lived here.

She grabbed a bag of apples from the kitchen counter and then headed for the front door, a smile on her face.

The cloaked figure standing there made Sharon take a step back.

'Oh,' she said, hand falling to her sides. 'I wasn't expecting—'

Her eyes widened as the gun was raised, that deadly circle of steel directed towards her. This had to be a joke, she thought, yet she had begun shivering as the hooded man lifted the weapon.

'You had it coming, bitch!' he spat, raising the rifle, his intention suddenly becoming obvious.

'No!'

Her scream was cut off as the bullet met her face, apples scattering onto the front step.

For a moment all was quiet as if the blast of gunfire had drowned out every other sound.

Then, turning on his heel, Sharon Carson's assailant walked swiftly down the path, his face hidden beneath the dark hood.

'It was the kids who found her,' the DI explained as he sat in William Lorimer's lounge. 'Came home after their Hallowe'en party to find their mother lying dead on the doorstep.'

Maggie clasped her husband's hand as they listened to the white-faced man relating what had happened to their colleague. She'd met Sharon Carson a few times at retirement parties, the officers at the MIT a close bunch when it came to celebrating one of their own.

And now, this. A talented young woman, one of Bill's own officers, cut down so savagely. Once the call had gone out Bill had gone immediately over to Dumbreck, needing to be there where it had happened. It was very late when he'd returned home again, hoping for a few hours' sleep, but that would not happen now that DI Derek Warner badly needed to unburden himself to the senior detective.

'Sharon was off duty.' Warner swallowed hard. 'Wanted to be around for the children. Mick isn't with her any more, you see …' He tailed off, putting his head in his hands. 'God what a mess.'

'It isn't your fault, Derek,' he said. 'Marriage breakdowns happen all the time, probably more often in our sort of job, you know that.'

'Aye, but if I hadn't … oh, dear lord, what will happen to the kids now?'

'Where are they?' Maggie asked gently.

'With Sharon's mother. She's in a state of shock herself, mind, but having the children with her is actually a help.'

Maggie nodded, remembering the times her own mother had been there for her.

'Look, you know the team's already mobilised,' Lorimer told him. 'It will be only a matter of time till they check everything, see if there's a link with the other shootings.'

'It has to be the same man,' Derek Warner insisted. 'Sharon's simply been another target.'

He looked from Lorimer to Maggie for support.

'It would seem a reasonable assumption,' Lorimer began, though making any assumptions at this early stage of an investigation was something he hesitated to do as a rule.

Though he was still stunned by the killing of his young colleague, he had begun to wonder about the difference between her death and those of the retired officers. Hers was such a waste of a life, full of promise, and with kids who would now never see their mum again. At least the older officers had known decades of service in their lives, though each death left ripples of grief in its aftermath.

'Take me through it again from your perspective,' Lorimer asked, glancing at Maggie and mouthing *tea?*

She nodded silently and got up from the sofa then headed towards the kitchen to put on the kettle once more, pulling her dressing-gown collar around her neck. It was after three in the morning and the central heating was off. She rubbed chilly hands together then slipped into the hall to turn up the thermostat before making another pot of tea for them all.

'Pathologist reckons she was shot around seven-thirty or so.' Derek Warner gave a sniff and wiped his nose with the back of his hand. 'But you know that anyway.' He gave a shuddering sigh. 'The light was on in the porch but the hedge at the front garden would have hidden her body from anyone passing by.' Warner paused then took a deep breath. 'Police were called by a neighbour. Kids had enough sense to run for help. They didn't realise what had happened. Thought their mum had just fallen on the doorstep.'

'That was something, at any rate,' Lorimer remarked gently, hoping to console the distraught detective who was now talking just to get it all out of his system, reiterating the facts of which the detective superintendent was well aware.

'Aye, suppose so. Anyway, I got called out soon after. Local station and all that. Couldn't believe it when I saw her lying there.' He looked up beseechingly at Lorimer. 'I just wanted to lift her up and hold her in my arms,' he whispered, voice choking with emotion. 'But I did what any officer would do. Even though it was breaking my h-heart.'

Derek Warner covered his mouth with his hands to stop from crying aloud but the muffled sobs were testament to his feelings of loss and guilt.

'How long had you and Sharon . . . ?'

'Over a year now,' the man told him. 'We wanted to get married as soon as she got a divorce. Kept it a secret from everyone to make it easier in the office . . . ' He bit his lip and looked up at Lorimer apologetically. 'Thought it might take a year or two, right enough, till everything was finalised with her husband . . . Mick . . . Oh, God, someone will have to tell Mick!' He looked around wildly as if at a loss what to do, half rising from his seat.

'Hey, the family liaison officer will have already been in touch,' Lorimer assured him. 'Sit down, stay here a bit. Maggie's making more tea.'

The white-faced man sank back into his chair, nodding, too numbed to talk any further.

Lorimer regarded him silently. DI Warner had been with the Major Incident Team long enough to know that he could trust him not just as his boss but as a friend. Yet there were things amongst his own fellow officers that had remained hidden from Lorimer until now. This particular one being the relationship between the DI and DC Sharon Carson, the young mother who had been gunned down on her own doorstep several hours before.

Warner had arrived on his doorstep, ashen-faced and exhausted, apologising for the lateness of the hour and asking if he could come in to talk.

The incident had been relayed to Lorimer mid-evening and he'd already visited the scene of crime, spoken to the immediate neighbours and talked to the on-call pathologist who had been packing up when he arrived. The woman's body was now at the city mortuary and the post-mortem would take place some time later today. Lorimer glanced up at the clock. It was not unusual for him to lose a night's sleep at the start of a major incident but he had hoped for a couple of hours at least, then the doorbell had started ringing and he'd discovered the detective inspector on his doorstep, tears streaming down his face.

He would insist that Warner take time off after he'd given another statement in the Govan office this morning, the DI's personal involvement now making it impossible for him to continue with the investigation. It would be a long day, Lorimer thought grimly, steeling himself for the hours that lay ahead, wondering what the scene of crime officers might report. Wondering how to tell the remaining members of his team that one of their own had been gunned down in cold blood.

Liam woke with a start and sat up, clutching the unfamiliar bedclothes around his chin. The streetlights outside weren't where they should be, streaming through the gap in the curtains to his left, and it took the boy a few moments to realise where he was.

This was Gran's house. The upstairs bedroom that he

stayed in sometimes for sleepovers during the school holidays gradually took on familiar proportions and he rubbed the sleep from his eyes, trying to figure out why he was here.

The dream was still vivid, his heart thumping from the fear of that monster chasing him through the forest. There had been monsters last night at the disco, his brain reminded him as the dream began to fade.

Then the little boy remembered. He saw once again that dark shape at his front door, heard Gran screaming then Aunty Julie bundling himself and Katie into the back of her big car.

Mum was dead.

Aunt Julie had told them late last night as she sat on Gran's settee, hugging him and his little sister tightly. *She's in heaven with the angels*, his aunt had said firmly and Katie had nodded, sticking her thumb in her mouth, wide-eyed.

'When's she coming home?' his wee sister had asked and Liam had closed his eyes then, the sudden understanding hitting him like a blow in his chest.

Dad was gone and now Mum too.

Eight-year-old Liam Carson began to cry, hugging his teddy bear to his chest, silent tears running down his cheeks as he wondered what would happen to them now.

CHAPTER TWENTY-THREE

The big man stared at the television screen, listening as the reporter talked to the camera, a microphone close to his face. Behind him he could see blue and white crime scene tape blowing in the wind, cutting off entry to the house where the atrocity had taken place.

His lips twitched as he heard the word repeated: Atrocity. This reporter evidently liked the sound of that, made the killing seem worse than it really was, of course. One shot to the head, or so the story went. He saw the camera pan over the doorstep where the woman had been killed.

'Police are certain to be working on the idea that this is the fourth in a terrible spate of killings directed against their own officers,' the reporter told the camera, his face set in grim lines appropriate to the news item.

The man watching the news flash sat back, his bulky shoulders moving in silent mirth. Then, unable to stop, he began to laugh out loud, big belly laughs that shook the room.

*

'Has to be the same gunman,' the Chief Constable said wearily. 'What other explanation is there?'

Lorimer glanced at the man by his side. Professor Solomon Brightman had been asked to join them this morning, his expertise as an offender profiler giving him a seat at the table.

'Solly?' Lorimer looked at his friend quizzically.

'It is possible, of course,' the psychologist began. 'Though there is the discrepancy of the latest victim actually being a serving officer, not retired like the others.'

Alan Marshall stared at the bearded man. 'A mere detail,' he said, waving his hand as though to brush the psychologist's point aside. 'Someone out there is targeting the police and it has got to be stopped!'

'We're doing everything possible, sir. Ballistics will be able to work on the case; the post-mortem is being carried out today,' Lorimer explained patiently. 'It's just that these killings appear so random . . . ' He shook his head. 'You know these are the most difficult to deal with. And this gunman, whoever he is, has been planning his assassinations carefully, probably staking out the movements of his victims. It's an impossible task to predict where he'll strike next.'

'You think there will be another shooting?' The Chief Constable sat back in his chair, alarm written on his face.

It was Solly who answered, however, nodding his head. 'Oh yes, this gunman, if it is just one assassin, has a list, I would think. Names of officers that he wants to eliminate.'

'But there's been absolutely no link between any of these officers!' Marshall exclaimed, fist thumping the table. 'We've spent hours and hours of manpower trying to see if they had any connection to cases in the past. Any common

162

felon seeking some sort of revenge. And there's nothing. Absolutely nothing!'

Lorimer heard a small sigh escape from the psychologist seated beside him.

'The gunman himself may be the common factor,' Solly murmured. 'But this latest killing, now, that does give me pause for thought.'

'Why?' Lorimer asked.

'A doorstep killing,' Solly replied immediately. 'It might be the mark of a professional hitman, someone paid to carry out an assassination. Two shots then away again. The others weren't all like that. One gun, certainly, but could there be more than one gunman?'

The two senior officers stared at the psychologist, knowing that what he said was true. Yet in Glasgow hits against gangland members had also been carried out from cars, something that McAlpine's and Ormiston's deaths might have had in common.

'It's different for other reasons too,' Solly said. 'If there was any sort of pattern then we might have expected the fourth victim to have been a retired officer in a different part of the country. Inverclyde, Inverness-shire, Glasgow ... ' he counted off on his fingers. 'Then Glasgow *again*?'

'What are you saying?' Marshall frowned.

'It looks a little as if whoever is behind the shootings deliberately wants to mix things up, annoy the police as much as he can. And I don't mean whoever was wielding that gun,' he added, looking up at them both. 'This is a highly organised operation, not a killing spree by one deranged gunman.'

'Go on,' Lorimer encouraged.

Solly paused for a few moments, gazing past the Chief Constable and fixing his eyes on the patch of sky he could see from the window of the man's office.

'I would have expected a fourth shooting to be somewhere else,' he said at last. 'Maybe down south or Edinburgh. The Borders, perhaps. Lothian and Borders?' He looked at each of the men as he spoke. 'One dead officer for each of the old regional forces. But, of course, I may be mistaken.'

Alan Marshall and Lorimer exchanged glances. It was a chilling theory but, if it was to hold water, then the recent death of DC Sharon Carson was not only an aberration but might not be part of this case at all.

'I don't believe that,' Marshall said at last, swallowing hard. 'And the public won't believe it either. Yet, what can we do? Can't wrap every officer up in Kevlar. It's an outrage. We swear to keep the public safe from violent men and yet we cannot keep our own officers safe!'

Lorimer did not voice his thought. It was not, perhaps, the right moment to remind the Chief Constable that George Phillips, Stephen McAlpine and Eileen Ormiston had become just that: ordinary members of the public once their time as serving police officers was over. And, as such, easier targets for a calculating gunman. So, a little voice asked, why not doorstep them like a professional assassin would have done? Was the man sitting by his side right in thinking there was more than one person using that same gun? He frowned, considering this idea. But the thought of officers from different parts of Scotland being targeted, now that was something to ponder.

What if Solly was wrong? What if there was a lone man with an old sawn-off rifle picking off people? That didn't make sense, though, did it? Not the way Solly had described it.

He rubbed his forehead. Either way, this whole mess has just escalated into the biggest and most complex case in his entire career.

Rosie Fergusson stood up and straightened her aching back. 'Thanks, everyone. Let's get all of this off as quickly as we can.' She met Lorimer's blue gaze through the viewing window and nodded up at him. 'We'll have the toxicology report to you as soon as. And ballistics will have their bullet within the hour,' she assured him. 'See you in my office?'

Rosie walked out of the post-mortem room, glad to have finished for the day. The body of Sharon Carson would be wheeled along to the refrigeration unit now and left there until such times as the Procurator Fiscal deemed appropriate. She stripped off the rubber gloves and flung them in the bin then removed her protective clothing. A quick shower with some scented gel to rid her of the cloying smell of death, then she'd get dressed in the trouser suit she wore most days to work.

There was a mirror in the small changing room that the female pathologists used and soon it would be steamed up, but right now Rosie caught a glimpse of herself, hair pulled back in a small knot, lines around her eyes and mouth where she had never noticed them before.

You're getting old, woman,' she muttered at her reflection, realising that those rays of sun streaming in from the window were being less than kind to the image in the mirror. She pulled the shower door aside and stood rigid under the cold spray, willing it to warm up. A few minutes under the hot water would wash away all of the smells that could linger on her body after a PM but no amount of standing there under that blessed flow of warmth could rid Rosie of the memory of the policewoman's body.

A young woman, really, same age as herself, Rosie had noted with a pang. Two wee kids, the elder boy not much older than Abby … and, according to Lorimer, the dad had not long left the marital home, some bother within the relationship that was only mentioned obliquely. And Sharon Carson had been one of Lorimer's hand-picked officers in the Major Incident Team, something that brought these killings a lot closer to home.

'Your husband seems to think DC Carson's death might not be part of a pattern,' Lorimer told Rosie as they sat either side of the pathologist's desk.

'Oh?'

Lorimer made a face. 'Alan Marshall has cancelled all leave within the entire force,' he sighed. 'That would have been a blow had it not been for the fact that we are dealing with fellow officers.'

'And each member of the force will no doubt be looking over their shoulder,' Rosie murmured.

'Won't do anything for morale,' Lorimer agreed. 'The latest government cuts were bad enough for our manpower but after this, well, what sort of recruitment are we likely to expect? And how many early retirements?'

'That won't save anyone,' Rosie reminded him. 'Your first three victims were all retired officers.'

'Aye, and senior officers at that. People who must have put away some violent men in their time.'

'What do you think is going on, Lorimer? Really?'

The detective stifled a yawn and Rosie could see from the way he was slumped on the chair that exhaustion was setting in.

'Oh, I think what everyone else is saying,' he replied. 'It's a former offender with a big grudge against the police in general and in those officers in particular.'

'But there hasn't been any kind of link between them,' Rosie protested. 'Solly told me as much.'

'No link that we've found yet,' Lorimer growled.

'So, what now?'

'Depends on several things,' he told her. 'Need to get the ballistics report first to see if that was the same gun . . . and . . . ' he stood up wearily then looked at his watch, 'in just over half an hour from now I have to face the press again.'

Rosie walked her friend along the corridor and watched as he left her department, shoulders hunched under his dark coat. It was not that long ago that Detective Superintendent Lorimer had seriously considered quitting the police force, a traumatic case sending him into a spiralling depression.

'Be careful,' she called but he did not hear her voice, or else had chosen to ignore it as he pushed through the swing doors and disappeared.

Two cups of black coffee had helped a little, Lorimer thought as he splashed cold water onto his face. It would be hours yet before he could drag his weary body into bed, a thought he had to dismiss as a yawn threatened to bring tears to his eyes. He pulled out a comb and ran it through his hair. That would have to do, he decided, the reflection in the mirror showing a man that looked suddenly far older than his forty-eight years. The blue eyes looked back at him, unsmiling. Vanity had never been part of his make-up, but a need to look respectable and reasonably alert made him straighten up to his full six feet four. The press could pounce on any sign of weakness from the representative of Police Scotland and Lorimer was not about to give them any more ammunition to damage the organisation he loved.

The usual flashlights made him blink as he strode onto the entrance to Govan police station, home to the MIT. He had asked for them to wait there, hoping that the cold wind on this first day in November might make them disperse a bit more quickly. Lorimer stood on the lowest step, but still towered above the pack of men and women, the paraphernalia of sound equipment and cameras pointed towards him.

'I am here to give a short statement about the shooting of Detective Constable Sharon Carson,' he began, looking down at the throng of reporters. 'DC Carson was one of my own officers working here as part of the Major Incident Team and her death has been a shock to us all.'

There was a murmur amongst those who had not been aware of the link to Lorimer, though most of them had already been briefed.

'This is the fourth death of a police officer in recent days, though do bear in mind that DC Carson was a serving officer whereas the first three assassinations were directed upon retired police officers.'

'Not the same man, then?' someone called out.

'We are at present running tests to determine a link between them all,' Lorimer admitted. 'And, as you are aware, there is only so much information we can give during an ongoing case.'

'There's a mad gunman running about, though, isn't there?' another shouted, the familiar voice making Lorimer look through the crowds to see the reporter from the *Gazette*, the middle-aged woman with flame-red hair who seemed to have a penchant for needling the detective superintendent.

'I cannot comment at this stage,' he said. 'But what I can tell you is that DC Carson was a fine officer and there are two young children who at this very moment are still in a state of shock after the trauma of last night.' He glared at them as he spoke, daring anyone to interrupt. 'We will stop at nothing to find whoever did this cowardly deed and robbed those children of their mother. All leave for police officers around the country has been cancelled meantime and I have no apologies to make about this.'

He drew a deep breath and continued. 'There are times in our lives as serving police officers when we have to make some sacrifices for this job and that is one of them.' He paused and stared at them all. 'But no single officer expects to join up and have to sacrifice their own lives. That is something I want to make very clear. We will find whoever is behind this,' he promised again. 'And the weight of justice will come down upon them as never before.'

Despite the clamour and calls, Lorimer turned and made

his way up the steps, leaving them with far less than they all wanted to know.

DS Molly Newton closed the door behind him and then caught him up as Lorimer headed for the stairs.

'Well done, sir,' she murmured. 'That can't have been easy.'

Lorimer looked at the tall blonde woman who had seen many dangers as a serving officer, almost losing her life when she had worked undercover before being invited to join the MIT.

'Thanks, Molly.' He slowed down a little to let her climb the stairs by his side. 'You were a friend of Sharon's, weren't you?'

He saw her blink for a moment as though to prevent tears then she swallowed before nodding her reply.

'Aye, we'd got to know one another quite well.' Molly sighed. 'She didn't deserve this.'

'None of them did,' Lorimer replied.

'No, but Sharon had so much of her life ahead of her. Plans for her future . . . ' Molly made a face. 'And these wee kids . . . och, it's horrible.'

'Molly,' Lorimer stopped at the top of the flight of stairs and turned to face her, 'did you know Sharon and her husband had split up?'

'Yes, I did. She told me a few weeks ago that Mick was out of the house.'

'And did she give you any reason for that?'

'Not really. Just said they weren't getting on any more.' Molly looked down at her feet as she spoke and Lorimer understood that the woman was trying to protect her friend.

'You knew about her and Derek Warner,' he said, making Molly look up at him, open-mouthed.

'Well ...'

'He came to see me early this morning,' Lorimer told her.

'Ah,' Molly sighed. 'Not many folk knew, honest. Sharon was keen to keep it that way till divorce proceedings were sorted. She didn't want Mick to accuse her of ...' She shrugged.

'Adultery?' Lorimer supplied.

Molly nodded miserably. 'I could see she and Derek were besotted with one another. Sharon told me once that Mick had never wanted her to join the police. Maybe he'd suspected something like that could happen,' she said slowly. 'Meeting another officer, I mean. Someone she had more in common with, I suppose.'

'Come on through,' Lorimer raised a hand, indicating that Molly should follow him along the corridor to his office. 'I think we need to talk about this.'

More black coffee and a plate of chocolate biscuits helped a little, though there was a dull ache beginning in his head as Lorimer listened to his detective sergeant's words.

'Sharon and Mick were an unlikely couple,' Molly told him, picking up a biscuit. 'He's a long-distance lorry driver. Makes good money, but that kind of work means that he was away from home quite a lot. Sharon's mum was great at looking after the kids. Katie's just started primary now so at least she only had to take them to and from school and have them till Sharon got back from here. It was harder when the wee one was at nursery,' she added.

171

'Tell me more about Mick Carson.'

'I met him a few times,' Molly continued. 'Nice-looking fellow, not that different from Derek, actually. You could see the type of bloke Sharon fancied. But he was ... how can I put it without sounding snobby?'

'Try.'

'Mick's a bit rough round the edges. Left school at sixteen, did a spell in the army. Think that's where he got his HGV licence. Not a great talker.' Molly set down her cup. 'He would leave most of the conversations to Sharon. I think he felt a bit out of his depth whenever she had her police pals round.'

Lorimer sat up in his seat. 'He was a soldier?'

'Yes.'

He felt a beat in his temples, an idea beginning to take hold.

'Molly,' Lorimer leaned forward, fixing her with his blue gaze, 'do you happen to know if Mick Carson has an old army rifle?'

CHAPTER TWENTY-FOUR

Flynn sang along to the radio as he drove to the garden centre that was several miles out from the city. This was one of his busiest times of year with arborists cutting back trees, leaving lots of paths to be swept clean of leaves, and hedges and lawns having their final cuttings before the onset of winter. Also, there were home owners that followed the seasons wanting new trees and shrubs planted before the frosts and Flynn knew just where to buy the best quality at the cheapest prices.

He knew this road well, the countryside between Barrhead and Lugton speeding past, slowing down for the tight corners near Uplawmoor and casting a glance now and then towards the hills and fields on either side. He could let his thoughts wander a little and nowadays most of these tended to focus on Erin and when he would see her next. Business had been good this year and his bank account was in a state of good health, making Flynn ponder on his next move. Would it be one where he might include Erin in his plans? There were several whitewashed cottages along this particular route, late annuals still brightening up their front gardens. He smiled as he considered the idea of a small house with a garden, somewhere they could be together. A sigh escaped him. But it was one of pleasure, the fantasy warming him as he embellished its detail in his imagination, rows of neat flowerbeds and blossoming fruit trees like the ones in the Lorimers' garden.

The sign for MacLaren's Nurseries came into view and he slowed down, his pleasant thoughts vanishing like mist evaporating off the hills on an early summer's morning. It was time to think of the purchases for one of his well-heeled clients, the money from this particular commission helping to bring his dreams a little closer to reality.

As he pulled into a parking space he wondered what Erin was doing right now and if her team were any further forward in identifying the remains he had found out in Houston. Who had he been? And what was his story? Flynn's smile faded as he remembered the small hole in the skull. Whatever had happened, there had been some bad folk involved in the poor guy's ending.

John Ramsay looked around the room at the other men seated there. He'd been acquainted with some of them for years, though in truth he really didn't know any of them at all. Their names and what they were in for was about as much as he'd picked up until the psychotherapy sessions had begun. Now he was learning more about his fellow prisoners as they opened up to the balding middle-aged man with the rimless glasses who sat cross-legged among them.

Rehabilitation. That was the new buzzword. Everywhere else in Europe prison populations were dwindling as the authorities sought ways to change the ways of violent men. He'd read that in the library, a book written by a former prison governor. But here things were different, overcrowding rife with more and more longer sentences keeping people behind bars till they were old grey men like himself.

Ramsay looked at the man in the centre of their half-circle with a cynical eye. He meant well enough, was probably trained up with the latest psychobabble, but what did he know about the day-to-day drudgery of prison life? The battles to maintain some form of street cred that left some men scarred, others cowering wrecks? The psychotherapist would walk out of here at the end of these sessions, no doubt pleased with himself, to some other kind of life; one that included a wife and children, a nice house somewhere and the ability to choose where he wanted to go and what he wanted to do. Freedom. That's what he had and that was what he would never understand until he was incarcerated like the men sitting around him. Like the Padre, this man was free to come and go, as his job dictated, not as the courts had demanded. Ramsay ground his teeth in silent frustration. Bloody waste of time! Sitting here with a guy who hadn't a clue what really went on in this place.

His thoughts turned back to the man that had attacked him in the corridor. Word had it he was a grade A nutcase with a history of random violence. The inmate had been sent to a different jail now and Ramsay was relieved he'd not need to cast eyes on him again. No questions had been asked of Ramsay but he'd seen a few grins directed his way when the subject came up of the man found groaning in that corridor. Someone had begun the rumour about the fellow being suicidal, running into the wall. But they knew what had really happened, Ramsay guessed, and not one of them would ever tell. That was the sort of morality that went on in here, something this trick cyclist would never figure out.

Still, he had to grudgingly admit that these sessions had made him think. What are your choices? the therapist had asked them all and one by one the men had opened up a little to talk about what they really wanted out of life once their release date was in sight.

'What about you, John?'

The question startled him out of his reverie and Ramsay looked up to see everyone staring at him, waiting for him to speak. He nodded, acknowledging the deference some of them still paid him not just as the oldest man in their wing but as one with a reputation that made them keep a safe distance.

'What about me?' he asked sullenly, a perverse mood making Ramsay want to spoil the therapist's day. It was more than he could do not to stand up and punch that soft white face and upset the class, but he unclenched his fists, noticing right away that the psychologist's eyes were directed at him, a small smile of amusement on his face as though he could read Ramsay's mind.

'You'll be out soon,' the therapist reminded him. 'What choices have you decided to make?'

It was old ground they were going over now, Ramsay thought; each man had been persuaded over the past few weeks to open up and talk about his past misdeeds as a way of coming to terms with them, as a way of preparing the individual inmates for a life beyond the walls of HMP Barlinnie.

'Health things mostly,' Ramsay grumbled, reminding them at one stroke of his ongoing illness and instantly receiving a different sort of smile from the therapist, sympathetic this time. 'Need to register with a new GP. Keep seeing the oncologist, I suppose.'

'Of course, John, we are all well aware of that as a problem you will have to live with but, really, my question related to your way of life. What choices can you make to stay out of trouble?'

Ramsay's eyes slid away from the man's scrutiny. If he could really read his mind the therapist would have been getting to his feet and pressing an alarm button. If he could rise from his place in this room right now he'd give this guy such a doing ... and he wanted to, wanted to see him with blood streaming from that pudgy nose, hear him cry for mercy. It took every ounce of self-control to keep still and focus on what was important: being released on the date he'd been told.

Once out of here John Ramsay would follow the instructions that had been issued to him, do what had to be done. Then he'd show them that old John Ramsay still had it in him to commit that ultimate act of violence.

'I'll do whatever has to be done,' he said at last. 'Like we all will,' he added, setting his gaze around on the other inmates, some of whom nodded as though they were all wee schoolboys in a class and Ramsay had given a correct answer.

For a moment the therapist caught his eye and John Ramsay saw that he had not fooled him with his oblique answer. If he could have read his mind, what murderous intent would he see there?

He blinked and looked away, the moment reminding him of another man whose blue gaze had overwhelmed him once, reducing Ramsay to weeping.

That had been the first time he had known regret for his actions, seeing finally the chaos they brought to his life, and the lives of his victims. Yet Lorimer had been kind, not condemning, talking gently to him, offering him a big cotton handkerchief as they talked in that interview room so many years ago. Once the tape had been turned off, they had talked a bit more, Ramsay asking the detective to look out for his family, see that they knew he was all right. And the detective had kept his promise, even visiting Ramsay once and bringing him some books.

He shuffled his feet as the end of the session drew near, wishing that his sentence had been longer. A couple more years and he'd have been carried out in a box. But now? A different sort of judgement had been passed upon John Ramsay and he would have to do the deed he'd been assigned or be killed.

Michael Carson was sitting on a settee in his mother-in-law's front room, a child cuddled in each arm, when Lorimer entered the room. He looked up and for a brief moment Lorimer saw the misery etched on the man's face. Carson looked as though he hadn't slept either, something that didn't surprise the detective.

'My condolences,' he began. 'It's just awful.' He shook his head. 'Sharon was one of our brightest prospects. I'd told her more than once that one day folk would be calling her "ma'am".'

Carson stared up at him blankly then turned his attention to little Katie who was nodding off to sleep, thumb stuck into her mouth. Liam squirmed out of his father's grasp, however, and, looking up at Lorimer, he paused before asking, 'Were you my mum's friend?'

Lorimer hunkered down to be on the little boy's eye level.

'I was *one* of her friends,' he said gently. 'Your mum had lots of friends where we worked together.'

'Police friends?'

Lorimer nodded. 'She was well liked,' he told Liam. 'And she used to talk about you, what a clever wee boy you are. She was fair proud of you, Liam Carson.'

The child stared back at him then looked at his father. 'Can I go out to play, Dad?'

'Not just now, son,' Mick Carson replied. 'Go on upstairs. I'll be with you in a wee while to build that Lego set. Okay?'

The child gave a brief nod, looked at Lorimer once again as though to seek his permission too then, when he saw the tall man smile encouragingly, he wandered away out of the room.

'Mr Carson, I'm so sorry for your loss but I hope you appreciate that there are things I need to ask you.'

Carson nodded wearily. 'Sharon used to tell me all about that, talking to relatives of folk that had died. It was the bit she hated most about the job.'

'She was happy in the force, though,' Lorimer said.

'Oh, aye,' Carson replied, a slight bitter note in his voice. 'It was all she wanted to do. All she ever talked about.'

179

'Was that the main reason for your splitting up?' Lorimer asked quietly, seating himself on the vacant armchair opposite the bereaved husband. 'I've seen it happen before,' he assured the man who was sitting back, his jaw tightening as though Lorimer had no right to ask such questions.

Then Carson looked down at the little girl who was now sleeping in his arms.

'Aye,' he said briefly. 'She had more in common with you lot in the end. I think we just ran out of things to say to one another.' Carson heaved a sigh and sat back on the settee, one hand stroking his daughter's hair.

'Mr Carson, I am really sorry to have to ask you this, but it is important.'

Was that a wary look in the man's grey eyes? Lorimer saw the shoulders beginning to rise, noting the familiar body language that spoke of tension.

'Do you happen to own a gun?'

There was a moment's silence before Carson shook his head, an expression of disbelief written on his face.

'I can't believe you just asked me that,' he began. 'Here I am with two wee children who've just lost their mum and you're pointing the finger at me?' His voice had risen and Lorimer saw Carson's arms tightening around little Katie. 'Oh, right,' he sneered, 'that old chestnut. Always the husband that does away with his wife? Is that what you're thinking? Eh?'

'We need to know, Mick,' Lorimer said gently. 'If you should require a licence for an unregistered weapon then we need to know about it. There are lots of things we have to do to eliminate people from our enquiries. You know that. Sharon must have told you how that works.'

'I do not have a gun,' Carson said slowly and deliberately. 'Okay? Never have had, never will have. So let's get that out of the way, right?' His eyes blazed with sudden fury. 'You think cos I was army that I must have handled a rifle? You wanting to put me in the frame for all these cop killings? That's insane! I was a driver. Pure and simple. Nothing else. Check if you like.'

We will, Lorimer thought, his words unsaid. But Carson's reaction was interesting, his protestations a bit over the top, that spurt of anger tinged with something else that the detective superintendent recognised, seeing the man begin to tremble. This was not just a man losing his cool, he thought. This was a man who was frightened.

'Who is this?' Lawrence Mathieson gripped the telephone tightly and waited for a response. But all he heard was a dull click as the caller hung up.

He stood for a moment, trembling. The voice had been heavily accented, suggesting someone from down south, someone from his past.

We know where you are, the man had said.

Mathieson tried to swallow but his throat was dry. It was all the fault of that stupid gardener, turning up a dead body. The news about that had travelled far, then. And now there were others eager to dig up matters that were better left alone.

CHAPTER TWENTY-FIVE

Nobody walking into the pub in Galashiels would have given the hitman a second glance and that was just how he wanted things to be; a figure who blended in, had no discernible features anyone might remember and who raised not a flicker of alarm amongst his fellow drinkers. That was how he had evaded detection much of his life, a master at his craft, never willing to show his face anywhere he could be remembered. Perhaps the barman might recall a stranger in their midst but it was doubtful he would be able to give an accurate description of a customer who'd come in for a pie and a pint.

He had chosen to sit in a corner giving him a clear view of the door as well as being able to see the comings and goings at the bar while watching the television screen fixed high on the opposite wall. A middle-aged man of medium height, wearing jeans and a brown crew-neck sweater, he seemed to disappear into the woodwork behind him, no overhead lights in this particular corner, the walls on either side of him casting a shadow even at this time of the day. The pie was finished now, just greasy crumbs he wiped from his hands and mouth with the paper serviette as he looked across at the television screen.

It was hard to make out the newsreader's words above the babble of conversations and the rattle of a metal barrel that was being rolled from a back room towards the hatch in the bar, but he could read the strip of writing as it rolled around the foot of the screen.

And what he saw made the man stiffen in his seat.

ANOTHER GLASGOW TRAGEDY.
POLICE OFFICER GUNNED DOWN
ON HER OWN DOORSTEP.

He leaned forwards, grasping the half-finished pint in both hands, watching as the reporter's figure filled the screen, microphone close to her chin. Then the image changed, replaced by a grainy black and white photograph of a uniformed police officer smiling at the camera, probably taken after her passing-out parade.

He shoved the drink away, fists bunched on the edge of the table.

This was not meant to happen! *He'd* been selected for the fourth hit, hadn't he? And *Glasgow*? That wasn't where the next hit was to take place. It was here.

Something had gone wrong and yet nobody had had the nerve to tell him. He gritted his teeth. Well, if that was the way it was to be played then sod the lot of them! He pulled the glass towards him and drained it in one draught.

Then, wiping the froth from his lips, the hitman rose from his corner, grabbed his coat and walked purposefully out of the pub and into a narrow street where the rain was slanting sideways.

He pulled up the hood of his parka, glancing ahead to where he'd left the van. Tomorrow was meant to have been the day for the hit. That was the date that his paymaster had insisted upon. But he was ready now, angry enough to take his chance and carry it out. Another day might make his mark a bit more wary in any case, he thought, quickening his pace as the rain began to batter the ground with an intensity that matched his mood. Now was the moment.

Eric Bryceland ran the short distance between the two cottages, one hand over his head to stop the rain soaking his hair, the other clutching a plastic bag. He pushed open the high wooden gate that divided their garden from next door's and he was through, stepping carefully on the wet crazy paving that had worked loose over the years, his mind composing what he would say to their neighbour, Margaret, about that. He'd offer (again) to mend it and he already anticipated her mischievous smile and shake of the head as she refused him politely. *Too independent for your own good*, he'd told her often enough. But she always just gave that throaty chuckle, evidence of another habit she was unwilling to give up. It was lunchtime here but to Eric it seemed like early morning, given the time difference in the US, and he guessed his body clock would take a bit of adjusting after the lengthy flights.

He knocked the grey-painted door briefly then turned the

handle, stepping inside and brushing his feet on the mat. The back door was rarely locked and the elderly lady was used to Eric's frequent visits. Besides, she'd want to hear all about their trip.

'Margaret? Are you there?'

Eric stopped for a moment, listening, then smiled. The sound of Classic FM was filtering through from the sitting room where he guessed the former police officer would be sitting, no doubt engrossed with her latest cross-stitch pattern.

He turned around in the kitchen, looking for a suitable plate on which to leave his gift of home baking. Since taking early retirement he had found the process of making scones, cakes and (more recently, thanks to a favourite television programme) different types of bread. Eric smiled to himself as he pulled a large willow-patterned plate from the rack below a glass-fronted cupboard. That was easily big enough. Margaret would be surprised but after the flight home, Eric had been unable to sleep, rising in the wee small hours, taking a notion to bake some decent home-made bread.

The loaf was still warm to the touch and Eric laid it almost reverently on the plate, placing it in the middle of the table where Margaret was sure to find it.

He was about to turn and retrace his steps back to the cottage next door when he heard the doorbell ring. Then footsteps along the hallway as Margaret made her way to the front door. Too early for the postman, Eric thought, wondering who was visiting his neighbour at this time of the day.

The sound was like an explosion, making Eric jump and let out a cry.

'Margaret!'

As the second shot rang out he heard a thump.

Then, propelled by some unquestioning impulse, he began to run.

'Margaret! Margaret!'

The black-hooded figure standing there made Eric shudder to a halt.

There, lying in an awkward heap on her doorstep was his neighbour, blood pouring from a wound on her head.

He felt his jaw slacken, wanting to cry out again. But somehow he could not utter a word.

Time seemed to stand still for a second.

Then, before Eric could move or speak, the gunman raised his weapon and fired twice more.

There was nobody in this quiet lane, he'd been certain of that, no other vehicle parked along the moss-covered stone wall that ran along the side of the two adjoining cottages. As he drove away, gunning the van out of the narrow entrance and onto the main road once more, the hitman cursed loudly, thumping the steering wheel with an angry fist.

That was not meant to happen. The woman should have been there on her own. He'd checked that out. No husband. No partner.

So, who the hell was the man he'd just shot?

CHAPTER TWENTY-SIX

C laire Bryceland put her foot on the brake and slowed the car down then turned into the lane that led to Maryvale Cottage. She sighed, glad to be home. The rainstorm was almost over now and she could see the first arc of a rainbow appearing over the nearby fields. Sunshine and showers, the weatherman had promised, so maybe she'd get into the house before another downpour began this afternoon.

The grey-haired woman parked her Golf beside the wall, a decent distance from her neighbour's old Saab so that each of them had easier access to turn back into the lane. Slamming the driver's door shut, Claire reached into the back and pulled the bags of groceries out. She should have waited for Eric, of course, asked him to carry the heavier stuff, but it was just a few steps around the corner to the back door and into their kitchen.

The smell of freshly baked bread met her nostrils as she pushed open the back door and a smile lit up her face. Soup and new bread for lunch, she decided, already gathering ingredients in her mind.

'Eric! I'm home,' she called out, dumping the bags onto the kitchen chairs.

There was no answer, so Claire shrugged then began to empty the contents, putting most of them in the big American-style fridge that was her pride and joy. Glancing at the clock on the wall she smiled. Time for a cup of tea before she began a late lunch. They'd sit in the conservatory and begin the *Times* crossword as they did every day, squabbling happily over their interpretation of the clues. Claire sighed, but it was a sigh of pleasure. She'd been relieved when Eric had taken early retirement from his job as a senior member of staff at the local high school, the stress of management putting a strain upon her husband that had threatened his health. Now they had all the time in the world, still young enough to enjoy life together.

'Eric!' she called again a few minutes later. 'Putting the kettle on now, dear. Tea of coffee?'

There was still no answer and so Claire strode through to the big airy room that looked out onto their garden and to the woods and pastureland beyond. But there was no sign of her husband.

'Eric?'

Puzzled now, Claire wandered through the house but sensed its emptiness even as she went from room to room.

Coming downstairs once more she stopped and grinned, the familiar smell wafting up at her. Bread! Of course, he'd have gone through to give a loaf to Margaret and probably stayed for a cuppa. Well, she'd just go in and take Margaret's copy of *The Times* with her. Now that they were home from their trip to the US, fetching her neighbour's newspaper was a daily habit Claire had resumed.

Leaving her coat on the back of a kitchen chair, Claire walked through the house and opened the front door. The high beech hedge that separated the two gardens was turning golden and by Christmas there would be a scattering of leaves to sweep up from the lawn. When they'd bought the cottage Eric had asked their neighbour if she'd wanted them to reduce its height but Margaret had just smiled and shaken her head, assuring them that she preferred having the privacy, but was glad to have them visit any time they wanted.

Claire bent to pull out a weed that had crept between two paving stones then placed it carefully on the path, making a mental note to pick it up and put it into the brown refuse bin on her way back. She straightened up, one hand on her back where it always hurt, before strolling down the path. Pushing open the front gate she stopped for a moment to admire the view of rolling hills, the clouds blown sideways by a vagrant wind, patches of blue sky emerging. Then she heard the familiar click behind her as the gate swung shut and she stepped along the front path.

Claire's hand was on her neighbour's gate when she saw the open door and the figure sprawled across the step.

'Oh! Margaret! What's happened?' She hurried towards the old woman, her first thought that the old lady must have fallen.

Then she saw the blood.

'Oh, no. Oh, Margaret . . . ' She stooped down to feel the old lady's wrist, frantically trying to find a pulse.

'Eric!' she shouted. But there was no response.

'Eric?'

Claire stood up, looking frantically into the darkened hallway.

It was then that she saw the second body lying there.

And, as she saw the familiar shape, and knew who it was, Claire Bryceland's whimper became a high-pitched scream.

'It's happened again.'

Lorimer's jaw hardened as he addressed the team. 'An older lady. Name of Margaret Woods. She was deputy divisional commander of Lothian and Borders way back in the eighties. Retired to a small place outside Galashiels more than twenty years ago.'

The faces looking at him around the table were uniformly grim.

The news about Sharon Carson had shocked the entire team and now another woman was dead, shot like those others.

'That's not all,' Lorimer continued. 'The gunman also fired at Miss Woods' next-door neighbour who was apparently visiting. Name's Eric Bryceland. He's critically injured and undergoing surgery at the Borders General Hospital.'

'Is he expected to live, then?' one of the team asked.

Lorimer shook his head. 'I don't know. Extensive blood loss, apparently. The doctor who spoke to me didn't commit himself.'

There was a shocked silence until Lorimer spoke once more.

'If this is a pattern of assassinations against police officers

190

then we may take a little comfort from this: up till now it seems as if every one has been meticulously planned, but I think the gunman was not expecting to see a second person in that house today. The Brycelands have been away in the US for over a month and their home was locked up, the car at a local garage.'

'Who found them?'

'Mrs Bryceland,' Lorimer replied. 'She'd walked up to the garage in the village around lunchtime to collect her car then gone for groceries. Like you do when you're first home from a holiday. We have set up the crime scene and a pathologist is heading down there,' he went on, looking round the room. 'But I'd like to be there myself. Plus as many of you as we can spare.' He stifled a sigh. The resources of the MIT were far from infinite and he continued to search the room till his gaze fell on Molly Newton and the man standing by her side. 'Molly, you and Davie come with me first thing tomorrow morning,' he decided. 'No point in going till then since Mr Bryceland is undergoing surgery even as I speak. There's still plenty to do up here to find out about Sharon.' Lorimer allowed the pent-up sigh to finally escape.

Claire Bryceland sat shivering on the chair in the hospital corridor, a rug around her shoulders, a plastic cup of coffee clutched in both trembling hands. The woman at her side (had she really said her name was Flo?) was regarding her carefully as though afraid that Claire might suddenly spill the contents all over her lap.

It was the waiting that was worst. Not knowing. She'd looked up beseechingly at every passing doctor and nurse but somehow the fact that they'd avoided her eyes gave Claire a heavy feeling in her stomach.

Eric was going to die. She blinked, not wanting to believe that. It was only yesterday they'd come home, giggling like two teenagers as they'd unlocked the front door at some ungodly hour of the night, careful not to disturb Margaret-next-door. The suitcases were still in the utility room, waiting to be unpacked, their bright holiday clothes still to be pushed into the washing machine.

Eric was going to die. They would never go away again together. Never sit side by side, hands clasped as a plane took off, each of them humming the theme tune to *Chariots of Fire* and sharing secret smiles.

A uniformed police officer stopped beside them and bent down to speak quietly to the family liaison officer at her side then glanced across at Claire. What did she see in his eyes? Pity? Sympathy? She strained to hear what was being said in case it was about Eric. Was he dead already, then?

But all she heard was one name; Lorimer.

'Eric?' She turned pleading eyes towards Flo.

'Still in surgery, Claire. We won't know anything for quite a while,' the woman murmured, patting Claire's cold hand. Then, looking at her as though to see if she was still in shock, she added, 'There's a senior police officer coming down from Glasgow tomorrow. He'll want to talk to you. Is that all right?'

'Yes,' she whispered.

'Sure you're okay with that?'

Claire nodded, though in truth she was not sure about anything at all.

CHAPTER TWENTY-SEVEN

'I don't think it's the same man.'

'What do you mean?' Rosie asked, looking up from where she was spooning cereal into their son's mouth and taking a quick glance at the kitchen clock.

'This one is different,' Solly said quietly, glancing at Abby who was now listening to the conversation between her parents.

'Are you finished your toast, pet?' Rosie asked, running a hand fondly over her daughter's blonde head.

Abby nodded and Rosie bent closer to wipe away a smear of jam from her mouth.

'There. Off you go and brush your teeth. Morag will be here any minute.'

With an exaggerated sigh that made her parents exchange an amused smile, Abby rose from the table, casting an envious look at her little brother who sat calmly in his highchair playing at feeding the teddy bear tucked in beside him.

Rosie looked at the puddle of Coco Pops and spilled milk

on Ben's tray and mentally thanked whatever kind fate had brought Morag into their lives.

Breakfast time at the Brightman household was a time of gentle chaos until Morag arrived at eight o'clock, allowing Rosie and Solly to drop Abby off at school before they began their own working day.

'What do you mean, Solly?' Rosie asked again, picking up the thread of their conversation.

'The gunman,' he whispered quietly so that Ben did not hear him. 'It's different.'

'What is?' Rosie frowned, her hand poised over the cereal bowl.

'The doorstep,' Solly began. 'It points to a different sort of execution.'

'In Galashiels? But the Carson woman . . . that was on her doorstep too, wasn't it?'

Solly nodded then stroked his beard thoughtfully. 'That wasn't part of the pattern either,' he murmured. 'It troubles me.'

The doorbell ringing made them both look up. Then the sound of their front door opening followed by Ben drumming his little heels excitedly as he heard a familiar voice call out.

'Morning!'

'We can talk about this later,' Rosie told her husband, giving him a warning glance before the nanny strolled into their kitchen, a beaming smile directed towards Ben.

They watched as Abby scampered off into the playground, pigtails flying as she joined her friends.

'Come on, I've got a pile of stuff to do this morning,' Rosie said, catching hold of Solly's hand. 'And I want to see if the ballistics report has come back from Gartcosh yet.'

Solly squeezed her hand and they set off up towards the University of Glasgow where they would part, Solly to his office in the department of Psychology, Rosie further into the campus to the forensic medicine department.

He was silent for most of the way, his thoughts still on the perpetrator of these horrific murders. There was no mark of it being a spree killing, he had decided, or of it being the work of one person. No, Solly decided, if he was correct in his deductions, the shootings had been carefully planned out beforehand. But possibly not by the person wielding that gun.

'Penny for them,' Rosie said, casting a glance at her husband's face. She knew that faraway look of his: something was going on in his mind, something that might or might not be shared with her.

Solly smiled and shook his head. 'Just thinking things through,' he said at last. Then he stopped and looked at Rosie gravely.

'Will you call me as soon as you have that report?'

'Yes, of course,' she promised, frowning. 'Why?'

But he had started walking again, still clasping her hand, a little shrug of the shoulders the only answer he was willing to give.

As soon as she had read the ballistics report, Rosie knew what he'd suspected. She sat back, hearing the whirr of the machine as it printed off a hard copy.

Rosie blew out a long exhalation. It was a similar bullet

that had killed the young detective constable, robbing two wee children of their mother: a .303. But the rifling marks showed that it had been fired from a different gun.

Sharon Carson's death *was* different from the rest. And Solly had known that. She shook her head slowly, amazed that he had come to that conclusion even before the words that danced in front of her eyes. Okay, so the woman was much younger than the rest of the victims, still in service. And that shooting had followed another one in Glasgow. Not part of the pattern, he'd told her. And very soon she would be letting him know that his suspicions were confirmed.

Rosie lifted her mobile and pressed the number that would take her through to Solly's office, wondering as she did what Lorimer would make of this.

The journey from Glasgow to Galashiels might have been a pleasant interlude for the three detectives as the Lexus sped along the narrow country roads, sun filtering through trees still burdened with autumn leaves, their colours bright against the rain-washed sky. They had left the city early in an attempt to miss the worst of rush-hour traffic, Lorimer picking up Molly and Davie from their homes, the darkness pierced by street lamps casting an orange glow. Now the sun had risen and Glasgow was far behind them, their thoughts on what lay ahead.

Would Eric Bryceland have survived that first night? He had been taken straight to a high dependency unit where his condition was stable but still critical, Lorimer had been advised by the DI who had been called to the scene. Would the medics allow them access to the man? And, more to the point, would Bryceland be in any fit condition to tell them what had happened?

Lorimer slowed down at yet another corner, his eyes looking out for any approaching vehicle that might be taking the breadth of the road. The Lexus had all the comforts he enjoyed, like these heated front seats (a blessing on cold winter mornings) but it was a big car and he had to take extra care on these narrower roads. Concentrating on his driving helped to take Lorimer's mind off the injured man and he'd even given an appreciative glance at the countryside unfolding before them, a river now running alongside the road, a flock of greylag geese in a waterlogged field nearby.

The phone rang out suddenly and he tapped a button by the steering wheel that connected him to his mobile.

'Lorimer.'

'It's me, Solly.' The familiar London accent came through clearly. 'Rosie wanted me to call you.' There was a pause but Lorimer waited patiently for the psychologist to continue, Solly's habit of deliberating no longer a source of irritation but one he was well used to after all those years.

'It was a .303 bullet that killed Mrs Carson,' Solly said at last. 'But it wasn't fired from the same gun as the others.'

'What are you saying?'

There was a longer than normal pause and Lorimer found himself biting the tip of his finger, anxious to hear something that he was already beginning to suspect. He glanced at the woman by his side, catching her eye. Molly and Davie were both listening intently to the conversation that was taking place even as he drove towards Galashiels.

'It's wrong,' Solly said quietly. 'It isn't the sort of pattern I thought we might see.'

There was another pause then he resumed. 'A professional hitman would doorstep his victim and depart as swiftly as he could, having made sure nobody was around to witness the victim's death.'

'Eileen Ormiston wasn't doorstepped and both George and Stephen McAlpine were out of doors.'

'Yes,' Solly agreed. 'But Sharon Carson and the latest victim were both shot dead on their doorsteps. Classic professional hits.'

'And yet the two guns were different.'

'There isn't a pattern, is there?' Solly murmured. 'Some are made to look like opportunist killings but I would be surprised if the first three had not been planned with great attention to detail.'

'And all from the same gun,' Lorimer said, slowing down as they approached a particularly tight corner of the road.

'Which brings us to this latest shooting,' Solly continued. 'It might have been planned to some extent but whoever pulled that trigger was completely unaware that the next-door neighbours had just returned from abroad. And he had no idea that poor Eric Bryceland was in the habit of popping in unannounced to her kitchen.'

'Something went wrong, you think?'

Lorimer could not see Solly nodding on the other end of the telephone line but he imagined that dark head affirming his question.

'I wonder about the shooting of Sharon Carson,' Solly continued. 'Different gun, you see.'

'And you think it might have been a different gunman?'

'Hm. I wonder.' Solly sighed. 'Hard to tell, but it broke a pattern of sorts, didn't it? Sharon was far from retirement and several people would have known she was alone in her house that Hallowe'en night.'

'What next?' Lorimer asked, running a hand through his hair.

'Oh, I think whoever killed Miss Woods will have gone to ground. Unlikely that there will be any trace of him whatsoever. A professional hit. But if Eric Bryceland survives, who knows what he may be able to tell you?'

'You heard all that,' Lorimer said at last, glancing to his side at DS Newton.

'We did.' Davie Giles leaned forwards from his seat behind Lorimer. 'This changes everything now, surely?'

'Depends on what turns up in Miss Woods' post-mortem. If it's the same gun that killed Sharon then we have two different weapons at large. But if not . . . ?'

'Sharon's death is at the hands of someone completely different,' Molly finished.

Lorimer nodded, his eyes on the road ahead. 'And if we find that to be the case I want you two turning over every single thing in Michael Carson's background. Means, motive, opportunity, usual way of eliminating every strand. There's something in what Professor Brightman says about Sharon's murder and I want to see her perpetrator brought to justice.'

Claire sat twisting one of Eric's hankies in her hands. It was hard not to weep and her head ached from the stress of thinking the same things over and over again. If only she'd come home sooner from the supermarket. If only Eric hadn't decided to bake bread this morning. If only ... She heard a sob heaving in her chest and clenched her teeth together, determined not to break down here in this public place. That would do Eric no good at all, would it? She had to stay focused, keep watching and waiting for someone to bring her news.

The three figures that rounded the corner of the corridor were unfamiliar but as soon as she saw them approaching, Claire knew they had come to speak to her. Two were tall, one dark-haired fellow and a woman with blonde hair swept into a ponytail, the other a little shorter, a good-looking young chap and, yes, they were all gazing at her with solemn faces. Was he dead? Had Eric perished on that operating table?

Claire stood up on trembling legs as they came closer.

'Mrs Bryceland? I'm Detective Superintendent Lorimer and this is DS Newton and DS Giles.' The man held out his hand and Claire took it, comforted by the strong grip for a very brief moment.

'How is Mr Bryceland?' He was asking the officer now standing beside Claire as she looked from one face to another, only half aware of the murmured response that there was no further news as yet. She saw sympathy there, the blonde woman nodding to her and coming to stand on her other side as though ready to take the elbow of someone who might soon be a widow and usher her back to her seat.

'I'm all right,' Claire told her, but nonetheless she was grateful to sit back down again.

'Can I get anyone a hot drink?' the younger man asked and Claire nodded, needing something else to keep her from shaking.

'Tea please. Milk, no sugar,' she said, looking up and meeting the man's eyes. She had already forgotten his name but recalled that he was a DS. Detective sergeant. And he hadn't let the other DS, the woman, go and fetch drinks. That was a point in his favour, Claire told herself as she listened to him taking orders. Suddenly the memory of her neighbour came to her, stories of high-profile cases she'd been involved with, watered down no doubt for the couple next door. Claire slumped in her seat, the memory of Margaret Woods' voice entering her mind as clearly as if she had spoken to her in this hospital.

Claire shivered, remembering other things now. The news items they had seen as they'd journeyed around the US, tragedies at home seeming so far away then, banished from their thoughts as they'd made the most of the beautiful colours of the fall. But, now? These murders had come not just to her own town but to the very heart of her being. And if Eric died . . . ?

'Mrs Bryceland, may I ask you some questions, please? Do say no if you don't feel up to it.' The tall man, Lorimer, was hunkered down by her side and looking up into Claire's eyes.

His voice was gentle, a west of Scotland accent, not broad Glasgow like some she'd heard. But it was his eyes that fascinated Claire, those piercing blue eyes that seemed to look right into her soul.

'Yes,' she told him. 'I'm all right. Still shocked, of course.' She let a trembling sigh fill the space between them. 'You need to ask things, of course you do.' She nodded, sitting up a little straighter and watching as the family liaison officer moved away to let him sit beside her.

It was never easy talking to a newly bereaved man or woman, doubly hard when the life of the victim was still hanging in the balance. Lorimer found himself admiring the way that Claire Bryceland had composed herself, sitting next to him. She had taken the carton of tea from Davie Giles and thanked him, then looked at Lorimer as though resigned to whatever he had to ask. He'd talked to her about the places they'd visited in the States, established that both the Brycelands were keen birdwatchers and shared a few anecdotes of his own; sightings of ospreys and white-tailed eagles. The woman was more relaxed by the time she took him through what had happened that morning. Her trip to the supermarket in Galashiels and the return home.

There had been nothing out of the ordinary. No strange car parked nearby as she'd left. They hadn't seen Miss Woods since their return and Claire Bryceland had told him that she had guessed her husband had taken a newly baked loaf next door. It had been a habit of Eric's to pop back and forth through the doors of their respective kitchens, the Brycelands on very friendly terms with their elderly neighbour. Lorimer had hesitated before asking about the dreadful scene on Margaret Woods' front doorstep. But she had answered his questions slowly and carefully, eyes closed as though to be completely certain she was still seeing those awful things.

'Thank you,' Lorimer said at last, placing a warm hand over her cold fingers.

Then, as the door to the room opened and a figure in blue scrubs appeared, everyone stopped talking.

He felt the woman by his side tense up, terror at what might be said. Then, a reassuring smile changed everything.

'Mr Bryceland is out of a very lengthy and complicated surgery now and in the recovery room but I can tell you that he's going to be all right,' the surgeon said, looking straight at Claire Bryceland then letting his eyes travel across the assembled officers in the room.

The cry that left her lips was like a howl of anguish, though, as she turned and sobbed into his shoulder, Lorimer knew that these were tears of relief.

CHAPTER TWENTY-EIGHT

Flynn whistled as he raked the damp earth across the raised bed as if he could blot out the mental images that still haunted his dreams. It was good that there were no longer police officers here, the scene of crime folk finished with the Mathiesons' garden at last. It was a cold day and he was glad of his fleece and thick leather gloves as he pulled the rake towards him, admiring the rich dark topsoil that he'd shovelled on the previous day. Whether anything would grow depended on how much light would get onto this place at the foot of their garden, shadowed as it was by the row of trees. He'd already hit a few roots whilst putting in the wooden frame and had explained to Mrs Mathieson the reason for raising the bed even higher with new soil. They might be lucky to sow salad veg in the spring but Flynn doubted that this area would be yielding healthy crops of vegetables year after year. He'd tried to tell them as much but it was clear that his clients didn't want to listen to the Glasgow man they had hired for the job.

He paused for a moment, straightening up to rub a knot in his back, listening to the sound of heavy wing beats. Ah, there they were, a pair of swans, flapping overhead, intent on heading to whatever field might provide a day's nourishment. He watched as they became smaller and smaller, finally disappearing against the pale clouds. Swans, he knew, mated for life. Lorimer had told him that once and he'd felt a surge of fondness for the huge white birds ever since.

Erin, now, would she be like that? Content to wed a gardener? Flynn shook his head. Early days for thoughts like that, he told himself, but here, alone in this country garden, he let his imagination wander to a time when he might ask her that very question. And then? A home together, wee ones on his knee? He smiled, contemplating the vision, while telling himself that such good fortune was pretty unlikely. They were at that lovely stage of a relationship when they were still finding out things about one another, sharing stories and confidences.

He looked back at the mound of earth, remembering when it had been thick with brambles, the years of neglect hiding that skeleton. She'd told him about that, too, how some woman expert down south had the skull away with her to see if she could give it a face. Flynn shuddered, recalling the first sight of these hollow places from which eyes had once gazed. No matter what sort of picture the expert made, that would be his lasting memory. Erin had been decent enough to keep him in the loop about some of her department's activities, probably knowing fine that Lorimer would have told him about further developments anyway.

Would they ever find out whose body had lain rotting in

the earth for all these years? Flynn drew the rake across the bed one last time and stood back, admiring the slight curve he had created to allow rainwater to drain off into the channels on one side. And if they did? What then? Would he be called to court one day as a witness to the dead man's final resting place? Flynn shifted from one foot to the other, uncomfortable with that thought. He had severed all ties with his former shady acquaintances but publicity like that might cause a few of them to make contact. He shivered a little. That was something he never wanted to happen, especially now that Erin was part of his life.

Lawrence Mathieson watched from the bay window as the gardener trundled a wheelbarrow up the side path towards his waiting van.

It was time to pay up, he thought, pushing the roll of banknotes deeper into his coat pocket. The garden would lie quietly through the winter months then, come the spring, there would be something new to keep his wife busy, her ambition to grow their own vegetables having kicked off the whole unpleasant episode.

Mathieson closed the front door carefully behind him and stepped out onto the drive, glancing up to see the gardener putting his tools and barrow in the back of his truck.

'Hello, there!' he called out and saw Flynn's head rise at the sound of his voice.

He walked briskly towards the vehicle and stood in front of the chap.

'Time to settle up, Mr Flynn,' he announced, pulling out the cash from his pocket.

The man's eyes slid onto the money but there was a frown, not the look of eager greed he'd expected.

'If it's a' the same to you, can you write me a cheque?' Flynn asked, eyeing Mathieson with a strange look. 'It keeps my books straight,' he added. 'Jist make it out to J. A. Flynn, Landscape Gardener.' He watched as Mathieson fumbled in his inside jacket pocket for his cheque book.

That was a surprise, Mathieson thought silently. Hardly anyone used bank cheques nowadays and it was rarer still for someone like this Glasgow fellow to pass up the chance of cash in hand. He shrugged, bemused by the fellow's insistence.

'I c'n add you to my list of clients if you like, though,' Flynn offered. 'Detective Superintendent Lorimer is my oldest client, as it happens. We're good friends, actually.'

Mathieson paused, Mont Blanc pen in hand, staring at the young man. He was a friend of a top cop? How had that come about? he wondered, blinking rapidly.

'N-no, thanks, anyway,' he stammered. Last thing he wanted was any further association with the police officers who'd crawled all over his property these past few days.

'Any news?' he asked as Flynn folded the cheque and placed it into his wallet.

'About the skeleton?'

'Yes,' Mathieson snapped. What did he think he meant? Of course it was about the skeleton.

The gardener cocked his head to one side and gave a faint smile as though he were making up his mind about something.

'Only what you read in the papers,' he said at last. But, as he turned away to open the van door, Mathieson was certain that J. A. Flynn knew far more than he was letting on.

As the banker watched the van trundle down his drive for the last time, he ground his teeth in frustration. It was too dangerous to ask the police questions about that skeleton in his garden: far better to keep his head down. Yet, as he rubbed chilled hands together and looked at the van disappearing round a corner, Lawrence Mathieson thought again about that threatening phone call and wondered just who might roll up at his door now that this discovery had been made so public.

'Can we keep this latest news under wraps for the time being?' Lorimer asked.

Claire Bryceland's head came up sharply. 'Why? What difference would that make? You heard the surgeon. Eric's going to be all right.'

'Mrs Bryceland, please hear me out,' Lorimer began gently, looking into the troubled eyes of the woman by his side.

'What is it?'

Lorimer sighed. 'It's a bit complicated,' he began. 'We're striving to locate the gunman, of course we are, but here's the thing.' He shifted in his seat, bending a little lower so that he could speak more quietly. 'We are convinced that your husband was not expected by this gunman, that he was shot at in a moment of surprise, catching the killer off guard. That is probably what saved his life. Your husband was a moving target as well, his injured hand getting in the gunman's sights as he aimed . . . ' He broke off as Claire put both hands across her mouth, her eyes widening.

'The bullet damaged his shoulder as well as grazing his head and it was most probably the pain and shock that made him collapse,' Lorimer explained. 'So far the gunman has no idea that his two victims are not both dead. And, with your permission, we'd like to keep it that way, for a while at least.'

'I see,' Claire replied slowly, never taking her gaze from his face. Then she looked down at her trembling hands. 'I keep thinking if I'd only come home earlier, been there . . . things might have been different.'

Lorimer nodded silently. She did not need to be told that it might have been three corpses, not just one that was heading to the mortuary. Eric Bryceland had been lucky, but if his wife had been there too, would the gunman not have made sure of all three targets? He imagined the hitman hearing an approaching vehicle and readying himself for a second shot. That had not happened. And Claire Bryceland could thank whatever it had been that had kept her from arriving back home before the gunman's departure. She'd work that out for herself, he thought. But right now the woman by his side was simply coming to terms with how lucky she had been and how grateful she was to have her husband alive.

Mr Khan nodded gravely as Lorimer explained what it was he wanted.

'I can't promise that every member of staff will be able to keep this a secret, but I do know every one of the team in high dependency,' the surgeon told him. 'We'll keep Mr Bryceland in a private room as soon as we can move him there and, yes, I will be glad to have an officer or two here for security.'

'Thank you,' Lorimer said, shaking the man's hand. 'It might make all the difference.'

He stood looking at the surgeon, noting the hollows under the man's deep brown eyes and wondered for a moment how to phrase his request. This man had spent hours in the operating theatre, his skills undoubtedly saving the man's right hand, the delicate surgery needed to reset so many bones a marvel to the detective.

'Mr Bryceland was lucky to have you here . . .' he began.

Mr Khan smiled wearily. 'Perhaps,' he murmured. 'I had been called to another patient who is not feeling so lucky today. We had to postpone her operation, I'm afraid. Not such good news for the profile of our National Health Service.'

Lorimer nodded, realising that the problems this man had were not confined to the operating theatre. His own job also involved a fair amount of PR, police occasionally coming under criticism for one thing or another, the general public often deliberately kept from knowing exactly why certain decisions had been taken.

'I really would like your permission to talk to him. As soon as possible, please,' Lorimer said at last, fixing the surgeon with a determined stare.

'Ah, this is not unexpected,' Mr Khan said. 'I guessed that you would want to talk to my patient. However, he is unlikely to be conscious for a while yet.'

The surgeon looked at his wristwatch and then focused his attention back to Lorimer. 'Give it about three more hours,' he suggested. 'But let Mrs Bryceland see her husband first. I can give you both about five minutes, if his nurse thinks he is up to it.'

'Thank you,' Lorimer said, allowing a sigh of relief to escape. There was no sign of fatigue in those skilful fingers, Lorimer thought as Khan gave him a firm handshake. Then the surgeon walked briskly away, his work done for now. Lorimer watched him retreating, marvelling at the dedication of those men and women who spent their days mending broken humanity, grateful for the surgeon's cooperation and understanding.

Molly Newton fell into step with Lorimer as they left the hospital, glancing now and then at his face, wondering what order he would give her once they reached the Lexus.

'Davie is staying as close to the Brycelands as possible,' Lorimer said as he held open the passenger door for her. 'Hopefully they'll be able to keep any reporters at bay.' He closed the door and came around to the driver's seat but simply sat back with a sigh. 'Local officers have been primed, too, and they will be liaising with our team back at Govan. Meantime,' he pulled on his seat belt and gave Molly a grin, 'I think we should have a bite to eat and have a look around Margaret Woods' cottage.'

Molly nodded, pleased to be going for some food; her stomach had grumbled several times in the past few hours as they had waited at the Borders General for news. That was one of the downsides of this job, snatching meals whenever possible, often having to go without a lunch or dinner when the pressure was on.

The scene of crime officers had spent that morning trawling the area around the two cottages and had left the lane as discreetly as possible, the scene of crime tape only at the entrance to the narrow lane where the residents' cars were parked. Molly sat back as the Lexus left the hospital parking area, wondering what was going on back at the MIT headquarters. Already she knew that Margaret Woods' professional life would be under scrutiny, like that of the other victims, officers poring over facts and figures, trying to make some logical sense of these killings. Would they find a link? Or, she wondered cynically, was there actually no link to be found, these shootings the work of a random gunman?

The professor smiled as she turned the three-dimensional model this way and that, glancing from time to time at the computer screen that had all the information she wanted, pixel by pixel. It was a satisfying task to recreate a person's face from their skull, art and science combining to achieve something rather magical to those unfamiliar with her methods.

He'd not been a very prepossessing-looking young man, she thought, though these missing teeth didn't help, adding to the overall impression of neglect. It was the blue eyes, of course, the colour prevalent in Scotland, that could make all the difference.

'The window to the soul,' Alice Morton murmured, wondering what he had really been like in life. Had he been someone's lover? Or father? She stared hard at the face, seeing the hollowed cheeks and then moving towards the screen and clicking to see the images she had created. There were several different possibilities of facial hair. The skinhead that looked unhappily back at her seemed to fit with that particular era twenty or so years back, another face with stubbled chin making him appear older than his years. The full beard didn't look right to her mind, but who was she to judge? All the pictures would be sent to the unit at Paisley where officers were trying to find the man's identity. And this, Alice thought with a smile of satisfaction, would undoubtedly help them.

'Who are you?' she murmured, turning back to the head and gazing into his artificial eyes. 'And who would have wanted to shoot you dead?'

CHAPTER TWENTY-NINE

It didn't matter what the Padre said, John Ramsay knew that he was a bad man with a bad heart. How could anything change? He was old now, weathered by storms of violence, years of doing things that would shock any decent person. No, he couldn't change.

The man's words haunted him nonetheless, and Ramsay had looked up the Old Testament passage in the Bible for himself, hiding the book under his bedcovers, frightened to be seen looking at it in case his co-pilot sneered at him or, worse, called him out about it in front of the other inmates. Losing face in here was as bad as it got and Ramsay knew the consequences for a man in his condition would be grave indeed. No, he'd continue to keep his head down. He was counting the days now rather than weeks and his heart thumped with a sort of excitement at the thought of fresh air on his face and days outside when he would be free to come and go as he pleased.

Of course he'd never really be free of the Big Man and

his power. Someone like that had arms that reached far and wide, his several henchmen trained thugs who had no conscience whatsoever about finishing a job.

That was the problem, Ramsay thought, with a deep sigh. It was as if the Padre had poked and prodded some dormant part of him, bringing it back to life. Conscience. Aye, he'd developed a troubled mind, all right, one that gave him sleepless nights worrying about things he'd never thought about before. Like the woman who'd be left behind, the colleagues who would mourn a man regarded as one of Police Scotland's finest. Lorimer. The man he'd been ordered to kill.

No, Ramsay thought bitterly, there was no way out for him now.

And yet, those words kept drumming in his brain. A heart of stone changed to a heart of flesh. Could that be possible?

Douglas Petrie knew that the old man would be in the library in a little while and possibly on his own. It would be a bit of a risk to be seen talking to him in case the other inmates of HMP Barlinnie were overly curious about why the minister was wanting to seek out John Ramsay. And yet he'd tossed and turned all night long, the thought gripping him. Petrie had prayed long and hard about it and at first light, rubbing the sleep from his weary eyes, he acknowledged in his heart that he'd been given a sort of summons. He grinned to himself, knowing that the ways of the Almighty were not always conducive to a good night's sleep. *A man's mind plans his way but the Lord directs his steps*; wasn't that what the Book of Proverbs told him?

And so here he was, walking along the familiar corridor, fingering his dog collar awkwardly as though to remind him of the status he held in the prison. The Padre, they called him, a catch-all title for a man ministering to all sorts of fellows who might have had allegiances in childhood to different strands of faith or, more likely, none at all.

When Ramsay looked up from his place behind the table it was as if he had expected to see him, Petrie thought at once, seeing the nod and that tired smile he'd come to know only too well.

'Aye, Padre, what brings you here?' Ramsay asked, glancing past him and looking at the prison officer who had accompanied the minister and was now in conversation with one of his colleagues at the far end of the library, mercifully out of earshot.

'I want to talk to you, John,' Petrie told him, pulling a chair over to the side of the table and sitting down as close to the man as he dared.

Ramsay gave him a strange look. 'Answer to my prayers, was it, Padre?' he whispered.

Petrie blinked in surprise. 'Maybe it was, John, maybe it was at that. I just feel ... ' How could he say it out loud without this man laughing at him? That God had sent him there to speak with this troubled soul?

'I read it again, you know,' Ramsay told him. 'All that guff about stone hearts. Describes me to a T, so it does.' He sat back and folded his arms as if to say that was the end of the matter.

Douglas Petrie smiled and shook his head. 'Well, God has ways of changing a man's mind, John. Even when we think we know it all, are sure about our present and our future, God can still surprise us.'

'Oh, aye? Like what happened tae St Paul?' Ramsay gave a small laugh. 'I'm no' a candidate for a Damascus experience, Padre, surely you know that by now?'

Douglas sat back and regarded the man thoughtfully, wondering how to choose his words then dismissing that same thought. God would speak through him if He wanted to change this man's heart.

'You remember the passage about God forgiving sins? How even if they are really bad he can wipe them out?'

'Wiping the slate clean, you mean? Aye, but He knows fine just how much I've done in my life. Far too much to wash away,' Ramsay replied, but Douglas Petrie heard that doubt in the prisoner's voice, saw the shadow cross his face.

'King David killed a man,' Petrie told him. 'Deliberately, I mean, not in a battle or anything like that. No, he had a man sent to the front where he was certain to be cut down by the approaching enemy forces. Quite deliberately. Know why?'

Ramsay shook his head, his eyes intent on Petrie's own.

'David wanted the man's wife for himself,' he said. 'And he took her as soon as he could. It was sheer lust, of course, and against God's commandments.' He looked Ramsay in the eye. 'D'you know what happened to David?'

'Naw, but I guess you're goin' tae tell me,' Ramsay replied with a faint smile playing around his mouth as if he were enjoying the conversation. 'God sent fire tae burn him up or somethin', right?'

'Wrong,' Petrie told him firmly. 'God forgave David after

David had been shown how terrible that deed had been. He was full of remorse for what he'd done and begged God to forgive him.'

'How wis that?' Ramsay unfolded his arms and frowned. 'He deserved tae be punished, just like I was.'

Petrie nodded his agreement. 'You're right,' he agreed. 'And every sinner deserves to be punished. Sent to eternal damnation.'

He saw Ramsay flinch at his words then Petrie leaned forward. 'You've served your time, John, but there is still an eternity in front of you to consider.'

'Ah'm no long fur this world, you know that,' Ramsay said, giving a dry cough as if to bear witness to his lung condition.

'And that's one reason why you need to listen to God.'

Ramsay frowned but said nothing.

'If you tell Him that you feel bad about what you've done, ask Him to forgive you and put a new heart into you, then He will.' Petrie paused. 'It's actually as simple as that, John.'

Ramsay shook his head and looked away, his mouth closed in a thin line.

'The gospel of John tells us what Jesus said,' Petrie told him, producing a well-worn New Testament from his jacket pocket. 'Look here. There's a story of a man called Nicodemus who came to see Jesus at night.' He read the passage then he paused and looked at the old man but Ramsay nodded as though to say *go on with the story*.

'They might be the most famous words in all of the Bible,' Petrie said slowly. 'John chapter three, verses sixteen and seventeen.' He looked up from the book and into the other man's eyes, not needing to read the words he knew by heart.

'"For God so loved the world that He gave his only Son, that whoever believes in him should not perish but have eternal life. For God did not send his Son into the world to condemn the world, but in order that the world might be saved through him."'

He stopped, noticing the old man's throat where he swallowed, the tears in his eyes ready to brim over. He stretched out his hand and grasped Ramsay's cold fingers, ready to pray with him.

'Lord, bless your child, John, make a new heart in him, for Jesus' sake, Amen.'

The small squeeze gave the younger man a glow of hope. Would John Ramsay accept Jesus as his saviour? Then he felt the hand drop and saw Ramsay brush his eyes with the back of his hand.

There was an acute silence for a moment between the two men, Petrie wondering what was in the prisoner's mind, yet feeling a sort of warmth within himself that told him these words had found their mark. Now it was up to the older man to make a choice that would change his life for ever.

The rest of the afternoon passed in a daze, Ramsay collecting a few books and placing them back on the shelves, handing out others, but saying almost nothing to the men who wandered in to the library. Why had the Padre come, uninvited, at exactly a time when he wanted to see him? That was a sort of wee miracle in itself, Ramsay thought. A coincidence? Or, and here he felt a shiver running all down his back, had God really sent the Padre to him today?

*

'Please may I speak to Niall?'

'Who's calling?' a woman's voice with a distinct Highland lilt asked.

'It's Douglas, Douglas Petrie.'

'Oh, it's yourself, wait a wee minute and I'll get him,' Eilidh Cameron replied. 'Niall, phone for you. Douglas Petrie.' He heard Niall Cameron's wife calling.

'Hello, Niall here. How are you, Dougie?'

'Grand. Sorry to disturb you at home. Especially when there's all this awful business going on.'

'That's okay. What can I do for you, Padre?'

Douglas Petrie smiled. Even his friends in the police were calling him that now, it seemed.

'I have an inmate here, name of John Ramsay. Just wondered if you'd ever come across him?'

'How long's he been inside?'

'Oh, he's almost at the end of a fifteen-year sentence. Word is he'll be out before Christmas.'

'Ramsay.' Cameron considered for a moment. 'Sorry, don't think I've come across the man. Why?'

Petrie heaved a sigh. 'Och, I just think he's been giving life and the hereafter a lot of thought. Reading between the lines I think he's beginning to understand the effects of what he did and remorse is finally setting in. Guilt and remorse. He feels he's too big a sinner to ever be forgiven.'

'Not true,' Cameron replied immediately. 'You know that and I know that, Dougie.'

'Well, maybe there's still hope for him before the end,' Petrie agreed. 'I thought maybe suggesting to him that he takes a look at your church. What do you think?'

220

'Everyone's welcome there,' Cameron replied. 'Aye, soon as he gets out he can make his way to us. I'll keep a look out for him.'

'Thanks,' Petrie replied. 'That really helps. We're not encouraged to keep in touch with inmates after their release so it would be good to know he was coming to your church.'

Once he had put down the telephone, Petrie bowed his head and closed his eyes, a feeling of relief and calmness settling over him. He did his job in Barlinnie but the real work happened in a man's soul. And that work was undertaken by a far higher authority than the Revd Douglas Petrie.

CHAPTER THIRTY

'Maybe I wasn't meant to die just yet,' Eric told her, his bandaged head deep in the pillows.

Claire held his good hand, the other swathed in dressings from the surgery giving it the look of a giant mitten. She tried to smile, forcing the tears that were gathered in her eyes to remain unshed, fearful of upsetting her husband. *Five minutes*, Mr Khan had warned her earlier. And she would make sure these were five good minutes to make Eric feel better.

'You've still plenty of damage to do,' she joked, her smile widening as they looked into each other's eyes. 'Once you're home we can begin to plan that next trip we spoke about. Canada next year. What do you think?'

Lorimer watched the couple as they spoke softly to one another, recognising the sort of bond that held the Brycelands together. He and Maggie shared that, this special connection that cemented a relationship. They were friends as well as lovers and somehow that mattered more than anything as the years went past.

It was hard to disturb them, intrude on this private moment, but it had to be done.

'Mr Bryceland? I'm Detective Superintendent Lorimer and this is my colleague, Detective Sergeant Newton,' he said, as they stepped into the room.

Bryceland's eyes looked up at them then across at his wife.

'I'll leave you to it, love,' she said, patting his good hand and rising from her seat. 'I'll come back later, though, I promise.'

Lorimer saw the wistful expression in her eyes as Claire Bryceland turned away, her feelings kept hidden from the man lying in the bed.

'I shan't stay long, Mr Bryceland,' Lorimer assured him. 'I just need to ask you a few things about what happened.' He sat beside the man in the recently vacated chair, nodding to Molly, who took a seat at the other side of the bed, her expression solemn.

'What can you remember, Eric?'

The man blinked and stared at Lorimer for a few moments then gave a small sigh. 'I remember ... taking a loaf ... to Margaret,' he began. 'My neighbour ... ' He looked up at Lorimer and the detective saw tears fill the man's eyes. 'She's dead, isn't she?'

Lorimer nodded but remained silent.

Eric Bryceland licked his dry lips. 'Can I have some water, please?' he asked, his eyes falling on the plastic tumbler with its straw on the surface of the locker.

Molly picked it up and held it for the man so he could take a few sips.

'Ah ... thank you,' Bryceland said with another little sigh. 'I remember ...' He closed his eyes and Lorimer saw the strain in his pinched, white face: pain could be eased by medication but conjuring up those images again must surely be hurting him deeply.

'I saw ... no, I *heard* it first. Such a sound, like – like an *explosion*,' he said, screwing his eyes a little tighter. 'Margaret was lying on the floor ... that man ... standing in the doorway ...'

Lorimer exchanged a look with Molly as they waited, knowing that, like him, she was fervently hoping for more.

Eric Bryceland opened his eyes. 'It all happened so fast,' he sighed. 'The man ... the gun ...' His mouth twisted as a spasm of pain seemed to grip him, then he closed his eyes again.

Was it too soon to be asking the injured man to recall what had happened? Lorimer wondered, looking intently at that bandaged face propped up on a bank of pillows. Already it seemed as though the effort of speaking had wearied him, lying there quite still, lips slightly parted as though sleep might take him at any moment.

'Do you recall what he looked like?' Lorimer's words broke the silence and he exchanged a glance with Molly. He saw her shoulders rose and fall in a shrug as if to say *that's all we're likely to get now*.

Should they simply leave? Lorimer wondered again, biting his lip for a moment.

Then he started as Eric Bryceland lifted his good hand a little. Not asleep, then.

'Some more water, please,' he whispered and once more

224

Molly held the straw to his lips, gripping the tumbler to keep it steady.

'An ...' Eric Bryceland broke off, coughing, then looked up at the detective. 'An ordinary man ...' He swallowed hard as if the words were choking him. 'He looked at me ...'

Eric Bryceland's eyes widened for a moment and Lorimer could read the fear the man was experiencing as he lived through that moment again.

'Didn't expect me to be there, did he?'

'No.'

'I remember ...' Bryceland paused, mouth open a little. 'I remember how he looked ... that's all.' He swallowed hard again and Lorimer could see from the man's drawn face how exhausted he was. He yawned, closing his eyes for a couple of seconds. 'Hard to say ... just an ordinary man ... Then ... I woke up here,' Bryceland said, a breathy catch in his voice. It was obvious from the way the man's eyelids drooped that he was close to falling asleep, the effort of talking to his wife then to two strangers taking its toll.

'I'm sorry to have tired you, sir,' Lorimer said, standing up and nodding to the man in the bed. 'If you can give any sort of description of your assailant later on, then please do. There will be an officer here at all times. Thank you for seeing us.' He stepped away from the bed, but Eric Bryceland's eyes were closed again and this time Lorimer doubted that he had heard another word. They would need more than this, he realised, thinking hard. Pictures of known hitmen, perhaps, shown to Bryceland in the hope that one of them might match whatever image was lodged in his mind. There was an outside chance he might make a connection, though it was more likely that this *ordinary*-looking gunman had evaded the police's scrutiny altogether.

'Do you think he remembers what the hitman looks like?' Molly asked when they were further along the corridor and out of earshot of any passing nurse.

'Possibly,' Lorimer admitted. 'But it would be such a fleeting impression. The shock would have been his primary feeling at that point. Who expects to see a strange man pointing a gun at you?'

'And he'd never have heard the shot,' Molly murmured.

'No. He'd have been on the ground, out cold,' Lorimer agreed. 'Sometimes people don't even know they've been hit, certainly don't hear the gun being fired.'

'But he remembers something,' Molly insisted. 'And perhaps he'll remember more as time passes.'

Lorimer did not reply. He was doubtful if that lasting memory was more than a look between the two men, the one hastening through his neighbour's home to find the cause of that first gunshot, the other taken by surprise to find another person in the former police officer's house.

The gunman had very little memory of the man, just an impression of his height as he stopped dead, emerging so suddenly around that corner. Had he held up a hand, as though to ward off the gun being lowered towards him?

Bryceland. Eric Bryceland, that was the name on the property register that he was now seeing on the computer screen. And the address ... he should have checked, made certain there was nobody there. But he had! His hand met the hard

226

surface with a thump. He'd done all the usual checks, ensuring the old woman was living on her own, neighbours away for several weeks, or so the postman had told him the day he'd sauntered along that lane wearing a hi-vis jacket. It was easy to pretend to be a workman carrying out routine gas repairs, a lanyard slung round his neck, clipboard in one hand. If you looked the part, nobody noticed anything more, did they? Besides, he had the advantage of being an ordinary-looking bloke, disguising his appearance further with the fake spectacles he'd worn on the day he'd carried out the recce.

He clenched his fists, wondering just how to find out what had happened to his second victim. Was he dead? This Bryceland had certainly crashed to the floor. But hadn't he been a moving target? The hitman tried to remember but it had all happened so fast and his main thought had been to get the hell out of there and put as many miles between himself and those two bodies as he could. He glanced up at the clock in the library of the village that was several long miles away from Galashiels. Surely there would be something on the early evening news to tell him? And, if he'd failed … His hand hovered in mid-air, a slight tremor as he paused above the keyboard.

The consequences of that were unthinkable. He'd done what had been ordered, carried out his part of the plan. What more could they expect? He gritted his teeth and thought of the remaining journey ahead, the narrow roads that must speed him out of this part of the country.

For, right now, he had another appointment to keep.

The gun was going back to Glasgow where the armourer would be waiting.

*

Solly looked out of his study window at the yawning darkness below then his eyes drifted towards the city lights dancing beyond the park. The rain had stopped at last, an east wind blowing the clouds back across the Atlantic. He had come in here to think, something that he often did after the children were finally asleep, Rosie stretched out on the settee, a book on her lap. Lorimer had told him about the history of that house near the village of Houston and how it had been left for months at a time, the previous owners off to see family in Australia.

What had happened to that gun? Solly felt that the answer to that question was quite important. An old army weapon, one of thousands like it, no doubt, but brought back when peace had finally prevailed. A weapon like that might be more than a trophy, of course. Many had been used in country estates for hunting game and it was possible this particular one had simply been kept for shooting foxes. Or maybe even rabbits? He winced, remembering the Beatrix Potter tale he had read just half an hour ago. Storybook bunnies in the city were a far cry from the way country folk saw them: as vermin that ate their precious crops or as something tasty for the pot. In the days following the war food was scarce, rationing in force for several years afterwards, a time Solomon Brightman was glad to have missed, though his grandfather had spoken about it when he'd been a lad.

The gardener was dead and gone now, Mrs Riddoch had told the police, but perhaps they would find out what had happened to that gun? Solly stroked his beard absently, thinking about the value of such a weapon if it had fallen into the wrong hands. There seemed little doubt that it was the same gun that had been fired in each of the 'cop killings', a heading members of the press were now using. Except in one case. But that was something they did not know. The young woman in Lorimer's team had been shot dead with a different weapon. And, for Solly, that was significant.

Why use the same gun against elderly or retired police officers? Had it been wielded by the same gunman? Had it been used for a specific purpose, perhaps? Solly nodded silently. There was a reason behind that. And if there was a reason then that indicated a reasoning mind, someone who had carefully thought this all out.

A sudden blast of wind rattled the window frame, making Solly shiver. Who would want to kill these police officers? The team at the MIT had trawled through their professional records in an effort to see if there was anyone from their past that could be a link. But there had not been a major arrest of the same criminal by any of them, a fact that perplexed the psychologist but also made him wonder if that in itself was a clue. What if . . . ?

He stared out into the gathering darkness, his mind roaming over several possibilities. And not one of them would leave Solly when he tried to sleep later that night.

CHAPTER THIRTY-ONE

Nitshill at one o'clock in the morning was shuttered and silent. The last drunks had staggered from the Nia Roo pub some time ago, rain lashing against the buildings that huddled close to the narrow road, their metal doors locked fast. Now only an occasional car passed under the old railway bridge, its tyres swishing on the wet tarmac. The last buses from the city had trundled back there again, the late train from Glasgow Central long gone.

Each street lamp seemed to quiver in the driving rain, scattering fragments of light across the slick wet pavements as he walked along to their meeting place. He'd been there before, of course, usually about this time when the world was asleep, yet he still looked intently into the darkness to make sure he was not seen.

There was nobody about as he crossed the road and headed along the lane that ran between the buildings, his feet making wet imprints on the ground. The gun was dry enough, though, slung under his coat on the makeshift sling that he'd learned to use so many years ago. Nineteen, that's how old he'd been for his very first hit, just a boy really, but the experience had confirmed his status as a man.

He noticed a thin line of light leaking from the doorway as he approached the shop at the end of the lane and he breathed out a sigh of relief.

It would be fine.

Hand over the gun. Get the money and go.

Those had been his instructions and all he wanted now was to carry them out and get as far away from here as possible. Aberdeen, maybe. Or one of those wee fishing villages along the Moray Firth. He'd been warned not to use his passport. Not yet anyway. And he wasn't too keen to disappear down south where his accent might be remembered.

Two sharp knocks on the door brought the sound of movement from within. Then the door was opened, he slipped in, closed it behind him and stood looking at the elderly man who was standing in a pool of light. He was wrapped in the same heavy tweed coat he always wore, a checked scarf wrapped around his neck. No matter how often he had to come here, the gunman was struck by the old fellow's genial appearance. Nobody seeing him could possibly imagine him as other than a kindly, grandfatherly figure. These bare walls with their locked cupboards hid many secrets, however.

'All right, son?' the armourer asked.

'Aye. Went like clockwork,' he lied, his eyes flicking sideways as he removed his coat and unstrapped the gun.

He felt the old man's eyes on the weapon as he handed it over, the gnarled hands taking it gently from his grasp and cradling it in his arms for a moment.

The gunman shuddered, a sudden distaste for the way McBride was looking at the gun as though it were more human than the man standing before him.

'What about ...?'

The armourer's eyes darkened as he finally looked at him. 'You'll get your money,' he said. 'That's all taken care of.'

The hitman shifted from one foot to the other, the cold air in the room making him pick up his coat once more and shove his arms into the sleeves, keen to wrap himself into its folds.

'Here.' A packet was being thrust towards him now and when he looked up, the gun was lying on a table behind McBride.

The hitman took the money and stuffed it into his inside pocket, pushing it down hard.

He had stopped to count the money, just that first time, but McBride had flown into a rage, as if the action had cast doubts on his integrity. The gunman always counted it later, of course, but not once had he been cheated.

'Right, I'll be off then,' he said, hesitating for a moment, but the armourer had already walked the few paces to the door, opening it to the darkness outside.

The wind whipped rain into his face as he ran down the lane and along the road. He'd parked behind the pub and, as he saw the van standing on its own there in the darkness, he was suddenly glad that it was all over. Nobody was ever going to come after him. McBride could be trusted and the Big Man would never reveal names. Besides, the whole idea was that nobody else would have any idea as to any man's identity, he told himself, grabbing the door handle and flinging himself into the driver's seat. He could be in Aberdeen by breakfast time, the all-night café he knew by the docks open for any long-distance traveller.

The old man wiped the gun carefully before swaddling it in the soft chamois and setting it back in its rightful place. The long cupboard was locked fast then he switched off the light, closed the door behind him and pulled down the metal shutters against any neds that might be more than curious to see what really lay behind this old man's workshop.

The armourer pulled his collar up against the slanting rain and walked along to the far end of the lane then turned towards a nearby block of flats, their brown pebbledash walls a nondescript grey against the night sky. In moments he was tapping the code on the security pad then entering the dimly lit hallway. McBride wrinkled his nose against the stale smell that pervaded the place, glad of the gloves that kept his hands from touching the cold metal handrail: who knew what sort of germs lingered? Its only advantage was the proximity to his workshop and the fact that he would be out of there first thing in the morning. He paid his rent to the council and nobody asked any questions of the old man who was seldom seen walking up a flight of stairs to the brown-painted door that bore no nameplate on the front. It needed two keys to enter his flat, security being necessary in this part of the world, though he doubted whether any of his neighbours had ever tried to break in, most of them elderly folk like himself.

He locked the door carefully, pocketing the keys before removing his coat and scarf then placing them over the back of a chair to dry. He gave a small sigh, wishing he was back in his comfortable bungalow instead. Still, there was a bed and a heater, a few home comforts, enough to help him through another night until he could catch a bus back into the city.

There Walter McBride would be safe, though each time he left the workshop with its hidden cache of weapons, especially the one returned tonight, there was that feeling of loss as though he were abandoning an old friend, a gnawing anxiety that the gun would somehow not be there when he eventually returned.

CHAPTER THIRTY-TWO

Flynn propped his elbow against the pillows, gazing at the woman sleeping beside him. It was a marvel, something he'd never expected to happen. Sure, he'd had a few one-night stands, but nobody had ever made him feel quite like this. And she was way above his league, a police officer, for goodness' sake! Yet, seeing her like this, her bare shoulders moving ever so slightly as she slept, Flynn told himself that this was actually all right.

His thoughts lingered over the events of the previous night, remembering the urgency of her kisses, the way she'd held him as they'd rolled together onto the bed. Erin had wanted him as much as he'd wanted her and there was no sign afterwards that she had wished to leave.

I take my coffee black in the morning, she'd murmured, closing her eyes with a yawn of satisfaction, a smile on her lips even as she began to fall into a sound slumber.

He'd make the coffee eventually, but for now he rolled onto his back, thinking how weird it was that a twenty-year-old skeleton had been responsible for their very first meeting. Twenty years ago he'd been scoring drugs, his life spiralling out of control as dealers set about using him for their own ends. Erin was still at school, planning a very different future for herself. If it hadn't been for Lorimer he might still have been on the wrong side of the law, far from the reaches of the woman dozing by his side. It was all so different now. Here he was, saving for a property of his own, his relative success as a self-employed landscape gardener giving him dreams for a future that, he hoped, included DC Erin Finlay. He glanced fondly, watching her as she slept; it was as if a spell had been cast over them both, protecting them from the world outside.

But only for a time, the reason they had come together still unresolved, the skeleton that Flynn had found becoming more and more of a real person every day. What had horrified him back then in the garden intrigued him now. And Erin was heavily involved with discovering the identity of who-ever these skeletal remains had once been. A man, maybe late thirties, older than Flynn, but still … to have that life cut short … He closed his eyes, remembering how excited Erin had been to tell him about the anthropologist's work. He hadn't seen the finished article yet, something Erin had promised to show him as soon as she could, and it was hard to imagine flesh on these cold bones he'd found buried out in that country garden.

There was something else she'd told him, something that had really caught the gardener's interest, not about old bones but about the soil itself. That professor, Lorna Dawson, was a scientist who could find out stuff from studying wee particles of soil and he'd seen her do amazing things on the

TV. Now, Erin had told him, she was going to work on the skeleton that he'd unearthed. Professor Dawson had helped Lorimer before with a case, hadn't she? They'd worked together to find a missing person ... Flynn opened his eyes. Had anyone missed this poor guy? Or had he been left to lie unmourned in the dark ground? He thought about the lumps of clay soil that he'd dug down to in that bramble patch and all the mesh of roots that had made his work so hard. What would the scientist make of that? It was a wonder that the very dirt he worked on day after day could yield clues to tell the story of who this man had been.

The woman in the light blue lab coat gave a small smile of satisfaction as she drew back from the microscope. Yes, here they were, tiny traces of pollen from plants that had not been in the thick clay soil out in that Renfrewshire garden. She had examined the scrapings from the victim's fingernails to find fly ash and red brick fragments that suggested a city environment but these pollen samples could help narrow down the options further. It was more likely to have been in a large suburban garden with managed lawn grass where he had first lain, given that the pollen had come from trees, bushes and garden plants. Had they tried to bury him there and found too many tree roots? She thought hard, trying to imagine a darkened landscape where shadowy figures dug deep into the earth, the victim wrapped in these layers of cold, black plastic.

Had they given up? Panicked as the dawn light rose across the city skyline? Perhaps they had had second thoughts and dug him up, afraid that the police might come around and search the home?

She had identified tiny grains of pollen from *salix caprea*, a type of pussy willow that could reach the height of ten metres, not a plant that Lorna would choose herself for a small garden. That, and the grains of pollen from sycamore flowers, told the soil scientist that it had likely been in springtime when the initial attempt at burial had taken place. She conjured up a vision of a large established garden close to the city centre, maybe with a line of trees creating privacy for some wealthy resident, wondering just where these soil samples would guide her.

It was now a matter of locating the exact place where such different components might be found, and Lorna Dawson relished the challenge.

Lorimer put down the phone, shaking his head in amused disbelief. The nature of the soil scientist's work both baffled and amazed him. She'd managed so far to tell him that she believed the victim had been buried – or an attempt made at burial – somewhere in a garden in the suburbs of Glasgow around twenty years ago, certainly during the spring months, maybe mid-April. He picked up the images of a man in his late thirties, one open-mouthed to show the gaps in his teeth, others taken from several angles as the forensic anthropologist had walked around her model, clicking on the camera button. The tiny traces of hair that remained had not shown up on any DNA database but had at least provided a clue as to the man's hair colouring, which was mid-brown.

Police Scotland's DNA database had been in existence for a little over twenty years. If this chap had ever been incarcerated, then it would have been before the mid-1990s, not an

238

impossibility. The odontology was still under investigation and DI Brodie's team had been working hard to establish any connections to Scottish prison records. Lorimer looked up as a shadow crossed his window, a crow, the black shape swooping past. The moment distracted him from his study of the pictures, making him think about the outdoors and Flynn, who was working in their garden today. A faint smile lit up his face as he recalled the gardener's news. He and one of Brodie's officers were an item, Flynn had told them shyly, his face colouring as he'd related how they had met. Strange how something so horrible had brought two people together like this, Maggie had murmured to him. Aye, life was never predictable, was it?

He looked down at the picture of a man, his narrow face and thin nose giving him a haunted look. He'd been no pin-up, this young man, had he? Malnourished, the pathologist and anthropologist had agreed from the extensive study of his bones. Had he been an easy target? A shilpit wee guy, too weak to run from a man with a gun in his hand? A gun that had recently been passed from one location to another, Lorimer reminded himself. Solly would want to know why, of course. Why had he been shot like this? Had it been a falling-out between two rival gangs? The nineties had been particularly bad for drugs in the city, different criminal factions vying for supremacy of the market.

A decision still had to be made whether to allow the image into the papers or not. For his part, Lorimer was keen to let it be publicised in the hope that this fellow's image might prick someone's conscience. Missing Persons had been shown it already but so far no match for this image had been found. Did that say more about the dead man? Had he been part of an underworld where a missing man would never be reported for fear of reprisals? Or, a sadder thought: was there never anyone to actually miss him?

Lorimer chewed his lower lip thoughtfully. It was a long time ago now, and perhaps any relative, mother or father would have passed on. The idea made him remember Mary Riddoch. Should he show this to her in the vague hope that she might have come across the man at some time?

The thought prompted him to shuffle the pictures back into their folder and slip them into his laptop bag. A long shot, probably, but certainly worth a try.

A quick phone call had told him that the residents were away at a theatre outing but he could come tomorrow, the receptionist had added. Mrs Riddoch would no doubt be pleased to have a visitor. Lorimer made a face. Tomorrow he would be back in the Borders to visit Eric Bryceland once more so any visit to Erskine Care Home would have to wait. He looked out at the gathering darkness, a typical November day of low clouds and leaden skies, days shortening as the year hastened towards winter.

The Big Man did not care about how cold it was outside, the feeling of warmth from his success wrapping itself around him. Everything was going to plan. He had thought about it for so long, the quiet of his days encouraging his mind along certain familiar lines. He'd always commanded respect, his authority unquestioned, and so his demands had been carried out now to the letter. The old woman had perished and soon it would be time for the next victim to meet his fate. It had been an easy thing to stoke the embers of different people's spite and he looked forward to the time when he would be reading about the demise of the man who had wrecked his own life.

But not yet, not until Ramsay was out. When it was time he'd instruct the old man where to go, though he knew perfectly well how to find McBride and pick up the gun.

The man lolled back in his chair, a satisfied smile on his pudgy face. By all accounts the cops were running around in circles like rats chasing their own tails. They would never know who might be next on his list, each one of them looking over their shoulders just in case it was them.

CHAPTER THIRTY-THREE

POLICE SHOOTINGS ESCALATE

Despite the extra manpower available throughout Police Scotland and the crack team under Detective Superintendent William Lorimer, police seem no further forward in their hunt for the gunman who has rampaged around the country, shooting dead five innocent victims at random.

'It isn't looking good,' Alan Marshall told her, throwing down the *Gazette* with disgust. 'The papers are making such a meal of this.' He paused, his face a mask of anger. 'Thank God they don't know we're looking at a different gunman for DC Carson's murder.' He ran a weary hand across his scalp then gave his deputy a baleful look. 'And did I tell you that seven cadets dropped out this week alone?'

Caroline Flint made a face and shook her head. 'That's bad,' she commented. 'We're undermanned as it is, despite the ban on leave, and any further resignations will just make the situation worse.'

'Can't blame them, of course,' the Chief Constable sighed, shoving his spectacles onto the bridge of his nose. 'Morale is at an all-time low after these killings.' And it was true, the initial surge of indignation by officers that their own were being targeted had dissipated and it was his belief that many of his younger officers were being pressurised by their family members to quit the force for good. The press hadn't helped, adding fuel to the flames of scaremongering they did so well. With each death had come shock and horror but now their attention had turned to the force itself and how hazardous police work really could be. Statistics had been printed about the dangers from actual deaths in the line of duty to things like PTSD, something Detective Superintendent Lorimer had suffered from a while back. He'd recovered, thank God, and was doing a sterling job now as head of the MIT.

Caroline Flint shrugged her shoulders. 'It's what we all signed up for, Alan,' she said. 'Nobody ever said it would be an easy job, but, hell, it's the best one in the world as far as I'm concerned.'

The Chief Constable did not meet his colleague's eyes. It was a matter of weeks until his own retirement and he had been advised that he might well be a prime target from this mystery gunman. Jennifer, his second wife, had been urging him to sell up and move abroad but Marshall was adamant that was not going to happen. Whatever else he might be, Alan Marshall was not a coward and if there was a bullet with his name on it . . . ? He shuddered, praying silently that his team in Govan would soon uncover the identity of whoever was wielding the weapon that had cut short all these lives.

'Sharon Carson,' Molly murmured, looking across at Dave. 'Different gun. Different killer? Lorimer thinks so.'

The pair had been working together on Sharon Carson's murder since their return from the Borders, Lorimer convinced that the dead officer's husband was hiding something.

'Any news about Mick Carson yet?' the DS asked.

'Aye.' Molly's expression was grim. 'He wasn't just a driver in the army like he told the boss. He'd handled guns, all right, and had been commended for that in training.'

'Interesting.' Davie Giles sat back, folding his hands behind his head. 'Omitting that little nugget suggests he may have had something to hide?'

'Sharon certainly did,' Molly replied grimly. 'She and Mick had parted acrimoniously and I bet you a month's salary her husband had got wind of her affair with another copper.'

'How is Derek?'

Molly made a face. 'Off on sick leave as ordered by Lorimer. D'you think Mick . . . ?'

'He had the motive,' Dave began thoughtfully.

'What about means and opportunity?'

'Well, he's bound to have known about the kids' Hallowe'en party along the road. He is their dad, after all,' Dave reasoned.

'Which brings us back to means,' Molly grumbled. 'A rifle, similar to the calibre of one that had dispatched three retired officers . . . a deliberate subterfuge?'

'Could be,' her colleague agreed. 'Made to look like it was part of the same pattern. But maybe, if it was Mick, he wouldn't know about the rifling marks on a bullet? How much do they learn in basic army training, do you think?'

'Come on,' Molly said suddenly, rising from her chair. 'I think we need to do what Lorimer has asked: look a wee bit closer at Mick Carson and where exactly he was at the time his wife was shot dead. Sitting here at our computers can only take us so far.'

Mick Carson opened the door.

'You can't come in here,' he whispered, looking along the balcony that ran the length of the flats where he was staying. The man in the black leather jacket pushed past him, shoving Mick against the door jamb, his silence more threatening than any spoken words.

'Nobody seen me,' the man said, as Mick closed the door shut and stood with his back against it. 'Anyhow, who's to mind an old friend visiting?' He gave a scornful grin. 'Condolences and all that?'

'Are you out of your mind, Eddie?' Mick hissed. 'Anyone seeing us together could ...'

'Could what?' his visitor sneered. 'Put two and two together and make five? Naebody will ever ken it wis me sold you that rifle.'

'Still.' Mick turned nervously as though expecting someone to come hammering on his door.

'Still what? You cannae keep no' seeing me, eh? Old mates, us. We're supposed tae have been drinking when it all happened. That's whit we agreed. Whit ye paid me thon

245

wee bit extra fur,' he laughed. 'And thon landlord knows fine ah'm in his pub every ither night. He'll no' remember which night, will he?'

Mick glared at the man as he sauntered along the hallway and into the lounge where a television was turned on, the replay of a previous weekend's football match in progress.

'Gonnae gies a beer?' The man had planked himself in Mick's own chair right in front of the TV, legs stretched out, and was looking up at him expectantly.

'Make yourself at home, why don't you?' Mick muttered as he left the room and went into the nearby kitchen, the man's laughter following him.

As he pulled a four pack from the refrigerator, Mick Carson's lips closed in an obstinate line. This was not the way it was meant to happen. He'd told Eddie to stay away, keep his distance, let things settle down till after the funeral. But here he was like a bad smell that lingered long after the rubbish bin had been put out.

When the sound of knocking came, Mick Carson leapt out of his chair, fists clenched. Had to be Eddie. But why had he come back? he thought, furiously stomping down the hallway, ready this time to stick his foot in the door. It had taken Eddie long enough to leave earlier but once the beer was finished, he'd made his move, assuring Mick that he would call in again some time.

'What—'

The appearance of the couple on his doorstep made Mick Carson close his mouth at once, the words he'd been about to shout at Eddie evaporating in the chill air.

'Can we come in, Mick?'

He stared at them for moment, swallowing the last dregs of his anger, trying to work out why two of Sharon's mates were here and if he really wanted to have them sitting in his lounge.

'Come on in,' he said at last, shuffling his feet as he drew the door open. 'Place is a bit of a tip,' he apologised, looking around frantically as he ushered the two detectives into the room where Eddie Burns had been sitting less than an hour ago.

'So sorry for your loss,' Davie Giles murmured, offering a hand to shake. 'Terrible thing, just terrible.'

Mick stood there, wondering if the shock at seeing the two detectives was perhaps playing to his advantage. Anyone would expect him to be in a bit of a turmoil, after all, his wife dead, kids distraught.

Mick followed the female detective's eyes as she took a quick look around the room, coming to rest on the four empty beer cans still sitting by the television. *What was her name?*

He saw her eyebrows lift slightly as though she disapproved of someone drinking in the middle of the day. Mick swallowed again, but this time his throat was dry.

'Cup of tea?' he asked hoarsely. 'Sorry,' he said, catching the blonde woman's eyes, 'I've forgotten your name.'

'It's Molly. DS Molly Newton,' she replied, giving him what looked like a sympathetic smile and placing a hand on his arm, 'Sharon and I were friends.'

Mick nodded, unsure how to reply. It was still hard to talk about his dead wife, finding the right words to say, especially to the kids.

'Here, sit down and let me make tea,' Molly offered. 'You look washed out, if you don't mind my saying.'

'Aye, sit over here, Mick.' Davie Giles patted the arm of the chair where Eddie had been sitting drinking the last cans of his beer.

Mick slumped into the chair, glancing across at Giles, who was perched on the edge of the settee, regarding him with pity.

'Hell of a thing,' Giles began. 'Can't tell you how we are all feeling about it. Losing her like that.'

Mick Carson took a deep breath then asked, 'Any further forward in finding that gunman?'

Giles shook his head. 'Clever bastard, whoever he is,' he admitted. 'Didn't use the same gun that was used to shoot the others.'

As he stared at him, Mick felt a sudden tremble in his legs.

'See, we think there might be more than one fellow running round the country with guns, Mick. That makes it harder to pin down Sharon's killer.'

'Oh, right,' Mick replied, his words coming out in a croak. *What was keeping that woman?* He really needed a drink, tea, anything to calm his nerves.

'I brought milk and sugar,' Molly said, emerging from the kitchen carrying a tray with three mugs, a half-opened carton of milk and a packet of sugar.

Mick Carson felt a moment of shame. Back in his own home Sharon would have poured milk into a jug, brought a sugar bowl, all the niceties that he had taken for granted.

He bowed his head, genuine tears of remorse wetting his cheeks, seeping through the fingers he held across his face.

*

Molly Newton set down the tea tray, glancing across at her partner. Signs of grief were not unexpected, but the suddenness of change in the man's demeanour puzzled her. Carson had looked almost belligerent on opening that door, his expression of fury changing instantly when he saw them standing there. Who had he been expecting? she wondered. And why had he broken down so suddenly now?

There was no smell of beer on the man's breath, Molly had noticed as she'd bent to shake his hand, so that only meant one thing: Mick Carson had had a visitor recently, someone who'd drunk four cans in one sitting. Unless Carson was in the habit of leaving his empties lying around, but the rest of the place was spotless, so that didn't add up, did it?

'Nice to see you've had friends coming round,' Molly said softly, pointing at the cans.

Mick Carson raised his head at her words and she read the first sign of fear in his eyes.

'An old friend? Come to pay his respects?' Molly held her breath for a moment as Carson shook his head. 'Nobody's been here,' he said abruptly, avoiding Molly's eye.

We'll let that one go for now, she thought, suppressing the smile that tugged at the corners of her mouth. *But you're telling us a great big lie, Mick, and we need to know why that is.*

'Milk? Sugar?' Molly allowed her smile to break through for a moment as she raised the carton of semi-skimmed.

'Ah, I needed that,' Davie Giles declared, setting down the empty mug on the carpet beside his chair. 'Sorry to have to do this, Mick, but we have a few questions that our boss wanted asked, just to clear up one or two things, you understand.' He'd been watching the body language of the man sitting next to him, noting the raised shoulders, a sign of extreme tension, and the way he had placed a hand on his knee to stop it juddering up and down. Was Carson on some sort of medication? Maybe, though it looked more to DS Giles as if this was a man thoroughly rattled by the presence of two police officers talking about their dead colleague, his own estranged wife.

'See back in your army days,' Giles began, 'you did a lot of driving. Gave you a chance to get your HGV, I suppose?'

He saw a sort of relief cross the man's face.

'Aye, that's right. What I told your boss, Lorimer,' Carson agreed.

'But you also told him you didn't handle guns, that right too?'

Carson looked from one to the other, his mouth opening but evidently unsure how to reply.

'Thing is, we have to dig a wee bit deeper into a case like this and we found that you were quite a dab hand when it came to guns,' Dave continued. 'Even got a gold star for doing so well in training. Too modest to share that with Lorimer, were you?'

Carson's eyes darkened in response to the tinge of sarcasm that Giles had allowed to creep into his voice.

'Now, I wonder why that really was? Maybe you didn't want anyone to know that you'd been so good with guns after your wife was shot dead on her own doorstep?'

'You lot only ever look for the nearest person you can find,' Carson sneered. 'Got to be the husband, is that the best you can do?'

'You had a good reason to be angry with Sharon, though, didn't you, Mick?' Molly asked softly, making the man turn away from Giles and glare at her instead. 'She put you out the house. A house you both paid for, I guess, long hours driving those big lorries from one part of the country to another. Now why was that? Had you done anything to deserve it?'

Giles noticed the man's leg jiggling again, an involuntary nervous reaction. Molly had hit a sore spot all right.

'And to see another man come in to the place where you should be, take over your bed, make friends with your kids ... ?' Molly left the rest of the suggestion hanging.

'He had no right!' Carson shouted, thumping the arm of his chair, his face twisted in rage.

'Derek Warner?' Giles asked.

'You knew?' Carson's face was red with fury now. 'You lot knew it was going on all the time? Sticking together, I suppose, laughing at me behind my back?'

'Where did you get the gun, Mick?' Giles asked, staring at the man until he looked away shaking his head.

'No, you're not pinning that one me,' he muttered.

'We dug a wee bit into other things, Mick, like your bank accounts.'

The man's head came up again. 'You ... what ... ?'

'We had a warrant from the Fiscal, it's all above board, Mick,' Molly assured him, her tone soothing, placating.

'Thing is, you drew out a helluva big sum of money the day before Sharon was murdered. Now why was that, Mick? And what did you need ready cash for, eh?' Giles asked.

'Funnily enough, we tend to know how much things cost in our line of work, Mick,' Molly told him, coming to sit on the arm of his chair. 'Like how much it costs to order a hit on someone.'

'I never . . . ' Carson looked wildly from one to the other.

'Or how much it costs to buy a certain type of gun,' Giles finished for her.

Carson slumped back, all colour draining from his face.

'Thought you were being clever, picking the sort of gun Sharon had mentioned? The one that blew away those retired officers?' Giles persisted.

The man stared mutely at his hands as though surprised to see the fingers trembling then he folded his arms protectively across his chest, tucking the treacherous hands out of sight.

'Only thing wrong with that plan—' Giles went on.

'To make it look as if Sharon's death was one of a series,' Molly put in.

'—was that ballistics found a discrepancy with the bullet.'

Carson risked a glance into each of their faces, a glance that revealed a moment of sheer terror in his widened eyes.

'Showed us that it had been the same calibre but a different gun,' Giles finished, staring hard at the man. Then Carson bent forward, covering his face, a low moan issuing from his lips.

The two detectives exchanged a look and a nod. Carson's defeated appearance was enough to convince them both. Then Davie Giles stood up and addressed the man who had shrunk back into his chair.

'Michael Carson, I am detaining you under Section Fourteen of the Criminal Procedure (Scotland) Act 1995 because I suspect you of having committed a criminal offence punishable by imprisonment, namely the murder of your wife, Sharon Elizabeth Carson ... '

There was no response from the man cowering in his seat, not even one word of denial and Molly listened as Dave completed the procedure, producing a pair of handcuffs, clipping one to his own wrist only after securing the first cuff around Mick Carson's. The man offered no resistance nor did he venture a look at either detective as they led him out of the flat and downstairs to where a squad car was waiting. From the way his head was hanging down it was as if he had given up altogether, Molly thought, yet she knew fine that once a solicitor was called things might well change. Would he confess? Or was this sullen silence a forerunner to a dreary interview punctuated with 'No comments'?

CHAPTER THIRTY-FOUR

At least one piece of the puzzle that surrounded the murder of several police officers (retired or not) had fallen into place. Former Superintendent Woods had been shot with the same gun as the first three victims, ballistic analysis confirmed. Lorimer gave a sigh of relief, partly because he had wanted to trust Solly's instincts but also because it meant that the officers from the MIT could channel their resources in a particular direction. Mick Carson was in custody, too, and that gave a sense of closure to what had been a disparity in the series of deaths. If the husband had shot his wife dead with a similar gun to that which had killed three other former officers in the hope that it would be taken as part of the pattern, then he was looking at a very long stretch in a Scottish prison.

Lorimer sat back and closed his eyes. Two wee children, robbed of their mum and now having their dad taken away from them. Somewhere in the picture there were loving grandparents to look after these poor kids, thank God, but that would never make up for the tragedies that had blown such holes in their young lives.

The scrutiny of each of the victims' past records as serving officers had produced masses of detailed information and, although there was no one name that linked them, Lorimer was still convinced that this was the work of some criminal who had been sent down in the past and was bent on revenge. Each of the dead officers had at least one high-profile case in those records and had been responsible for sending someone down for a lengthy stretch. It made some sort of sense: these officers were now retired from the job, some of the men and women they'd put away now released into society having served their sentences. He'd instructed members of his team to delve into the present whereabouts of several of those high-profile prisoners, just to see if his theory held water. What if, he had asked himself, what if one of them had been so set on retribution that he had targeted not only the officer that had apprehended him but several others? Did that make any sort of sense?

He looked up as the door of his office opened.

'Solly! Thanks for coming in.' Lorimer rose from his place by the window and walked across the room, shaking his friend's hand warmly.

'You wanted to talk to me?'

'Yes, come in and sit down. As I explained on the phone, we are now looking only at those officers that were retired,' Lorimer began. 'The way I see it, targeting these particular officers suggests to me that whoever killed them may have been seeking some sort of revenge.'

'A disaffected villain?'

'Aye. Someone who'd held onto a grudge against the person responsible for putting them in prison,' Lorimer agreed.

'Nursing their wrath to keep it warm,' Solly paraphrased quietly.

Lorimer's eyebrows rose in surprise. 'Didn't expect you to be quoting *Tam O'Shanter*, Solly,' he said.

'Oh, I was always a great fan of Burns,' the psychologist told him. 'We had a Scottish head teacher at our school and she encouraged the English department to let us loose on your bard's poetry. Always did have a soft spot for that particular poem.'

'Well, the sentiment is possibly justified if my idea is correct. Imagine this,' Lorimer said, leaning forward. 'Someone nurses this sense of vengeance all throughout his imprisonment and then, when he gets out, goes to seek the person he feels responsible for putting him away.'

'Go on,' Solly murmured.

'We've found that there are at least six men who were released prior to the deaths of Phillips, McAlpine, Ormiston and Woods. George collared quite a few nasty characters in his day, some of whom have been released in the past two years, others still in various establishments in Scotland. Miss Woods has a similar track record, one name in particular made me sit up and think.' He leaned back and took a file from his desk and handed it across to Solly.

The psychologist opened the file and Lorimer pointed at a small photograph that was attached at the top right-hand corner.

'That's him: Stanley Miller. Last job was on a bank in Edinburgh. They shot three people dead. You maybe don't remember? No?' Solly shook his head. 'Well, you'd still have been down south at that time, of course. Got the mandatory twenty-one years for one of the shootings and was released about two months ago. Margaret Woods was SIO on that case.'

Lorimer sat back, a grim expression on his face. 'I've put out a request for Intelligence to look at Miller's movements since then. See if he has been seen anywhere in the Galashiels area.'

'You think he targeted a woman in her eighties as revenge for her putting him in prison?'

Lorimer gave a sigh. 'I don't know,' he admitted. 'There's something nagging away, telling me there should be an obvious link to all of their deaths ...'

'But you haven't found it.'

'No, and perhaps I shouldn't be looking for anything too easy to find. After all, you did say we were looking for someone clever.'

Solly stroked his dark beard thoughtfully. 'Hm, I do like your idea of revenge,' he began, 'and someone who has a spiteful grudge simmering away as they serve a long prison sentence also has plenty of time to work out a plan to carry out a series of killings.'

'However,' Lorimer smiled slowly and shook his head, 'that only works if it is one gunman who has decided to avenge himself on a police officer. And there is not one single person who was arrested by all of the victims at any time.'

Solly nodded. 'Perhaps we need to look at it from a different perspective,' he murmured. 'Think about the possibility that we have not one gunman driving across Scotland committing these crimes but several different hitmen.'

'But there's just the one gun,' Lorimer objected.

'That's true,' Solly agreed. 'But a gun can surely be passed from hand to hand?'

Lorimer rubbed his chin, considering the idea. 'We need to find who was recently released from jail about the same time as Miller, then.'

'Perhaps,' Solly said, frowning a little.

Lorimer looked at his friend's face, wondering if Solly had some doubts about this theory already. 'What?'

'I don't think that someone planning a series of executions on former police officers would make it easy for us to find them,' Solly said. 'And, if I'm correct, we need to look just as closely at the gun as we do at whoever fired it.'

Lorimer sat back, remembering his words to Maggie.

'The armourer,' he said suddenly. 'If it is one gun being passed around, then maybe, just maybe, these men are all using the same armourer.'

'A person that provides them with weapons?'

'One weapon,' Lorimer corrected him. 'One old gun that has seen service in a war then . . .' He stopped and thumped his fist against his open palm. 'We need to find out more about that lad Flynn dug up out near Houston,' he said. 'If we knew who he was that might help lead us to who killed him twenty years back.'

'Rosie showed me the image of his reconstructed face,' Solly said. 'Poor-looking individual.'

Lorimer nodded. 'I have to make a decision about releasing that man's face into the media,' he said. 'But there's someone else I'd like to show it to first. Mary Riddoch, the former owner of the house where he was found.'

He rose from his chair. 'Thanks for coming in so early this morning, Solly. I needed to run this past you before I went back down to Galashiels today.' He took the file back from Solly's outstretched hand. 'It's a long shot but I would like to show this photo of Stanley Miller to Eric Bryceland. See if it jogs a memory of that gunman.'

Solly picked up his briefcase and headed for the door. Lorimer had given him plenty to think about but there were things about this case that he had already begun to consider, not least that the entire series of killings was at the behest of one particular individual, a man that dealt out death.

And the gunmen? Others with grudges to settle, perhaps? All being played like puppets on strings that were held firmly in the grasp of their puppet master.

Galashiels seemed to be crouching under a blanket of grey raincloud when Lorimer arrived at the Borders General Hospital, any sign of the local hills blotted out. All the way down he had experienced a dull headache as though the low cloud was pressing on his brain. It had been a very early start, Solly coming into Helen Street before seven and then the drive south, meeting rush-hour traffic on the ring road as he passed Edinburgh, the windscreen wipers moving back and forth rhythmically as rain battered against the Lexus.

Lorimer pulled into the hospital car park, grateful to have arrived at last.

He could easily have had the photo of Stanley Miller sent electronically, saving him the hassle of a long drive there and back, but he had wanted to talk to Eric Bryceland again, to see if he had remembered anything else about his dreadful ordeal. It would be a bonus if Bryceland were to recognise his assailant from this picture.

Lorimer climbed the stairs to the corridor where Eric Bryceland was being kept in a private room, a plainclothes officer sitting outside the door reading his newspaper. The officer stood up abruptly as Lorimer approached.

'Sir,' he said. 'Mrs Bryceland's in with her husband at the moment.' He turned and nodded towards the closed door.

'Thanks. Dennison, isn't it?'

The man nodded and smiled. 'DC Dennison, yes, sir.'

Lorimer gave two short knocks on the door, waited a couple of seconds then entered the room.

Two pairs of eyes turned his way.

'Sorry to interrupt. Any chance I can have a quick word, Mr Bryceland?'

Claire Bryceland gave a small frown of annoyance then stood up. 'I'll be downstairs, dear,' she said. 'Won't be long.' She gave Lorimer a meaningful stare.

'No, I won't keep you,' Lorimer assured her, stifling a sigh. It had been hours since he had left his own home and there were still things to be done before he could spend any sort of time with Maggie. But this couple needed to be together much more, if only to reassure themselves that their horrible ordeal was coming to an end.

'How are you, Eric?' Lorimer asked, sitting down in the plastic seat that Mrs Bryceland had just left.

'Sore,' the man said shortly. Then, as Lorimer studied him, Eric Bryceland raised his good hand. 'They tell me it will be weeks, maybe months before I'll be back to normal.'

Lorimer nodded. 'Just keep telling yourself that you're one of the lucky ones,' he said.

'Oh, I do, believe me, I do,' Bryceland assured him. 'But sometimes I see it all over again ... ' He squeezed his eyes shut.

Good, thought Lorimer. *Maybe something's coming back?*

'I brought a picture to show you,' he said, reaching down and taking the file from his case. 'Just wondered, have you ever seen this man before?'

Bryceland stared at the picture that Lorimer out to him. Taking it in his fingers, he looked carefully then handed it back.

'No, sorry. Never saw this man before. Is that who you think shot us?'

Lorimer did not reply to the question but posed one of his own instead.

'Can you remember what he looked like?'

Bryceland paused for a moment before answering. 'I have this mental image of him,' he began. 'Medium build, not as tall as me. I'm six two,' he said, catching Lorimer's glance. 'Brown hair ... well, not fair, not dark, mousey-brown the women call it, I think. Just an ordinary-looking man. Except for that gun in his hands ... '

'And can you recall how he moved?' Lorimer asked. 'That might give a clue to the man's age and level of fitness.'

'No. It all happened so fast. Sorry.' Bryceland heaved a sudden sigh and grimaced as pain caught hold of him once more.

'Shall I call a nurse?' Lorimer offered.

'It's okay,' Bryceland replied. 'I can press this button.

Keeps me full of whatever drugs they're dripping into my system.' He lifted a clear plastic wire that was concealed beneath a fold of the bedclothes leading to a drip attached to the back of his hand. 'It wasn't that man. The one you showed me.' Bryceland's head was sinking deeper into the bank of pillows. 'I'm sorry to disappoint you.'

'That's all right,' Lorimer told him. But the detective superintendent gave no more information about the photograph of the man he had brought with him. It had probably been too much to expect to find that Stanley Miller had returned to gun down an old lady who had put him behind bars all these years ago. Miller would be a good age himself, now, after all, and maybe was just relieved to be a free man at last.

'I hope you feel better soon,' Lorimer told him, standing up and pushing back the chair. 'We'll be keeping a steady watch on you both meantime, don't worry. Everything is being done by the police officers down here to make sure you're safe.'

'Thanks,' Bryceland said softly. 'Appreciate it. Specially for Claire. She's hardly slept since it happened.'

The door behind him opened again and Lorimer stepped aside to let Claire Bryceland enter.

'Just leaving now. We'll be in touch again to let you both know if anything transpires,' he said with a smile, choosing his words carefully so they were both reassuring and vague. Having a police guard might be a good thing at present but eventually the couple might come to see it as some sort of threat to their future peace of mind. Would they return to that idyllic cottage? Or was it to be for ever tainted by bloodshed?

*

262

The drive back to Glasgow was marginally more pleasant than the earlier journey, the rain easing off and clouds lifting a little to reveal a line of brightness across the horizon. Once on the motorway, Lorimer kept the big car on the outside lane, driving as fast as he dared. If he was back along the M8 at junction thirty before midday there was a chance he might see Mary Riddoch before the residents of Erskine Home were shepherded off for lunch.

Sure enough, the digital clock registered eleven forty as he parked the Lexus and switched off the engine. In minutes he was heading down the long corridor of the home and then taking the lift one floor up to Pearson House.

The door to room seven was ajar and he peeped in, relieved to see Mary wrapped in a bright pink cardigan and seated in her wheelchair in front of her television, watching some quiz show.

'Hello.' He rapped on the open door and saw her turn to look up at him. Then her face lit up.

'Oh, it's you!' she gasped, hand to her throat. 'What a nice surprise!'

'Hello, Mary, mind if I sit down?' he asked, indicating to the chair beside her.

'Be my guest.' She beamed. 'So, what brings you to visit me today, Superintendent?'

Lorimer lifted his briefcase onto his knees. 'Something I wanted to show you.'

The old lady's eyes brightened. 'Mm, something exciting, I hope?'

Lorimer lifted the plastic folder that contained the image of Flynn's mystery man and set it on his lap.

263

'Remember I told you about the skeleton we discovered in your old garden?'

She nodded, still looking at him expectantly.

'Well, we've been given some help from a forensic anthropologist,' he began.

'Someone that digs up treasures and stuff?'

Lorimer shook his head. 'No, that's an archaeologist, but you're not far off the mark. This lady does what is called cranial reconstructions. In other words she can take a skull and, with digital technology, recreate what the owner of that particular skull may have looked like. And,' he went on, 'she's just let us have an image of her findings.'

Mary made a silent *oh*, and nodded slowly.

'Here he is.' Lorimer drew out the picture and held it in front of her.

'Not as handsome as you,' she quipped, glancing up at Lorimer flirtatiously. 'Do I know him?' she murmured, frowning a little. 'He does remind me of someone, right enough ...' She put one hand to her mouth, biting the edge of her index finger.

Lorimer waited silently. It would be another waste of time, he decided gloomily, just like showing Eric Bryceland that picture earlier.

Then Mary Riddoch's face cleared and she gave a tiny gasp.

'Of course, that's who it is!'

Lorimer looked at the image once more, the thirty-something man staring back at him from beyond the grave.

'It's Wattie's boy, Luke,' she said, excitedly. Then her face fell. 'But what was he doing buried in our garden?'

'Are you sure, Mary?'

Mary Riddoch sat back, an expression of indignation on her face. 'Sure I'm sure,' she told him. 'Knew him since he was a wee boy. Used to come around with his daddy during the summer holidays. Our two loved playing with him, though they were a bit older than Luke, of course.'

'When did you last see him? Can you remember?' Lorimer felt a pulse beating in his throat, the excitement in the room almost tangible.

'Oh, now you're asking,' Mary said, her face falling as she let the picture fall onto her lap. 'Wattie was most upset when his boy left home, I do remember that. Think there was some sort of a row between Luke and his mother. We got the impression that Luke had fallen into bad company in his teenage years,' she murmured sadly. 'But what on earth made him come back ... I mean ... why our garden?' She shook her head and looked back down at the picture of the reconstructed face.

'Poor Luke Watt,' she said. 'You did come to a sad end, didn't you, son? Just like your old ma said you would.'

'We've got a name!' Lorimer burst into the main room at the MIT and strode across to the whiteboard at the front where pictures of five victims were displayed, dates and times written in red pen beneath their names. He fixed the image he had shown Mary Riddoch and turned triumphantly to those officers assembled in the room.

'His name is Luke Watt and his father, Malcolm Watt, was the gardener during the time that Ladybank House was owned by the Riddochs.'

Lorimer looked up as the door opened and two men and a woman entered the room.

'Ah, this is DI Brodie, from the Cold Case Unit, who is known to some of you already,' Lorimer said, coming forward and shaking Brodie's hand.

Brodie glanced around and nodded to the rest of the Major Incident Team.

'DS Evans,' the other man said.

'DC Finlay,' the woman added, giving a hesitant smile.

Lorimer's eyebrows rose a fraction. So, this was Flynn's new girlfriend, was it? He could see why Flynn had fallen for her. She was a bonny lass right enough, and her intelligent eyes regarded him thoughtfully.

'Welcome. I'm glad to see you all here,' Lorimer continued, leading the trio to the front of the room where chairs had been set out.

'This,' he turned to the whiteboard and pointed to the image he had recently fixed there, 'is Luke Watt, son of the late gardener who worked for the previous owners of Ladybank House.'

He saw all three of the officers from Paisley sit up a little straighter, delight on their faces at this latest intelligence.

'I am just back from speaking to our old friend, Mary Riddoch,' Lorimer said, turning to Brodie. 'She knew almost at once who this was.'

'Did she know him twenty years ago, then?' Brodie asked.

'Possibly,' Lorimer replied, 'but she remembers him more as a youth. Seems he got into a bit of bother back then and was estranged from his family.' He looked over their heads and nodded to his own team. 'We need to find out as much about Luke Watt as possible. That's a priority,' he commanded.

'We thought he might have been in jail at one time,' DC Finlay commented. 'Poor teeth and, now that we have his face, we can see he was a bit run-down-looking. Suggests he wasn't that good at looking after himself. A chaotic lifestyle, perhaps?'

'These are definitely things we want to know,' Lorimer agreed, warming more and more to DC Finlay. 'And hopefully by tonight we will have plenty of answers to these questions.'

He thought for a moment about Professor Dawson. It would take a bit more time for her to come up with a location but she had reported that it did indeed look as if the victim had been buried somewhere else before being transferred to the Renfrewshire garden where Flynn had found him twenty years later.

CHAPTER THIRTY-FIVE

'And your release date has therefore been brought forward. So, John, you'll no longer be with us this time next week.'

The governor of HMP Barlinnie beamed at John Ramsay as if he were conferring some gift upon him, then, leaning across the desk, he offered a hand for the inmate to shake.

Ramsay took it, still reeling from the man's words. There had been some administrative cock-up and here he was being released weeks earlier than he'd expected. Just a matter of days from now he would be a free man, the governor had told him.

'You'll be going home. In plenty of time for Christmas,' he'd said with a huge smile that would have done justice to Santa Claus himself.

He stood up as the governor waved him off, ready to be escorted back to his cell. All the way along the corridors he heard the familiar sound of the prison officer's keys jangling by his side, their footfalls echoing as they reached the huge open space, ranks of cells on either side, men fitted into their places like pallets of groceries in a supermarket warehouse. It had been the place he'd endured for so long now that it was odd to imagine being anywhere else.

The door shut behind him with a clang and Ramsay stumbled across to his bed, relieved to be alone. He didn't have a cellmate at present, nor would he have company for the remainder of his time here, which suited him just fine.

He lay on his back, arms behind his head, looking around the place that had been a substitute for home these past fifteen years. The walls had been painted battleship grey at one time but were scuffed and faded with age. A bit like myself, Ramsay thought, seeing the tiny room as if for the first time. Various men had come and departed during his imprisonment, leaving traces of their stay; the calendar one had been sent last New Year from home that was still attached to the wall with lumps of Blu-tack. (No nails here, they could be made into chibs or used to self-harm.) The November picture was a dull landscape with misty hills and a Highland cow in the foreground. Ramsay had never bothered to look and see where the picture had been taken; he had no real interest in places he was unlikely to see other than the city where he'd been born.

You'll be going home, the governor's words reverberated in his brain. Well, that was a matter to consider, now, wasn't it? Where was home these days? His wife had upped and left a long time ago, the council reletting the wee cottage flat that they'd shared for all those years. Couldn't blame her, of course. No life for a woman waiting for her man to come out of jail, wondering how long it would be till he was back in and she had to go through it all again. The kids had stopped visiting a long time ago, an' all, so there was little chance that he'd find a welcome there. Who'd want their weans to see a granddad who was a jailbird?

He closed his eyes, remembering the Big Man's promise. One shot was all it would take and he'd be comfortable for the rest of whatever life was left. He'd been given an order and it was sheer foolishness to forget that. One shot, just one direct hit and then scarper away to be safe from the thugs who'd be waiting to see that he'd done the job. Anyone could have done it, but the Big Man had this fancy idea to pay them all back by using the ones who'd been hurt the most, hadn't he?

But first there was the matter of what he had to do once he was out. It wouldn't be the one who had been responsible for putting him away fifteen years ago he'd be gunning down, but the one against whom the Big Man had such a bitter grudge. Ramsay heaved a sigh, wondering if he was really that bothered any more. The Big Man had whispered to him, suggested a way to seek revenge and, at the time, he'd been fired up enough to give him a name. But then he hadn't known the consequences, had he? Nor had he felt the way he did now, doubtful if he could carry out his order successfully. Or, indeed, at all.

You do this one for me and there will be someone to do yours, the man had whispered, the poison seeping into his brain. He'd imagined how wonderful it would feel to hear that his oppressor was dead and gone. But that feeling had disappeared and now Ramsay was stricken with doubt and guilt.

He was a bad man, he'd told the Padre. There was no salvation for him, no matter what the Bible said.

He shifted uncomfortably, as if the book beneath his mattress was pressing against his spine.

It was almost a reflex action to sit up and fumble for the old worn book, taking it between his hands and running his thumb across the faded red edge of the pages encased in black leather. *This will give you all the help you need*, the Padre had said once during a Sunday morning service, holding up his own copy of the Good Book.

Well, perhaps it was time to put that to the test, Ramsay thought grimly, taking the book and looking to see whereabouts it might fall open.

A Psalm, number 31, written by David, the footnote told him. **A Prayer of Trust in God**, it said at the top in darker print. Ramsay gave a disdainful sniff and began to read.

> *You are my refuge and defence;*
> *Guide me and lead me as you have promised.*
> *Keep me safe from the trap that has been set for me;*
> *Shelter me from danger.*

The trap that has been set for me. His eyes flicked back to those words. The Big Man had set a trap all right and now he was ensnared by his plan as easily as if he was a fly caught in a spider's web.

'Oh, God!' Ramsay groaned, putting the book aside and holding his head in his hands.

'John.'

His eyes flew open, his first instinct to look towards the door, expecting to see a figure standing there, the key unlocking the cell while he'd been engrossed in this passage.

But there was no one there.

He'd heard it. His name. He knew he'd heard it. Dear God, was he going mad?

'What can I do?' he cried aloud, his face contorted with terror.

'Trust me,' the voice said.

There was no echo, nothing to suggest that someone was playing tricks from outside. Nor, Ramsay believed, was this voice simply inside his own head.

His whole body trembled and he clasped his hands together tightly, fearful of what was happening to him.

Then, looking down at his fingers, Ramsay saw that they were ready for prayer.

'Help me, God, oh, help me. I don't know what to do!'

Was that a sigh of wind? And did he really feel a faint touch on his shoulder as something passed him by?

John Ramsay sobbed into his hands, grief for what he had caused in his life overflowing, the tears soaking his clothes, drowning his remorse.

CHAPTER THIRTY-SIX

It was the second thing that had gone wrong. Third, if you counted the young female detective constable's death, though that had simply played into his hands. The Big Man grinned. Then his face resumed its customary look; teeth clenched, jaw rigid with an anger that simmered just below the surface. Margaret Woods' death had not been kept to the exact timetable that he had instructed, the hitman taking the matter into his own hands.

Of course he didn't have access solely to contract killers and, besides, where would the fun have been in that? Paying money to some cold-hearted men who had no personal interest in their target. No, this was much more amusing and carried just the smallest of risks. Still, he ground his teeth together in frustration at the many imponderable events that were so out of his reach.

Now, this; Ramsay's release date was changed and so he could not afford to wait to deliver the final execution as he had planned. Christmas Eve, that had been his idea, a wee present to himself, catching the detective superintendent off guard. It would have to happen sooner, that was all. Ramsay would be hedged about with social services and parole board worthies as soon as he was out. Medics too, if the old lag was really on his way out. But it would not be Ramsay's turn yet; not before the next name on his list was scored off.

He sat back, only half listening to a football match on the television, his attention drawn to the darkening sky outside his window. The shadows had fallen earlier tonight, the year closing in. Soon it would be time to set things in motion once more then sit back and watch as officers from every part of the country scampered about like headless chickens, not knowing what to do or who to blame.

The sigh that escaped him was one of sheer pleasure, the anticipation one has before a long-awaited event. Not long now, a little voice reminded him. Not long till he witnessed the facts on his television or read about it in the papers.

What might the heading be?

Head of MIT gunned down on his own doorstep?

Another top cop killed?

Or, more simply:

Lorimer shot dead.

CHAPTER THIRTY-SEVEN

A lot had happened in the fifteen years since Tony Weir had stood in the dock, a witness for the prosecution in John Ramsay's case. He'd been SIO in plenty of cases, though none quite as high-profile as that one way back when. It was years since he'd thought about it, time having softened the former detective inspector, though he still enjoyed getting together with former colleagues and reminiscing about the old days.

Tony put down his pint glass with a sigh of satisfaction. It had been a good evening, the lads talking about the current spate of killings, of course, but the conversation had veered away from the present as it always did to people and places from their past. He was last to leave the pub this time, the others with trains to catch from Perth railway station, their journeys to different parts of the country beginning there. Tony settled back in the padded bench seat, glancing up at the clock. Another ten minutes and Fiona would appear at the door of the pub ready to drive him home, their car parked along the road. These reunions happened every couple of months and this time it was Weir's turn to have the others come to his town. He'd ended his career in Tayside, happy enough to relocate there, one eye on the retirement to come; a decent enough police pension plus Fiona's salary as a primary school teacher keeping them comfortably off.

His thoughts turned to one of the old cases they'd brought up and the man he'd sent to prison for a good long spell. John Ramsay. God, that was so long ago now and the guy might easily be dead, for all he knew. It had been in all the papers at the time: a robbery gone horribly wrong, three men gunned down by attackers in balaclavas before the police had swooped down on the place, armed reinforcements overpowering them. Ramsay had shot one man dead in cold blood; several witnesses had testified to that and he'd been convicted and sentenced accordingly.

They'd tried to make him confess to the other killings, hadn't they? Well, *he* had, at any rate, Weir thought, remembering the other man in that interview room, Bill Lorimer. He'd done all right for himself, though; head of the MIT now, the Chief Constable's blue-eyed boy, by all accounts. Weir had pushed Ramsay as hard as he could but Lorimer had stopped the interview at one point, taking him outside and telling him to ease off. That still rankled. Weir had always played hard, never letting the villains off with the least wee thing. He'd thought the DCI a bit soft at the time, wondered how he could have had so many convictions under his own belt, but Weir at least had the satisfaction of being the SIO that had taken credit for John Ramsay's arrest and eventual sentencing.

He picked up the glass, saw that it was empty then set it down again on the table. Too late for another. Fiona would be here any moment now.

A movement by the door made Weir look up and sure enough his wife stood there, her eyes searching the room for her husband. She gave him a wave and Weir stood up with a sigh, his night of reminiscing over for another wee while.

'Car's just down the road,' Fiona told him, tucking her hand into his arm. Weir nodded and smiled. It was a fairly new acquisition, a black SUV with just over three thousand on the clock, and he looked forward to sitting in the passenger seat, looking down into other people's windows as he was being driven home.

The wind blew a scattering of leaves along the pavement as they set off, the city closed up for the night, darkened windows and shutters making the streets no place to linger.

Weir glanced behind him out of habit but the place was deserted, most folk sensibly in their own warm homes in front of a telly or tucked up in bed.

'Nice night?' Fiona asked, trotting along beside him, her heels click-clacking on the cracked paving stones.

'Aye, usual crowd. Tommy, Mack, the Edinburgh lot … most of the talk was about these murders,' he added, then wished he hadn't as Fiona shook his sleeve impatiently.

'Nothing bad like that will happen up here,' she said, her voice light. 'This is *Perth*, after all.'

Weir bit back a retort. He knew the underbelly of this city by heart but Fiona had always claimed that it lived up to its Fair Maid reputation, a nice middle-class place where nice middle-class people did nice middle-class things. Frankly,

Weir was bored with the turn his life had taken since retirement, Fiona insisting they enrol in ballroom dancing classes and join the indoor bowling club. He blamed *Strictly Come Dancing*, the TV programme his wife obsessed over, but there was no arguing with Fiona once she had made up her mind that they were going to do something together. She reminded Tony often enough of the lonely nights she'd spent waiting for him to come home, worrying herself sick every time she heard a siren.

The car was a welcome refuge from the cold and Tony climbed in, grateful for the heated seats in this newer model. He closed his eyes, content to let Fiona drive off into the night, their home a ten-minute journey from the city centre.

He was almost asleep, drowsy from the beers he'd consumed and the warmth from the car, when she pulled up outside their home. Weir gave a smile at the sight of the detached villa, a bigger house than they needed but with every luxury that a good builder could provide. Bloody hell, he'd earned it and he was going to enjoy it for years to come.

'I'll put it away. See you inside,' Fiona said as Weir slipped down from the passenger seat. The detached double garage was a few yards further along the driveway and she would come back around to the front door once the car was safely locked up for the night.

'Put the kettle on?' Fiona suggested, before he closed the car's door.

'Aye, sure,' Weir said then put a hand into his pocket, fumbling for his keys as he laboriously climbed up the three steps to the front door.

Former DI Anthony Weir had no time to turn around as the muzzle of the gun touched his head.

No time to think as the bullet punched into his skull.

No time left at all.

'Fifth one down,' the voice told him.

There was a click then the call was cut.

The Big Man secreted his cell phone, conscious that he had to keep it hidden, a piece of evidence that might condemn them all. One more call. One more killing. That was all he craved, like an addict promising himself his final high.

He pulled the blanket over his body and lay motionless on his bed, wondering why the notion of finishing this filled him with a slight sense of dismay. Soon it would all be over.

Then what? He closed his eyes, refusing to think about that any more, consoling himself with the thought of what further mayhem he had just spread tonight.

CHAPTER THIRTY-EIGHT

'Tony Weir?' Lorimer slumped down in his seat. 'Tony ... used to be at Stewart Street ... moved to Tayside before reorganisation.' He looked at DCC Flint and shook his head. 'I knew him,' he said. 'Hard man, always wanted to get a suspect to admit his guilt. Sometimes went over a line to do it, as well,' he mused. 'But a decent enough cop. Never saw him after he left Glasgow.'

'They got him on his doorstep,' Caroline Flint told him. 'Two shots. Textbook execution. And not a trace of anything to identify our hitman. Forensics have scoured the area. No CCTVs in that particular part of Perth though we're still accessing all the routes nearby.'

She gave Lorimer a quizzical look. 'You knew him, Lorimer. Any ideas?'

He shook his head then stopped.

'There is one man that springs to mind,' he said slowly, gazing at Flint. 'Suspect we both interviewed in the wake of an armed robbery. Horrible business. Three civilians shot dead.' He paused.

'Go on,' Flint encouraged.

'John Ramsay,' Lorimer said at last. 'If anyone could have held a grudge against Tony it might be him.'

'Why?'

'Tony was a bit heavy-handed with Ramsay,' Lorimer admitted. 'We could never prove anything, mind, but Tony had been down in the cells the same night that Ramsay ended up with a sore face.'

'Was this reported?' Flint asked sharply.

Lorimer screwed up his face. 'Ramsay said he'd run into the wall. Nobody really believed that but there wasn't the will to press Tony on it. He was SIO, after all.' He breathed in hard. 'Got a commendation for bravery as well. He was one of the armed squad that went into the premises. Got Ramsay and the others to throw down their weapons.' He looked at Flint again. 'You can't drop an officer into it after something like that.'

Flint nodded her understanding. 'And this Ramsay? Will he be out and about now? Has an old score to settle so he goes looking for Anthony Weir, perhaps?'

Lorimer hesitated, trying to calculate the timing. 'Could be,' he said at last, a faint smile on his face. 'Perhaps this is the breakthrough we've been waiting for?'

It made sense, Lorimer told himself, heart thudding with excitement. If Ramsay had been released a couple of months ago, then maybe he was the gunman who had been responsible for all of those deaths? He'd known his way around a sawn-off rifle back then. Who was to say that he hadn't been plotting and planning this spate of killings during his prison sentence?

It didn't take long for the detective superintendent to be put through to the prison governor. But what the man told him left Lorimer with a bitter taste in his mouth.

'No joy,' he sighed. 'It can't be John Ramsay. He isn't due for parole till next week.'

She must be reading the disappointment in my face, he thought as he gazed towards the DCC.

'Pity,' Flint replied. 'That would have made our lives one hell of a lot easier. 'Right.' She rose from her seat and patted Lorimer on the arm as he accompanied her to his office door. 'Looks like we're after someone else, then, now that this Ramsay character is out of the picture. It simply isn't possible for him to have been the hitman, is it?'

John Ramsay turned over onto his back. It had to have been some sort of dream, he told himself. Things like that just didn't happen and it was only nutters that heard voices. He'd been overwrought, that was all, he reasoned. Yet he could remember with absolute clarity the tone of that voice and the sensation of someone passing him by, touching him, even.

He'd slept for hours after that, a dreamless sleep, or at least one where he had no memory of a dream. Or nightmare. Funny thing was, how calm he felt this morning. There was no tension in his body and he hadn't even had a fit of coughing, something that surprised Ramsay, given that it was a normal occurrence on waking each morning.

I've changed, he told himself. Then, *Nah, loada rubbish.* But he dismissed this second thought, knowing full well that something had happened the previous night. His thoughts turned to the Padre. Should he tell the man who'd given him that old Bible? Or would Petrie pass it on to the rest of the staff? Maybe they'd change their minds about releasing him next week if they thought he'd flipped his lid? *No*, he thought, *keep it to yerself, man*.

A few more days and he'd be clear and free.

But would he really ever be free from the promise the Big Man had extracted from him?

Trust me, that voice had said. Well, maybe that was what he should do? Get out of this place and see what happened next?

Ramsay closed his eyes and thought hard. It had been decades since he had thought about saying a wee prayer. *Now I lay me down to sleep*, his granny had taught him. And *Our Father who art in heaven* … But neither seemed to be the right words to say.

'See all this mess I've got myself intae? Gonnae help me get out of it?' Ramsay said aloud, then murmured, 'Please?'

There was no answer. No voice inside his head or in the empty cell.

Had any Divine Authority heard his prayer? Or was he just kidding himself after all?

'Tony Weir's deid.' The prisoner laid down the book in front of John Ramsay. 'See thae Val McDermids? Any chance you've goat wan I huvnae read?' he added with a grin at Ramsay's startled expression.

Ramsay looked down at the A4 sized notebook that showed all the recent borrowings. Then he looked up at the man staring down at him.

'How about *The Last Temptation*?' he offered.

'Sounds kinda my thing,' the man grinned. 'See if you kin get it fur me, eh?' He leaned forward, dropping his voice to a whisper. 'Oh, and I'll tell the Big Man I passed on his message. He'll know how made up ye are, John.' A frown crossed the man's face. 'That's right, eh? You're chuffed tae bits about the news?'

'Christ, aye,' Ramsay assured him, then as the man walked away from the library counter, he bit his lip, wishing that the word 'Christ' hadn't slipped out quite so glibly.

So, Tony Weir had been shot dead. Well that meant only one thing. The Big Man would be expecting John Ramsay to keep his part of the bargain.

CHAPTER THIRTY-NINE

I t didn't make sense, Solly told himself. If there had been a common name that linked these officers then the police would have swooped down on the man but, no, each of the dead officers had mostly served in different parts of the country. He'd dismissed the idea of a lone gunman seeking retribution for past injustices despite the fact that it was the same gun used at each execution, the very thing that had tripped up Mick Carson.

Try as he might, Solly could not shake the belief that there was more than one gunman, despite the evidence that the same gun was being used at different locations. Whoever was behind this had it all carefully planned out, the victims chosen in advance.

Solly stared out of the window, not seeing anything in the street below, the moment frozen as he considered the question, *why?* Why these particular victims, especially when none of them had been involved in the same case. It wasn't a random thing, Solly didn't believe that for a single minute. No, this was a carefully worked out pattern by someone whose intention was to cause as much grief to Police Scotland as he possibly could. And yet ... it seemed as though the officers had been chosen for a reason. Could it be that whoever was pulling the strings had coerced his hitmen (hitman?) into gunning down a particular individual?

John Ramsay was in prison, due for release, Lorimer had told him, his friend's voice betraying his frustration and disappointment. It would have made some sense had it been Ramsay shooting Tony Weir dead, after all.

Solly picked up a pencil and scored a line down the middle of a fresh page in his notebook. On one side he wrote the names of the dead officers, excluding Sharon Carson for the time being, on the other he began to write down Gunman a), Gunman b) until he had reached the fifth name opposite. What if there was no correlation between the gunman and his victim? What if ... ? Solly stared into space once more, pondering the idea that had come to him.

'DCI Cameron speaking. Oh, Solly, how are you?' Niall Cameron sat back in his seat, a smile spreading across his face. He liked the professor a lot and had become used to his eccentricities over the years, appreciating the usefulness of Solly's keen, puzzle-solving brain.

Cameron's smile spread into a grin as Solly treated him to one of his lengthy pauses, as he deliberated how to phrase a particular idea. They were worth waiting for, Lorimer had once joked, but it was true.

'The killings,' Solly began. 'Lorimer thought that it might have been a chap called John Ramsay that carried out the latest shooting. Seems he had reason enough to hold a grudge.'

'But Ramsay is still inside,' Cameron reminded him.

'Yes, and that is what got me thinking,' Solly replied. 'Ramsay will be out very soon and it made me wonder . . .'

There was another pause and Cameron stifled a sigh.

'He was convicted of killing an innocent bystander in a warehouse robbery that went horribly wrong. With a sawn-off shotgun.'

'Go on,' Cameron said, intrigued to hear what was coming next.

'Could he be planning to kill again, once he's out?'

There was a silence between the two men for few moments.

'Anything's possible,' Cameron admitted slowly. 'Though I happen to know Ramsay is a very sick man. He'll be out on life licence, of course, carefully monitored by social services. I could talk to whoever is going to be his caseworker, if you like?'

He could hear the sigh over the phone. 'He's been suffering from lung cancer, Solly,' he added. 'I'm not sure how fit he would be to take part in a spate of killings.'

'It might be a good idea to keep an eye on him, nonetheless,' Solly said. 'But I do take your point, Niall. I know how squeezed you all are for resources right now with the investigations covering such a large part of the country.'

'You're not wrong there,' Cameron agreed. 'The MIT's officers are spread pretty thinly at present given the different locations.'

'Hm, I wonder . . .'

But DCI Cameron never found out what it was that Professor Brightman was wondering as the call was suddenly terminated.

That was what he wanted, Solly told himself, clasping his fist and shaking it in a gesture of triumph. Maximum disruption. Taking the officers of Police Scotland all over the country. He looked back down at his notebook. Had he got it all wrong? Had the person behind it all simply mixed up all those names, chosen different places, deliberately making it harder for the police to carry out their investigations?

Inverclyde, Inverness, Glasgow, Galashiels, Perth ... and where next? Aberdeen? Somewhere in the former Grampian Division that pre-dated the existence of Police Scotland? Or, and here he sat very still, were they simply intended to think that?

Solly looked back down at his notes. Did the man behind all of this also have some sort of a list? A list of names that were being scored off one by one?

He felt a presence somewhere, a person cunning and full of hatred, a mind that he needed to understand in order to work out why these deaths had happened. And if they were ever going to stop.

'He asked what?' Lorimer shook his head. 'We can't spare any more officers to shadow Ramsay. Besides, I'm told he's a sick old man now, no hope of ever working again. The governor tells me that there's not much chance of him being here in a year. Lungs shot,' he added wearily. 'Poor creature.'

'Some would say that he got what he deserved,' Cameron replied.

'But you don't believe that, do you?' he asked. It was well known that Niall Cameron was a card-carrying Christian, his upbringing in the Free Church in Lewis now tempered by a less rigid but staunchly evangelical outlook.

Cameron shook his head. 'No,' he said. 'The Church tells us that Redemption can happen for anyone. Maybe this old man will find it before he shuffles off that mortal coil.'

'Why do you say that?' Lorimer frowned. 'Sounds as if you know Ramsay personally.'

'Never met him,' Cameron replied, 'but I do know Douglas Petrie. We were on several Seaside Mission teams back in the day and we've kept in touch now we're both in Glasgow. He's the chaplain at Barlinnie,' he explained. 'He spoke to me recently about the inmates and how he was finding it hard to persuade them that no one is ever too lost to find forgiveness.'

'Aye, I can believe that,' Lorimer agreed. 'But what's that got to do with John Ramsay?'

'Oh, well, he mentioned the man's name. Asked me if I had ever come across him. Which I hadn't. Then he said that Ramsay had been asking questions about faith.' He shrugged. 'That's all.'

Lorimer nodded. 'Makes sense for an old guy facing death to reach out to a man of the cloth,' he agreed. 'Right. Thanks for that, Niall. And I think we can discount any worries Solly has about Ramsay being our next gunman.'

CHAPTER FORTY

DI Brodie was looking around the room, regarding each member of the Cold Case Division as they waited for the latest update. They'd worked their socks off trying to find out about Luke Watt, thought Erin, and now they had plenty to pass on to Lorimer and his team. She watched the boss as his eyes travelled around them all, then he stopped at Erin, giving her a nod.

'Erin,' he began. 'This will all be going to the MIT and I am certain that Detective Superintendent Lorimer would pass it on to Mr Flynn. However,' he cleared his throat and gave a knowing smile at the other officers, 'you have my permission to tell him yourself.'

'Go, Erin!' someone called then several wolf whistles and hand-clapping broke out as Erin Finlay blushed bright red. She'd made no secret of their blossoming romance, even being sensible enough to bring it to the attention of DI Brodie in the early stages.

'Not every day we find a skeleton with a hole in his head that plays Cupid,' the DI added with a wicked grin.

'Thanks,' she said shyly, then, turning to her colleagues she shook her head and gave a mock sigh of despair at their antics. She'd tell Flynn all right when they met later this evening but she'd omit this particular little scene!

'Right, what we know now is this,' Brodie began, turning to the whiteboard that had details of the current case, including several photographs of the skeleton and the forensic archaeologist's impression of what Luke Watt might have looked like. 'Our chap was not as pure as the driven snow, in fact we've turned up several hits on the database regarding his previous record.'

Erin nodded, listening. They'd begun to think their victim had form, right enough, when they had seen the state of his teeth, a feature that indicated a poor diet and neglect, something that was more prevalent in prisons than elsewhere. It was not unusual, either, for a victim of violent death to have been involved with the more sinister characters of the criminal underworld and, as Erin listened, this appeared to be the story for Luke Watt.

'Some petty thieving when he was a boy, escalating to dealing in drugs, then he was jailed for his part in an armed robbery. He got off with a three-year stretch on that occasion seeing as how he was just the lookout and was never on the premises. Nor had he ever handled a firearm as far as the records show.'

'Do we know why he was killed?' a voice asked, and Erin turned to see who had spoken. It was DS Evans, standing with his arms folded, regarding the DI hopefully.

'Not yet,' Brodie replied, 'but I am coming to that. Luke mixed with some nasty people back in the day. The Cooper gang for one. He and Shay Cooper hung about together from what we know.'

There was a murmur from the assembled officers on hearing that name.

'The older officers among us will know all about Shay Cooper,' Brodie said, 'but for those of you who don't, let's just say he was one of the notorious family that had held far too much of the city in thrall to drugs some years back. A violent man, given to terrible rages, he ended up inside on a life sentence after beating his girlfriend to death.'

Erin shuddered. It was horrible thinking of men like that, though their vicious actions were sadly all too common to the officers around her.

'Now,' Brodie rubbed his hands together. 'We are waiting for Professor Dawson's report into the samples that were taken from the grave in Houston. It looks at the moment as if the original burial site is somewhere in Glasgow.' He smiled and raised his eyebrows. 'So let's see if the famous professor is as good at pinpointing that location as she was on that TV programme.'

Erin heard the ripple of laughter and felt a frisson of excitement. Lorna Dawson had been challenged by a television team to find the partner of a wellington boot by examining the soil around it, and she had located the exact place where it was buried, out in Mugdock Park near Milngavie. Not only that, but Flynn had told Erin about a more recent case where Lorimer had been helped by the soil scientist to locate a missing woman. If Professor Dawson were to find the place where Luke Watt had originally been buried, well, that would really push this case on.

'There are few family members left to mourn Luke Watt,' Brodie continued. 'He never married, both his parents died years ago and there are some cousins up in the islands related to Mrs Watt who never even met Luke.'

That was sad, Erin thought. Nobody should have been so alone in the world that his absence was never noticed. Yet in their line of work that was something that often happened; a person disappearing only to turn up as a corpse decaying in an unmarked grave.

'No one will take the slightest bit of notice if you disappear,' the man by his side whispered. 'Social workers won't care and the cops aren't going to spend time looking for an old guy like you.'

The sound of crockery being cleared away and men's voices rising and falling were enough to prevent the words being overheard.

Ramsay nodded as he slowly chewed the beef hash, scraping the bits of vegetables and potatoes into the gravy on his plate. It was one of the few times when he was given any sort of information outside the library, the screws all too busy at mealtimes to be bothered with dozens of hungry men.

'Hearing what I'm saying, Johnny boy?'

Ramsay did not look up but continued to fork the food into his mouth.

'Cat got your tongue?'

'I hear you,' he said at last, glancing at the younger man sitting beside him. His dinner companion was a cut above most of the inmates, the educated accent giving him an edge over the others, plus his connection to the Big Man. This fellow might be dressed like all the others in regulation jeans and sweatshirt but somehow managed to make it look as if he'd chosen the clothes rather than been forced to wear them.

'Right, then. Our *mutual friend*,' he paused and gave a low snigger, 'our mutual friend says he'll send someone to pick you up, all right? You've to look for a dark blue Beamer. Driver'll be on the watch for you as soon as you walk out of here.'

John Ramsay scratched his nose and then gave the man a quick look, nodding to show that he'd understood. 'What about ma social worker? Thocht I wis meant tae be picked up by her?'

The other man gave a lazy shrug. 'I was reliably informed that would be taken care of,' he said, giving Ramsay a wink. 'Ways and means, eh? Ways and means.'

He laughed at his own innuendo then leaned closer to Ramsay.

'Big Man'll send you all you need to do the job after that. Usual way.' The man pushed his plate to one side and stood up from the long table. 'Keep a lookout for returned books. Okay?'

Ramsay did not watch him leave, knowing that it was better to distance himself from any of the messengers. This one had been sent to dictate how he was to behave the moment he was released from here. Plus reinforcing the threats of what would happen if he did not comply with his orders.

294

He had only once come into contact with the Big Man himself and was not relishing a second meeting. That wouldn't happen, he told himself: far too risky for the guy to actually keep in personal contact with him. Though, come to think of it, what did the man behind all these shootings have to lose? Not as much as John Ramsay did if he failed to carry out the hit.

Later, once the noise of men stamping back to their cells, the clanging shut of doors and rattling of keys had died down, Ramsay lay on his bunk and wondered why it was that he felt no fear at the threats that man had made. Had the cancer and its aftermath drained him of all the terrors life could bring? Or was he simply tired of life itself? It was true that nobody would miss him if he ended up dead, beaten and tortured by the same thugs who would be waiting for him several yards along the road from HMP Barlinnie.

And yet, and yet … the idea of being out of here and breathing cool fresh air that was not being breathed in by hundreds of other men had such an appeal. He closed his eyes, imagining a room with a soft bed, pillows that sank beneath his weary head, and decent food he could afford to buy. It was all his if he just did what they wanted.

And they trusted him, didn't they? The plan would be carried out to the last detail, old John Ramsay taking out the one person that the Big Man really wanted dead. That was what they believed, what was expected. An old man with dodgy lungs wouldn't throw up the chance of a cushy few months sitting back enjoying the fag end of his life, would he? What was his alternative, after all? Signing on to the homeless register and hoping some dingy, damp council flat would come up?

Ramsay closed his eyes and breathed in deeply.

'You said tae trust you,' he murmured. 'Well, see and sort this mess out for me, will you?'

There was no voice disturbing the silence in his cell, no cool breeze to signify a passing presence. And yet as Ramsay lay there he felt a sense of peace as though a great burden had been lifted off his shoulders.

CHAPTER FORTY-ONE

The street map showed a line of large residential houses close to a park, homes for wealthy men and women that had been built over a hundred years ago when Glasgow had been famed for its shipbuilding and trading with countries overseas. Lorna smiled, wondering just what she would find along this particular street. Would there be a match in one particular garden for the soil samples she had so painstakingly analysed? Or would she find that several gardens contained the same mixture of plants, obfuscating the exact place she wanted to locate?

The professor had packed an overnight bag and was preparing to set off by train to Glasgow. A wee trip to the affluent suburbs coupled with a guest appearance at a local writer's book launch made the journey doubly worthwhile. And she looked forward to working with Detective Superintendent Lorimer again. He had put his faith in her before and together they had solved part of a particularly difficult case. And he wasn't the only police officer who came asking for her help; Lorna's work involved being an expert witness in many cases where her expertise had proved that a person had been at a scene of crime, the soil attached to their shoes or car an indisputable fact that often helped the prosecution to put someone in jail.

Her smile faded as she thought about the police officers whose lives had been so cruelly taken. After dedicated service they had all deserved to enjoy a long and fulfilling retirement. Instead, they had been cut down by some gunman. The newspapers had suggested that it was revenge by some felon for being imprisoned decades before. But Lorimer had told her they had no link to make amongst these officers, no common name of any offender who had held a grudge all through his sentence. It was a mystery, but perhaps she would help to solve at least one part of it. The bullet that had killed Luke Watt had been fired from the same gun. And so, perhaps locating the original site of the young man's burial could give a clue as to who had owned that particular weapon after it had been taken from Malcolm Watt, the Riddochs' gardener.

Lorna stood up and massaged the base of her spine. It would be good to be out walking that particular Glasgow street after the hours spent sitting over a microscope. Good to be part of the team that was working round the clock to discover any sort of clue in this case. She stretched her arms and rolled her shoulders, wondering what lay ahead of her in Scotland's biggest city.

'Shay Cooper got out a few months ago,' Lorimer said slowly, turning in his chair and facing Solomon Brightman.

'Hm,' was Solly's response as he regarded his friend thoughtfully. 'And, remind me, what was he sent down for?'

'Nearly killed his girlfriend,' Lorimer growled. 'She was left with only partial sight in one eye after he battered her senseless. The trial was horrific. Bad bastard made the family go through the whole thing again, pictures of the woman's injuries shown to the court. It was disgusting.'

'You put Shay Cooper away?'

Lorimer shook his head. 'No, not me. It was George Phillips who was SIO in that case. But I was required to give evidence since I'd been part of the squad that took him into custody.'

'Shay Cooper was out before George was shot,' Solly mused.

'He wasn't the only rotten villain George put away in his time, but, yes, he is certainly a person of interest to us, given the timescale of his release. And now, this.'

'Interesting that he had a connection to Luke Watt,' Solly murmured. 'However, what I would really like to know is this. If Professor Dawson is correct in thinking that the Houston garden was not his original burial site, why did they take him all the way out there from Glasgow?'

'That's a question that's been troubling me too,' Lorimer admitted. 'But, before we get onto that, there's something else I need to tell you about our skeleton.'

'Go on.'

'I think I know why he was shot,' Lorimer said. 'Since we identified him from the archaeologist's model, we've been scouring every old record to do with Watt and we've turned up another old name from the past: Len Murdoch.'

Solly's dark bushy eyebrows rose in response. 'The chap who was Kirsty's partner?'

'The very same,' Lorimer replied. Kirsty Wilson, the daughter of Lorimer's former colleague DI Alastair Wilson, had been a serving officer in several cases in Glasgow, along with Len Murdoch, now retired from the service.

'Wasn't there some question about his . . . ahem . . . integrity?' Solly asked, choosing his words carefully.

'Aye, there was. But Murdoch had some assets that we used from time to time. Human assets,' he added, with a wry grin.

'Informants?'

Lorimer nodded. 'I think you met one of them? Tam McLachlan?'

'Yes, of course. What a life that poor soul had,' Solly murmured, remembering the old drug addict who had helped the police.

'Well, another of Murdoch's touts just happened to be Luke Watt.'

'My goodness,' Solly said slowly. 'That certainly gives a motive into his death twenty years ago, doesn't it? Rosie did describe the injury as a textbook execution.'

'And twenty years ago Len Murdoch was part of a team investigating the Cooper gang,' Lorimer told him. 'There were several factions vying to be top dog back then. I remember coming across a few incidents involving guns fired from cars. It was like Glasgow was a mini war zone the way the different gangs tried to compete for territory.'

'So,' Solly continued, stroking his beard thoughtfully, 'we have motive, means and opportunity, do we not? A villain found out to be informing the police behind their back, an old firearm that seems to have been kept in very good condition and ... well, what? A dark night when this Watt lad was lured somewhere he felt safe? I wonder where that might have been?'

'We may not have much longer to wait till we know that,' Lorimer told him. 'Professor Dawson is on her way here today and,' he looked at his watch then started to rise from his chair, 'I'd better get a move on if I'm going to meet her train.'

Waiting at the barrier in Queen Street station, Lorimer looked around him, seeing how much had changed over the years since he had worked in this city. Security had heightened here, as everywhere, of course, and he doubted whether it would be possible for the ladies of the night to ply their trade in the station as they used to do. A memory came back to him of a foggy night, the station cold and dank, a woman's body discovered in the lifts that separated the upper and lower levels. And she had not been the only poor soul to be targeted by a deranged killer. That man was locked up for good, however, the state mental hospital his home for the remainder of what life was left to him.

'Lorimer!'

He looked up as Lorna Dawson approached, smiling at him.

'Hello.' He grasped her hand. 'Can I take one of those?' he offered, looking at the bags she carried.

'Thanks, this one's pretty heavy,' Lorna agreed. 'Stuff for a lecture in Edinburgh tomorrow.'

'You're going to be busy,' Lorimer remarked as they made their way through the station to where his car was parked.

'They don't mind you leaving your car there?' Lorna asked, indicating the line of private taxis curving around the outside of the station.

Lorimer chuckled. 'They all know me,' he told her. 'And the Lexus has in fact been mistaken for a taxi before now. Had a nice young woman jump into the back one day, asking to be taken to Bellshill. She nearly had a fit when she saw my warrant card and I told her I wasn't a cab driver.'

Lorna laughed. 'Well, I'm happy to travel in style,' she said as Lorimer opened the passenger door for her. 'Jolly cold out here.'

'Right, ma'am, where exactly are we going?' Lorimer asked as they drove around George Square and headed along St Vincent Street.

'Southside,' Lorna told him. 'I think this is the address we want. And here's the postal code,' she added, holding a piece of paper so that Lorimer could see what was printed.

He blinked and read it again, just to make sure. But there it was in black and white.

An address that he had once visited and the memory of a particular man he would not easily forget.

He screwed up the letter in his fist, teeth clenched in sudden fury. After all he'd done to cover his tracks!

Mathieson stared at the wall of his office where his diplomas were hung in gilt frames for all to see. That was the man he wanted to show to the world, not the one he'd discarded after all the things that had happened.

He had three choices: do what they asked, ignore it and face the consequences or . . .

His eyes flicked across to the window and the buildings across the street. He'd settled so well into this position in Glasgow; the kids were happy in their new school and everything had been fine till that idiot Flynn messed it all up by bringing the police to his home.

Mathieson closed his eyes, recalling every detail of that day, particularly the tall detective who had questioned him.

He gave a sigh, admitting to himself that his next step was inevitable. It was Lorimer, he realised, that was his third and only choice.

CHAPTER FORTY-TWO

This might be his last chance, Douglas Petrie told himself as he made his way along to the prison library. He had lingered after Sunday's service in the hope that John Ramsay could snatch a brief moment or two to talk but he had trooped out with all the other men, head down, as though deliberately avoiding Petrie's glance.

The door was open and from where he stood it looked like any other small library, shelves full of an assortment of books, overhead strip lighting making the place bright. There were posters on the walls, too, one advertising a play that had been put on by David Hayman, the actor, some months previously. Douglas had missed that but the governor had assured him that the performance had been well received by the prisoners.

The old man was seated at his usual place behind a desk writing in a large notebook. He had been acting as assistant librarian ever since Petrie had arrived in Barlinnie and the chaplain paused for a moment, wondering how much

Ramsay would miss the routine and the responsibility that job had given him.

'John,' he said quietly.

Ramsay started back in alarm and dropped the pencil he had been holding, then, seeing the chaplain standing there, he swept a hand across his brow.

'Gave me a wee fright there, so you did, Padre,' he said, swallowing hard. Petrie tried to hide his bewilderment. That grin on Ramsay's face was a little forced, surely? He glanced at the open notebook and the pencil rolling to one side but there was no sign of Ramsay hiding anything.

'Wanted to see you one last time before you leave, John,' Petrie said. 'Mind if I sit down?' He looked around for a chair and walked to a corner of the room where there were several plastic chairs stacked up.

By the time he had returned, Ramsay appeared to be back to his normal self. Whatever had startled him? Petrie put the thought to the back of his mind, intent on having this final conversation with a man he regarded as one of his parishioners.

'Just tidying everything up,' Ramsay said. 'Don't know who'll take over once I'm gone.' He shrugged, looking down at the rows of neat handwritten titles and names opposite. 'Wan thing I wis always good at in school,' he admitted. 'Top marks for spelling, though my arithmetic wis rubbish,' he chuckled. '"Know how many beans make ten," my old ma used to say and I daresay that was enough fur me.'

'Well, you don't need a calculator to work out how many more days till your release,' Petrie said warmly. 'How do you feel about that, John?'

The man sat back and folded his arms, regarding the chaplain as if he was some daft wee laddie.

'How d'you think?' he frowned. 'D'you imagine I want tae stay here a moment longer than I need to?'

Petrie shook his head. 'Things will be very different from how you remember them outside, John,' he warned. 'And I wanted to see if I could help with that.'

The old man opened his mouth as though to protest but Petrie raised his hand to stop him. 'Oh, I know you'll have social services looking after your needs, John, but there's more to rehabilitation than just sorting out somewhere to stay and having enough money to live on.'

Ramsay gave a slight nod as if to encourage the chaplain to continue.

'I've been speaking to a friend of mine who attends a church in Govan, near the place where you're going to be staying.'

'How did you know where I'll be?' Ramsay snapped, unfolding his arms and bunching his fists by his side.

'The governor told me,' Petrie said, surprised at the man's sudden belligerence. 'You gave an address of a friend, that's right, isn't it?'

Ramsay slumped back in his seat, avoiding eye contact with the younger man. 'Aye, right enough. Jist a share in a room. Till ah get oan ma feet.'

Petrie saw the way the man avoided his glance. What was happening here? Was it something to do with the people who were offering accommodation? Had Ramsay been ashamed to admit that there was no returning to a family home? Once again, the chaplain was struck by the way John Ramsay was behaving.

'Well,' he said, taking a folded paper from his inside pocket, 'here's the name and address of the minister and the church. He's a nice guy and will welcome you any time you want to attend a service or just go along to the manse for a chat.'

'What have you told him about me?' Ramsay said suspiciously.

Petrie raised his shoulders in a shrug. 'The truth, of course. That you're a man who is questioning your faith. That you want to make a fresh start.' He leaned forward and made eye contact with Ramsay. 'You do want that, don't you, John?'

There was a moment's silence then Ramsay looked away.

'Aye,' he said shortly. 'You know that, Padre, but it isnae always that simple.'

Petrie heard the long sigh then the old man began a fit of coughing, his back bent as he pulled a handkerchief to his mouth. It was a stark reminder that this poor soul's days on earth were numbered.

'Do you want to pray with me, John?' he asked quietly. The man nodded and then closed his eyes, clasping the handkerchief tightly between his fingers.

'Dear Father,' Petrie began, 'help John as he goes away from here tomorrow. Be with him every step of his new journey and let him know your presence in his life. Even when doubts arise and temptations happen, shield John from danger and keep him close to You. In the name of Jesus, Your Son and our Saviour, Amen.'

He heard the shuddering sob and when he opened his eyes to look at the man across the desk, he was astonished to see him holding his head in both hands, openly weeping.

Glancing around, Petrie saw the prison officer standing in the corridor chatting to another inmate who was coming towards the library.

Ramsay must have heard the voices, too, for he sat up again, scrubbing his face with the tissue and looking over Petrie's shoulder with a worried expression.

'You cannae be here, Padre,' he hissed suddenly, sitting forward and looking fearfully at the pair outside the door.

'What's wrong, John?' Petrie asked gently, concerned that there was something really troubling the old man.

'Ah cannae say.'

Petrie held out a hand and made to grip Ramsay's fingers but the old man brushed him off roughly and grimaced as though any physical touch was abhorrent to him.

'Jist you keep praying fur me, awright? There's something ah hiv tae do wance ah'm oot o' here.'

Petrie sat back and frowned, surprised at his manner.

'Of course I will John,' he promised. 'And you won't be alone. Remember you are God's child and he is always with you. Here.' He pulled out a bookmark from his pocket. 'I meant to give you this,' he said.

Ramsay gave it a cursory glance then pushed it underneath the open notebook.

'Thanks, Padre, it's been good tae have had our wee chats,' Ramsay said. Then, as his eyes travelled past Petrie, he shuffled in his chair.

'Be seein' you,' he whispered, clearly wanting the chaplain to leave so that the lumbering figure of an inmate approaching the desk could have the old man all to himself.

He left the library hastily, aware that John Ramsay did not

want him there. It happened of course, inmates embarrassed to be seen talking to a man of the cloth as though it were some sort of weakness. He gave a quick glance as he turned into the corridor, wondering who that particular inmate might be, a broad-shouldered fellow who seemed to fill the small room with his bulky presence as he seated himself opposite John Ramsay.

There was just a flicker, as the old prisoner looked up to see him go, just a fleeting expression crossing his pale face before he began to cough. It was an expression that Douglas Petrie had seen too many times to doubt.

Whoever this man was, he could see that Ramsay was truly afraid of him.

The closed cell was a sanctuary now, Ramsay told himself, lying down on the bunk, the sweat chilling on his body. The Padre had given him a shock, there was no doubt about it. Saying his name . . . that had sent a real shiver down his spine. It had been like that voice in here, in the place where he now felt safe. But it had only been the kindly chaplain, coming to see him one more time before he was released. He'd thrust the bookmark into his Bible, not even giving it a second glance. A wee memento, he supposed.

Ramsay sighed, relieved that the chaplain had left the library when he did. If he'd been seen greetin like that . . . ? It didn't bear thinking what sort of impression that might have given the man who'd walked in and taken the Padre's place. No, he was just a tired, worn-out old man, that was all. Who could blame him if his eyes watered a bit? All that coughing . . . Ramsay breathed in and out slowly, confident that he had managed to appear pretty normal to the man who'd sat there glowering at him, his very presence a threat.

He had made a promise, of course he had. He wasn't stupid. He'd looked the Big Man in the eye and listened to everything he had to say, nodding at the right times, assuring him before he left that he understood exactly what it was he had to do. McBride would be at the same place as usual out in Nitshill. Then the job should be carried out exactly when he'd been told it should. He had enough time for a recce on the house out in Giffnock, time to know when the policeman would be at home, time to do the job and finish off the final name on the list.

Ramsay had smiled back when the Big Man had risen laboriously to his feet and grasped his hand.

'Good luck, Johnny,' he'd said. 'Enjoy your retirement.' He'd chuckled then strolled off into the corridor to walk side by side with the prison officer who'd been waiting outside.

Somehow he'd managed to play the system in here, gain certain privileges that had eluded normal folk like John Ramsay. Money. That was what made the difference, of course. And power. And, despite his incarceration, the Big Man still had them both.

CHAPTER FORTY-THREE

'You've been here before?' Lorna Dawson sat back, her face a picture of astonishment. 'That's a coincidence,' she exclaimed. Then, tilting her head to one side she looked at the tall man by her side and gave a little smile. 'Or, perhaps not?'

Lorimer gazed out of the window at the house where he had parked the Lexus. The professor had taken him to an area in the suburbs that fitted her analysis and Lorimer had driven directly to this particular property, a place he remembered well. It was more than a hunch, he told himself grimly. The man who had lived here had been the perpetrator of all sorts of criminal activities. The hedge was in need of a trim, its foliage masking the lower part of the big house, but apart from that the place looked exactly the same as it had on his previous visit.

'You know who owns this place?' Lorna asked, curious.

'I do,' Lorimer nodded. 'Question is: was he the owner when Luke Watt was killed twenty years ago?'

It would be easy enough to find that out, but meantime he wanted to see if there was anybody occupying this large pale sandstone villa.

The iron gates swung open as he pushed them and he saw at once the black-painted storm doors closed fast across the main entrance. Behind them, if he remembered correctly, was a vast porch with an art deco lantern that had lit the place up at night. The windows, too, were shuttered, the entire house locked up against anyone who might dare to break in.

'Last time I was here, the owner invited me in,' Lorimer said slowly.

'Oh, and where is he now?'

'As far as I know being given hospitality at the pleasure of Her Majesty. Not quite sure where but I can find out. Could be Shotts, might be somewhere else. They can be moved about depending on their behaviour,' he told her. 'But you know these things, Lorna, don't you?'

The professor nodded. She was accustomed to court cases, knew more about the law and justice than many of his own colleagues.

'Tell me more,' she said, evidently wanting to find out a bit about this old case.

He stood there at the end of the path, his eyes travelling across the extensive garden grounds, the soil scientist's particular remit.

'His name is Gallagher. Jack Gallagher,' Lorimer said at last. 'He was head of a drug ring and had a hand in several other schemes, one of which was the disposal of sick and elderly people.'

Lorna Dawson frowned. 'He killed them?'

'Only in a manner of speaking. Someone always did Gallagher's dirty work for him. He raked in the money that people would pay to have the lives of their nearest and dearest brought to an end.'

'Involuntary euthanasia,' Lorna murmured.

'Something along those lines, yes. Occasionally it was out of a sense of pity. Mercy killings, some folk call them. A lot of the time people simply wanted the money left to them after a relative died.'

'Bloody hell,' Lorna exclaimed. 'And this guy, Gallagher, he was the one behind it all?'

Lorimer shook his head. 'No, as it happens that was a different person, a man who somehow managed to inveigle his way into Gallagher's operation.'

'But, you caught them?'

'Eventually,' Lorimer admitted. 'But there was a lot of collateral damage, including one rather bent senior officer who is also serving time for what he did.'

'Goodness! No wonder this place looks so neglected,' Lorna said, sweeping her soft brown hair from her face as a gust of wind caught it.

'Well, shall we get on?' Lorimer raised his hand and ushered the professor across the lawn to see if she had indeed found the place she had been seeking.

The grass was long now and the flowerbeds full of weeds, but the overgrown state of the place was just what she had wanted, botanical elements like the willow showing their presence to confirm that the garden out here in Pollokshields was the place where Luke Watt had been buried. It did not take very long to see that every trace of pollen that had been extracted from the soil samples as well as the layers of soil themselves were a match for this particular section of the garden.

It lay out of sight from the public, behind the house and to one side, a patch of bright green grass concealing what had once been a flowerbed, the stone edging still partially in place. If Luke Watt had been buried here two decades previously then a deep pit must have been dug into the soil and covered over again. After the hasty exhumation – why did she imagine that? Was it the badly constructed piece of lawn here? – someone had laid turf from an adjacent part of the lawn on top, an attempt to disguise the original grave. But there it was; a suite of flowering grasses, seeds plus pollen, just as she had established back in the lab.

'This is where they buried him,' she said at last. 'See?'

She pointed at a patch of grass that was ever so slightly different from the rest, though almost invisible to an inexpert eye.

'Fertile patch of nutrient-rich grass,' she murmured, bent down, fingers parting the long stems of grass. 'And no clover.'

Probing into the dark soil surface was especially satisfying, the humus colour decreasing as the depth of the soil changed to dark grey and there were fewer roots to bind the soil together.

'How long was the body there before it was dug up, I wonder,' she said aloud.

'Any way of telling?'

'Not easily,' she admitted. 'But the burial site out in

Renfrewshire was well established, whereas this one ... well ... weeks? Months? Impossible to tell.' She looked up at Lorimer and shook her head. 'Only the men who buried him here can give you that information now,' she replied at last.

'Barlinnie,' DCI Cameron told him. 'And, yes, Jack Gallagher has owned that house for more than twenty years.'

Gotcha, Lorimer thought grimly. 'Think a visit to Riddrie might be in order?' he said instead, a slow smile curving along his mouth as he mentioned the district in Glasgow where HMP Barlinnie was situated.

Gallagher had indeed been part of one of Glasgow's biggest organised crime gangs, even, at one time, its head. Now in Barlinnie for his crimes, he had questions to answer about the man who had disappeared all those years ago only to be turned up by the garden fork of Joseph Alexander Flynn. It would be interesting to see what the man had to say for himself, Lorimer thought. Though whether Gallagher had actually pulled the trigger of the gun that had killed Luke Watt would be impossible to prove.

The gun, though, that was the interesting thing. Would Gallagher be willing to shed any light onto its use to murder five retired police officers? Well, that remained to be seen, Lorimer thought, picking up the phone and dialling the number for DCC Caroline Flint.

'Good work,' Flint said when they met up in her office.

As Lorimer looked across he saw her eyes crinkling with a passing smile but he could also read the strain that the DCC had been suffering for over the past weeks. It was hard being near the top and having to field the barrage of questions fired at her from members of the press. Yet she could still give a little credit where it was due.

'Would you like company?' she added.

'You want to meet him?' Lorimer asked, surprised.

'What sort of man is he? Would he be less comfortable with a woman there, do you think?'

Lorimer paused to consider. There was no Mrs Gallagher, nor ever had been, and his only knowledge of Gallagher's private life were the rumours about women he had put up in various flats around the city, high-class prostitutes who had no doubt melted into the shadows after Gallagher's arrest. Perhaps a senior officer like Caroline Flint in her uniform might give him a bit more leverage with a man like that?

'Yes,' he said at last. 'I thought of having Professor Brightman with me but it might do more good to have someone he's never met before. And you can tell me afterwards what you make of him.'

Caroline Flint rose from her seat. 'Right, let's get an application made straight away. The governor won't be able to refuse a deputy chief constable access to his prison for very long, will he?' The smile lit up her narrow face again and Lorimer could see an eagerness to be part of the ongoing investigation that reminded him of when Flint had been an undercover officer, back in the Met.

Sometimes prison ages you, other times it keeps you looking young, an inmate had once advised Lorimer. That particular man had looked like a teenager when he'd been in his early thirties, fresh-faced and so innocent-looking that it was hard to imagine he had taken the life of his best mate in a drunken brawl.

Gallagher, however, had not fared so well, Lorimer thought as the man ambled into the room. He had put on a lot of excess weight, the flab above his waistband spilled out under a loose-fitting denim shirt and pale grey cardigan and his eyes were sunken in folds of flesh. His hair was thinner too and greyer than Lorimer remembered from the last time he had seen him in court. Then he had stood in the dock wearing an expensive suit, the silk tie and cufflinks all part of a show of bravado, a show of power. How he had managed to become so heavy in here was a bit of a mystery; the exercise regime was mandatory for the prisoners and everyone had the same amount of food served at mealtimes. It made the detective think for a moment: had Gallagher wangled some sort of special deal with those passmen who supplied his food? Or did he have a hold over the other inmates to bring him extra high-calorie treats?

'Hello, Jack,' Lorimer said as the man sat down heavily on the plastic chair, a prison officer hovering behind him.

The glower as he looked back at Lorimer was enough to tell him that there was no love lost here, Jack Gallagher no doubt remembering their tussle in that house in Milngavie when he'd disarmed him, saving the life of another senior officer in the process.

'You not retired yet?' The question was like a taunt but Lorimer tried to ignore it. No doubt this was Gallagher's way of needling them about the killings of these former officers.

'This is Deputy Chief Constable Flint,' Lorimer

continued, raising a hand to introduce the woman seated by his side.

Gallagher gave her a look, up and down, a grudging nod as he took in her uniform and the braid. Did he feel flattered by her presence? Lorimer glanced across at Flint, wondering if that was why the DCC had offered to accompany him to Barlinnie. Good move, he told himself.

'How do you do?' Gallagher said slowly, a tinge of sarcasm in his tone, but not enough to make it an outright sneer. Perhaps he really was a little impressed by Flint's seniority. A man who'd been in control of a major crime organisation would recognise another person who wielded power, after all.

Then he turned and looked at Lorimer. There was no mistaking how he felt about the tall man sitting opposite, the clenched jaw and mulish cast to his small, mean mouth showing that for two pins Gallagher would have leaned across this table and taken a swipe at the man who'd put him inside.

'We're here to ask you a few questions, Jack,' Lorimer began.

'*Mister Gallagher*, if you don't mind,' Gallagher replied with a hiss.

'Mr Gallagher,' Lorimer repeated, conceding the point. There was little to be gained from antagonising the man from the outset if they were to get any sort of information from him.

'It's about your garden,' Lorimer continued.

Gallagher's reaction was almost comical as he sat up suddenly, eyes widening.

'My garden? Did you just say my *garden*?' He frowned, evidently puzzled and quite unprepared for this.

'That's right,' Lorimer agreed smoothly. 'It's been the subject of an investigation.'

'My garden?' Gallagher repeated, shaking his head. 'Is this some sort of a joke?' he asked, looking now at Flint.

'No joke, I assure you, sir,' Flint replied. 'We have been looking at a particular part of your garden in Pollokshields that is believed to have been a temporary burial site.'

'Oh.' Gallagher sat back, suddenly deflated, his podgy hands sliding down by his sides. He looked down then threw a glance between the two officers opposite, not meeting Lorimer's steady blue gaze.

'About twenty years ago the body of a man was buried in your garden,' Flint went on. 'We have forensic evidence to prove that,' she assured him. 'And we also have the man's identity.'

Was that a flicker of anxiety he could see in those piggy little eyes? Had this unexpected news brought back a memory of something vile in the man's chequered past?

Gallagher shifted in his seat then pulled his cardigan closer around his rotund form, his body language suggesting that he was being protective of something. A hidden secret, perhaps?

'Don't know what you're on about,' he mumbled.

'No?' Lorimer asked quietly, staring directly at the man, willing him to look him in the eye. 'Not even when I tell you that it was Luke Watt?'

That did provoke a reaction. Gallagher seemed to freeze where he sat, the rigid jaw clamped over gritted teeth, no sound coming from him as though he were actually holding his breath.

'Luke Watt,' Lorimer repeated slowly. 'He was one of your boys back in the day, isn't that right, Mr Gallagher?'

There was silence from the man now and Lorimer wondered if that indicated a shock or if Gallagher was frantically thinking of some lie to tell them.

'We have been talking to some of the folk who knew Luke,' Lorimer said truthfully, hoping that Gallagher would interpret that statement as if the police had been interviewing some of Gallagher's own former criminal colleagues and not simply an old lady in a care home.

'Watt's remains were discovered out near the village of Houston,' Flint put in as they both watched the man across the table.

'It looks very much as if someone was eager to get rid of him,' Lorimer continued. 'Classic shot to the skull. Buried in your garden then moved to the countryside. Fancy telling us what happened, Jack?'

This time there was no objection to the use of his Christian name but neither was there any response from the former gang boss. His head had drooped and his eyes were closed as though to shut out the sight of the two police officers.

Had they been in an official interview situation then there was little doubt that a response of 'no comment' would have been given to their questions at this juncture.

'We also have evidence that you had a gun licence at one time,' Lorimer went on. Gallagher remained very still although Lorimer could see a tiny movement beneath his eyelids, a sign that something was happening in that crooked brain.

'The gun used to kill Watt just happens to be the very

same that was used to execute five retired police officers,' Flint commented.

'Five? Thought there had been six?' Gallagher's eyes flew open and a menacing expression began to cross his face, a reptilian smile that did not reach those eyes.

There was a moment of silence as Gallagher looked from one of them to the other, his confidence obviously regained.

'What do you know about this?' Flint demanded sharply.

'Me?' The man grinned at them, his hands spreading in mock innocence. 'How can you pin anything on me?' he said. 'Here I am inside, impossible to be involved in anything like that, surely?' His grin widened. 'Don't know where you got that information.' He shook his head. 'Never handled a gun in my life.'

Then, closing his thumb over two fingers he pointed towards Lorimer.

'Pow!' he said then blew on the gun shape, threw back his head and laughed. 'Gotcha!'

Flint looked across at Lorimer with a look of concern. Had the guy suddenly flipped?

Then, without any warning, Gallagher rose unsteadily to his feet.

'We finished now?' he snarled, hands on the table and leaning towards Lorimer. 'Because I'm finished with you.'

Both officers rose to their feet knowing that it was not in their power to detain the man any longer in this particular room without some sort of official warrant for his arrest.

'We may be back to see you again,' Lorimer told him as the prison officer came forward to accompany Gallagher back to his cell.

Gallagher turned slowly and took a couple of steps towards the tall detective.

'I don't think so,' he said, a smile creasing his features. 'No, I don't think you will.' He turned away, chuckling to himself.

'What was all that about?' Flint asked as they walked along the corridor together.

'Haven't a clue,' Lorimer replied with a frown. 'Probably just his way of trying to dominate the conversation. Have the last word.' Yet, as they made their way to the prison governor's office, Lorimer felt a sense of unease that had nothing to do with the investigation into Luke Watt's death.

CHAPTER FORTY-FOUR

The clothes he had arrived with had been laid to one side, the trousers and jacket now several sizes too large for his thin frame. He would be walking out of here in borrowed garments, a much-washed pair of denim jeans and a grey pullover plus the regulation white T-shirt that they'd said he could keep. At least his socks and trainers still fitted okay, though the shoes looked as if some of the rubber sole had perished over the years. John Ramsay picked up the navy anorak with a sigh. It looked new enough but how many other men had worn it before? It was old-fashioned, its hood with a drawstring the sort of thing that elderly folk might choose to wear. Ramsay shook his head. Aye, well, he was an elderly person now too, wasn't he? A senior citizen with claims on several official agencies, or so the woman from social services had assured him.

A bus pass, she'd said. A way of travelling around the country for free. (The country! Not just the city!) And then there would be a state pension, not a great deal, of course, but something to sort out with some department or another. They got a few quid too, on release. Eighty pounds, was it? Ramsay wasn't too sure, but that sounded like a fortune to him. Free travel and money every month, not bad for a man who'd seen the inside of a jail cell for the past fifteen years, counting pennies to buy a fag or two. Even that had stopped now, the smoking ban extended to inmates, and that vaping nonsense just hadn't cut it with Ramsay. No, a packet of fags would be his first purchase once he was shot of this place, dodgy lungs or no.

The prison officer came to the door of the room where Ramsay had been changing into his clothes.

'Ready?' he asked, then handed him a plastic carrier bag that contained all his meagre possessions: his wristwatch, a few books (including the old Bible), some faded photographs that had been stuck and re-stuck to the walls with Blu-tack, and a slim brown wallet. It was made of real leather and had been a gift from his ex-wife a long, long time ago, in the days when they had exchanged presents on a Christmas morning, the kids running around like daft things, playing with the plastic toys they insisted on having but that never seemed to last very long.

Ramsay opened the wallet and saw the twenty-pound notes pushed into one side.

'Okay?'

'Aye.' Ramsay shoved the wallet into his pocket, zipped it shut and followed the man along a corridor. They walked briskly through a series of locked doors, more corridors and a flight of stairs until they were out in the open air, bare flower-beds across a stretch of tarmac and, to his astonishment, a huge sculpture of a horse and plough fashioned from barbed wire.

'Where did that come from?' Ramsay stopped for a moment, admiring the work of art.

'Come on,' the officer replied. 'We haven't got all day.'

Ramsay continued walking, following the man back inside the building until they reached a gate that reminded him of the football turnstiles of his youth.

He was pushed through then made to walk between two large plastic barriers and out towards a glass door.

'Right, that's you,' the prison officer said. 'Don't forget you need to have a weekly meeting with the parole board from now on as you're out on life licence.'

Ramsay nodded. He'd heard all of this before, the prison authorities drumming it into him how he could be back inside if he broke any of the terms of his parole.

Shooting dead a senior police officer? Would that count? he wondered as the door finally opened and he walked out of HMP Barlinnie towards freedom.

The wind was cold so he zipped the anorak right up to his neck and pulled the hood over his head, his ungloved hands shaking as he attempted to tie a wee bow beneath his chin. Above, the skies were dark, clouds scudding swiftly from the east, the threat of rain or snow in the damp air.

The social worker had told him to be there but after fifteen minutes there was no sign of her. No way was he going back in, he told himself, glancing towards the building over-shadowing him. Besides, hadn't he been told to look out for someone else? Someone sent specially to pick him up and take him to the address he'd given the prison authorities?

Ramsay walked steadily down the hill, looking this way and that to see if the car was there, like he'd been promised, but each corner seemed deserted. Then, as he approached a main road between two lines of tenement buildings, Ramsay heard a beep and turned round.

There it was, crawling along the road, its driver grinning at him.

'Get in the back,' he shouted as Ramsay opened the passenger door.

Obediently he closed the front door and climbed into the back of the BMW.

Inside it was warm and Ramsay sank back, glad to be out of that freezing wind.

Thanks,' he said huskily. 'Social worker never turned up.'

The man's grin as he turned around told Ramsay all he needed to know. Somehow they'd managed to stop his social worker getting there on time.

A series of frantic beeps from within the car made the driver brake suddenly and turn again, this time to glare at him.

'Put your seat belt on, old man!' he commanded, in a voice that to Ramsay's ears was definitely foreign. Eastern European? Weren't there lots of Poles and Romanians here now? He'd met some of them inside and thought he recognised the accent.

Once the belt was clicked into place and the insistent beeping stopped, the driver took off again and drove through a maze of streets until they came to a motorway junction.

Ramsay stared out of the window, absorbed by a view of the city he'd known so well yet had never see from this perspective.

'Where are we?' he asked, leaning as far forwards as the safety belt allowed.

'M74,' the driver called back. 'New since your time, old man.' Then he laughed.

It might have been the skyline of a foreign city, unfamiliar shapes, strange-looking buildings dominating the horizon. But there, hidden amongst them, was Glasgow, his own city. He could make out the spire of the university, a place he'd never been inside, then the white towers nearby. As the car sped along he marvelled at the way the old place looked from this angle, a conglomeration of buildings and styles no doubt, but to John Ramsay it was the best thing he'd ever seen. Then the car swept around and entered a highway of several lanes, making Ramsay clutch the edge of his seat. What the hell sort of road was this? And were they really heading for that address in Govan?

It was not long, however, before he saw some familiar signs: *Clyde Tunnel, Ibrox, Braehead, Renfrew*. They were like beacons of light leading him home, Ramsay mused. He dismissed the fancy with a small grunt. There was no home for him now, was there? Only a share of some place provided by the generosity of the Big Man. And even that was to be regarded as temporary accommodation, the money he got from the hit setting him up somewhere better. That was what he'd been told, the bait dangled in front of him by the man who wanted Lorimer dead. And, of course, he'd taken it.

The slip road took them away from the thundering roar of cars on every lane and soon they were heading into an area that he remembered. Ramsay sat up now as they drove slowly along past familiar tenements, scowling now and then at newer flats with their garishly coloured balconies and turning his head as the driver took an unfamiliar route.

'What? Is this the right way, son?' he asked, a sense of alarm seizing him.

'New one-way system,' the driver called. 'We'll be there in a minute.'

Sure enough the car drew up outside an old tenement in a part of Govan that seemed to have resisted all attempts to bring it into the twenty-first century.

Ramsay got out slowly and stood on the cracked pavement, breathing in the smell of stale fish suppers and a whiff of something salty in the wind that might have been blowing from the docks. He savoured it all. And, for once, there was no spasm of coughing to follow.

'Up there.' The driver pointed to the top flat, four storeys above them. 'Top flat.' He grinned as though he found it amusing to make his elderly passenger walk up all these flights of stairs.

He watched the man press the buzzer and then they were inside the close, its gloomy stone floors and white tiled walls echoing as they stepped up and up.

Ramsay stopped at each landing to catch his breath, letting the younger man climb ahead of him. He could hear a door opening and discern voices above him, no doubt the driver telling whoever was inside that he'd brought his passenger back as ordered.

The pain in his chest made him hunch over as he reached the top step. The door was open and he could see a long hallway with a strip of worn green carpet down the middle, an ancient runner that instantly reminded him of visits to his aunties down in Pollokshaws. All dead and gone now, of course. And no one else in his family left to remember them.

He walked along the narrow hall, his bag of possessions clutched in one hand, following the sound of the voices until he came to another open door and turned into a kitchen where the driver and another man turned to regard him.

'Where do I put my stuff?' Ramsay asked. But the stranger seemed to ignore him, looking back at the driver and conversing with him in some foreign language or other. Polish? Romanian? Sometimes it sounded a bit like Italian but Ramsay really hadn't a clue what language it was.

'Can ye no' speak English?' he asked, a little annoyed at being so excluded from whatever it was they were saying.

The driver looked at him with a disdainful expression.

'I speak good English,' he said, tossing his head. 'My friend here,' he laughed and said something else to the other man, 'not so much. Not at all.' He began to giggle as if the joke was on Ramsay. 'His name is Andrei. He'll take you to your room.'

The other man seemed to understand this at any rate and nodded in a surly fashion to Ramsay who followed him out of the kitchen and across the corridor into another room.

The man grunted something, pointing at a single mattress shoved up against the wall with a rolled up sleeping bag and a pillow at one end. So, this was his bed, was it?

Ramsay looked around the tiny room that was not much larger than the cell he'd recently left. There was a single bed against the opposite wall and the man called Andrei stood, legs apart, arms folded defiantly and nodded towards it then tapped his chest, indicating ownership and glared at Ramsay

329

as though he was furious at having to share any of this space with the old man.

'Fine with me, pal,' Ramsay said, slinging down his bundle and beginning to remove the anorak. 'Cup of tea would be nice,' he murmured hopefully, but the man had left the room and Ramsay could hear the resumption of their conversation in the kitchen.

He sat down on the mattress with a sigh, glancing around the room. The wallpaper was peeling at the edges where it met the ceiling but at least there was no sign of dampness, no telltale specks of black around the window. There was, however, a smell of cigarette smoke and the sudden longing for a fag made Ramsay pick up his jacket again. If that pair weren't prepared to be hospitable, then maybe he could slip out for a wee cup of tea in a nearby café, buy a tin of baccy and some Rizlas to roll his own the way he used to.

He pushed the bundle of his belongings to one side then, reached forward as the old Bible began to slip onto the floor.

'Ach!' he exclaimed, picking it up and noticing the bookmark that the Padre had given him.

Curious, he read the spidery script. It was a sort of a story, really, he realised, blinking at the words. A story about God and a man at the end of his life having a wee chat. *Footsteps in the Sand*, the story was called. For a few minutes John Ramsay sat and chewed his lower lip then he put the bookmark back carefully into the Bible and folded over the bag. *Thanks, Padre*, he thought with a faint smile, comforted by the thought that somewhere in this city there was someone that still cared about his welfare.

*

'Where's my key?' Ramsay demanded as he entered the kitchen once more.

The two men looked at one another then Andrei pulled a set of keys from his own pocket, unclipped one of them and handed it to Ramsay. *So,* he thought, *you do understand some English.*

He shivered for a moment, remembering his jailers and their bunches of keys. But he was free now, wasn't he? Free to come and go as he pleased?

'I need to see my parole officer this afternoon,' Ramsay told them. 'I'll be back later.'

The driver looked at him and shrugged. 'I won't be here when you get back,' he said.

'Well,' Ramsay shuffled his feet, 'thanks for picking us up, son,' he said, holding out his hand.

The driver grinned, shook Ramsay's hand then said something to the other man and both of them began laughing once more.

Ramsay turned on his heel and left the flat, a rising sense of fury at being treated as an outsider by two men who were incomers to his own city.

Outside, the day had brightened and he walked along the road, trying to find a café where he might sit for a while and sip a decent cup of tea. But the place he had in mind was no longer there, its windows long since boarded up, graffiti scrawled across thin plywood sheets. As Ramsay walked further away from his temporary lodging he blinked in astonishment at the changes. Gone were the bookies and the corner shop that had been run by several generations of Pakistanis; gone, too, was the old entrance to the

Underground, a newer and shinier sign showing where to go deep below the city streets. He might travel that way some time, Ramsay thought, but not yet.

He had reached the end of the road and found nothing that resembled a café and so, waiting for the traffic to clear, he decided to cross the road and retrace his steps, maybe find a place on the other side?

It was the sound of laughter that drew him from the pavement at first, children running over the pathway that led to the church's open door. Something made him take a tentative step towards the railing and read the notices fluttering from a large wooden board. One in particular caught his attention, the picture of a teacup and coloured-in cake making him lick his lips hungrily.

WOMEN'S GUILD COFFEE MORNING 10.30 TILL 1 PM, the notice read.

He kept on walking up the gravel path, ignoring the children's curious stares, and entered the old church building, following the sound of human voices.

'Hello, come on in.' A small woman with frizzled grey hair wearing a floral apron bustled past Ramsay. 'Tickets are two pounds fifty pence and you get refills and a couple of cakes or scones.' She beamed.

Ramsay followed her into a large hall where tables had been set out with teacups, plates and saucers. For a moment he was seized with a desire to run, so many women's faces turned to look at this stranger.

There was a lady seated at a table smiling at the stranger, the black money box for ticket money open in front of her. Once he'd have grabbed it and scarpered but now all that John Ramsay wanted was to pay for his tea and cakes.

'Two-fifty,' the lady said, her hand hovering expectantly towards him.

Ramsay drew out his wallet and handed her a twenty then waited quietly while she counted back his change then handed him a slip of paper.

'Someone will come round with the teapot. Or coffee if you prefer,' she said, nodding him towards the tables where several women were seated talking loudly to one another. Looking around for an empty table, he was relieved to spot an old guy in a wheelchair sitting on his own and headed to join him.

'Awright?' the wheelchair man grunted, nodding at Ramsay as he sat down opposite, the familiar Glasgow greeting warm to his ears.

'No' bad. Cold outside,' Ramsay replied, rubbing his hands together.

'What'll you have?' Another woman with an apron was suddenly standing there, the big teapot handle cushioned between folded tea towels.

'Is that tea?'

'It is. Freshly brewed,' she told him.

'Aye, that's fine, thanks,' Ramsay said watching the brown liquid flow into the tiny cup.

'I'll be back in a wee minute to fill it up,' she assured him then walked away.

Ramsay picked up a small porcelain jug with trembling fingers and poured a little into his cup. Before him were two plates full of cakes and scones. He glanced at the other man.

'Help yersel',' he was told. 'I cannae take much nowadays. Diabetic, see,' he growled, wiping a bony hand across his mouth.

Ramsay wasted no time in stuffing the food into his mouth, relishing the unfamiliar taste of home baking.

'No' seen ye in here afore,' wheelchair man commented.

'Jist moved back tae the district,' Ramsay muttered, reluctant to begin a conversation that might lead to awkward questions about where he had been before. However, that was not to be as a tall young woman came from a side door and walked across to their table.

'Right, Grandpa, time to go,' she said and, with a faint smile and nod to Ramsay she wheeled the old man across the room and out of the church.

'More tea?' The wifey was back again, and Ramsay nodded, pushing the wee cup towards her with a sigh.

'Tell you what,' she leaned forward conspiratorially, 'how about I fetch you a mug?'

'Aye,' Ramsay said. 'That would be smashing,'

He watched her go, a nondescript sort of woman with greying hair that he might have passed in the street without giving her a single glance. But here, with that kindly offer and a twinkle in her eye as if she knew he was feeling a bit lost, she seemed to Ramsay to be some sort of angel from heaven.

'Mind if I join you?'

Ramsay's smile faded as the balding man with the dog collar hitched his trousers and sat beside him. No doubt this guy was curious about the stranger in their midst, he thought cynically.

'You wouldn't be John Ramsay, by any chance?' he asked.

Ramsay blinked in astonishment. 'Aye. How did you know . . . ?'

'A pal of mine, Douglas Petrie, said you'd be in this area today. I'm really glad you came here so soon, John.' The minister clapped Ramsay on the shoulder. 'I'm Alan Powell,' he said, regarding him interest.

Ramsay let the man shake his hand, noting the hazel eyes flecked with green, the crinkles around deepening.

'I . . . well . . . ' Ramsay struggled to explain. 'Just fancied a cup of tea,' he admitted. 'Didn't realise this was the church the Padre had told me about.'

The minister's smile broadened. 'Ah,' he said, 'the good Lord works in mysterious ways, right enough, eh?'

Ramsay shifted uncomfortably under the man's gaze. Then he looked at his watch, struggling for an excuse to leave.

'Need to get going,' he mumbled. 'Appointment with the parole officer.'

'This afternoon at two o' clock,' Powell retorted, clearly amused at Ramsay's attempt at subterfuge. 'Douglas gave me all your details, including the address along the road. Is it all right?' he asked as Ramsay looked away.

'It'll do for now,' he replied, then sat back as the nice lady reappeared with two mugs full of tea.

'One for you, Mr Powell,' she said, setting one in front of the minister. 'And one for your friend,' she added, her eyes frankly curious about the sallow-faced man sitting there.

'This is John,' Powell said.

'Oh, nice to meet you,' she replied then walked away back

across the room and disappeared through a door that might have led to a kitchen.

'So, John, what's it like being back in Govan?'

Ramsay waved the man off as he stood outside the office at five minutes to two. It wasn't that far from his church but the minister had insisted on driving John Ramsay to his appointment, the rain now lashing down on these grey city streets.

They had talked for a long time after the tables had been cleared and the ladies all taken their leave, Powell becoming more serious as the former prisoner had begun to explain how he felt about the changes he'd seen that morning. One thing had led to another and he'd begun to tell the minister about the strange things that had happened ever since the Padre had given him that old Bible. It felt like a release, being able to talk about the voice he had heard, Powell listening with a sympathetic look on his face. And then, he'd asked the big question that had been bothering him ever since: *Do you really think a person like me can change?*

CHAPTER FORTY-FIVE

I t had to be the gun. That was the only link that joined up those deaths. And yet... Lorimer looked at the names on his list, a painstaking result from his officers after trawling through five police officers' records and cross-referencing them with each and every villain they'd sent down during their tenure.

Shay Cooper, though, that name did stand out. Cooper had the opportunity, having been released from Inverness prison scarcely two months previously, his term ending up in the Highland jail after being transferred from Barlinnie. And one of the dead officers had been shot not all that far from the Highland city. And yet the fact remained that Cooper had never been arrested by Stephen McAlpine, since the dead officer had spent most of his working life in Dundee.

Lorimer drew a heavy sigh.

Solly had insisted there was a pattern to it all, a certain logic behind the shootings, but so far he was at a loss to see what that might be. Still, that one common factor was being rigorously investigated, officers pooling their resources across the entire country.

An armourer, Lorimer had decided, was perhaps the only person that could tell him where that gun had originated. Was it the same weapon that Mary Riddoch's late husband had entrusted to his gamekeeper/gardener, Malcolm Watt? And had it fallen into the hands of his son, Luke, perhaps, with tragic consequences? Gallagher knew something, he suspected, from way back when the fatal shooting of the informant had taken place, killing Luke Watt with the very weapon he'd filched from his own father. That had been no random shooting. That had borne the hallmarks of some gangster's deliberate elimination of a grass. And moving the body from the garden grounds in Pollokshields made a sort of sense, he admitted grudgingly, if Gallagher had been unaware of Luke Watt's death at that time. Who would want their own garden to be under suspicion, after all, when the cops were keeping a careful eye on your every movement? No, maybe Gallagher had been speaking some sort of truth when he had denied knowing about Luke Watt; besides, it was the kind of thing he would have delegated to one of his heavies.

Lorimer clenched his teeth. They'd done everything possible at each of the locations; every senior officer had spent hours interviewing members of the public in specially equipped caravans that doubled as mobile incident rooms. Traffic had trawled CCTV cameras for miles around each of the sites where the retired officers had been gunned down and the door-to-door foot soldiers had submitted reports including possible sightings of a man carrying a lengthy object that might have been a gun. There were so many things to follow up and none so far yielding a scrap of useful information to push the case further forward.

Despite the fact that he had been allocated a huge amount of resources, with all leave cancelled meantime, the press were hounding him for answers to the main question: who was this gunman and why had he targeted these particular officers? Some of them speculated, of course, substituting imaginary ideas for hard facts and adding fuel to the fire that was beginning to feel like a simmering panic amongst the public in general and the police force in particular. Resignations were trickling in and Lorimer feared that as time went on that trickle would become a flood, reducing Police Scotland's manpower to critical levels.

He looked up at a gentle knock on his door which swung quietly open to reveal Solly wearing a long brown overcoat, a multicoloured woollen scarf wrapped around his neck.

'Hello,' he began, unbuttoning the coat and pulling off the scarf without any preamble.

Solly sat down and leaned forward, his hands clasped in front of him, eyes twinkling at Lorimer.

'You've found something?' Lorimer knew at once that this was no casual visit as Solly began to smile and nod his dark curly head.

'I think so,' he replied, drawing out a much-folded piece of paper from his jacket pocket. 'It took me a while, but I think I have discovered the pattern we've been looking for. Here.' He pushed the paper across the desk.

Lorimer ran his eyes across the rows of names, noting the arcs drawn in pencil that connected them.

He read it carefully then looked up, frowning. 'Shay Cooper, Archie Corrigan, Stanley Miller and John Ramsay,' he said at last. 'But Ramsay wasn't out of prison when Tony Weir was killed,' he said slowly. 'And you've put his name against a question mark.'

'Correct,' Solly agreed. 'But,' he leaned forwards and pointed to another name on the list. 'There is a sort of pattern, isn't there? If you look at the person each culprit most wanted dead then it stands that the person wanting Margaret Woods killed – and you thought that could be Stanley Miller – would be the person that dispatched Tony Weir.' He paused and looked at Lorimer to see that he was following him. 'I've put their initials after the officer they most wanted to see killed.'

'And whoever killed Miss Woods had already seen their bête noire gunned down by someone else? Is that what you're saying?' Lorimer sat up, his face alight with the realisation that Solly could be on to something.

'Look at Eileen Ormiston's file. Who would have wanted her dead more than anybody else?' Solly asked.

'An ordinary-looking man, that's what Eric Bryceland told me,' Lorimer said slowly.

'Doesn't Archie Corrigan fit that description? He was the one I'd selected from Ormiston's file.'

'I'd have said so,' Lorimer replied, sitting back and thinking hard. 'He was a known hitman in his day, did stuff as a free-lance, if you can call it that. Never affiliated himself with any particular organised crime gang. But it was Eileen's team that finally put him behind bars.' He looked thoughtful. 'It wasn't a particularly lengthy sentence, but he was prevented from attending his wife's funeral, as I recall. That would maybe be enough to make a person feel a lasting sense of bitterness.'

He steepled his fingers, thinking aloud.

'And since the previous killing of Eileen Ormiston was the one he'd really have wanted to do then he was committed to do the next one on the list. Is that what you're saying?' Lorimer asked, looking back at the chart.

'Exactly,' Solly grinned. 'Each gunman was selected to kill not the person against whom they have a personal grudge, but the one *after* that on this list,' he said triumphantly. 'Do you see?'

'And no doubt given a lump sum as well as the satisfaction of already knowing their old enemy was dead,' Lorimer said slowly. 'But what about George? And Stephen McAlpine? You've put a series of question marks against their names. Who do you reckon shot them, if this theory is to stand?'

Solly lifted his hands and shook his head. 'Who knows?' he said. 'But my guess would be that there was at least one double murder going on here. Perhaps someone else was responsible for the first two killings?'

'Okay, let's go with that for the moment,' Lorimer said slowly. 'A person unknown as yet kills Phillips and McAlpine.

Shay Cooper guns down Eileen Ormiston, Corrigan takes out Miss Woods and then you have Ramsay figured to be the next hitman on that list?' he frowned again, shaking his head. 'But why kill two people within a day of each other in different parts of the country? That doesn't make sense.'

'It does if you want to make it really hard for a national police force,' Solly said quietly.

Lorimer looked at him and saw the serious expression of his friend's face.

'You think whoever is behind this has been pulling our strings all this time?'

'Perhaps,' Solly agreed. 'And how better to ensure the maximum chaos within the force than to have officers chasing all across the country?'

'And, the gun?'

'Ah, that was clever, don't you see? Made us all think there was just one person behind it all. But, after the first two shootings, it wouldn't have been too hard to pass a weapon on from one person to the next.'

'Or to use an armourer as a middleman.' Lorimer was quiet for a moment. 'So, who's next?' he asked softly. 'And, if it is John Ramsay's turn for the gun, where on earth will he strike?'

Molly Newton stood in his doorway, a quizzical expression on her face.

'Someone here to see you, sir.' Lorimer rose from behind his desk. 'Mr Mathieson,' she added. 'He's waiting downstairs. Do you want to see him right now or shall I ask him to make an appointment when it's more convenient?'

'I'll see him right now, Molly,' Lorimer decided, intrigued

to find out why the banker had given up his precious office hours to come into Helen Street.

'Mr Mathieson.' He strode across the office to shake his visitor's hand, sensing that there was something troubling the man. Lawrence Mathieson looked ill and beads of sweat stood out on his pale forehead. Either the man was going down with a fever or he needed the detective's help.

'Please, sit down.' Lorimer ushered the banker into a comfortable chair. 'Can I get you a glass of water?' he asked, motioning to the jug and tumbler on an adjacent table.

'No, no, really, I'm fine,' Mathieson said, sweeping a hand across his brow.

'What can I do for you?' Lorimer gazed intently at the man.

Mathieson pulled out a crumpled piece of paper from his coat pocket and held it up.

'It's this,' he said, his voice breaking under the strain. 'I'm being blackmailed.'

He passed the letter to Lorimer then sat, head down, hands clasped on his lap as though he could not bear to say any more.

Lorimer read the contents of the letter, his frown deepening as he turned it over and reached the end.

'There is no mention here that you did anything illegal?'

Mathieson's head came up. 'I didn't,' he protested.

'I can see you're afraid,' Lorimer said kindly, 'but, if you are an innocent man, why do you think these people have any hold over you?'

'It's what they can do to my reputation,' Mathieson mumbled. 'I'd made a new start here, put it all behind me, the redundancies, the whole sordid business . . . It wasn't my fault what happened,' he said, his voice rising in a petulant whine.

'But someone died, all the same,' Lorimer said quietly.

Lawrence Mathieson put his head into his hands and groaned. 'Oh, God! If I could turn the clock back, I would. How was I to know the guy was suffering from depression?'

Lorimer did not answer but inwardly he thought: *You were his boss.*

'Sacking him was the final blow, seemingly,' Mathieson admitted. 'I was advised to seek out a new post. Promotion, would you believe!' he exclaimed with a short ironic laugh.

'Look, I can't promise that the press will leave you alone,' Lorimer told him, 'but I can deal with these people. Blackmail is a criminal offence and I think this matter can be dealt with discreetly without further injuring the family of this poor fellow.'

'It's them who are trying to injure me!' Mathieson snapped.

Lorimer remained silent. He would do what he could to stop the threats against the banker but in his heart he felt for the anguish Mathieson's junior associate must have suffered to take his own life. It was human nature to want retribution, after all. But the law stood firm against civilians who were set on taking matters into their own hands.

As he showed Mathieson out, Lorimer thought about Flynn's discovery. Strange how that was turning out well for the gardener and his budding romance with Erin. And yet, disturbing that body buried in the ground for so long was casting several shadows from the past.

CHAPTER FORTY-SIX

It was the sort of place he and Helen had dreamed of back in the old days. Some time, he'd promised her, they'd have enough money for a place of their own and be able to move away from the council scheme that was their first and only home.

Ramsay looked along the street, admiring the mature trees waving in the wind, most of their leaves now skittering on the pavement and choking the gutters. It was good to feel the wind, hear the sough as it filtered through the massive beech and oak trees. He walked steadily along, casting glances as he went, not loitering (which might alert a nosy parker) but striding out as though he had every right to be there. He'd picked up a haversack from the kitchen cupboard in the Govan flat and stuffed it with flyers advertising a new curry house that had been left inside the downstairs hallway. It was his cover should anyone stop and ask him who he was and why he was in the avenue that day. But nobody did.

It was easy enough to find the house he wanted, the

detached property with its neat garden and porch. There was no nameplate on the white front door but an arch of greenery with star-like yellow flowers branching above the lintel caught his eye.

Ramsay imagined the moment when Lorimer would open that door. It would have to be dark, of course, late enough to do the business. There was a security light on the apex of the garage and a lamp fixed on the roughcast wall by the porch. One way or another he'd be seen by the man as soon as he opened that door. It would mean being quick with what he had to do. *One shot is all it takes but give him two*, he'd been told, the memory of the man's chuckle still in his ears.

He continued walking around the cul-de-sac, scoping the area out and looking for a route that might take him beyond the crescent of houses and into the adjoining gardens of the next street. There was a narrow path at the end leading to a garage set way back from the street and Ramsay made his way along, glancing up at the house to see if there was any sign of life. The back garden had a thick hedge all around but in the far corner was an old wooden shed and it was to this that the ex-con swiftly moved.

A grin appeared on his face as he slipped between the back of the shed and the hedge. Here the privet was wispy and it would be easy to push his body through and into the neighbouring garden beyond. Now it was just a matter of walking along the next street to see what sort of exit that might allow.

The sound of a dog barking made him beat a hasty retreat. No, that wasn't going to work, was it? He'd just have to skip back out the way he'd come and hope to hell the place was deserted late at night.

He stopped briefly outside Lorimer's home, lips pursed as he thought about the nice lifestyle the senior cop enjoyed in this leafy suburb of Glasgow, trying to summon up a feeling of animosity towards the man. Warmth, food, and a wife, no doubt. No kids. Where had he heard that? Ramsay scratched his head, such details defeating his memory. Yet, try as he might, he could not lose the thought that Lorimer had earned this just as he had been given the justice that had landed him in jail for all these years.

He would come back another time, early evening, maybe, when darkness had fallen. This needed careful consideration if he were to carry out the hit exactly as the Big Man wanted.

Maggie turned the car radio off as she slowed down into the driveway, her fingers pressing on the remote that lifted up their garage door. The interior space lit up automatically and she sat for a moment, too tired to slide out of the driver's seat. It had been a long day and there was a pile of marking to do, the prelim exam papers stuffed into her briefcase on the back seat.

With a sigh, she opened the car door and stood up, massaging the base of her spine. In a few moments she had heaved the bags from the car and slammed shut the doors, tottering under the weight as she left the bright interior and aimed her key fob towards the garage.

Behind her the doors swung shut with a dull clang. The path was still wet from an earlier shower of rain so Maggie carried the bags into the porch and set them down before fumbling in her coat pocket for her house keys.

Perhaps it was a swirl of leaves or a bird in flight but whatever had caught her peripheral vision made Maggie Lorimer turn and stare into the darkness for a long moment.

Was there someone out there? She shivered, eyes straining across the street.

Nothing. No movement, not even the sound of a distant breath.

Still she stared, wondering if she were becoming paranoid in the wake of all these awful killings.

I'll be all right, Bill had reassured her. *It's retired officers they're targeting.*

'Hello?' The word was out of her mouth, falling dully in the cold air.

There was no reply but Maggie still had a sense that something was watching and waiting out there.

Tiredness and imagination, her sensible self chided as she turned and unlocked the door, stepping thankfully into the light and closing the door behind her, the key turned once more, the chain securely fastened.

She was bonny, Ramsay thought as he stood by the massive beech tree, hidden from the woman's sight. It was too dark to make out her features in any great detail but when she'd stood there, the wind ruffling her long dark curls, he'd felt a pang of grief.

How would she feel seeing her husband lying dead on that doorstep? What would she do?

He'd heard her call out into the darkness and for a moment

Ramsay was tempted to reveal himself to her, say that he'd changed his mind after all. But he stood still, a statue carved from misery, his true intentions hidden in the shadows.

He could see them waiting for him as he approached the corner of the street. Had the Romanians blown it, then?

Ramsay turned on his heel, heart thumping. He had enough in his pocket for the bus fare but first he would need to get well clear of Govan.

He skipped across the street, avoiding a delivery van, and headed to a narrow lane that ran between the tenement buildings. Once he had known Govan like the back of his hand, every wee back court and alley imprinted like a map in his mind. Now, with the police looking for him already, Ramsay truly needed that advantage.

In minutes the old man was puffing, his chest aching with the unfamiliar effort of jogging on hard pavements. He neared the bus stop and, seeing a single-decker emblazoned with its destination, he joined the lengthy queue, just one more old guy shuffling along to visit his relative in hospital.

He sat down beside a mother with a toddler on her knee, turning his face from the window, his anorak hood scrunched into a makeshift collar.

As the bus began to move away from the stop, Ramsay held his breath, terrified to look and see if the police cars were still nearby.

It was not long till the vehicle disgorged its passengers at the door of the Queen Elizabeth Hospital, a huge building that made Ramsay shake his head in awe. *The Death Star*, he'd heard some of the other inmates call it. The last time he'd been here it was dark and he had seen very little as they'd stretchered him to the waiting ambulance. His lasting memory of the place was a private room heavily guarded by uniformed cops until he could be moved back into the prison.

It would take a couple more buses to get to where he really wanted to be, Ramsay decided. But would he find the man he was looking for? And, more important still, would he have the gun?

'Ramsay reported to his parole officer okay,' DCI Cameron told Lorimer. 'Nothing seemed to be worrying him, we're told. So, maybe he'll just head back to that address later tonight?'

'I hope so,' Lorimer said. 'And we're still looking for Shay Cooper, Archie Corrigan and Stanley Miller. Miller and Cooper are both on life licences and neither has done anything to break their parole. So far as we know,' he added grimly. 'Corrigan seems to have gone to ground, though.'

'There are warrants out for their arrests,' Cameron assured him, 'and we've got all road patrols and railway stations on full alert to pick them up.'

Lorimer blew out a huge sigh. It was dark outside and he'd been working since early that morning, nothing new in that, but he was beginning to feel as if the walls of this room were starting to close in on him.

'Look, it's after nine now, and I'm heading off home. I suggest you do the same, Niall. We've got officers working round the clock and we'll be called the moment one of them is picked up. And they will be,' he added defiantly.

Cameron nodded wearily. It had been a stressful day since the professor of psychology had made his theory known to Lorimer.

'Right, see you in the morning,' the DCI agreed. 'Unless I turn up on your doorstep with good news.'

Lorimer looked out of the window seeing nothing beyond the street lamps but an inky darkness. He'd hardly spent any time with Maggie for days now and suddenly he needed to be at home with her, talk for once about normal things. With a sigh he turned and pulled his coat on and headed out of the door, careful to switch off the light as he left.

CHAPTER FORTY-SEVEN

It was bitterly cold as he made his way along the road from the bus stop, hood pulled up tightly, hands thrust into anorak pockets. Already there was the sting of sleet against his cheeks, the wind gathering strength as he struggled against its icy blast.

The street lamps seemed to sway above his bent head, scattering fragments of light across the darkened pavements as Ramsay crossed the main road and headed towards the line of shops, now shuttered for the night. It was a road he'd tramped often enough in the old days, the rendezvous known to a select few in this city. He huddled close to the buildings on his left, glancing up to see the entrance to the lane where the workshop lay. Would he be there tonight? Or was this a futile exercise, the police hunt clamping down on the Big Man's plans?

It was with a sense of relief that Ramsay turned the corner and saw the line of yellowish light that filtered out from the doorway. He was there.

Two raps on the door brought the sound of footsteps from within, the sound of bolts being drawn back, then Walter McBride appeared.

In seconds Ramsay was inside, the door shut fast and the locks secured once more.

'Everything all right?' McBride looked up at him with rheumy eyes.

'Aye,' Ramsay lied. 'Bloody arctic out there,' he added, looking over the armourer's shoulder to the cupboard where he knew the guns were kept.

'A bad night to be out, right enough,' McBride agreed, nodding his head and rubbing his hands together as if Ramsay's entrance had blown the cold air into the tiny room.

'I need to be out of here as fast as possible,' Ramsay told him. 'Job needs to be done tonight.'

'Oh?' McBride regarded him carefully then shrugged his shoulders. 'No business of mine, of course. Just make sure you bring it back by this time tomorrow, then,' he said, fumbling in the pocket of his jacket for a set of keys.

Ramsay watched as he unlocked the gun cupboard and withdrew a cloth-covered weapon.

'Got somewhere to conceal this?' McBride frowned, regarding Ramsay's anorak.

Ramsay stood still for a moment. In his desperation to get here, he'd not thought about how he was going to carry the weapon.

'Here.' McBride pulled open another door to reveal a small cloakroom. 'You can borrow this,' he said, handing Ramsay a fine tweed coat. 'But I want it back tomorrow, mind.

Good quality cloth, that. Bought it in Slaters,' he grumbled as Ramsay took the garment and pulled it on. 'And you'll need this.' He opened a drawer and fished out a rolled-up piece of twine.

Ramsay nodded. He'd make a sling for the gun and secrete it under his arm, winding the string through one sleeve of the coat, an old trick they all used to hide a rifle.

'Got a car waiting, I suppose,' McBride mumbled.

'No,' Ramsay admitted. 'Can you call a taxi for me? A local one, mind. I know you always used to have friends who could help you out?'

McBride frowned at him. 'This all sounds a bit irregular,' he began. 'Are you sure you want to involve someone else?'

'It's fine,' Ramsay assured him. 'Just need to get back into the city.'

The old armourer shook his head but then took out a smart mobile phone and made the call.

'Taxi to the Nia Roo. Name of Smith.' He nodded at Ramsay and gave a smile. 'He'll be there in two minutes,' McBride told him. 'So get your skates on.'

Once more Ramsay was out in the freezing rain, the gun clutched to his side, feet slipping on the icy ground as he walked as fast as he could towards the pub.

Sure enough there was a black Skoda, the driver watching his approach.

'Smith?' he asked and Ramsay nodded, yanking open the car door and sliding into the back seat.

He gave the driver the address that he'd memorised, hoping against hope that the house he was heading for would be in complete darkness, the man he sought home and in bed, too sleepy to react quickly, an easy mark at this time of night.

His heart beat faster as the vehicle sped through the dark. He knew he could do this, he told himself. He'd done crazy stuff like this before. So surely he could do it again?

CHAPTER FORTY-EIGHT

They'd talked for hours then fallen into bed, clutching each other like lovers who had been separated for months. Maggie was dead to the world now, her breathing deep and regular, but Lorimer had been unable to sleep, thoughts of Solly's theory and the renewed effort to locate the men who might be responsible for these killings uppermost in his mind.

Gathering his clothes up from the floor where he'd dropped them, Lorimer began to get dressed once more. He'd go downstairs, make himself a sandwich and maybe have a glass of whisky. That might do the trick. He crept quietly from the bedroom and felt his way down the stairs, one hand on the banister.

His hand was on the light switch near the foot of the stairs when he heard the knock. Just two sharp raps, but enough to make him alert to the possibility that he was being summoned personally back into HQ. Had they found the gunman, then?

He unlocked the door and stood back, ready to admit a fellow officer.

At first it was a shadow falling across the porch. Then he saw the light glinting on the metal, knowing in an instant who it was and why he was here.

As their eyes met, Lorimer froze.

Was this how it was going to be? A quick and bloody death?

'No . . .' he cried out, breaking that moment of disbelief

Lorimer tried to push the door shut but was too late.

As the man with the gun moved towards him Lorimer was forced to take a step back into the house.

His eyes fell on the man's hands. Any moment that finger would pull the trigger.

He would not even live to hear the bang.

The gun was pointing straight at him, the gunman an older and thinner man, to be sure, but still recognisable as John Ramsay.

The last name on Solly's list.

William Lorimer, the final victim.

And then Ramsay gave him an odd little smile and lowered the gun.

'Hello, Mr Lorimer,' Ramsay said. 'I think you've been looking for me.'

Lorimer stood absolutely still, waiting for the old man to raise the gun again and pull the trigger.

'Here,' Ramsay said suddenly, holding out the weapon. 'You'll want this.'

Lorimer took it from the man's outstretched hands, blinking in disbelief.

One moment he'd been facing certain death and now he

was standing on his own doorstep watching as John Ramsay shuffled his feet as though embarrassed at having disturbed the detective.

'Can I come in?' Ramsay asked, giving a quick look behind him. 'It's bloody freezing oot there and your lads are all waitin' for me back in Govan.'

Lorimer stepped aside and ushered him into the house, setting the gun down on an angle of the stairs. The safety catch was off, he noticed. Had been when Ramsay arrived.

'It's okay, son, it isnae loaded,' Ramsay chuckled. 'Sorry tae disturb you, but I had promised to look you up. If you know what I mean?'

There was a moment as the two men looked at each other then Ramsay nodded his head. 'Aye, you worked it all out, I suppose,' he said at last. 'But ye didnae know yours wis the last name on his list, did ye?'

Lorimer shook his head, stunned by this strange turn of events.

'Don't suppose ye can offer me a wee cup o' tea?' Ramsay asked. 'It's been a gey long day since ah got oot o' the Bar-L.'

If he had ever to write his memoirs, this would be top of the weirdest night of his career, Lorimer thought as they sat side by side, the whisky bottle on the table between them.

John Ramsay had told him everything, even down to the location of the armourer's workshop in Nitshill and the council flat where McBride spent some nights. Already a patrol car had been dispatched to pick him up. But it was the tale about the Big Man that fascinated him most.

'How did he do it?' Lorimer wanted to know. 'How could Gallagher manipulate so many of you from a prison cell?'

'Some screw must've slipped him a mobile phone. They tape them tae the underside of their desk drawers,' he said with a shrug. 'Never had one of my own, right enough,' he added, draining his glass and regarding it fondly. 'Ah, nice stuff this.' He gave a throaty chuckle. 'Even Gallagher cannae get this where he is right now.' He raised his glass appreciatively, evidently expecting it to be refilled. 'See you've done all right for yourself, Mr Lorimer.'

'But how did he manage it all?'

Ramsay raised his eyebrows. 'Money, always money,' he said softly. 'That's whit drives maist o' us intae this business in the first place. Wantin' things that we cannae get ony ither way. Fancy cars, nice hooses, holidays abroad … Ach, ye begin tae wonder why a' that stuff wis important back then,' he mused. 'Gallagher, now, he wis loaded. Still is, though I cannae say where he has it all stashed. Some o' his boys must hae it locked away to be able tae gie it tae these shooters. Five deid?' He looked at Lorimer sorrowfully. 'An' word has it the young lassie in yer ain team wis done in by her fella. 'S that right?'

Lorimer nodded.

'So someone outside still has the power that Gallagher once had. Someone he trusts enough to dole out ten grand a time to folk like you?'

Ramsay frowned. 'Here, ah'm no' tae be considered amongst that lot. Okay, well, I suppose ah did say ah'd do this job fur him, but ma heart wis never really in it,' he said. 'You're no' a bad fella, Mr Lorimer. And even if it costs me, I couldnae dae a thing like that.'

'You've no need to worry, John,' Lorimer told him. 'We'll look after you. Witness protection will see you safe till ...'

Ramsay chuckled. 'Till I pop ma clogs? Ach, son, that willnae be long. Doc hasnae given me longer than one mair Christmas.' He shrugged. 'That's awright. We a' hiv tae die o' something. Jist rather mine wis the big C and no whit Gallagher'll have in mind.'

Lorimer nodded slowly. 'Maybe he won't have to know that you didn't carry it out,' he began, a plan forming in his mind. 'Look, I have to make a few more calls, but I think you should stay here meantime.'

If Maggie Lorimer was surprised to see a figure wrapped in a duvet and slumbering on her settee the next morning, she never showed it. The night had been broken several times with noises of feet coming and going, the telephone ringing and then a whispered 'See you later' from Bill as he bent to kiss her cheek.

'Hello, Mrs Lorimer. I think we better brief you on what we have in mind today.' Caroline Flint rose from Maggie's favourite rocking chair, glancing at the pair of uniformed officers who were stationed by her lounge door.

'Oh.' Maggie looked from the Deputy Chief Constable to the shape on her settee and then back again.

'Mr Ramsay has been sleeping it off,' the DCC explained with a wry smile. 'Not used to the hard stuff after fifteen years inside. And we would appreciate it if you called in sick to your school today.' She looked straight at Maggie with a penetrating stare. 'And, we might need you to remain indoors. Is that all right?'

Maggie nodded. She'd lived with her husband long enough to expect the unexpected, even when it impinged on her own life. Stifling a sigh of resignation and trying not to think who would cover her classes, she turned her thoughts to the practicalities of the day ahead.

'Have you all had breakfast?' she asked, thinking about the contents of her fridge and whether it might withstand a siege.

CHAPTER FORTY-NINE

Jack Gallagher threw back his head and roared with laughter. He'd done it! Lorimer was dead and gone, the man who had curtailed his prosperous life, taking him away from his home and destroying the empire he had taken years to set up. He was dead. No future for the man from the MIT. No more years of looking up at the sky, breathing the fresh air that was denied to people like himself. He gave a huge sigh of satisfaction. Good on Ramsay. He'd done the sensible thing, taken the money and scarpered, by all accounts.

He pulled the desk drawer out again and smoothed the mobile phone back with the gaffer tape that held it there, hidden from sight. The screws had been given backhanders to keep them sweet and knew not to cross the Big Man.

He'd taken chances, trusting an old friend to be his banker, the money he'd accumulated stored safely away where no one else could find it. And, once he was out (given early release, surely, for being a model prisoner), he would begin to rebuild his business. Not here, in this godforsaken city. No, he'd sell the place in Pollokshields and move; Spain, perhaps. There were enough ex-pats amongst his acquaintances to give him a wee start-up over there.

It was a matter of timing, Molly Newton thought as they waited outside the block of flats in Perth. Stanley Miller had been faithfully attending his parole board meetings each week and so they expected to see him emerge from the door of the flats at any moment.

Sure enough, the figure of the man they suspected of having shot Tony Weir opened the door and walked out into the sunshine, blinking as he looked upwards.

They were out of the car in moments, Davie on one side and Molly on the other, holding Miller's arms tightly.

'Stanley Miller, we're arresting you ...' Molly began, a smile spreading across her face as the man groaned in disbelief. *One down*, she thought even as she declared the caution, hoping that by the end of the day the rest of the team would have rounded up the other killers.

Lorimer paced around his room, an anxious expression on his face. When the phone rang, he snatched it up.

'Yes?'

'We've got Corrigan,' a voice assured him. 'Bringing him in now.'

Lorimer breathed a huge sigh of relief. According to McBride, who had talked non-stop since his arrest earlier this morning, these were two of the men he'd paid on behalf of Jack Gallagher. It just remained to locate Shay Cooper, the man who'd been given the chance to exact revenge on

Stephen McAlpine by agreeing to execute Eileen Ormiston, the third name on Gallagher's list. McBride had sung like a Linty. However, he had so far refused to reveal the identity of the first man, the mysterious gunman who had shot dead both George Phillips and McAlpine.

He looked down at Solly's chart, finally understanding how it had all worked. Unable himself to wield a weapon and take his revenge on William Lorimer, Gallagher had concocted this bizarre plan. He'd manipulated several men who were due for release into agreeing to carry out these hits, the promise of a lump sum enhanced by the knowledge that the officer who'd put them away would be killed by the time they came to carry out their own particular job. Executing a stranger was perhaps easier in cold blood for killers like that, Lorimer mused. But how much had the thought of money influenced them, compared to the need to know that a particular officer was dead and buried?

It had been clever, though, Lorimer had to admit. None of the gunmen had carried out the hit on the officer against whom they'd held a grudge. That had confused the whole issue from the beginning, as had the single weapon passed from hand to hand, via the old armourer who was now languishing in custody.

So far no other name had appeared that matched a vengeful gunman in either of the first two officers' files. McBride had insisted that the man was unknown to him, but he had at least been able to say that the gun had been held for several days, the man returning to Nitshill and being given the money Gallagher had promised: twenty thousand pounds in return for taking the lives of two innocent men. Photos were being shown to the armourer, but of course, they were from banks of pictures of known gunmen who had been in prison.

Lorimer had an uneasy feeling about this one. What if Gallagher had known this particular man before his jail sentence had begun? And what if that hitman had never been caught by the police for committing a single offence? He bit his lip, thinking hard. It had all begun with that skeleton out by Houston, hadn't it? And the discovery that Luke Watt had been in Gallagher's payroll all those years ago made Lorimer wonder if the man who'd shot him dead then originally buried him in Gallagher's garden was the same person who had carried out the first two executions on his boss's list – not Shay Cooper, after all.

Jack Gallagher was perhaps the only person now who could tell them who this was.

Lorimer imagined the triumphant look on the ex-gangster's podgy face when he had been told about the 'successful' hit against Lorimer. They'd gambled on this piece of subterfuge, hoping that the last part of their plan might actually work. It was a huge risk and might actually backfire on them all. But, if they could find out the identity of the man they sought, it would be well worth it.

CHAPTER FIFTY

The timing had to be right. One half-hour too soon and he'd suspect something was wrong. If Lorimer could catch him as he slept, perhaps the shock might make him blurt out the truth.

Being alone in a prisoner's cell was totally unorthodox but, with the wire well hidden and the Fiscal's approval, Lorimer left the governor's office, accompanied by the man himself.

It was silent here in the dimly lit corridors and Lorimer started as the governor grasped his sleeve.

'This is where I leave you,' he said softly. 'Good luck.'

Lorimer nodded and began a careful ascent of the staircase, his running shoes making no sound on the metal treads. Every prison officer had been brought into the plan, except for those who had taken an unhealthy interest in the prisoner known as the Big Man. Right now there were several men being questioned back at Govan, their integrity as HMP officers called into question.

As he reached the top of the staircase, Lorimer looked

at the rows of locked cell doors, imagining all the men that slept there. Did they dream at night of the lives they had left behind after making bad choices? Or were some of them so hardened that they only thought about the next job after their release?

Gallagher had been given his usual hot milk and syrup, a special treat from one of the prison officers who'd already admitted being in thrall to the gangster, claiming threats against his family had made him bow down to his demands. Lorimer stood perfectly still outside the cell door, listening. But all he heard was a distant thrumming of a generator somewhere in the bowels of the building.

There was no need to turn the key in the lock, the last officer to check having left it open, simply attached by a stout piece of string.

Lorimer unfastened it and gently pulled the cell door open.

There was no sound at all as he slipped inside and closed the door behind him. Then, walking a few paces closer to where the man slept, he could make out heavy breathing and knew that Gallagher was fast asleep.

There was a chair by the desk so he lifted it up and set it down next to the bed, looking at the man who had wreaked such havoc within the country. For a moment his hands bunched into fists as he thought of those five dead officers, cut down before their allotted time. Retribution, he told himself. It was an age-old instinct but as a senior police officer who believed firmly in the law of the land, he had to ignore the impulse that made him want to give this evil man a thrashing. He sat for a few more moments. Gathering his thoughts, trying to relax into the role he had to play.

'Jack,' he said. 'Jack Gallagher.'

The man stirred in his sleep but did not waken, so Lorimer leaned forward and whispered in his ear.

'Why did you do it, Jack?'

'Eh?'

The Big Man leapt to one side, cowering against the wall as he caught sight of Lorimer.

'Wh ...? You? You're dead ...!' he whimpered, covering his face with both hands, eyes widening in horror.

Lorimer nodded and stared at him, fixing him with the blue gaze that had broken so many villains in the past.

'Why did you do it, Jack?' he asked quietly, sitting as still as he could, wondering what was going through the man's mind at that moment.

'You're dead,' Gallagher repeated. 'You're dead now. Don't come near me ...!' he called out, his cry like that of a scared child.

'I can leave you in peace,' Lorimer said in a breathy tone, 'but not till you tell me who killed my friend.'

'Who ... who?' Gallagher's voice cracked, a soft moan issuing from his lips.

'George Phillips,' Lorimer said softly. 'Who killed George Phillips, Jack?'

The man stared at Lorimer and for a moment the detective thought that he was awake enough now to see through this fakery.

'McQueen,' he said at last. 'Nicol McQueen.'

'Ah, one of your old chums,' Lorimer replied. 'The man that killed Luke Watt, yes?'

Gallagher frowned and sat up, huddled against the wall.

368

'You're not real, are you?' he asked, pulling the blankets up to his chin. 'This is just a dream, right?'

Lorimer nodded very slowly and deliberately. He had to keep this man under his stare, keep him focused on answering these questions.

'Where is he, Jack? Where is McQueen?'

Gallagher opened his mouth to reply then closed it again, swallowing dryly. 'You lot never found him then and they won't find him now,' he replied, a sliver of his old bravado returning. 'Nobody can find McQueen,' he said. 'And no one ever will!'

Lorimer stood up and leaned over the bed, watched by the terrified man who was attempting to hide under the covers. 'Is that right, Jack?' he said in his normal voice.

'What the . . . ?'

Gallagher's jaw dropped as the cell door was swung open and the governor appeared, followed by two of Lorimer's team from the MIT.

'Jack Gallagher, I am arresting you for conspiracy to commit the murder of five former police officers . . .' Lorimer began.

'You should've seen his expression,' Davie Giles laughed as they sat in the pub the following evening. 'Wish someone had taken a photo.'

'Well,' Molly chimed in, 'at least we got the recording all right. I could listen to that all night!'

Several people joined in with the laughter as they celebrated the conclusion of a case that cast such shadows across the entire police force. Nicol McQueen had been located in a terraced house in Kirkintilloch, a pleasant leafy suburb that had kept him hidden amongst decent folk for all these years. Once they had him in custody they had arranged for McBride to take a look at the man as he sat quietly in his cell. The armourer had agreed that, yes, this was the fellow who had rented the gun for the job in Inverkip, his compliance with the police no doubt showing some hope of a more lenient sentence when this all came to court.

Molly glanced across the pub to where a couple was sitting in a darkened corner. Erin and Flynn might be discussing the case but the way he was holding her hand suggested that their conversation might have taken a rather different turn. She smiled indulgently at them, silently wishing them well.

'Where's Lorimer?' someone asked. 'And where's Professor Brightman?'

Molly and Dave exchanged a look but kept silent. This evening was for celebrating the team's success and no doubt the boss was doing that in his own way.

'He put a stack of twenties behind the bar,' Dave said with a grin. 'So let's enjoy ourselves.'

Across the city two men gazed out on the river, the coloured lights from the bridges reflected in the water.

'Aye, it's bonny, right enough,' John Ramsay said. 'No' like in my day, mind.'

Lorimer laid a hand lightly on the old man's shoulder. Soon there would be a car coming to take Ramsay away to a secure place, far from the city, where he could spend his last months in peace.

'It wis that voice that done it,' Ramsay said wistfully. 'D'you know what I mean?'

Lorimer shook his head. He and Maggie had listened to the tale of the old man's change of heart, the strange calling of his name that had made him finally believe that there was something greater out there than any human authority.

'Padre tried tae tell me,' he said. 'Redemption. Didnae know what that meant at first. Didnae think it wis fur the likes o' me onyhow. Back then I jist saw it all in black and white.' He shrugged. 'Can ye imagine how it felt? An auld guy like me bein' given a second chance?' He sighed. 'That ither minister, the wan doon in Govan, he gied it a name, so he did.'

'Oh?' Lorimer regarded him curiously.

'Aye,' Ramsay said, a smile on his wizened face. 'He called it *grace*. Like in that song. Amazing Grace.'

Lorimer looked at the old man, marvelling at the serene expression on his thin face. Something had happened, right enough, something real that defied explanation, unlike his own ghostly act in Gallagher's cell.

'Here it is,' he said, looking down at a car that had stopped below them. 'Well, good luck, John. I hope everything goes well for you.' He shook the old man's hand.

'Ach, once the trial's over you'll no' hear about me again,' Ramsay chuckled. 'Till ma funeral,' he added with a sly smile. 'See you and that nice wife of yours come tae see me off then, eh?'

'That's a promise,' Lorimer said warmly. Then, as three men approached, one carrying a small suitcase, he stood back and let Ramsay walk towards them, safe in the know-ledge that some sort of freedom awaited the old man.

He saw them all get into the big car and then watched until it had driven across the bridge, its tail-lights disappearing into the night.

'Good luck,' he murmured.

But, even as he uttered the words, Lorimer knew that John Ramsay had found something far better than luck.

ACKNOWLEDGEMENTS

I've fair enjoyed writing this book for lots of reasons but one has to be coming into contact with so many professional people who give me generously of their time and expertise.

Thanks to my good friend and former ballistics expert Alistair Paton for his thoughts on sawn-off rifles. You were such a help, Alistair, and made it possible for my imagination to take wing and use the sort of gun you suggested. Thanks, too, to Dr Marjorie Turner for her insight into dead bodies, both old and not so old. Rosie is grateful, as always! To Tom Halpin, former Deputy Chief Constable of Lothian and Borders and now CEO of SACRO, my heartfelt thanks for coffees, chats and lots of stories and also, of course, for enabling me to talk to other professionals, notably former prison governor Don Gunn. Don, your insights helped such a lot and your knowledge of prison chaplaincies gave me a securer understanding of their roles.

Thanks also to Sharon Stirrat, Director of Operations at

SACRO, for letting me have more insight into what happens once a prisoner is released back into the community. That was very useful indeed.

The reader should know that I take some liberties by suggesting that HMP Barlinnie is a place for long-term offenders. It is not, but, like several of my fellow writers, I am beguiled by its atmosphere and use it as such for the purposes of fiction.

While he was not directly asked any questions about this book, it would be remiss of me not to mention my friend Professor David Wilson, whose book, *My Life with Murderers*, was extremely useful for research.

Thanks to Janice Rae in South Africa for letting me use her late mother in the story. May (Mary Riddoch) would have been delighted to feature in one of my stories. She was a good friend of our family for forty-four years and did indeed spend her last days peacefully in Erskine Home for ex-servicemen and -women.

Thanks, too, to Lisa Walsh who won an auction to name a character in this book. Hope you like them as much as I do, Lisa!

Big thanks, again, to Professor Lorna Dawson for her help in solving yet another mystery with her fabulous knowledge of soil science and the intriguing way she can pinpoint a place from the particles found at a scene of crime. Lovely to have you as yourself in this novel, Lorna. Lorimer was very grateful!

My thanks to former DS Mairi Milne for being there whenever I need to check details. Hope this book doesn't give you shivers now that you are retired from Police Scotland!

As ever, I could not manage to see this book to its proper conclusion without the amazing editorial skills of Lucy Dauman and the excellent input from the Sphere team including Liz and Thalia. Gratitude as always from one who has a limited knowledge of all things technical! It is always a relief to know that I can rely on my agent, Jenny Brown, to read the preliminary draft and make sympathetic comments. I am most fortunate to have a friend who supports my work like this. And always there is Donnie, putting up with the strange vagaries of a writer's life, being my roadie and helping to keep me (more or less) sane.

Last, but not least, thanks to my son John for encouraging me away from this laptop and into the world of birds, trees and hills. Lorimer would approve!

ALEX GRAY 2019